IDEAL
a SNAPshot novel
image

by

FREYA BARKER
& KT Dove

Ideal Image
a novel

Copyright © 2017 Freya Barker & KT Dove

All rights reserved.

No part of this publication may be reproduced, distributed, or transmitted in any form or by any means, including photocopying, recording, or by other electronic or mechanical methods, without the prior written permission of the author or publisher, except in the case of brief quotations embodied in used critical reviews and certain other non-commercial uses as permitted by copyright law. For permission requests, write to the author, mentioning in the subject line: "Reproduction Request" at the address below:
freyabarker.writes@gmail.com

This book is a work of fiction and any resemblance to any person or persons, living or dead, any event, occurrence, or incident is purely coincidental. The characters and story lines are created and thought up from the author's imagination or are used fictitiously.

ISBN: 978-1-988733-08-1
Cover Design:
RE&D - Margreet Asselbergs

Editing:
Karen Hrdlicka
Joanne Thompson

BLURB

In one blinding flash, the very fiber of her existence is shredded.

For criminal lawyer and single mother, Stacie Gustafson, a dependable career, a well-organized life, and an immaculate image, had always been her armor. Without it she's left exposed and struggling to create a new existence for her and her daughter. No matter how hard she tries, she is unable to avoid her history.

All it takes is one look at the blue-eyed woman, for Nicolas Flynn to be transported back ten years. Sure, her appearance has changed, but then so has his, since he turned his life around. His devotion to his small-town law firm is tested with the arrival of this bittersweet blast from the past, making for a persistent distraction. One that drags along more trouble than she left behind.

DEDICATION

To those visibly or invisibly marked by trauma
they've sustained in their life.
In hope that Stacie's words may resonate for you.

I have scars, but they don't get to define me.

*I am a sum of my parts, and I've been forgetting about a lot of my parts, focusing only on the part of me that has changed, not the parts that have stayed the same.
I'm still me.*

Before you start…

It is highly recommended you read Shutter Speed, and Freeze Frame prior to reading Ideal Image!

PROLOGUE

Ten years ago

"Are you...coming back?"

My voice is slurred and I have to blink to clear my vision. I'm drunker than I thought I was.

This was supposed to be my last hurrah before forcing myself into a corporate suit and adopting a professional demeanor, suitable for a brand-new lawyer in the market for a placement. A final party saying goodbye to what otherwise has been a long and rather boring road to graduation. On Monday, I'd be diving back into the books to prepare for the bar exam, but this weekend I was going to let my hair down.

It would appear I've let my hair down a little too far.

All I can see is the dark hair, wide shoulders with what looks to be a tattoo of a Celtic cross between his shoulder blades, and tight ass disappearing out the door, but for the life of me I can't remember his face. His cum is still running down my leg, and I can't remember what the hell he looks like, let alone his name.

Did we even exchange names?

I can't concentrate. I know I should be concerned about the sticky residue he left behind, but I just can't bring myself to worry. I'm too busy trying to keep the room from spinning.

I may have dozed off for a minute, but the second I open my eyes, a violent bout of nausea hits me, and I can barely roll myself to the side of the bed to find the trash can. Puking does not feel good. My eyes blur with tears, my head pounds, and I'm so disoriented I don't know where I am.

Wiping my mouth with a corner of the dingy sheet, I wrestle myself into an upright position and reach for the jeans and panties still tangled around one ankle. My bra and shirt have been shoved up under my armpits and I manage to pull them back in place. I think.

I suddenly want to be home. Back in my own apartment, where I can crawl into my own bed and sleep.

Still trying to button up my jeans, I stumble out of the room, right into a body. I tilt my head back to see, but the movement brings on another wave of nausea, and I feel myself shoved into a bathroom and bent over a sink, right before it all goes black.

-

I don't know what wakes me up, but it's daylight outside and I'm facedown on a towel on my couch, my Ikea salad bowl on the floor beside me. I have no fucking clue how I got here.

-

Three months later, my bar exam behind me, I sit on the edge of an examining table in a sterile room wearing only a paper gown, still wondering how the hell I got there. The party may have been reduced to a slight ripple in my history, but the impact is long-lasting, as I discover.

My promising and bright future grinds to a halt at the hands of the fresh-faced doctor, who with three words instantly changes the course of my life.

"You are pregnant."

I'm not sure what first attracted me to her.

Sure, she's beautiful, but so are a good number of the other students. All I know is that the first time I saw her walk into the auditorium, her blonde ponytail bouncing with every step and her ready smile brightening the dark and somewhat intimidating space, I simply couldn't look away.

Highly inappropriate—she is much younger and a student. I'm a staff member for crying out loud. Besides, it's not like she noticed me. I'm not exactly a noticeable guy; it's easy for me to blend into the background.

Three years I watched her come and go for lectures. Three years of surreptitious glances on my part and a rare nod of acknowledgement on hers. Whenever her eyes did land on me, however briefly, it felt like my heart stopped.

I spotted her coming out of a favored coffee shop a while back, carrying her book bag and a travel mug. I wasn't thinking, and ended up following her to an older, three-story apartment building.

There I stood outside in the parking lot, watching as she made her way along the third floor gallery to a door about halfway down. The instant the door slammed shut behind her, the almost trance I'd seemed to be under, as I followed her here, snapped. Shame and disgust washed over me as I glanced around me to see if anyone saw me gawking.

After that I'd done my best to avoid her.

Until tonight.

-

"You should come," Derrick, one of the other TAs said, elbowing me as we walked out of the campus gym where we started working out a few months ago.

"I don't know," I hesitated, not sure whether going to a student grad party was a smart move.

"Just for a beer or two. It should be fun."

I guess his definition of fun and mine are not the same.

I've been nursing this one beer for about an hour, leaning my back against the wall as I watch. The alcohol is flowing freely and more than once I've had to wave off someone offering me a shot of one thing or another. No one seems to recognize me, which is interesting, since I recognize a large number of them.

Maybe it's because I finally bit the bullet last week and shaved my head. At twenty, I started losing my hair at an increasingly rapid pace, leaving me with a sizable bald spot at barely thirty. Oddly enough, shaving what little remained resulted in me looking younger, rather than older. It gives me a bit of an edge, and apparently makes me more noticeable to the opposite sex. I guess the bald head is an attraction, despite the fact I still wear the same glasses and I'm still carrying a few extra pounds, although a few months at the gym have made a difference. It's a new reality for me.

With these thoughts going through my mind, as I wave off yet another offer of tequila, I almost miss the familiar blur of blonde hair in my peripheral vision.

It's her.

She seems drunk off her rocker as a big muscular guy, I'm not familiar with, drags her into the back hall where I know the bathroom and bedrooms are. It's like a punch in the gut. I know she's not for me—I get that—but that makes watching her go off with that muscled jock no less hurtful. I'm actually a bit disappointed. In my fantasy, I had her built up into someone who'd be able to look further than outward appearances. Someone who would appreciate the person, not the package, but it seems I was wrong.

Despite the churning in my stomach, I keep an eye out. When not ten minutes later I see the guy come out of the hallway, still zipping his jeans, with a cocky grin on his face, I push myself off the wall. There's no sign of her.

I keep an eye on the jock, who slips into the kitchen for a while, to see if he's going back down the hallway. At some point, I realize I haven't seen her appear and make my way to the back of the house to investigate. I stop, trying to listen for any sounds coming from the bedrooms, but the damn music is so loud, I can barely hear myself think. I knock on the first door I encounter, before carefully pushing it open. It's a bedroom and although it's empty, the thick smell of sex still lingers in the air. I guess this side of the house is seeing its share of activity.

I skip the next door on the left, because I know that's the bathroom, focusing instead on the last door on the right side. Just as I reach out to knock, the door flies open and she comes stumbling out, barreling straight into my chest. She smells of booze, puke, and sex, and I almost push her off me when she tilts her head back. One of her hands flies up to cover her mouth and I can guess what's coming, so I quickly shove her into the bathroom and over the sink.

Next thing I know, her knees collapse and I can barely prevent her from hitting the floor. I wrestle her onto the toilet, where she slumps against the tank, and wet a hand towel under the tap. She's mumbling incoherently as I wipe her face clean. I step back and contemplate what to do next, when the bathroom door slams open and her jock boyfriend steps in.

"Perfect," I mumble, handing him the wet rag I'm still holding. "She's wasted, you should take her home."

He looks at me funny, and then glances at her with a look of disgust.

"Not my fucking problem, dude. I don't even know the chick; she's just a warm hole, man. Just a warm hole."

I've never been a violent person, but my fist shoots out before I can even think about what I'm doing. I can almost hear my knuckles crunch as I catch him right on the chin, catching him by surprise. He stumbles back, hits his head on the edge of the door and slides down to the floor, where I leave him to go find some help.

I need to get her home.

-

I've crossed so many lines tonight.

I take one last look at the couch, where I left her to sleep off her bender. Her long blonde hair wiped back, a towel under her face, and a bowl in case she needs to puke. It's tempting to stay and make sure, but already I don't feel comfortable with the liberties I've taken. I don't want to run the risk of her waking up and freaking out at the sight of me.

Best for me just to go—walk away. Not just from her, but from my obsession with her.

She's not for me.

CHAPTER 1

Stacie

"Mak! You're not going to have time to eat if you don't hurry the hell up!"

Ever since school started last week, Makenna has been dragging her ass every morning.

She didn't have any problem getting out of bed during the summer break; she'd be out the door and by the riverside, with that damn fishing rod my brother got her, before I had my first coffee. Thank goodness Ben put the fear of God into her about the Dolores River right across the street. His recounting of the lives the fast-moving water has claimed over the years was enough to scare her into the life vest he insisted she wear.

With her fishing now limited to the weekend, she's lost her interest in getting up at the crack of dawn. In fact, she's missed her bus, more often than not, so I've had to drive her to school most mornings. Not really a problem, since I work from home, but being out in public still makes me uncomfortable.

People gawk.

I can't really blame them, because I have a hard time looking in the mirror myself, which is why I've taken most of them down. The scars I was left with, as the result of an explosion earlier this year, are pretty prominent along the left side of my body and draw looks. I'm still due for some plastic surgery, but after the initial months of constant prodding and poking at my body; I need a break.

I've barely had a chance to settle into the new house and my new reality. Days are so much longer without the constant pressures of working in the very busy Albuquerque District Attorney's office. I'd barely been in the hospital a week, when the phone calls started coming, wanting to know when I would be back in the saddle. I already knew that wouldn't be anytime soon, since an ADA is in the public eye quite a bit, and the public wouldn't want to see me like this.

My life has been turned upside down and I'm still finding my feet.

As is my nine-year-old daughter, Makenna. Although she loves the idea of living near her Uncle Ben, Isla, and their baby, Noah, she wasn't happy about giving up her school, friends, and home permanently when I decided to settle here. Displeasure she is more determined every day to drive home.

"Makenna! Now!"

Christ, that kid drives me up the wall.

I toss a few muffins in a container and grab an apple from the crisper drawer in the fridge. Looks like my recalcitrant daughter will be eating on the fly again. Loud footsteps come pounding down the stairs, and Mak comes stomping into the kitchen, a scowl on her face, but at least she's carrying her backpack.

"No time, kiddo. Told ya the first time." I hand her the muffins and turn her around so I can stuff the apple in her pack. "Get your butt out to the car. We're pushing it already."

"Why can't we have Pop-Tarts or donuts? Normal people do," she complains all the way out the door.

I roll my eyes heavenward, and count to ten, before snagging my phone and keys off the counter and following her outside. By all counts, I have ten or so more years of this before I can legally show her the door. The thought is enough to get me drinking at seven forty-five in the morning.

-

"Regular?"

Jen spots me coming in right away. Doesn't matter that there's a bit of a lineup, she waves me through to the back right away.

"Do Stace a macchiato when you have a minute," she calls out to the barista before following me into her office. "I need to pick your brain," she says to me after sitting down at her desk.

"About what?"

"Isla's sent me the edits from your shoot with her—I cried," Jenn says, dramatically flapping her hands in front of her face. "So gorgeous. Anyway, with the campground booked all the time, still nursing Noah, and the upcoming fundraiser, she's running ragged. I need your help."

"Sure," I offer, shrugging my shoulders. "What do you need?"

"You know she's planning to auction off some of your shots at the gala, right?"

I nod, I do know, it was the whole purpose for allowing her to photograph me in all my *glory.* The Children's Burn Foundation is a cause I've thrown myself into the last months. I'd never heard about them until I got to talking to a mom of one of the kids in the burn unit at Durango Mercy Regional Hospital. Her little girl had sustained burns to her face and chest, in an accident with hot oil, and was there for her eighth surgery in two years. Her mother mentioned that if not for the foundation, she would not have been able to afford the additional plastic surgery to reconstruct the little girl's nose and mouth. When I mentioned the foundation to Isla a month or so later, it was her idea to do something.

Well, that *something* has turned into a huge silent auction and dinner fundraiser. Through some of Isla and Ben's connections, we managed to get a Durango art gallery to donate artwork, and the Strater hotel in Durango is donating the space.

Isla worked on me for months, but I finally conceded to let her use me as a subject for a series of art photographs, showing the beauty of imperfection. It was an interesting experience. Other than a quick peek here and there at the digital screen on Isla's camera, I haven't seen any of the shots, let alone the edited ones.

To say my curiosity is piqued is putting it mildly.

"Yes. The whole series from what I understand," I confirm.

"She picked certain shots for that, yes. She shot over three hundred images though. There are plenty more." Jen leans forward on her desk and lowers her voice. "I want to do a photo book with a selection of the leftover images," she whispers, but immediately rears back with her hand up when she sees the concern on my face. "Isla wanted to do one herself, and was crushed when she was in here earlier this week that she wouldn't have the time to tackle it before the event. So I thought I would do it for her," she says hopefully. "With your help, of course."

"I don't know…" I begin, a feeling of panic threatening at the idea of having my face, my body, in a book. I mean a few exclusive original prints in the hands of a few people are one thing, having a book full of my pictures for anyone to buy is another.

"I get it," Jen quickly states. "Which is why I need your help. I need to know which images you'd be comfortable with including."

"Your macchiato?"

The blonde girl provides the perfect interruption, allowing me a moment to settle myself down. By the time she's put the extra large cup, almost overflowing with whipping cream, on the desk in front of me and backs out of the office, I'm a little more in control of my thoughts.

"Where are the pictures?" I ask, lifting my cup to my mouth and slurping off the best part of my coffee, as Jen flips open her laptop and turns the screen around.

-

I'm surprised when I note the clock as I walk out of Jen's office. Over two hours have passed, and I'll have to hustle to get back home in time for my eleven o'clock conference call. I have a standing appointment with the Denver lawyer I'm doing some freelance research for.

In my hurry to get home, I fly out of my spot outside the coffee shop, nearly ramming a gray Audi just pulling into the parking lot. I barely manage to slam on the brakes in time, as the driver lays on the horn. I raise my hand in apology and edge forward, so he can pull in around me.

I start rolling down my window to apologize in person when I recognize the person getting out of the car, and instead slam the gear in reverse and hightail it out of there.

Nicholas Flynn.

A man so eager to snag me for his firm when he discovered a former ADA might be settling in town, he almost hounded my brother for my number. He never got so far as to contact me. Instead he very obviously reconsidered whatever offer he was going to make me when we were introduced at Ben and Isla's wedding. Mr. Flynn got his first good look at my damaged appearance and could barely look at me. Needless to say, I never heard from the man.

That was one of the reasons I decided to try and find some work to do from home, at least until I was ready to talk to the plastic surgeon about possible next steps.

I'm in pretty decent shape financially, especially since the sale of my place in Albuquerque, but it doesn't hurt to have a little extra coming in. Hence the research from home.

Resolutely pushing a certain tall, bald, well-dressed asshole and his shiny car out of my mind, I park the car on the dirt shoulder outside of my yard and rush inside, snatching the ringing phone off the counter.

Nick

Normally I hit the coffee shop on my way into work at around seven a.m.

This morning I'm running late, because one of the horses got tangled up with some barbed wire. Not sure where the damn wire came from, since we don't use it on the small ranch my dad and I own just out of town, but her front leg was pretty mangled and we had to call in the vet early this morning.

Dad and I bought the place maybe six years ago, after my mother passed away suddenly. Mom had always been the driving force behind the large farm we had not far from Durango. It was too much for Dad to manage on his own, since ironically Mom had been the healthy one of the two of them. Of course, all eyes had been on me to drop everything and take over. The truth is, as much as I enjoy a bit of physical labor, I knew in the long run, farming wouldn't have been enough to satisfy me.

So, seeing as I wasn't ready to give up my practice in Cortez, and my dad wasn't quite ready to give up on farming, we managed to work out a compromise. Dad sold the farm, I sold my place in Cortez, and together we put in on this small ranch in the Dolores River valley. My father brought a few of his horses and we have some chickens for fresh eggs, so with their daily care and the vegetable garden he likes to grow, Dad keeps himself busy.

The ranch house is all one level, with a central living area and kitchen right off the foyer, and a hallway going off on either side. One runs behind the kitchen to a separate bed and sitting room with bathroom, which my Dad claimed as his space. He liked being closer to the kitchen. On the other side, behind the living room, are two smaller bedrooms, a bathroom and a den. I guess Dad's staying in what was originally the master suite, and I have one of the smaller bedrooms on the other side, but I also have my home office in the den.

The layout makes it so we don't have to be in each other's space all the time; we retain our independence, yet at the same time, I know I'm around whenever Dad needs me. Like this morning when he found his favorite mare injured.

The arrangement works for us.

My mind is still chewing over how that tangle of barbed wire could've gotten in one of the pastures when I'm almost sideswiped by a late model, navy Subaru SUV. I lay on the horn, which clearly alerted the driver, since the car abruptly comes to a halt, but my heart is beating in my throat. That was close. I could've cared less about another ding on my own pickup truck, but Dad wanted it to check along the fence lines today. I'm driving Dad's prized possession. The one indulgence he allowed himself after selling the farm.

It would've been a blow if his pretty baby got scratched up, and I'd never live it down.

I manage to pull around the back of the SUV and step out of the car, turning toward the rolled down window. I barely have a chance to register who's behind the wheel before they back out and fly off with squealing tires.

"Was that Stacie Gustafson?" I ask Jen when I walk up to the counter.

"Morning to you too, Nick," she fires back smartly.

"Morning, Jen," I dutifully respond, trying not to roll my eyes too loudly. "May I have an extra large please? And by chance, was that Stacie?" I try again.

"You may, and it was." She turns her back without elaborating, and I grit my teeth, knowing I'm being toyed with. "You're late this morning?"

"One of Dad's horses got injured. I spent most of the morning trying to get her corralled and waiting for the vet to get there. It's gonna be a late one tonight. Hence, the extra large," I explain.

"She going to be okay?" Jen wants to know as she sets my coffee on the counter in front of me.

"She should be, pending any complications. Doc cleaned and stitched the wound, gave her a tetanus shot and wrapped her up. Dad's keeping an eye on her in the stable."

"Good." Jen nods, tilting her head to the side, a twitch at the corner of her mouth. "Stacie was here to do some work on the gala. Have you two met?"

"We met briefly in April. Haven't really had a chance to talk to her, though."

"Odd," she concludes with a twinkle in her eye. "I would've thought the two of you have tons in common. You both practice law, you're both involved with the foundation, funny your paths haven't crossed more often."

I don't bother telling her that as far as I know, Stacie is not even aware of my minimal involvement in the Children's Burn Foundation. All I did was help set up the original framework for the organization a few years ago, since then my involvement had just been through my support and donations.

I also don't want to let on that I've purposely avoided Ms. Gustafson these past months. Ever since I got my first glimpse of her at Ben and Isla's wedding. Instead I pull my billfold from my back pocket, toss a five on the counter and grab my coffee.

"Doesn't matter," Jen says, breaking through my thoughts. "You'll get your chance in two weeks, at the fundraiser."

"I guess I will," I concede, with a friendly smile as I back out of the door.

The smile is gone the moment I turn toward the car. I haven't quite figured out how to avoid her at an event I'm supposed to be hosting. That had been Isla's idea, and I said yes before I knew her sister-in-law was deeply involved in the fundraiser.

At least this time I know what to expect. I had no idea that Ben's sister, an assistant district attorney, was her. The first name threw me off. Stacie Gustafson was not necessarily an uncommon or exotic name.

Anastasia was.

CHAPTER 2

Stacie

"Thanks for doing this, Al."

Isla's uncle looks up from his great nephew's bassinet and smiles.

"Happy to have Mak help me watch this little guy. He's growing so fast, I'm afraid he'll be running circles around me soon."

Mak and Al got pretty close over last Christmas. Other than Ben, she hasn't really had any male figures in her life, so she took to Al, a gruff but kind and decent man, like a fish to water.

"Can you help me with this?" My big brother Ben walks into the joint living room of their suite, fussing with his bow tie. I bite down a chuckle, because the only other time I've seen him in a suit, of any kind, was the day he and Isla got married.

My brother is more a jeans and T-shirt kind of guy, with his tattoo-covered body and his new, edgy, gray goatee. He looks pretty fantastic in a tux, though.

"You look cute, Uncle Ben," Mak says, and I have to bite down a grin at the instant look of horror on his face. No matter how ornery my daughter can be with me, she absolutely worships the ground her uncle walks on.

"In a totally manly, handsome way. Right, Mak?" Isla rubs her husband's bicep soothingly as she walks in with a big smile for my girl.

"Right," she responds eagerly, and I miss having the look of adoration she bestows on my sister-in-law directed at me.

"Done," I whisper at Ben, tugging the loops of his tie so it lies flat against his throat. "And she's right," I add, under my breath. "You do look kinda cute." I laugh at the low, ominous growl he responds with.

"We should get going," I announce. "Jen is probably already waiting for us downstairs."

The Strater is a beautiful historic hotel in downtown Durango, which is serving as the venue for our charity dinner and auction. Rather than make the two-hour drive back to Dolores tonight after the event, we decided it would be simpler to just all stay here. More convenient for Isla for sure, since she's still nursing Noah. They have a two-bedroom suite that houses Al as well, and Mak and I have an adjoining room.

I'm eager to get Isla downstairs, because Jen was adamant she wanted to show her the beautiful photo books she picked up from Southwest Printing just this afternoon. It had been a collaborative effort and a mad rush to get them all done, but when Jen phoned me earlier she said they were beautiful. The book will be a surprise for Isla.

Truthfully, I'd rather be the one to stay up here with Mak and Noah, but I know I can't. I committed myself to this event, to this cause, and although the temptation to run and hide is overwhelming, I couldn't do that. I couldn't do it to Isla and Jen, who've put so much of their time into this project, because of me.

Mostly I have to do this for my girl. I have to show her that I'm stronger than that. Stronger than the looks, the whispers, I encounter every time I'm out and about. She's not stupid; she's seen the way I hide away so I don't have to be strong. That's not a lesson I want to leave my daughter with, though.

Mak was the first one to see right through the scars and the bandages, straight through to the soul of me. Oh, she'll look at my scars from time to time, but in such a purely clinical and matter-of-fact way, that it doesn't feel rude or invasive. She looks at them like she would at a new haircut or a fresh manicure: as a part of me, but not defining me.

Jen is waiting right there, the moment the elevator doors open on the main floor.

"Hurry," she urges us down the hall to the Henry Strater Theater, which has been converted into a large banquet room. She leads us to a table butted up against the stage, which is covered with a white sheet.

"What's all this?" Isla wants to know.

"I...I mean, *we* thought...you were so busy..." Jen stammers, for once at a loss for words. Finally she just throws up her arms and grumbles, "Oh, why don't you just have a look?"

Isla pulls the sheet off the table and immediately her hands come up to cover her mouth. I have to admit, I have tears burning my eyes when I look at the beautiful job Jen has done on the cover.

I had no part in that; I simply selected images I thought were beautiful. It was difficult. Looking at the new version of yourself and trying to find beauty there is a challenge, to say the least. But what really strikes me is the image Jen picked for the cover.

A starkly contrasted close-up of my face, partially covered by my hands. It looks like I'm slowly revealing the new, scarred, me.

Rebranding Beauty, is the title Jen came up with and it is perfect.

"I don't know what to say," Isla sniffles, stroking her fingertips over the cover. "I love it so much." Suddenly she swings around to me. "Were you in on this? Are you okay with this?" I just nod, smiling wobbly.

"It's all Jen though," I confess. "I just helped select the images.

After hugs, tissues, and quick makeup repairs, Isla does a final round of the space, before opening the doors to the already well-filled foyer.

-

When I finally find my way to the table I've been assigned to, I've had it up to my eyeballs with the sympathetic, and often pitiful, glances and smiles.

I keep wanting to shift my head so that they're forced to look me in the eye, instead of avoiding my face altogether.

Christ, I'm not *that* hideous.

The edge of anger feels good. Better than the shame and occasional self-pity I sometimes find myself overwhelmed with.

Too bad for Nicholas Flynn, who finds himself in the unfortunate seat right across the table from me. When his eyes travel my body from the top of my head to where my legs disappear from vision under the table, it's like someone poked me with a cattle prod.

"They're still there," I snap at him. "They haven't disappeared in the past few months since the first time they repulsed you."

Whoa.

I blanch at my own vitriol. Not quite sure he deserved that kind of lashing, but it was out of my mouth before I could put a lock on it. Judging by the stunned look on his face, he's as shocked as I am. Before I can say or do anything in apology, the rest of the table guests start arriving, and the moment is gone. Or more honestly, I grasp at the distraction my tablemates provide.

I manage to avoid looking in his direction during most of dinner, although the few times I do, I find his eyes on me. I can't quite figure out whether he is scrutinizing me, like a bug under a microscope, or simply assessing me curiously. Regardless, even when I don't look, I can feel the heat of his eyes on me.

"Dance with me?" I startle at the weight of a hand on my shoulder and the determined invite in my ear.

I smile my apology at Ryan DeGroot for the interruption. He is the gallery owner who has donated several pieces of art for the silent auction, which I was in the middle of discussing with him.

"Excuse me," I tell Ryan before dropping my napkin on my plate and turning around to address Nicholas.

His face is much closer than I'd anticipated and I'm surprised at the warmth I see in his eyes. That's not what I was expecting. I'm so taken aback, I don't have a chance to formulate my excuse before he takes my hand in his and pulls me right out of my seat.

"Actually..." I try, but it's too late, he's already dragging me to the dance floor.

Rather than make a scene that will only result in more people staring at me, I drop my chin to my chest, and let him lead me. I try not to curl into his big body when he lifts our linked hands to his chest and slips his other arm around the small of my back, pulling me close.

It's hard not to feel drawn in by his gentle sway and the touching words of Sarah McLachlan's, 'In The Arms Of An Angel'.

Nick

I'd known last week when I almost ran into her—or rather she almost ran into me—that my attempts to avoid her wouldn't last.

What I didn't expect was the sharp tongue-lashing I got.

Not entirely underserved, as I realize after the initial shock wears off. After all, I did rather rudely avoid looking at her at the wedding, although that was more out of self-preservation than anything else. She's still fucking gorgeous, and as expected, my IQ dropped significantly in her presence.

To her, I'm sure, it would have come off as rude, to say the least, but I'm shocked to find she assumed I found her repulsive. Nothing could be further from the truth.

I observed her during dinner; mulled about how impossible it would be to continue to try and ignore her. Finally deciding that perhaps the right way to look at this would be to see it as a very fortuitous second chance. The one thing Mom told me, time and time again, was that if you weren't open to possibilities, opportunities would pass you by.

Stacie is not the kind of opportunity you let pass by.

The waitress conveyed my musical request to the DJ, and the moment I heard the first keystrokes of the piano, I was out of my chair.

She smells amazing.

Even just leaning over her, the light hint of lime, and maybe vanilla, is enough to make my mouth water.

I don't give her a chance to refuse and don't even try to fight the smile on my lips when I wrap her in my arms. I have her hand pressed against my chest and I wonder if she can feel the thundering of my heart.

It's pathetic, really. I'm a forty-year-old man, behaving like a teenager scoring a dance with his crush on prom night.

"Why?"

I barely hear her mumbled question; she's speaking so softly.

"Why what?"

"I don't understand," she says, slowly lifting her face. "You could barely stand to look at me a few months ago. And now you're staring at me all through dinner and ask me to dance? Why? Is this a bet or something?"

I can feel my blood heating as, "Are you for fucking real?" flies from my mouth unchecked. Stacie takes a step back, looking alarmed, but I have my arm still firmly around her waist. Taking a deep breath in I try to calm myself down. "Look, I…" For a moment I contemplate explaining my behavior to her, but I'm afraid right now it will only make her more, and not less, wary of me. "All I want is a dance, and a chance to get to know you a little. If I've done something to offend you, I can assure you it was unintended." I watch, as her eyes soften a little, but not quite all the way. "As for my behavior tonight, it's not often I get slapped down like that, and you also happen to look beautiful. So yeah, you piqued my interest. It's possible I may have been staring a little," I add with a self-deprecating smile.

"A little?" she snorts, taking a step closer and moving to the music again. "I was afraid I'd grown an extra eyeball on my forehead or something."

"On the contrary," I correct her. "You're quite beautiful. It was hard to look away." I can feel right away it was the wrong thing to say. I wish she wouldn't make me forget every smooth line and move I've mastered over the years, and have me behave like the shy farm boy I once was.

"Don't insult my intelligence with your flattery, Mr. Flynn. I am well aware of my appearance." Her tone slices, making it clear that I will have my hands full convincing her that I mean every word.

"But you don't know what I see."

-

Pops is already in bed when I get home a little after midnight. I'm glad, because I'm not quite ready to explain the large print I'm carrying in.

I walk straight through to my bedroom, peel the brown paper away, and lift it to sit on top of my dresser.

It's a little unnerving to watch eyes, which I've imagined on me, follow me around the room as I strip and hang up my clothes. In the bathroom, I quickly go through my nighttime routine, before flicking off the lights and climbing into bed. I stuff the extra pillows behind my back and fold my arms in my neck. Those beautiful ice-blue eyes, the only color in the stark black and white photograph I bid a ridiculously large amount of money on, stare right back at me from across the room.

"Who…who are you?" She could barely keep her eyes open as I backed out of her apartment.

"Just go back to sleep. I'll pull the door shut behind me."

It hadn't been easy to get her into a taxi, and more than once, the driver threw a concerned look in his rearview mirror. I ignored him; I had a hard enough time trying to keep her from falling over.

Thank God I had enough cash in my wallet to pay for the cab, otherwise I would've had to go through her purse in front of him, and that could've been awkward. As it was, I had to dig through that purse for the keys, but at least I could do it without the suspicious eyes of the cabdriver on my back.

I contemplated taking her clothes off so she'd be more comfortable, but in the end, I just took off her shoes and unbuttoned her jeans. I spread the quilt I found folded on the back of the couch over her, and that's when those gorgeous blue eyes popped open, and zoomed right in on me.

I recognized something the moment the question left her mouth. I'd never even registered on her radar. Not after years of walking the same hallways, even teaching an occasional class, did she know who I was.

It was then I decided to walk away.

Ironically, all it took was those ice-blue eyes to turn on me ten years later, to bring the fire I thought I'd doused long ago, back to life.

CHAPTER 3

Stacie

"Mom, can we go already?"

I'm trying to blow-dry my hair with one of those wall-mounted hotel dryers. I barely feel the air move with this damn thing. Mak has been bouncing off the walls since she opened her eyes this morning. I don't know what Al fed her last night, but I need to ask. I'd give anything to have her this ready to go on school days.

Today, not so much.

"Give me a minute!" I yell at my daughter, who is fast losing patience outside the bathroom door.

I toss the useless blow dryer on the counter and flip my hair upside down, ruffle my fingers through it, and straighten up in front of the mirror.

Ugh. At home I can do all this blind. I know exactly how to style my hair to cover as much of the left side of my face as I can. That's not going to work with wet hair though, and I promised my daughter breakfast in the swanky restaurant downstairs.

Not about to break my word to my girl, I do the best I can with my hair. Nothing on my face but my day cream, which has a tinge of green to cut down on the red in my face, and a light brush of mascara. It is what it is.

"Let's go, chicklet," I tell Mak, walking into the bedroom to grab my purse and the room key, before ushering her out the door.

"Uncle Ben and them are probably done with their breakfast by now," Mak grumbles as we get on the elevator.

"Honey, they knocked on our door just five minutes ago, they haven't even had time to order."

I get an eye roll and silence in response. That's fine, I need a little caffeine before I can handle much more anyway.

Mak makes a beeline for the large table the moment she spots my brother and his family. I follow a little slower, my eyes down to the carpet in front of me so I don't have to see the looks I get. Usually by the time I go out in public, I have been properly caffeinated and have my game face on, but that's not the case this morning.

I'm probably not the only one who feels less than perky this morning. Last night was unexpectedly fun. After the introductory speeches, dinner had been fabulous, and the surprise book reveal Jen orchestrated resulted in amazing sales. People had been bidding like crazy on the artwork displayed, including the prints of pictures Isla took of me. I tried not to look too much in the direction of the display, because my face and body were pretty prominently displayed.

The largest print was a close-up of my face and the one I loved best. The others were a selection of full or partial body shots, where my face and much of my body was kept in the shadows. A lot of light play in those, showing me mostly from the back. When you look quickly at those, all you see is a mostly nude woman. Only on closer inspection do you see the thick ridges of scarring running along my left side. I had to swallow a few times when I first saw them all set up on their stands.

A few stiff drinks helped.

I blame those same drinks for not putting up more of a fight when Nicholas Flynn pulled me onto the dance floor. I hate to admit how much I enjoyed that. It's never been particularly difficult for me to draw male attention. Something I'll freely admit I've used to my advantage both in and outside of the courtroom. Those days are over, which is why he caught me off guard.

I totally had him pegged as an arrogant ass, but he surprised me. Some of what he said sounded quite genuine, although that might have been the alcohol talking.

I enjoyed the dancing, but we were interrupted when Jen stepped up to the mic, at some point, and called everyone's attention for the results of the silent auction. I took that opportunity to slip out of the party and disappear upstairs to my room. Once there, I shot a quick text off to Isla to let her know I was calling it a night, before crawling into bed where my baby was already sleeping.

"Morning, lightweight," Ben says in a teasing voice.

"Bite me," I tell my brother, as I bend over the stroller where Noah is happily chewing on a toy. "Morning, my handsome little fella," I coo at him before kissing his fuzzy little head.

"You bailed early," Isla pipes up, giving me an eyebrow lift.

"I was just suddenly wiped," I explain, not really lying, because I'd fallen asleep the moment my head hit the pillow.

"They've got a buffet," Al says to Mak, who's been quietly eyeing his plate of food. "I'll take you, I need some more toast."

I shoot him a grateful smile as he walks off with a chattering Mak. I'll need some coffee first, before I tackle breakfast.

"Yes, please." I smile at the waiter, who comes by with a large thermos, and hold out my cup. "Ahhh, this is just what I needed," I groan, closing my eyes as I take my first sip of coffee.

"Not as good as Jen's."

My eyes pop open, at the sound of the deep voice, to find Nick pulling out the chair beside mine and putting down a plate overflowing with food. He must have been sitting there before; because he picks up the cup I'd seen on the table and takes a sip. Dark brown eyes appraise me over the rim of the cup, and I shift in my seat.

"True, but it'll do the trick in a pinch."

"You should grab some breakfast. They've got quite the spread," he says, before shoving a forkful of scrambled eggs in his mouth.

"Maybe I will." I take another swig of my coffee before shoving back my chair. I notice Isla looking at me, an eyebrow raised and a faint smile on her lips. "What?" I ask, less than graciously, but she's not impressed. In true Isla fashion, she breaks out in a big grin and shrugs.

"The French toast is good," she offers with a smirk.

By the time I get back to the table, Ben is in deep conversation with Al and Nick. Something about a doubleheader, which tells me sports, which also means I can dive into the stack of blueberry pancakes I scored at the buffet in peace. However, it seems Nick has other ideas.

"So what are the chances I can get you to come work with me?" he suddenly asks, catching me with my mouth full of sweet, fluffy deliciousness.

Have you ever tried talking with a mouth full of pancake crumbs? Not recommending it.

"With you?" I blurt out, spraying all over his clean white dress shirt. "Jesus, I'm sorry!" My apology only adds to the problem.

"Swallow first, Stace," my brother says helpfully, chuckling at his own joke.

I throw him a glare before dunking my napkin in the nearest water glass. Turning back to Nick, I try not to look up in his face, but focus on his pristine shirt, rubbing furiously at the little blue specks I've left all over it. I pretend I don't notice the heat from the solid body underneath my hands, or the chuckles and giggles I hear around the table.

Luckily, Mak's cheerful banter—a full stomach does wonders for the kid—quickly distracts everyone from my more than embarrassing moment. The conversation around the table seems to fade into the background, and all I hear is the pounding of my own heart.

"It's fine."

Nick's voice is soft, but clear as a bell against the background noise.

"It's fine, don't worry," he repeats, and still I don't look up.

When my hand is stilled by a steel grip around my wrist, I do look up, straight into Nick's dark, but highly amused eyes.

"Okay."

I feel dumb. I fucking sound dumb. There's too much going on here I can't wrap my head around, or even want to attempt trying.

"I'm sorry if I threw you with my question," he says. "I've wanted to ask you since Ben told me you were settling here. Well, in Dolores," he quickly corrects himself. "I left a few messages for you earlier in the year, but I never followed up. Then summer hit, and it got busy, but I'm still interested."

"Even after I ruined your shirt?"

I watch with interest when his eyes crinkle and lines pop up all over his face as he smiles. *Age looks good on him.* I'm not sure where that thought comes from, but it's true. Nicholas is one of those guys who will probably continue to improve with age. Utterly unfair, if you ask me. Still, he strikes an imposing character: with his dark eyes, clean jaw, white smile, and bald head.

"Plenty more shirts, but only one you," he replies smoothly, his face now straight, but his eyes still smiling. "Unless you have no interest, we should set up a time for you to come into the office," he adds, leaning back in his chair to let the waiter top off his coffee. "We can chat, I can tell you what I'm thinking, and you can have a look around."

I'm not sure what prompts me, and from the surprised looks on Ben and Isla's faces, they're as shocked as I am at what comes out of my mouth.

"I'd love to."

Nick

I don't know what wakes me at the crack of dawn this morning, but the moment I open my eyes to the picture on my dresser, I realize I screwed up by not staying at the hotel last night.

It doesn't take me long to get dressed, and I catch Pops sitting at the kitchen table, already having his morning coffee. Years of getting up early to tend to the farm is a habit that's hard to shake. Even after several years of retirement.

"Off so early?" he asks, when I grab my keys from the bowl on the counter. "You know it's the weekend, right?"

"I know. I'm meeting someone for breakfast in Durango," I tell him, and watch as the corner of his mouth twitches into a smile.

"Might've been easier just to stay the night there," he offers, with a shrug.

"Probably," I admit. "I'll pick up some steaks for us for dinner tonight."

"You going to that organic place? Pick me up some dried prunes, will ya? Been plugging up a little."

With a roll of my eyes and a wave, I head out the door.

Last night's events play through my mind as I drive the two hours into the mountains.

I'd had every intention of staying the night; I'd booked a room. Then when they started with the winning bids, Stacie disappeared from the table and never came back. I kept my eye out for her as the lucky winners went up to the stage to collect their items. When Jen announced the winning amount for the last item, entered by an anonymous bidder, my attention was drawn by the collective gasp that went up.

I'm still not sure why I didn't want anyone to know I was bidding on that shot of Stacie. Probably, in part, because when people noticed me bidding furiously on that print, it might have raised some eyebrows. Not just Stacie's, but likely Ben and Isla's as well, and I'm not quite sure what to give as explanation.

"I don't give a rat's ass why," she'd said when I approached her at the coffee shop earlier. "An extra grand, on top of the highest bid, is good enough for me. I'm just interested in raising as much money as we can, so if you want to throw that kind of money around, be my guest." She turned around, set my coffee down, and placed her hands on the counter, leaning into my space. "I will have you know that if ever that girl is hurt as a result of whatever it is you're up to, I will shove my fist so far down your throat, I can tickle your balls."

"Last thing I want to do is cause any harm," I told her, grabbing my coffee and backing out of her shop.

Then last night when I slipped out of the ballroom and met her behind the stage to collect the print, I just wanted to take it home, so I packed my stuff in my car and took off.

The check I handed over had been substantial, but very much worth it to go to sleep feeling her eyes on me.

-

"I'd love to."

I asked the question, I must've at least considered the possibility she might say yes, but still her answer surprises me, as much as it apparently does everyone else at the table.

This is a conversation I was hoping to have last night, but I never had a chance. Maybe I was too distracted having her so close.

When Ben initially mentioned his sister, before I even knew who she was, I'd been very interested.

My firm is small; I have one associate, who specializes in family law, and I focus on mostly corporate stuff. Diversifying is always a good idea when you service a relatively small community. It's why the mention of a former ADA got my attention. It got me thinking about adding criminal law to our services.

Then I was introduced at his wedding and realized who she was, even though she clearly had no recollection of me. It had been reason enough to put my thoughts of adding new expertise to the firm on the sidelines. It would be awkward.

I've come to realize since then, that avoidance is impossible, no matter how hard you try. Living in the same small town, it's a small miracle we didn't encounter each other before we nearly collided in the parking lot of my favorite coffee place.

She still doesn't have a clue who I am, not yet anyway.

"Are you eating that, Mom?"

I hadn't paid the little girl much notice, but her voice draws my attention. *Mom*? I turn to see her look at Stacie.

"You already had French toast, Mak. You're gonna make yourself sick."

I lean back in my chair and grab my coffee to give my hands something to do. She has a daughter. Does that mean there's a father? My eyes flick down to her hands, but there's no ring and not a hint of a suggestion there recently was one.

"I could eat more," the little girl says, shrugging her shoulders.

She is not at all how I would have pictured a daughter of Stacie's. Not that I pictured one at all, but the short dark hair and the shirt with the Grateful Dead logo, completely throw me off. She can't be much older than…ten maybe?

"I'm sorry," Stacie says, suddenly turning back to me. "I don't think you've met my daughter? This is Makenna, but she wants to be called Mak, so we do," she explains with a shrug before directing her attention to her daughter. "Mak, this is Nicholas Flynn. He's a friend of Uncle Ben's."

I reach a hand over the table and shake her much smaller one. Eyes, as blue as her mother's, regard me with some curiosity.

"I know you," she says, startling me. "You were at the wedding."

"I was." I chuckle at her direct manner. "Nice to *officially* meet you then, Mak."

"Ditto," she says smartly.

"Mak!" Stacie snaps, and Isla's uncle barks out a laugh.

I barely manage to stifle a chuckle myself when I see Mak's wide-eyed innocent look to her mother. Stacie sighs deeply, rolling her eyes, while she shoves her plate in front of her daughter.

"Just eat," she instructs her, before turning back to me with a mouthed, "*Sorry.*"

"So when would be a good time for you?" I ask, steering her right back to our earlier conversation.

"She's flexible—aren't you, Stace? She works from home," Isla interjects with a smile, ignoring her husband who is growling at her. Stacie throws a glare in her direction with bulging eyes, clearly not appreciating the input, and I can't hold back the chuckle.

"Good to know," seems the safest response.

By the time I climb back behind the wheel to head over to the organic market, I have an appointment booked in my iCal and a phone number added to my contacts. I'm wearing a big grin.

CHAPTER 4

Stacie

"What are you doing here?"

I'm surprised to find Isla with baby Noah on my doorstep, as I'm heading out for my daily walk.

This morning, Mak was actually in time to catch the bus, and I've already managed to get a few decent hours of work in. I want to get out for a bit before my meeting this afternoon.

It's tempting to just sit here at my desk all day long, but my body just gets stiff. My walks along the path by the river make for a nice break, and during the week, I hardly ever see anyone on there. Perhaps just the occasional fisherman, or once or twice a raft on the river, but overall it's quiet.

"I have something to show you," Isla announces with a serious face.

Already I'm lifting Noah from her arms as she walks past me into the house. The little guy manages to get a fistful of my hair, which is finally at a length again where I can pull it in a ponytail, and brings it to his mouth. Not that I bothered with that this morning, to Noah's delight.

She pulls her laptop from her messenger bag and sets it on the kitchen island, when I walk in with the baby making a wet spot on my shoulder.

"Your son is hungry," I tell her. "He's starting to chomp on my shoulder."

"Just a minute, sweetheart," she coos at Noah, throwing him a distracted smile before turning back to the screen. "Okay, here it is. Check it out," she says, stepping back and taking the baby from me.

On the screen she has pulled up some kind of graph I don't understand.

"What is this?" I turn to where she's taken a seat on the couch.

"Sales for *Rebranding Beauty*," she says, Noah already happily nursing. "I check that site daily to track all my sales, and saw that this morning."

"This peak?" I point out a sharp incline for today's date on the screen. "Is that since this morning?"

"Yup. Sales are skyrocketing."

"What happened between last week and today?" I want to know.

"Remember that article in the *Durango Herald* from last week? Apparently, it ran in a few other newspapers and this morning was picked up on *USA Today*. It's all over the Internet."

"That's fantastic!" I blurt out, until I see the worried look on her face. "What?"

"They've added some background that was not with the original article. Ben is going to flip over this," she sighs dramatically, as she drops her head back on the couch. "Remember how we decided to keep your name out of it?"

A feeling of dread uncurls in my stomach. One of the stipulations I'd had in participating with the images was that I would not be listed as contributor. I may not have walked away from my years of prosecuting criminals, leaving only friends, so it had been a calculated omission to leave my name out. Also for Makenna's protection.

"I'm so sorry," she whispers. "I don't know how."

"How bad is it?" I ask, shaking off the shock as my fingers fly over the keyboard, pulling up the *USA Today* website. "*Shit!*"

They apparently found an editorial image that shows me outside the doors of the Bernalillo County courthouse in Albuquerque, being interviewed after a particularly harrowing case we tried, and won. This was a few years ago, and the picture shows the top half of my body and a straight on view of my still undamaged face. Next to this picture they posted one of Isla's images, with half my face marred. I guess for contrast?

I don't even need to read the explanatory writing underneath, I can take a safe guess, but my name is listed clearly and in bold.

"Can we get them to retract?" Isla asks from behind me.

"No. The information and picture they used was previously published. Public record. They've done nothing wrong, other than some quick investigative journalism to find the link. Even if we had a case, it's all over the Internet; there's no retracting that."

"I'm sorry," Isla says again.

"Stop." I turn around to face her. "This is not your fault and it was a risk I took knowingly. Besides, focus on the good; look at those damn sales! Amazing."

I'm not sure my attempt at focusing on the positive have the desired effect on Isla. When I help her buckle Noah in the car seat half an hour later, she is still apologizing.

"Enough of that. Go home. I have to get dressed for my appointment." That perks up her attention.

"Appointment? With Nick? Is that today?"

I roll my eyes at the overt enthusiasm in her voice. She's been my biggest cheerleader when it comes to stepping out of my comfort zone: the images, the fundraising gala. If not for her, I would probably still be sitting inside the house with the curtains drawn.

My circle is small, so to think my sister-in-law would not clue in immediately would be wishful thinking. There is no privacy in such a small community.

"Yes, so let me get ready," I tell her, unable to stop the smile when I look at her widely grinning face.

"Call me after!" she yells, as she gets in her car.

I wait until she disappears around the corner and head back inside. My walk will have to wait for another day; it's time to make myself presentable.

Thirty minutes later, I'm starting to panic. I've pulled just about every designer outfit I own from the closet, and discarded them on the growing pile on my bed. Everything looks ridiculous on me. Especially my ultra feminine suits with pencil skirts. I can't wear any of those without wearing my hair in a chignon, and I'm not about to do that, because it would leave my face uncovered. Already it's not going to be a picnic to walk around Cortez, I definitely don't want to do it drawing all kinds of attention to myself with an outfit.

Trouble is, other than my power suits, the only other things I own are jeans, yoga pants, and a handful of summer dresses.

I guess I could wear one of those.

By the time I get in my SUV, wearing a long navy blue tank dress with a cropped white jean jacket, I'm already running ten minutes behind, and I hate being late.

I know my day has gone from challenging straight into fucked when a few minutes later, just outside of town, I see flashing lights in my rearview mirror. It takes everything out of me not to cry as I obediently pull over on the shoulder.

"Officer, I—" I start as I lower my window.

"In a hurry?" The familiar face of Drew Carmel, Montezuma County's sheriff, peeks in. I'd dealt with Sheriff Carmel a few times after the explosion, and he was a nice enough man. At least I hope so, seeing as he just caught me speeding.

"I'm sorry," I apologize. "I'm late for an interview in Cortez. Flynn and Associates? I know I was speeding," I quickly add. Better to lay it all on the table.

"You were," he says, a smirk on his face. "Is he finally talking you around?"

"Sorry?"

"Nick. He mentioned to me months ago he hoped to talk you into joining his firm. In fact, if I remember correctly, he told me he couldn't wait to see you wipe the courtroom floors with me." The sheriff chuckles, and I'm not sure if he's amused at Nick's expense or mine. "You probably will," he adds, still smiling. "Nothing as intimidating as having a former prosecutor at the defense table."

He holds up his finger to stop my almost objection and to my surprise, pulls a cell phone from a clip on his belt and dials.

"Yeah, Nick? I'm afraid Ms. Gustafson is going to be a few minutes late. There's a bit of a traffic hold up just outside Dolores...No, nothing like that...Yes, she'll be on her way shortly." He nods at me as he tucks the phone away. "One less thing for you to worry about," he tells me. "Now as for the speeding…"

Minutes later I'm back on the road, with just a warning, and a much better understanding of the small-town dynamics. It looks like possibly being on opposite sides of the law at some point doesn't create anywhere near the division it would in the big city. Prosecution and law enforcement are not often seen socializing with criminal defense lawyers, in my experience. It would be too difficult to eviscerate someone in the courtroom that you just had drinks with the night before. Not impossible, but difficult.

"How may I help you?" The impeccably dressed, slightly older woman behind the reception desk eyes me suspiciously, but I don't get a chance to answer.

"Stacie?" Nick comes walking out of one of the two hallways on either side of reception. She startles at the sound of his voice, and swings around in her chair before turning back to me with renewed curiosity.

"Hi," I tell him. "I'm sorry I ran a bit late."

Late at this point is closer to half an hour, since finding parking was a bitch. The small, but tastefully decorated offices are located on the east side of town, but apparently parking here is at a premium.

"Not a problem," he says to me before turning to the other woman. "Hold all calls, will you? And get hold of Urquhart; tell him I won't be able to make lunch and set something up for next week. Then call Tequila's and reserve a booth for one o'clock? Thanks, Sheila."

I barely have a chance to nod at the woman before he grabs me firmly by the elbow and maneuvers me down the hall; into a spacious office with large windows, looking out on Mesa Verde in the distance.

Nick

"Sheila is our legal assistant," I explain, after guiding Stacie to the small sitting area in my office, where she settles in the leather couch. I sit across from her in the single club chair, before continuing. "She basically runs the office, and probably us. She and Doug have the two other offices on this side of the building. Doug Grant is my associate. He specializes in family law, and is stuck in court all day. We also have a receptionist, who helps with some clerical work, but she called in sick this morning." I know I'm almost rambling, but I can't seem to help myself; I don't want to mess this up. "Do you want coffee? Or something else?"

"I'm fine, thanks." She gives me a nervous little smile, and somehow that settles me down.

"Corporate law is my area," I explain, although I'm pretty sure she's aware of that already. "A bit boring in comparison to criminal law, or even family law, some days.

"Why corporate then?" she wants to know, and I have to think on that for a minute.

"I guess when I picked a direction, I wasn't comfortable with the amount of litigation that often comes with family, but especially criminal law."

"Really?" she reacts surprised. "You must know you're charismatic; you'd make for an impressive figure in the courtroom." The slight blush on her face is cute and I can't hold back a grin at the compliment.

"Thanks for the vote of confidence," I tell her. "I probably could've used that ten years ago. Even at almost thirty I was a bit awkward, to say the least."

"That's hard to believe."

"Oh, believe it. It's amazing what laser eye surgery, a good gym, and a pair of twelve dollar clippers can do," I confess.

"Clippers?" she repeats, her eyebrows raised.

I run a hand all over my bald head.

"You didn't think I come by this without some help, did you?"

The resulting snicker I get from Stacie is like music to my ears. She visibly relaxes after that, and I finally get around to the reason I asked her here.

"We only have two lawyers who practice criminal law in Cortez. One does so exclusively, and the other as part of his general law practice. Given the increase in the number of calls we receive weekly, looking for a defense attorney, I'd like to offer a third option." I wait for a moment to see if I can gauge her reaction, but her face is pretty expressionless. Not a surprise from a lawyer who is used to sporting a poker face in the courtroom. "On the other side of reception is a second hallway that houses a washroom, a kitchen, a file room and another office with an exterior door. You'd have a quiet space to work from, close to all amenities, and you could almost slip in and out undetected."

"Why aren't you in there then?" she asks, with a grin.

"I was," I admit, smiling back. "But I discovered I much prefer being close enough to Sheila so I can yell, instead of trying to master the intercom system on the phone," I reveal, shrugging at my admission.

"A Luddite," she remarks, accurately.

"So it would seem. I know how to use my cell phone, and after many hours of instruction, I can now work our office software and the email on my laptop, but I'm lost if even the smallest thing goes wrong. I'm not savvy. In fact, I paid someone to hook up my TV and program the remote; one look at the instruction sheet had me break out in a sweat."

"Something we have in common then," she discloses, with an almost shy glance through thick lashes. "However, I have a nine-year-old daughter, who excels where I fall painfully short. And what she doesn't know, she Googles. She has no fear, unlike her mother."

Part of me wants to disagree with that statement; Stacie is probably one of the most courageous people I know. I'd like to know more about her. I'd also dig a little deeper into the existence of her daughter and what role, if any, her father plays in her life, but decide against it. For now, at least. Last thing I want to do is come off as too interested or invasive. Too obsessed—even if I am.

"So what are your thoughts?" I ask instead.

"I have a commitment to a trial lawyer in Denver, I'm doing some research for from home."

"Is that ongoing or on a per case basis?" I inquire.

"Per case. When I took it a few months back, I wasn't ready to commit to anything."

"And now?" I jump right on that comment, making her smile.

"I might be ready," she says, and there's no way I can hide the shit-eating grin.

-

I wipe my fingers and my mouth with my napkin after devouring my last tamale, and find Stacie staring at me with an amused look on her face.

"Did I miss a spot?" I ask, doing a second swipe just to make sure.

"No, I'm just amazed at how fast you downed those things."

I'm happy to see her so much more relaxed.

It had been touch and go when I told her those reservations I had Sheila make were intended for us. I'd just finished showing her the facilities, and the empty office, when she mentioned needing a few days to think about the logistics. She was preparing to leave when I mentioned going across the road to Tequila's. I think maybe the mention of their tamales was what swayed her to come.

"I was hungry," I tell her by way of explanation.

"Clearly," she deadpans, grinning as she takes a bite of her own.

I could tell when we walked in she was uncomfortable, keeping her head down and her hair covering her face. I thought she might, which is why I had Sheila ask for a booth. She shot me a grateful look when I offered her the left side of the booth. That way her scars would be facing the wall.

"So you're willing to give it a shot?" I ask, sitting back in the booth and watching her finish her own meal. "Six-month trial period. Three days a week to start, giving you some time to adjust. And just to clarify, I understand you have to honor your commitment to this case you're working on, and that's fine."

"Six-month trial, where either one can walk away without question?" she inquires.

"Of course," I say easily, lying.

I have no intention of letting her go.

CHAPTER 5

Stacie

"Can Becca stay for a bit, Mom?"

Mak doesn't waste any time when she gets off the school bus and comes charging toward me. No hi or hello, but straight to the point.

I've dreaded this moment, where she'd ask to bring home a friend after school. Mostly I've dreaded the parents. Kids can be quite pragmatic and will either ask straight up, or they will quickly accept something as normal, especially at this age. It's the parents who will tell their kids it's rude to stare or to ask questions, when it's their own silent judgment that is most insulting.

I look at the little redheaded girl with glasses, who got off right behind my daughter. She's a skinny little thing and looks about ready to bolt. My Mak has a rather powerful and strong-willed personality, and easily bulldozes over other kids her age. Not that she does so maliciously; she's not a bully. On the contrary, she's the collector of lost souls, my Mak is. Find her a kid who's shy, is picked on, or is treated like a misfit, and she'll show you her new best friend.

It's a miracle she hasn't brought home an entire menagerie of lost and lonely creatures, both two and four-legged.

"Hey, Becca," I greet the girl, bending down a little so I can look her in the eye. I notice she doesn't even flinch at the state of my face. "You're welcome to come play with Mak, honey, but we'll need to check with your parents first." That gets a reaction from the little girl, her expression one of concern as her eyes flit between Mak and me.

"She can just call from our house," Mak offers, but I notice the girl, Becca, turns to look a little forlornly at the school bus, which is just disappearing around the corner.

I can't leave the child standing on the street, so I wave her over. She hesitantly closes in and follows my daughter up the porch steps and in the house.

"So let's call your parents," I suggest, after sitting the kids down at the kitchen counter with a glass of chocolate milk and a muffin, and I hand Becca the phone.

She stares at it like it'll bite her, before turning her worried eyes on me.

"My mom is probably still sleeping," she says in a surprisingly raspy voice.

It's the first time I'm hearing it; she's managed with just nods so far. I'd expected something high-pitched, to match her small frame, but her voice sounds like whiskey.

"Sleeping?" I inquire, trying not to be too nosy but needing some information all the same.

"She works nights," Becca explains. "And sleeps during the day."

I can't help but wonder what kind of work the mother does, but I bite my tongue. "Is it just you and your mom?" I ask instead.

"And my older brother," she clarifies. "He drives to school in Cortez and doesn't usually get home until later."

"Okay," I tell her, making a split-second decision since I don't want to put the girl out. "You're welcome to stay for an hour, but then I'm driving you home. We'll clear things with your mom and go from there."

Becca doesn't look too pleased, but Mak more than makes up for that when she whoops out loud, grabs her friend's hand, and drags her to her room.

I sit back down behind my computer at the dining room table.

It's been almost a week since I ended up having lunch with Nick. I'd come home after that and immediately got cold feet. It felt like I might have jumped on his offer a little too eagerly. The offer was fabulous, and I can't deny I felt a surge of excitement at the prospect, but I should've taken some time to consider. It's not usually like me to decide on the spot, but it seems like I lose all independent thinking when I'm around that man.

I called him right away and let him know that I would prefer to finish my current assignment before embarking on something else, and he appeared very understanding.

Right now I'm writing up the final report with my findings to send off, and then I'm officially done with my last case. I promised Nick I would call as soon as I felt ready to make plans, which may be the reason why I've been dragging my heels on this one. For someone who lived by her appointment book and her promises most of her adult life, I certainly have grown an aversion to commitments these past months.

I've barely even opened the file when my phone starts buzzing on the counter.

"Hello?"

"Stacie? This is Linda at Dr. Ashrad's office."

"Hey, Linda! It's been a while. Did I forget an appointment?" I ask, quickly pulling up my iCal on my laptop to check.

"No, no," she hurries to assure me. "You didn't. You weren't due until the second week of October."

"Pre-op on October thirteenth, I'm looking at it," I confirm.

"Dr. Ashrad has had a cancellation September fourteenth, are you interested?"

"For the pre-op?"

"No, for the surgery."

My heart instantly starts pounding in my chest. After the last surgery on my arm, earlier in the year, I decided to take a break and had half-heartedly booked the final surgery on my face toward the end of the year, thinking it was far enough away. September fourteenth is in two weeks and I don't know if I'm emotionally ready for it.

There's something comforting about knowing there is still room for improvement, but that'll be gone once that surgery is done. What I end up with afterward will be as good as it gets, and *that* scares the crap out of me.

What if it's a disappointment? What if they can't lift the outside corner of my eye and get rid of that droop? What if they aren't able to smooth out the edges of the graft? And, God forbid, what if I end up with another infection like the one in my arm and the scarring only gets worse?

Funny as it may sound, I'm just now getting used to my face. These past few weeks, I've looked in the mirror more than I did in the months prior. After this surgery I'll have to start all over again.

"Stacie? Are you there?" Linda's disembodied voice drags me from my swirling, slightly panicky thoughts.

"Yeah, I'm here. I'm just...what does it mean? I mean, I know what it means, but when do I come in for my pre-op appointment? What time is surgery? Will I see Dr. Ashrad before?" I ramble, the many panicked thoughts now freely tumbling from my subconscious. Linda softly chuckles on the other side.

"Two days prior, eight forty-five, and yes. In that order," she answers, amusement in her voice. "Normally this could be done in day surgery, but he may want you to stay for one night to keep an eye out for infection."

"Isn't it a proven fact that the chance of getting an infection is highest in the hospital?" I point out, half joking, but half not.

"Not on Dr. Ashrad's watch," is the firm response. "Trust him to be invested in what's best for you, Stacie. I understand this is your face we're talking about, but for Dr. Ashrad it just emphasizes the need to be extra vigilant."

"Understood," I concur. I guess for a plastic surgeon, his patients become his walking advertisement. Or downfall, depending on how you look at it.

"By the way," she says. "I'm looking at you right now."

"Sorry?"

"Did you not see him at the gala? Dr. Ashrad? He bought a couple of your pictures for the clinic. They're gorgeous!"

"I had no idea he was there," I tell her truthfully, and a tad ashamed. Clearly my mind hadn't been functioning on all cylinders. "Which ones?"

"Not to worry, he purposely chose ones where the face is not or barely visible. Only reason I know it is you is because he told me," she clarifies.

So not the large close-up of my face. Isla mentioned it was bought by an anonymous bidder, and the thought of some stranger looking at my face is slightly unnerving.

When the girls come charging into the kitchen half an hour later, I haven't done a lick of work on my report. I am, however, scheduled for pre-op at ten-thirty on the twelfth, and am to check in at six-thirty a.m. the day of surgery.

-

"Is this your house?" I ask Becca, pulling up to a rundown double-wide in the trailer park across the road from the Baptist church. She'd told me to drop her off in the church parking lot initially, but I made it clear I wasn't about to dump a nine-year-old in an empty parking lot. It took some doing, but she eventually told me she lived in the trailer park on the south side of the road.

"Yes," she says, not quite meeting my eyes in the rearview mirror, but not making a single move to get out.

"Becca? Could you see if your mom is awake so I can meet her?"

I roll down my window and watch as the little girl reluctantly makes her way to the side of the trailer, where an upside down milk crate serves as a step to get in. Before she even has a chance to touch the door, it's already flying open, almost knocking Becca on her ass.

A slightly disheveled woman, blonde hair tied back in a lopsided ponytail, wearing men's boxer shorts with a tank top, grabs Becca rather firmly by the upper arm and pulls her into the trailer. Not before shooting a scathing look in the direction of my car, though. I guess that means we won't be friends.

A quick glance in the rearview mirror shows that Mak did not miss that. She looks sad and stares at the trailer.

"Hey," I call back, getting her attention. "How about we head over to the Depot for some fries and a shake?"

The smile and the enthusiastic headshake are instantaneous, but when I pull away, I catch her throwing a last look at the trailer out the rear window.

Nick

"Tomorrow let's tackle the roof on the small barn. Last week when we had that rain come through, the horses stayed drier under the overhang covering the outside pen than they did inside the barn itself."

I'm glad we're onto more palatable dinner subjects now. As my Pops ages, his choice of casual conversation over a meal, more often than not, includes the day's special on ailments or a detailed report on bodily functions.

Today's topics of choice had been ingrown toenails and the effects of the latest pinto bean crop on a senior's digestive system. Yeah, my dad can be a laugh-and-a-half at the dinner table.

"Absolutely," I say, trying not to sound too relieved at the change in topic. "Do we still have a few of those corrugated roof panels we used on the shelter for the woodpile?"

"Probably just one or two," Pops answers, before taking another massive bite of his hamburger.

"Maybe we'll head into Cortez in the morning?"

"We can hit Denny's for breakfast," he says, slurping the dregs of his milkshake loudly.

Pops is a man of simple pleasures: a regular constitution and a hearty meal. Throw in a beer occasionally and he's a happy man. He also likes predictability, which is why I've made it a point, in recent years, to keep my schedule clear on Friday afternoons. We go out for an early meal—Pops likes to eat at five—and catch up on our weeks, before planning out our weekend.

I don't have much of a life outside of work. Sadly, my father is responsible for the bulk of my socializing. Friday dinners at a restaurant of his choice, and the weekends mostly putzing about our property. There are days when I feel more like sixty than the barely forty years I'm old.

"Now there's a sight for sore eyes."

I barely register Pop's voice as I focus on my chicken-fried steak sandwich, until the melodic cadence of a familiar voice pierces my awareness.

"First pick a booth, Mak, and then we'll order."

I swivel around in my seat to find Stacie's daughter staring back at me.

"Hey," I offer in greeting, my eyes immediately looking for, and finding, Stacie behind her. I can feel my face crack open in a big smile.

"Hi," is the cheerful reply, along with Stacie's more subdued, "Hello."

"You friends of my son?" Pops pushes half out of his seat, the paper napkin he habitually tucks in his collar to catch the inevitable crumbs and stains flutters down to the floor, as he sticks out his greasy hand in greeting.

Instead of bouncing my head off the table a few times, which I'd like to do, I also stand up.

"Stacie, this is my father, Henry Flynn. And, Pops, this is Stacie Gustafson and her daughter, Makenna. Stacie is a colleague." I'm not quite sure why I add the last, but the moment I see my father's eyes narrow on Stacie's face, a feeling of doom settles in my stomach. My pops is not exactly known for tact or subtlety.

"Why don't you join us?" I quickly ask, hoping to avoid what I know is sure to come. Stacie opens her mouth with what I fear will be an objection, but Mak easily slides into the booth beside Pops.

I feel bad for Stacie, who is left standing a little awkwardly next to the table. I grab her hand and gently pull her to sit down. I try to glare at Pops to warn him off when he leans over the table, his head slightly tilted to the side, but he's like a dog with a bone.

"What happened to your face?"

And there it is.

I'm still contemplating my father's imminent demise, while desperately seeking for ways to soften the shocked expression on Stacie's face at the impact of his words, when her little girl pipes up.

"She got burned in an explosion. Gnarly, right? You should see her arm."

I watch Stacie's eyes pop open at her daughter's callous description, but Pops is immediately distracted.

"The explosion up on the mountain last winter? That was your mom? Damn, I heard that was bad."

"She almost died," Mak says, her face somber.

"Yeah, but she didn't, did she?" Pops counters sagely, and I throw up my hands, there's no way to stop this train wreck. "Looks pretty alive to me."

Stacie's eyes, round as saucers, turn to me. Surprisingly, I see a glimmer of humor in their depths.

"Thank God," her daughter blurts out dramatically, and the whole situation suddenly becomes comical in the most surreal way.

"Yeah—thank God," Pops echoes, a smirk on his face as he winks across the table at Stacie, who promptly bursts out laughing, and I can't hold back a chuckle. "Besides, they can fix that, you know?"

"Oh, I know," Mak says wisely, tucking her paper napkin in the collar of her shirt, mimicking my dad. A move that makes all of the adults at the table smile. "Mom's having her face done in two weeks."

After a little confusion—during which the waitress shows up to take Stacie and Mak's orders, and Pops takes the opportunity to order another milkshake and an order of fries—I manage to glean that *having her face done* means Stacie apparently has another surgery scheduled.

I'm happy for her, but I'm also a little apprehensive. I don't want her to back out of my job offer. Distractedly, I'm picking at my fries with half an ear on the chatter between Pops and Makenna. Apparently sweet potato fries are far tastier and healthier—according to Makenna. My father is of a different opinion, and loudly touts the beauty of the original spud. If I weren't distracted by thoughts of the woman sitting next to me, I'd probably laugh at their harmless bickering. They sound like an old married couple, except one is nine and the other seventy-eight.

A warm hand lands on my forearm and I turn my head to look at its owner. Stacie sends me a faint smile.

"Surgery was scheduled for later in the year, but they had an opening earlier. I thought it was probably better to do it now, because later it might interfere with active cases? Hope that's okay with you," she says, searching my face for answers. I'm trying to hang on to my blank expression, because I'm worried the big grin that is itching to break free would seem too maniacal. "I'm sure I'll be on my feet in a few days," she adds, probably interpreting my silence wrong.

"God, that's a relief," I blurt out on a sigh, resulting in surprise and then a snicker from Stacie.

So much for my self-restraint.

Without really thinking it through, I lean in and lightly brush my lips over hers.

"Something you want to tell me, Son?"

I ignore Pops and keep my eyes on Stacie's face. An entire gamut of emotion plays out over her features, and finally lands on a blank poker face.

As if I didn't just kiss her out of the fucking blue, Stacie picks up her hamburger, opens wide and takes a humongous bite, chewing with perhaps a tad too much vigor.

I sneak a peek across the table, where Mak is still stuck in shock, and Pops has a grin on his face and shakes his head at me.

Me—I don't know if I just fucked up or scored big.

I'm at a total loss.

CHAPTER 6

Stacie

"Mom, are you coming in?"

Mak's voice pulls me right back to the here and now, which is parked on the dirt shoulder outside of my own house.

Don't ask me how I got here. I don't think I could tell you, even though the restaurant we just left is around the corner. Years spent in courtrooms have trained me never to show whatever plays out inside my head or my heart. I can appear unaffected, while falling apart emotionally.

Kind of like what just happened in that booth.

I don't know what happened. One minute I'm laughing at something he says and the next his really nice, firm lips are pressed against mine. The kicker is, I didn't even move. I just let him kiss me; in a booth at a restaurant, with his father and my daughter sitting smack across from us, and I did not even consider stopping him for one second.

Unable to process, I did what I do best. I let years of training take over and dismiss the entire incident as a just vague blip on my radar. For appearances only, because inside my head, and my heart, it's chaos.

"I'm coming," I mumble, grabbing my purse and getting out of the car.

Once inside, Mak immediately flicks on the TV to catch her favorite show, and after a perfunctory, "Homework done?" to which I received an affirmative, I disappear into my bedroom. I change into a pair of soft, flowy lounge pants and an old T-shirt, and walk into my bathroom to wash my face.

The lighting over the vanity is purposely harsh. I had Ben change out the light fixture that was here before, because it gave off a muted, softer light. If I'm going to look in the mirror, I want to know exactly what others are looking at when they see me outside. I don't want to delude myself into thinking it's not as bad as it is and be surprised or hurt by reactions.

A fine theory, but the reality is that even if I'm looking at the same thing they are, I have no way of knowing what they see. Or how they will react. More than that, I don't even seem to control my own reactions, because I still get upset, or hurt, by the way some people look at me. The irony is that I can be just as judgmental, just as quick with my knee-jerk response to how others react to me. It's the monkey on my own back that colors the way I see the world now.

I scrutinize my face in the mirror, and try closing my eyes for five seconds before opening them again, to see what part of my reflection I automatically focus on first. Hardly a viable scientific test, but even knowing the scars are there, I find my eyes first, every time. The eyes, then the one droopy side comes into focus and from there the scarring.

I'm not exactly sure what it proves, but it makes me feel a little less confused about that kiss.

I am a sum of my parts, and I've been forgetting about a lot of my *parts*, focusing only on the part of me that has changed, not the parts that have stayed the same.

I'm still me.

I've tried so hard to become someone who fits the ten percent of me that's changed, that I've been ignoring the other ninety percent.

The people I care about; Mak, Ben, Isla, and even Al, they see all of me. And for some reason, it appears Nick does too.

I have scars, but they don't get to define me.

"Can I have popcorn?" my daughter yells from the kitchen, interrupting my lofty self-analysis.

Nothing like a call for food to bring you back to basics.

-

"I know. It's soon. I almost said no," I admit to Isla.

With Mak tucked away for the night, I called to tell her and my brother about the pending surgery. Ben answered and was quick to offer me a ride to the hospital in Durango the day of. When he suggested Mak should stay with them the night before, Isla apparently had exercised as much patience as she could muster, because suddenly I had her on the phone.

"I'm glad you didn't," my sister-in-law expresses. "It's time. You're so ready to be out there, instead of wasting away inside."

I don't have the heart to tell her I've been *out* more than she knows. Both Ben and Isla have been absolutely wonderful during my recovery, looking after Mak, helping me find a place to live. Isla really made me push my self-imposed envelope with the photo shoot, and all of it helped me to get to this point. But I've always been independent, self-sufficient, and capable, and it's time I reclaim that.

Both my brother and Isla would have a thing or two to say about my recent social and professional interactions with Nick, for instance. Ben would want to protect me, and Isla would probably try to throw us together at every opportunity. All very sweet and lovable, but also completely unnecessary. I can figure this out on my own.

"I've hardly been wasting away," I counter, a smile in my voice. "I'll have you know, I've packed on thirty pounds since I got out of the hospital."

"Only because you lost at least twenty of those by the time they released you," she fires back. "I hated you skinny." I snort out a laugh. Isla is always bitching about the size of her ass. A feature my brother clearly adores, and one I wish I could complain about. I have hips, I have solid legs, but my ass is flat. No cute bubble butt here.

"Oh, before I forget," she says with some urgency. "Ben is dropping Uncle Al off at the airport tomorrow, Ginnie has developed pneumonia, the nursing home called earlier."

"Awww, I'm sorry to hear that."

Ginnie is Al's second wife. The man already buried one, and it would break my heart if he had to bury another, but Ginnie has Alzheimers and has been in a care facility for a year and a half. Some might argue that death would be a blessing, and that might well be true, but that doesn't make the loss any less painful.

"Part of me hopes that like the other scares, this will pass as well, but there's this other part of me that just wants this to be over. It is going to happen, we all know it, so rip off the Band-aid already."

I completely understand where Isla's coming from, even though I know she will be devastated to have to say goodbye to the third mother figure in her life. She'd already lost her birth mother when she was twelve, and her uncle and aunt took her in and raised her. Just five years later, her aunt died suddenly. Losing Ginnie too will be difficult.

"I hear you," I commiserate, staring out the kitchen window. There really is little else to say.

I think I see movement outside and I sit up to get a better look. It's hard to see anything because the kitchen light is on and it's dark outside. Probably just the lower branches of the tree out there. The next thing I know, there's a sharp knock on my front door and my head swivels in that direction.

"Tomorrow morning was the first flight out…" I listen to Isla detailing Al's travel plans, while I get up and walk to the door to peek through the peephole.

"Honey, can you give Al my best?" I jump in the first break I get. "Mak is calling for me."

It should worry me how easily the lie rolls off my lips, but I can't think about that right now. I can hear the pounding of my heart in my ears as I pull the door open.

"Hey," Nick says, looking a little sheepish as he leans against the doorpost.

"What are you doing here?"

Not exactly very warm and welcoming, but it is past ten o'clock on a Friday night, and I'm more than a little flipped out. I just don't know whether it's Nick that's freaking me out, or the feelings he evokes, randomly appearing on my doorstep.

It's mild outside, albeit a tad windy, but still I fold my arms around me defensively. A move that does not go unnoticed by Nick, whose eyes have dropped down to where, I'm just now remembering, my unrestricted boobs are now pushed up and out. I immediately drop my arms, which really doesn't help, since it also removes any support. So my boobs plummet to their now natural resting place, somewhere at the level of my bellybutton.

A big rack is fun when they're perky and appropriately harnessed. My lady lumps are free-flowing and my perky left the building about eight years ago, when Mak quite literally sucked the life out of them.

I'm about to blast the man for staring, when he reaches out with his hand and strokes his fingertips over the grooves and ridges on my left arm.

Shit.

―――――◯◯◯―――――

Nick

I know I'm staring, but fuck, her forearm looks like it's been through a meat grinder. I guess I never quite picked up on the fact she was always wearing something that covered her arms, or at least this arm.

"Does it hurt?" I ask, stroking my fingertips over the scar tissue on her arms. When she doesn't answer, I lift my gaze to her face. She seems focused on the movement of my fingers over her arm. "Stacie?" That startles her.

"Not really," she says, as if she's assessing as we speak. "Parts of it feels dead, like it's not attached to me, and then other parts feel hyper-sensitized, almost bordering on pain."

I immediately withdraw my fingers.

"Sorry. That was forward of me," I apologize, but to my surprise, Stacie snorts.

"*That* was forward?" she asks with a healthy dose of sarcasm. "You kiss me in the middle of a restaurant, with your dad and my little girl at the table, completely out of the blue, and you're worried that touching my arm is too forward?"

I chuckle, because she has a point.

"About that kiss," I start, and her face turns serious instantly.

"Maybe you should step inside. Doesn't really seem like something to discuss on the doorstep."

"Right."

She steps aside and I walk past, into her house. Living and dining room as well as an open kitchen make up the large open space. There's a hallway off to the right that I assume goes to bedrooms and a bathroom.

"Have a seat," she says from behind me. "Do you want something to drink? I think I may have one of Ben's beers floating around the back of my fridge, or otherwise there's always wine, or water."

"I'm good, thanks."

"All right," she says, walking into the kitchen anyway. "I think I'll need some wine."

I sit down on the couch and watch as she pours herself a healthy serving. She prefers white wine, a bit of information I file away. I didn't expect her to fall in my lap, but still I find myself a little disappointed when instead of taking a spot next to me on the couch, she curls up in an oversized chaise on the other side of the table.

"I won't apologize for my attire," she says without preamble. "You knock on my door at this hour of night, you'll have to take what you get."

"Okay," I answer simply. There really is nothing else to say to that, besides, you won't hear me complaining.

"So about that kiss," she prompts. "What exactly am I to make of that?"

I grin at her forward approach. Typical lawyer, she goes straight for the point.

"Not sure myself, but I'm not apologizing either," I challenge her, just like she challenged me a minute ago. "I did come here to explain though, Anastasia."

Pops grilled me all the way home. At first I just kept my mouth shut, but then he'd said something that hit home: *"You don't play games with a woman like that, Son."* He was right, and I ended up telling him everything. His instant reaction had been: *"Don't wait any longer telling her."* So I got in my car and drove back into town.

I watch her eyes open wide with curiosity, whether at the sentiment I expressed or the use of her full name, I don't know, but I make use of her undivided attention.

"I remember you from college. We didn't move in the same circles," I quickly explain when I see her expression.

"I don't remember you," she says, almost apologetically.

"That doesn't surprise me," I chuckle. "I had hair then and I didn't socialize much, but I noticed you. So when Ben introduced me to his little sister at the wedding, it was a shock to find it was you."

"But I don't understand; why not say something then? I thought…" she starts, but I interrupt her.

"I know what you thought, and it couldn't be further from the truth. I was just shocked, and I don't know why I didn't say something. Maybe I was a little embarrassed," I admit, shrugging my shoulders. "Like I said, I wasn't the most social guy at the time, and I wasn't exactly the most confident either."

"Well, that's clearly no longer an issue," she deadpans, and I chuckle.

"Clearly. Anyway, long story short, I kissed you because I could. Scratch it off my bucket list, so to speak."

"So that's it? I'm an item on your bucket list that's now taken care of?" I smile at her incredulous tone, as I get up from the couch.

"Not exactly," I confess, reaching out a hand to her, that she hesitantly accepts, and I pull her to her feet. "Kiss Anastasia is off my bucket list, but that kiss just added about five more pages to my list," I half joke. "I've said it before and I mean it; I want to know you. I want to know about Mak, and although it scares the crap out of me, I want you to know me too."

I try to gauge her thoughts by her expression, but her face is a mask once again. She hasn't pulled her hands from mine though, so I'll take that as a good sign.

"Okay," she finally says, lifting her eyes, and they tell me a lot more. Fear, excitement, reservation, and heat. Especially the heat I recognize. I want to drop to my knees and bury my face against her soft skin, but I hold back, instead I bend down and rest my forehead against hers. Her eyes close, fanning her lashes over the top of her cheekbones, and I watch as her mouth relaxes, and the tip of her tongue slips out from between and slicks her lips.

"Okay?" I want to make sure.

"Yes. But wait," she suddenly steps back, planting a hand in the middle of my chest. "What about the firm?"

"What about it?"

"Do you still want me there? Won't that be…I mean, isn't that awkward? A risk, even?"

"Not exactly conventional, and not particularly advisable, but yes; I most definitely still want you there…" I pull her against my chest, wrapping one arm low around her waist, and sliding the other up her back so my hand lands between her shoulder blades. "And I want you here," I assure her, brushing her lips with mine once, twice, before tilting my head and slanting my mouth over hers. Her arms curl around my neck, pulling me closer, and I feel her breasts press against my chest.

The moment her tongue curls around mine, my chest is full and my cock feels heavy. The urge to imprint myself on her so strong, but I'm afraid to lose control. I reluctantly drag myself away before I drown in her kiss. Her eyes blink a few times before she focuses on me.

"Wow," she sighs. "Heady stuff."

It sure as fuck is, and it will get headier in a hurry if I don't get out of here.

I resolutely step out of her reach and start toward the door.

"I'd better go," I say, my hand already on the doorknob, as I turn to where she is staring after me, still a bit dazed.

"I know," she says, making me feel a little better for my abrupt behavior.

"One step at a time," I offer, and she softly repeats.

"One step at a time."

CHAPTER 7

Stacie

To say I'm in a panic would be an understatement.

And here I thought I was on top of everything. Goes to show control is just an illusion: one phone call and everything changes.

"Not to worry," I tell my brother, lying through my teeth. "It'll be fine. I'll just bring the dog here, it makes it easier."

"I just don't know how long it'll be," my brother says, concern lacing his voice. "This fucking timing sucks."

"I don't think the timing is ever right for this, Ben," I offer.

"I can't have her go through this alone, Stace. You know I'll do my best to get back in time."

My wonderful brother is referring to my surgery, which is scheduled for Friday. Today is Tuesday, and there is no way in hell he'll be able to make it back here.

Apparently Al called early this morning and told Isla that if she wanted a chance to say goodbye to Ginnie, that she should come now. The general consensus seems to be that it won't be long, but who knows? Sometimes people hang in for days before they're finally able to let go.

Ben didn't hesitate for a second and already has all three of them, baby Noah included, booked on a flight to Phoenix for this afternoon. Not only that, but he's got

Nick looking for someone to look after the campground. I offered to help, but I was categorically shut down and told my job was to look after myself.

"I'll be fine, Ben. I'll pick up the dog this afternoon and bring him here. I'll call Jen, she'll be able to help and if she can't do it herself, she'll know who can. And as for the surgery, it's not like Mak is a baby, there's stuff she can do to help. It's not going to be an issue. You need to go and be with your family. And tell Isla and Al they are on my mind and in my heart."

"I'll call," he says and I can hear Noah fussing in the background. Sounds like he's cuddling with his dad.

"Yes, please. Keep me in the loop."

There's a pregnant pause, and for a moment I think perhaps he's hung up on me, but then I hear him clear his throat.

"Love ya, Sis."

My eyes tear up when I hear those words in his *I-don't-do-emotion* growl. The times I've heard those words from anyone, other than my daughter, are few and far between.

"Ditto, you big lug. Safe travels," I manage, and quickly end the call before the first tears roll down my cheeks.

I hate losing people. I really, really do. Although I don't know Ginnie, I know how important she is in Isla's life, and it hurts me that she has to say goodbye to yet someone else she loves. I just hope Al will be around for her for a long time to come yet.

Sometimes the idea that Ben and I are now the oldest generation of the Gustafsons, the last ones standing so to speak, scares the heck out of me.

-

It took me all of twenty minutes after Ben's phone call to get myself organized by making lists.

I made a grocery list, featuring mostly frozen meals and easy snacks for the days right after surgery. I wrote another list with things I needed to get done before Friday. Then there was one for the few things I might need help with after surgery, mostly around Mak and Ben's dog.

It's those things I needed to talk to Jen about.

"You're a little late for your regular," Jen says from behind the counter when I walk into the Pony Express. "Shall I make it a decaf?" she asks, glancing at the clock that shows it's only half an hour before Mak gets home.

I'm going to have to hustle to grab Atsa as well as his dog bed and paraphernalia and get back down the mountain in time to grab her off the bus. Good thing I already have groceries done and packed away at home.

I was so focused on what I needed to do, I didn't even notice anyone staring; the way I usually do. Perhaps it is true, that I see what I expect to see, not necessarily what is visible. Maybe I am projecting my own issues on the world around me. In which case, you'd think it's also in my power to chance that.

I remember someone saying to me once that you receive back what you put out into the universe. In her case I think she was using it as a tool to get rich, which I had my doubts about. But that's not to say there isn't some truth to it.

Maybe it's not the judgment of other people I should worry about, but my own.

"Hit me full strength," I respond after those heavy thoughts on an already heavy day. "I'm gonna need it today."

"What's today?" she asks, turning around to work coffee magic with that big shiny machine of hers.

"Al's wife isn't good," I explain. "Ben is taking Isla and the little one to Phoenix. They're probably at the airport by now."

"I'm so sorry to hear that." Jen sends me a sad little smile before turning her attention back to the production of my macchiato.

In the silence that follows, I try to come up with the right words to ask Jen for a hand. Asking for help is not one of my strong suits.

"What can I do?" I look up at Jen, who easily solves my dilemma. She sets a foaming cup of sanity in front of me on the counter, with a half smile on her face.

Instead of trying to sort out what to ask of her, I just pull out the list of things I need to source out.

"What about the campground?"

"Ben called Nick to find someone to look after things. I'm actually off to pick up Atsa now, and I'll check in with Nick to see if he has things sorted, or else I'll head back up there after dinner and make sure everything is okay."

"What about Friday?" she asks, looking over the list she's holding.

"My main worry is Mak. Technically she could get herself on the bus in the morning, but she'd need someone looking after her after school and overnight. Chances are I'll have to stay at least twenty-four hours."

When I rush out fifteen minutes later, my macchiato in hand, I have peace of mind that my little girl will be in good hands. Jen suggested she take Mak and the dog Thursday night to stay with her. She'll bring her in to the coffee shop for breakfast, and run out to drop her at school around eight. She'll be able to get off the bus in front of the Pony Express in the afternoon.

It's too late to get up the mountain and grab the dog and get back in time, so instead I head straight for the school, where I can maybe catch her before she gets on the bus.

"Makenna!" I yell, standing on the running board of my SUV and waving my arms at the bus. She was about to climb on board when I pulled into the vacant slot. Luckily she sees me, and comes jogging in my direction, her backpack bouncing on her shoulder.

"Where are we going?" she asks, clipping her seatbelt and turning to me.

"We're picking up Atsa," I explain as I pull out of the school parking lot. "Uncle Ben and Isla had to go see Uncle Al in Phoenix."

"Are we picking up Noah as well?" she asks, a big smile on her face.

"No. They're taking Noah along," I assure her, hesitant whether I should let her know about Ginnie or not. I decide against it for now. When she passes away it's a different matter.

"Have I been to Phoenix?" I love how she still looks to me as the keeper of her life. I'm not sure how long that will last, but I will treasure these brief moments of high dependency in the meantime.

"Not Phoenix, but you've been in Flagstaff once. I think you were two."

"Where else?"

Nine years old and blissfully easy to distract. With poor Al and Ginnie all but forgotten, the rest of the drive up the mountain is spent discussing all the places Mak has seen in her young years.

To say Atsa was happy to see us does not do the dog's enthusiasm justice. Even though it's only just been a few hours since his owners left, his big body practically vibrates with excitement. Mostly for Mak, who is treated to a wave of doggy kisses, when I have to make do with a quick sniff and nuzzle.

Either Ben or Isla had already packed up the dog's stuff and left it, along with a big tub of his kibble, on top of the kitchen counter. It takes me just minutes to load up the SUV while Mak lets Atsa out for a piddle.

I'm just about to pull the front door closed, when I hear the crunch of gravel. A vaguely familiar truck pulls up next to my Subaru, just as Atsa comes barreling out of the woods, barking loudly, Mak following behind.

"Thought that was you," Nick says, climbing down from the cab.

―――――∞―――――

Nick

The second I got off the phone with Ben, I called Sheila into my office.

"What is on the docket for the rest of this week?"

"The Marx merger has to be finalized. James Marx wants to make an announcement before the end of the week. You have two closing dates we have to get checks and paperwork ready for, and you have to be in court on Friday for that continuance hearing in the Masotti case," she listed, flipping through my agenda.

"I'll handle the Marx merger. You can get the paperwork and checks ready for me to sign on the real estate deals, other than my signature, you can deal with the clients," I delegated and watched her take notes. "As for the hearing on Friday, contact counsel for the other side and inform them that we won't contest the continuance as long as they can assure us we will bring this case to a conclusion within a reasonable timeframe. No more yearlong delays," I told her, rubbing a hand over my head where the stubble is creeping up on me again. "I'm sure they'll be happy to have that taken off the court docket."

"I'll take care of it," Sheila assured me when she finished her notes. "Anything else?" she wanted to know, curiosity shining through her question.

"I've had some personal stuff come up this week. I'll be in tomorrow to finish the Marx contract, so get him in on Thursday morning to sign. I'll be out of commission from midday Thursday until sometime after the weekend, but I'll have my cell on me for emergencies."

Next on my list was a call to my pops, to see if he'd be willing to help keep an eye on the campground. I should've known he'd jump at the opportunity, I think he misses feeling useful. When I told him where I would be, he just chuckled.

That leaves just one last obstacle, if you can call her that: *Stacie*.

My plan had been to do a quick drive around the campgrounds to empty the garbage bins, as Ben had explained needed to be done daily, and replenishing the bathrooms with toilet paper. He dropped off keys on his way out of town earlier and mentioned that I didn't need to worry about cleaning, since he hired a service to come in twice a week after Noah was born. I just need to be there to unlock the sheds.

I'm just locking the gate to the dumpster, after tossing the last garbage bags in there, when I spot Stacie's SUV turning up the steep drive to Ben and Isla's house on the cliff. I quickly wash my hands at the outdoor tap and wipe them dry on my jeans, before following her up the mountain.

I can hear Atsa barking up a storm as I pull in beside Stacie's ride, and the moment I open the door, the large dog is all over me.

"Thought that was you," I direct at Stacie as I get out, handling Atsa with both hands as he jumps up on me. "Down, buddy."

"What are you doing here?" she asks, making me chuckle.

"You seem to be asking me that a lot," I tease her. "It's probably just easier to accept that wherever you are, I might not be far behind."

"I'm not sure if that was your intent," she says, pensively tapping her finger on her chin, "but that's actually a mildly disturbing comment to make."

"It's only disturbing if you don't want me around," I offer, one eyebrow raised. It takes a minute for her to respond, but when she does it's with a little smirk on her lips.

"Jury's out on that," she quips.

I want to kiss her again, but Mak walks right up to us, so I ruffle her short hair in greeting, before leaning down to kiss her mother on the cheek.

"I'll take it," I whisper in her ear. "And in answer to your earlier question," I explain at normal volume. "I was actually coming over to your place. I was just doing a quick drive around to make sure everything is okay here. Ben forwarded the emergency number for the campground to my cell phone, but I wanted to have a look for myself."

"It's not busy," she says, walking up to the edge of the cliff that overlooks the campground and the reservoir below. I'm right on her heels.

"About half the spots are taken."

"Kids are back in school so you don't get many families. The season rush is done," she points out, turning her head to watch Mak and the dog darting in and out of the bushes on the side of the house. Seeing they are safely within range, she moves her eyes to me. "So what did you need me for?"

"Dangerous territory, counselor. So many ways to interpret that question, and so many more ways to answer it," I tease, as she slugs me in the shoulder. "I promised

Ben I'd look out for you, so I wanted to get some times down for Friday."

"I can look after myself," she snips.

"I'm sure you can, but when a friend calls and asks you to look out for his little sister—you don't argue that point—you do as he asks," I clarify, before I add carefully, "especially when that frees him up to look after his wife and baby." I can see she gets the message when she casts her eyes down.

"So noted," she affirms curtly.

"I assume you've got Mak covered?" I prod gently, lifting her chin with my knuckle.

"Jen is taking her and Atsa on Thursday night. I need to be in the hospital at six thirty in the morning, so I don't know how good you are at waking up early, but—"

"We'll grab a hotel in town the night before," I interrupt, the opportunity too good to pass up. "We'll drop Mak and Atsa off at Jen's and drive straight to Durango. We'll go to the Derailed Pour House for a bite to eat and some great music. I'm not sure if you're allowed any alcohol the night before, but they do a mean Dickel Pickle." I grin at the expression on her face.

"Anything you said after Durango is like a different language to me," she says.

"Derailed Pour House is a great place on Main Street, and the Dickel Pickle is one of their signature drinks that involves sour mash and pickle juice."

"Ixnay on the Ickelday Icklepay. I'd rather suck a raw egg."

"Deal," I jump in before she can throw out any more objections. "No pickle juice for you. I'll get a room at the

Strater for Thursday, the Derailed Pour House is one block further down Main."

Just then Mak comes darting out of the trees with the dog bounding along at her heels.

"I'm hungry, Mom!"

"Just a minute, honey," Stacie admonishes her daughter. "I'm just talking to Mr. Flynn."

"I think we're past the mister part," I point out. "Besides, I have to get going, I promised Pops a hand with the fencing for the corral."

"A corral like for horses?" Mak pipes up, her little ears clearly well attuned.

"Exactly like that. We have a few at the ranch. There's one mare who got hurt a little while ago. She can't go out into the pasture until she's healed, but she doesn't like it and keeps escaping." I smile at Mak's big hungry eyes.

"I didn't know you had horses," she says a little breathlessly.

"We do—you should come see them sometime."

From the corner of my eye I can see the firm line Stacie presses her mouth into at my impromptu invitation, while her daughter is jumping up and down with excitement.

"Pushy," she hisses at me after telling Mak to wait by the car.

I quickly press a kiss to her tight little mouth. "I warned you," I mumble against her lips, before stepping around her to saunter off after Mak.

CHAPTER 8

Son of a bitch!

Another wasted fucking day at the unemployment office. What's the damn point? Once the human resource assholes look at my application and see felon, they fucking show me the door. But to keep my jackass parole officer off my back, I have to come in every week to get a new list of dead ends from the employment counselor.

Not my fucking fault the little slut at my bachelor party was underage; she sure didn't blow like a sixteen-year-old. After she had all my friends, I went for the only untouched hole—her mouth. It sure wasn't worth eight damn years when she cried rape to her daddy. Blonde little bitch! I swear every woman who has ever screwed me over has been a fucking blonde: the little slut, my wife, and that fucking ADA in Albuquerque. There's little else I've thought about for the past eight years, other than ways to make those bitches pay.

Six goddamn months I've been coming in, six fucking months in that slum of a halfway house because I can't get a job. Nothing changes, same faces, same furniture, same damn magazines. Why the hell would someone looking for a job give a shit about what's in USA Today? Who the fuck cares about that shit when you can't even get on with your life? They never throw these damn papers out, nothing new, same old crap.

Reaching to grab the top paper, I'm shocked to find it's one I haven't read at least once before: this one's only two weeks old. I flip through the pages while waiting for my appointment, when a picture of a woman catches my eye. Something about her face is familiar. A quick scan of the article reveals some poor slob spent a small fortune at a charity auction to own the portrait, what a dumbass. You know what they say about fools and money.

I almost flip through to the next page when I spot a name in the caption underneath the photograph. The sight of it is enough to have the hair on the back of my arms stand up, Anastasia Gustafson. My eyes flick back to the image for a closer look. The blonde hair isn't as long, and one side of her face looks mangled, but I'll never forget those eyes—the ones that stole my future.

One of the computers in the waiting room is not being used, so I look up the charitable foundation mentioned in the paper. The online article is more detailed and outlines how Anastasia Gustafson was injured in an explosion earlier in the year. That picture was taken by her sister-in-law; who apparently owns a campground in the mountains near Dolores with her husband. I'm just jotting down the name of the place, when my name is called. I tuck the slip of paper in my pocket and mumble under my breath, as I head into the counselor's office.

"Someone blew the bitch up," I mutter, disappointed I didn't get the opportunity first.

Stacie

"Are you sure you don't mind? It's in a garment bag in the closet, and the shoes are somewhere underneath in the pile. Shouldn't be too hard to find, since they're the only high-heeled shoes I own."

I quietly let Isla ramble on the other end of the line. She's coping her own way.

Ben called earlier this morning with the news that Ginnie had passed away during the night. They'd all been in the room with her and hadn't even noticed when she finally slipped away. He mentioned Al seemed to deflate, but Isla immediately went into action mode, bossing around the nursing staff and making arrangements. I suggested that was likely for each of them their way of coping with the immediate sense of loss.

So I thought I was prepared, when Isla called, but I was wrong.

I barely had a chance to say hello before she launched into a list of things she would need me to ship overnight. It's heartbreaking to listen to her rattle on in the slightly elevated pitch, which doesn't quite hide the pain right under the surface.

"I've got it," I assure her again. "Black dress in garment bag, black heels, Ben's navy suit, white shirt, paisley tie, and dress shoes. I still have a FedEx wardrobe box I can use to pack it up. I'll call them right now; see if they'll pick up, otherwise I'll drive it into Cortez. Not to worry, I'll get it there by Monday."

Apparently Ginnie's funeral is being arranged for Tuesday. A small, private affair, from the sound of it, as per Ginnie's own wishes. I offered to come; actually contemplated canceling my surgery for tomorrow, but that was met with vehement resistance, both from Ben as well as Isla.

"I'm sorry," I suddenly hear Isla sniffle. "I wasn't thinking. You have other things on your mind right now. I don't really need—"

"Stop it," I cut her off, immediately softening my tone. "I promise it's not a problem. I'm actually glad you're giving me something to do. It keeps my mind busy."

I hear some rustling, and then the deep rumble of my brother's voice as he mutters comforting words to his wife.

"Stace?"

"Still here," I tell him. "Go take care of her. I'll make sure the clothes get there. I'll text you the tracking number when I have it. Tell her I love her."

"Are you all set for tomorrow?" he asks. I can hear the struggle in his voice.

"All taken care of. Mak and the dog are going to be at Jen's and Nick has volunteered as my chauffeur. I'll be fine."

"Sure?"

"Positive," I reinforce with as much conviction as I can muster. "Now go look after your wife and give that little stinker a raspberry kiss for me."

I set my coffee mug in the sink after hanging up, and head out to the shed where I remember tossing that garment box.

-

Atsa, who's had his head over my shoulder and out my window the entire drive up the mountain, almost launches himself over me the moment we turn up the driveway to my brother's house. But when I roll to a stop in front of the door and turn the engine off, I can feel the tension radiating from him, a low growl rumbling from his chest.

"What is it, bud?" I reach out to stroke his head, but he dodges my hand, too focused on something out there.

I'm well aware there is wildlife out here—I remember all too well that Mak was almost attacked by a mountain lion last winter—but they usually hide until the weather gets a little cooler.

I'm trying to open my door carefully, so I can get a decent grip on Atsa's collar before he takes off on me, but the dog is too fast. He's over the backrest in a flash and forces himself against the door, ripping it through my hands. Before I can even call his name, he's bounding off into the tree line behind the large shed. I rush out after him.

I can't hear him bark again, which worries me. Atsa may be a good-sized dog, but if a mountain lion or a bear gets in his path, I'm not at all sure he'd walk away alive. There simply is no way Isla would be able to take another loss. She adores that dog.

I'm already well into the forest behind the house when I realize it might have been smart to grab a weapon. I have a 9mm Smith & Wesson that Ben gave me when I started working for the DA's office. He insisted I needed to be able to defend myself in that line of work. I never liked keeping it in the house because of Makenna, so I kept it in the glove box of my car. Of course that doesn't help me much now.

I spot a thick stick on the side of the barely visible trail in front of me, and bend down to grab it, when I hear the sharp snap of a branch behind me. Quickly grabbing the improvised weapon from the ground, I whip around and hold it up defensively.

"Whoa!" the older man scrambles back, both hands raised protectively, just as Atsa charges out from the underbrush.

"Atsa—no!" I yell as the dog leaps at Henry Flynn, the poor man looking like he's about to have a heart attack. I make a quick grab for his collar and pull him back a safe distance from the startled man in front of me. "Henry? What are you doing here?"

Before he has a chance to answer, there is more rustling in the dense brush and a disembodied voice calls out, "Pops!"

"I called him," Henry says clarifying his son's sudden appearance. Not that it helps me much, because I still don't know what he's doing up here, although he does seem to have rediscovered his equilibrium now that I have Atsa contained.

"There you are," Nick says, as he steps out onto the trail and almost casually walks up to drop a kiss on my lips. Of course now the dog's tail starts wagging furiously, as he's immediately drawn to the other alpha in the pack.

The moment I release my hold on him, he's nudging his big head under Nick's hand for a rub. Traitor. "What happened, Pops?" Nick turns to his father.

Exactly. I'd love to know what it is we are doing, standing in the woods on the side of a mountain.

Nick folds his hand around the back of my neck, his thumb absentmindedly stroking the ridged scarring that disappears under the neckline of my shirt, as Henry starts talking.

"I was just taking care of the garbage bins like you asked, when I see this guy walk up to the office trailer. I was just emptying the bin down by the boat launch when I noticed him. He was looking around, peeking in the windows. I thought he was looking for a spot, but then he disappeared around the back of the trailer, so I beelined it up there. By the time I got that damn golf cart up the hill, there was no sign of him. I didn't think too much of it, until I was coming out of the shed where I'd just returned the cart: I spotted him standing on the cliff by the house and that's when I called you," he says, looking at his son almost apologetically.

"And I told you to stay put," Nick says, his fingers flexing against my neck.

"He could've been breaking into the house," the old man protests.

"So what?" Nick fires back.

"You asked me to look after the place, and now you're being a burr up my ass when I do?"

"I didn't mean play some kind of vigilante cop and risk your ass traipsing off into the woods," Nick barks at him.

"So what happened when you got up here?" I interject, biting my lip not to bust out laughing as I try to desensitize the situation. It works, because both men turn their eyes to me simultaneously.

"*How* did you get up here?" Nick fires the question right on top of mine.

"On foot," Henry says. "I wanted the element of surprise and the sound of an engine would've alerted him." In my peripheral vision I see Nick rolling his eyes heavenward, and I suppress a snort. Barely. "Anyway…" Henry drawls, a pointed look in his son's direction. "Something spooked him because by the time I got up here, he was running past the shed and into the woods."

"Probably my car coming up the drive," I suggest, before reaching out and putting a hand on Henry's arm. "And for the record, my brother installed a state of the art security system. It wouldn't be easy to get in the house, and even if he did, his mug would be on camera; he wouldn't get away with it."

"Good to know," the old man grumbles as he starts walking down the trail, and with Nick's hand still firmly on the back of my neck, we follow him down.

―――――⧄―――――

Nick

"What brought you up here?" I ask her when we get to the cars. Pops doesn't stop and keeps going down the drive. I can catch up with him later.

"Ginnie died last night," Stacie explains. "I need to overnight ship some things Isla needs for the funeral." The words have barely left her mouth when I wrap her in my arms, pressing my cheek to the top of her head.

"I'm sorry," I mumble.

"I never met Ginnie," she explains, pushing out of my arms and I reluctantly let her go. "But I'm hurting for Al and Isla. They've lost so much already."

"She was a firecracker," I tell her. "She'd have to be, to be a match for Al. She loved Isla, like she was her own flesh and blood. And she loved being here in the summer, but as soon as the season would draw to an end, she couldn't wait to get back to Arizona. She did not like winter."

"I'm sorry," Stacie says, her hands covering her mouth. "I didn't realize you knew her that well, I wouldn't have blurted it out like that."

"It's all good," I promise her, pulling her hands away from her face. "I'm just going to have to chase Pops down the mountain so I can tell him; they played cards together for years. I don't want him finding out through the grapevine."

"Of course," she says, a little flustered. "I'll just pack up the stuff for Isla and run it into Cortez to send it off. I've got to hustle anyway so I'm back in time for Mak to get off the bus. And given the circumstance, I think I'll just call for a shuttle into Durango tomorrow."

"Like hell," I bark, grabbing her by the shoulders when she turns toward the house. "I'm going to talk to Pops while you box the stuff up. I'll meet you back here; I'll take the box back to Cortez with me, and get it sent off. I'll be back at your place at five, like we agreed, and you'd better have your bags packed."

"You're bossing me around," she says, her eyes sparking fire. "Just so you know, I don't do well with bossy men."

"Then don't say stupid shit," I fire back, watching her jaw go slack in shock. "I keep my word; if I say I'm taking you, then that's what is going to happen."

I get a particularly dirty look, but rather than argue with me, Stacie presses her lips into an angry line, before stomping off. I don't even make an effort to hide my grin as I watch her disappear inside.

-

Pops takes it better than I expected. I guess when you get to be a certain age; death no longer has the power to shock.

"Get going," he mutters when I ask a second time if he's okay. "I'm fine. I'm heading home, I'll do a drive around tonight, and I'll be back here tomorrow. You go take care of that girl, I get the impression you'll have your hands full with that one."

CHAPTER 9

Nick

"Are you nervous?"

I look over at her profile, her jaw is tight and the scars on her face seem more pronounced than before. I reach for the clenched hand in her lap and fold it open, twining my fingers with hers. Her palm feels a bit clammy.

She throws a quick glance my way before focusing back on the road in front of us, with just a sharp little nod in acknowledgement.

With instruction for Pops to call the sheriff next time he thinks he sees something suspicious, instead of chasing after them, I tossed my overnight bag in the car and drove into town. Stacie had been pacing the porch of her house. She'd already been in her own zone and barely said hello. We loaded Mak and the dog up and dropped them off at the coffee shop with Jen.

Aside from a quick hug for Makenna, Stacie had been staring through the windshield, her hands silently wringing in her lap. I tried to leave her in peace, hoping maybe the drive would settle her down, but by the time I leave Mancos in the rearview mirror, I realize that's not likely to happen.

"Stacie? Will you talk to me?" I rub my thumb over the top of her hand encouragingly. "I'm not sure if I can help, but let me try?"

"I don't even know why I'm this anxious," she finally says, still staring straight ahead. "It's not like this is the first surgery I've had. I can't remember being this nervous before."

"Maybe it's because it's the last?" I suggest carefully. Still she swings her head around and looks at me sharply.

"What do you mean?"

"My guess is with previous surgeries there perhaps was less pressure? This supposedly being the last one, I'd think your—your hopes—would be higher."

"What if it doesn't change anything?" she whispers, and I can hear the emotion thick on her voice.

There's an outlook point up ahead and without a word, I pull the truck right up to the railing. I kill the engine, unbuckle my seatbelt, and turn sideways in my seat so I can look at her.

"What if it doesn't? What if it's all perception anyway?" I ask her gently. "Will it change the way people see you? Or perhaps the way you see yourself? For me, even now I can't see how they could possibly improve on what I see as beautiful already."

Her eyes lift, from our entwined fingers on her lap she's been staring at, to meet mine.

"Flatterer," she accuses, but with a hint of a smile.

"Simply telling you what I see," I offer with a shrug. "We all have a different perspective on what is, and I can guarantee that your surgery tomorrow will not change that." I lean in to kiss the frown forming on her forehead. "But what it could do, is change how you perceive yourself, and perhaps that's the important transformation you should be looking for."

"How'd you get to be so wise?" she says, brushing at the moisture gathering in the corner of her eye, as she unbuckles her own seatbelt, and scoots closer. I wrap my arm around her shoulders and tuck her closer to my side.

"Not wise," I confess, staring at the beautiful landscape. "I just know that the way the world sees you is directly related to the way you see yourself."

"Tell that to the gawking parents picking up their children at Mak's school," she scoffs. "Or the cashier at the Food Market, who flinches whenever I get into her checkout line."

"Do they matter?" I ask, and she turns her head to look at me, confused.

"I don't understand what you mean?"

"Those parents, that cashier, and any of the other people who gawk at your scars; do they matter in your life? Are you having this surgery for them?" I know I'm pushing, but this is an area I'm at least a little familiar with.

"Of course not," she bristles.

"The people who do matter in your life, do you think it would make any difference to them whether you have this surgery?" I smile at the sudden fire in her eyes.

"That's a stupid question," she spits.

"It is," I agree. "We both know it wouldn't make a lick of difference."

We sit in silence for a while, each lost in our own thoughts while looking out the window, when Stacie suddenly turns to face me.

"You know a large portion of my left side is burned, right?"

"I guessed. I've noticed you dress to cover up. I also saw your arm the other day, and assumed the scarring would go beyond that. Why do you ask?"

A deep blush crawls up her face at my question, giving me a bit of a hint.

"I'd convinced myself I was going to be daring," she confesses, her voice barely audible. "I was going to throw caution to the wind tonight."

"I booked a suite," I blurt out with a confession of my own. "Two bedrooms. I'm not gonna lie and say I'd complain if we ended up sharing one, but that wasn't the objective here," I try to reassure her, cluing in that her surgery may not have been the only thing causing anxiety. "A relaxed dinner and a good night's sleep is as far as plans go for tonight, and we'd better hustle to make our reservation."

-

"How is it?" Stacie shouts over the music in the Derailed Pour House.

A great spot with good music, but not exactly conducive to any kind of conversation. All through dinner we tried, but quickly gave up, eating what was a nice meal, but barely speaking. That was not how I imaged tonight would go.

"Not really my thing," I admit, looking at the signature Dickel Pickle that I just had to try, to Stacie's great hilarity. It's actually fucking disgusting. "I'm pretty sure it took the enamel right off my teeth."

Stacie throws her head back and laughs. Completely uninhibited and utterly beautiful. Exactly the way I remember her.

"What are you thinking?" she wants to know when she catches me observing her.

"That we should pick up dessert, head back to the hotel, and watch a movie." I can see the wheels turning as she eyes me sharply, before she finally nods.

Twenty minutes later, we're walking back to the Strater, a container with two slices of cheesecake in one hand, and the fingers of the other tangled with Stacie's.

"Gorgeous!" A deep voice calls out from across the street.

I watch a tall, silver-haired, and rather distinguished-looking man step off the sidewalk, crossing over to us. A big smile, focused on Stacie, splits his face and immediately the hackles on my neck stand up. Abandoning the loose hold on her fingers, I quickly lift my arm and wrap it around her shoulders, tucking her tight to my body as I watch him approach. He looks familiar but I can't quite place him

As if I'm not even here, the guy steps squarely in Stacie's, and therefore my, space and leans in to kiss her on the cheek.

"How are you, lovely? What are you doing roaming the streets of Durango?"

"Good! We're just on our way back from dinner. Ryan, surely you remember Nicholas Flynn? You must have been introduced at the fundraising gala?"

"Of course, the lawyer," he says, wearing an all-knowing smile as he offers me his hand.

"And you're the gallery owner," I return, finally able to place him. "Nice to see you again."

"Absolutely," he directs at me before turning his full attention on Stacie. "So I haven't seen too much of you in Durango. What's the occasion?"

I listen as Stacie explains she has some medical appointments early in the morning, observing how easy she seems to be around Ryan.

"Our cheesecake is melting," I finally throw into their casual chatter, earning an amused smirk from him and an irritated glare from her. Both clearly on to my distractive tactics.

"I won't keep you any longer," Ryan says, running a hand through his thick gray hair, before extending it to me. "Good to see you again, Nicholas. And you, my sweet," he addresses Stacie. "I wish you the best of luck tomorrow and you must come by soon."

I grind my teeth loudly when he leans in and kisses her again, breathing a sigh of relief when he crosses the street. I turn back to Stacie, only to find her already halfway down the block, marching at a stiff clip back to the hotel.

Son of a bitch.

Stacie

"You're an asshole."

Nick's head snaps up when he walks into the suite.

I had totally left him standing on the sidewalk after that little display of male posturing. I'm not some kind of fire hydrant he can mark. Men can be such babies.

Instead of the elevator, I take the stairs, two at a time, to burn off some of my frustration. I let myself in with my room key and fully plan to hide in my bedroom, when the sound of another key in the lock has me swing around.

"I think I fucked up."

"Ya think?" The sarcasm is oozing as I work hard not to melt at the contrite look on his face. "What the fuck was that?"

"He had his hands all over you," he protests, visibly realizing it's the wrong thing to say the moment the words leave his mouth.

"First of all, he's a friend, and a good one at that, so if he wants to touch my arm or kiss my cheek, he absolutely can." I take a deep breath, walk a step closer, and rise on my toes so my nose is just inches from his. I'm only just getting started. "Secondly, who the hell are you to say anything? You kissed me in front of my kid, in the middle of a restaurant. And need I remind you that was nowhere near my cheek? For your information, not that you deserve any clarification, but Ryan is like a brother to me."

"He's into you," the idiot persists.

"Not that it's any of your business at this point, because whatever this may have been—" I wave my hand between him and me, "—is no longer anything, but Ryan is only interested in Jen. *We* are done," I hit him with my parting shot before marching into my bedroom and slamming the door shut.

I'm not sure what I'm expecting, but I find myself surprised when I step out of the bathroom thirty minutes later, after a nice long shower, and there's no sign of him or a sound to be heard from the living room. It's tempting to peek, but instead I get ready for bed, setting my alarm for the butt crack of morning.

The soft click of a door wakes me, and a glance at my alarm tells me it's barely midnight. A bump, followed by a mumbled curse, and then silence again. I guess he must've gone out while I was in the shower, and only now returns. I try not to wonder where he's been, any right to an answer for that went out the door when I ripped into him earlier.

I'd fallen asleep, still self-righteously angry, but now, lying awake in the middle of the night, I'm starting to slide down from that moral high ground. Here is a guy, who has rearranged his schedule, and gone out of his way to make sure I can go into surgery tomorrow, relaxed and rested, and I totally blew him off. Sure, he was behaving like an ass, but that's no reason for me to behave like one, too.

Thinking about it, I wonder if my overreaction wasn't at least partly motivated by the prospect of spending time alone in a hotel room with him. Not so much my lack of trust in him, as my lack of trust in my own response to him.

I drive myself nuts with this emotional teeter-totter I'm on. One moment, I want to let go of inhibitions and grab hold of whatever comes my way, and the next I'm tied up like a frigid little schoolgirl who's never been touched. My problem is: I don't know what I want, and I'm taking it out on him.

I slip my legs over the side of the bed and get up. I quickly pee, pull on a pair of lounge pants, and carefully open the door to the living room.

Only the glare of the muted TV screen outlines the still form of Nick slouched in a corner of the couch. His head turns when I approach.

"Hey," he whispers softly, but he doesn't move. He seems to wait cautiously for my cue.

"I was a bitch," I tell him, as I sit down in the opposite corner from him, tucking my feet under me. "I'm sorry."

"Shhh," he hushes me, as he reaches out and tags one of my feet, pulling it into his lap.

I find myself almost purring at the firm pressure of his thumbs on my instep as he massages my foot. I drop my head back on the armrest and close my eyes as he works the last bit of tension from my body, with only the touch of his hands.

I'm almost asleep by the time he's done with my other foot. My eyes pop open when I feel him lift them, kissing the instep of each of my feet, which sends shivers down my back.

"I'm the one who's sorry," he mumbles, his lips vibrating against the sole of my foot, making my toes curl, before placing them both in his lap. "I was hung up on talking about some things with you tonight, and things just didn't exactly pan out as expected. I reacted like an ass. I'm sorry."

"Where did you go?" I ask, not quite able to help myself. "Just now I mean. I heard you come in."

"I went down to the bar. Did some soul-searching with the aid of a good scotch."

"And? Find out anything interesting?" I nudge him with my foot.

"I did. I found out a couple of glasses of good scotch in a hotel bar costs almost as much as a room, and I discovered that I no longer can hold my liquor the way I used to." I giggle at the painful grimace on his face.

"Don't tell me it's hurting already," I tease him.

"Not yet, but I'm warning you, I have limited control over the things that come out of my mouth."

"I'll try not to hold it against you," I promise.

"I'd be much obliged," he says with a wink.

The banter is relaxing and I'm comfortable, my legs stretched out, my feet resting on his thigh, and his arm reaching for me along the backrest. I touch his hand with mine, and as if by rote, our fingers lace together.

"What did you want to talk about?" I finally break the silence.

"You, mostly," he says with a light shrug of his shoulders. "Your work, your life, your daughter… anything that matters to you, I want to know about."

"Not much to tell," I admit. "I love the law, in all its forms, and from all angles, which is why I was able to work both sides of the equation. It taught me a lot. My life, well, it commonly consists of work and Makenna, with little room for anything else. So much has changed since the beginning of this year, and so much change is yet to come, I'm just focused on settling down."

"Makes sense," he says, giving my fingers a squeeze. "You like Dolores, though? Being close to your brother?"

I chuckle, because I'm actually surprised at how much I do enjoy small-town Dolores.

"Never thought I could move away from the big city, but look at me now," I joke, smiling. "I like it. I like that we're not too far from the amenities that Cortez or Durango have to offer, and I really love the fact that I have not hit a single traffic jam since moving here."

"We don't have many of those," he admits, grinning. "What about Mak?"

"Oh, she loves it here. It's perfect for her; she has Ben, whom she adores, close by, and Isla's uncle, Al, has become another important male figure in her life. She was sorely lacking positive male influence before."

"What about Mak's father?" he inquires, and I resist the urge to shut down the conversation. It's not like I didn't open that door myself, and I won't lie.

"Let me first say that Mak is the best thing that ever happened in my life," I confirm, before clarifying. "She's the result of a college indiscretion. One that unfortunately has no face, no name, and little in terms of memory attached to it."

Nick's thumb, which had been rubbing circles on my skin, stops abruptly, as his whole body stills. I look for judgment in his face, but there is none, just the same friendly impassive expression. The moment his thumbs resumes its stroking, I relax back in my seat.

"So there's no father in the picture," I finish. "There never was."

CHAPTER 10

Nick

The moment I pull the truck up in front of Stacie's house, Mak comes running out, the big dog at her heels. She pulls the passenger door open and leans in.

"Let me see," she demands. I'm about to tell her it'll be a while longer before those bandages come off her mom's face, when I notice it's not her face she's interested in, but her wrist. "Yup, it's you," she says, rubbing a small tattoo of a four-leaf clover on the inside of Stacie's wrist.

"It's me, baby," Stacie confirms, running her hand over her daughter's short haircut.

I observe as Mak helps her mother out of the truck, while I grab her bag from behind my seat. She's very mature for a nine-year-old. At least she seems to be. I don't really know that much about kids, I don't have any myself and no nieces or nephews either. I guess this is not the first time she's seen her mom wrapped in bandages.

I'm realizing how scary this must've all been for the kid: the explosion, the multiple surgeries. Especially since, as it turns out, Stacie is the only parent she has.

When Stacie shared a little about herself two nights ago, what she said about Mak's parentage threw me. The fact she can't remember anything, about that night, is perhaps both a curse and a blessing. I'm afraid though;

that the truth has a way of floating to the top, no matter how much easier it would be to let sleeping dogs lie.

I can't wait too long. I'll have to tell her soon.

"How are you feeling?" I hear Jen, who was waiting inside, ask Stacie.

I follow inside, after dropping her bag in the hallway, and see Mak installing her on the couch, spreading a blanket over her legs. I have to bite down a chuckle, because it is pretty damn hot outside to be needing a blanket, but I don't have the heart to say anything.

Seeing that she's looked after, I step outside on the porch and give my dad a call.

"Pops, how's things?" I ask, when he answers on the third ring.

"Interesting. But first tell me how she's doing."

"She's fine. Her doctor says to take it easy for a week or two, but that she'll be good to go after that. The full effects of the surgery won't be visible for another month or two, he says," I fill him in on what I know.

"Good. Glad to hear it."

"Now what was interesting?" I want to know.

"Probably nothing," he answers, but without a lot of conviction. "Remember that fellow I saw at the campground the other day? I think he may have been back last night. When I went to unlock the shed to grab the golf cart this morning, it looked like someone had tried to get in. The chain was cut, but the deadbolt on the door was still locked. It looked like they tried to force it."

"Did you call the sheriff?"

"I did, but before he showed up one of the hunters camping down by the water's edge walked up. He mentioned last night he and his buddies had come back from a night out in Cortez, drove by the shed, and saw someone sprinting away from the building. He didn't think much of it at the time, but seeing me this morning made him curious."

"So what did the sheriff say?"

"It was one of his deputies, and he said since nothing was actually taken, there wasn't a whole lot they could do." Pops sounds more than just a bit irritated. "I didn't want to alarm Ben, and I knew you'd be back in town today, but I'm telling you, something fishy is going on."

"Okay, Pops," I pacify him. "I have my overnight bag in the truck, I'll get Stacie's key to the house. Maybe I'll just stay there for a few days. Keep an eye on things. I'll give Drew a call too."

"Give me a call when you're heading up and I'll meet you there with the rest of the keys," my dad offers, sounding a bit relieved.

"Sounds like a plan, Pops. Talk to you soon."

I end the call and immediately dial another number. Drew Carmel is the sheriff of Montezuma County, and someone I've grown to respect over the years. He's a friend of Ben's as well, so when I fill him in and mention my plan to stay up at Ben's place to keep a close eye on the place, he assures me he'll be sending some extra patrols up the mountain.

Stacie

"Can I get you anything else?"

I lift my hand to indicate I've had enough. I know Jen means well, but right now, I'm just exhausted.

When they wheeled me into surgery yesterday morning, I'd had perhaps two or three hours of sleep the night before. I'd ended up falling asleep on the couch, my feet still on Nick's lap. Both of us were cursing the next morning, with our necks and backs hurting from sleeping in awkward positions, and two perfectly good mattresses just steps away.

Anesthesia seems to affect me more and more with each surgery, and this time it just seems to drag on, leaving me feeling sluggish and tired.

I hear Nick and Jen talking behind me, but I can't seem to focus on what they're saying. It's almost like being underwater, in my own little world.

"Lie down." I suddenly hear clear as day, as Nick's face swims in front of my eyes. I feel myself being moved, and quickly close my eyes to a wave of vertigo at the sudden shift in position.

-

"She's awake!" Mak yells right by my ear.

"Shhhh," I try, but at this point it's moot.

I crack open my one free eye to find my daughter hovering over me, a smiling Nick pulling her back.

"Easy, tiger," he says to her, with a wink for me. "Give your mom a chance to wake up."

"I'm okay," I croak, my voice a little rough from a dry throat. I gratefully accept the bottle of water Nick hands me and take a deep drink. "God, that feels so much better. Thank you."

"Guess what?" Mak half screeches, or maybe it just sounds that way. My head is still a bit sensitive.

"What?" I ask, playing along.

"Nick said we'll order in, but we had to wait for you to wake up. So can I have a milkshake? Please, can I?"

I have apparently slept most of the afternoon. Sadly, I didn't get a chance to thank Jen for looking after Mak and the dog, because she had to get back to the shop. The good news is that I feel a lot more myself now than I did earlier. That horrible fog has lifted and my senses are a lot sharper.

Unfortunately that also means that I hurt like a son of a bitch. It feels raw, like someone took a giant cheese grater and used it on the left side of my face.

Before I have a chance to respond to Mak's request, Nick drops a couple of tablets in my hand.

"Just T3s," he clarifies. I guess I must've told him at some point about my aversion to strong narcotics. They make me loopy.

I toss them back and take another long drink on the bottle, before turning to Mak.

"I think we can do a milkshake." I smile at her excited fist pump. "Who were you calling?"

"That depends," Nick answers. "I suggested The Depot, because they're around the corner, but then your daughter here, announced she loves Sonic. If you're okay for half an hour or so, I'm more than happy to pick something up at the drive-thru in Cortez."

"I'm gonna come!" Mak announces loudly, and I wonder what happened while I was sleeping that made these two thick as thieves.

"Can you use your inside voice, please, Mak?"

"Sorry," she mumbles, looking guilty, and I turn back to Nick.

"I'm fine. I don't mind; if you don't mind having my kid hyped up on the prospect of Sonic in your car. You think this is bad? Wait until the sugar from the milkshake hits her," I tease, grinning when I see a shadow of doubt pass over his face. "Make sure she's in the back. I don't want her driving in front yet."

"Mo-om!"

"No argument, missy," I threaten when she starts whining. "I can also say no and make you stay home. Up to you."

Makenna is not a fan of my way of tossing the ball back in her court, but I do it every chance I get. I figure it's the best way for her to learn she always has a choice, but that with every choice there are consequences. She likes the choice, but not always those consequences.

In the end, she dutifully gets in the small seat behind Nick, but not without shooting a glare to where I'm watching them from the window.

Also not new.

-

"Can I have your key to your brother's place?" Nick asks, after dinner. Mak has already disappeared to the river, wearing her life vest and carrying her tackle box and rod. "My dad said there may have been an attempt at a break-in at the campground last night, so I think I'll spend the night up there."

"Seriously? Have you called Ben?" I'm thinking my brother would probably like to know.

"No," he says, surprising me. "There's really nothing urgent to report, and besides, I'm sure he has his hands full with Isla and Noah, and preparations for the funeral."

Shit. I can't believe I forgot about Ginnie.

"Of course," I consent, quickly digging through my purse to find Ben's keys. "You should take Atsa," I suggest, when I hand over the key ring. "He's a great watchdog."

"I might, if Mak doesn't mind."

In the end, Mak is easily convinced. Especially when she's promised a trip to see the horses on Nick's ranch for tomorrow.

"I need to help my dad with a few repairs," he explains, leaning down with his arms braced on either side of me. "Won't be more than a couple of hours, but I figure you might be due for a nap sometime late morning. I'll pick up Mak and the dog and take them with me. They'll have a good time, and you can sleep."

"Sounds good," I agree easily, as I look up into his dark brown eyes.

"Maybe when we get back, we can barter some favors."

I find myself squirming in my seat a little at the heavy innuendo in his words and the heat in his eyes. A kid is normally a perfect distraction from even the possibility of arousal, but she's not here. Besides, I can feel the deep rumble of his voice everywhere.

"What did you have in mind?" I can't even recognize the sultry sound of my own voice.

I've all but forgotten that half my face is swaddled in bandages, and the best I can hope for is perhaps seducing a mummy, but certainly not this large, striking man leaning over me. I've seen him in suits a few times, but my favorite look on him is this one; faded jeans and a fitted Henley, with the sleeves pushed up over a pair of strong forearms. I can't seem to stop my hand reaching out to touch him. Even the shape of his skull is appealing, as my palm rubs his bald head.

"I'll cook you dinner," he starts, lifting a finger to trace my bottom lip. I inadvertently run my tongue along the slight burn his touch leaves behind. He follows my move with great interest. "God, you make it hard."

"Sorry," I whisper, not sorry at all.

"I'll cook you dinner," he repeats, before lowering his mouth to mine, sweeping his tongue along the same path before slipping it between my lips. All pain is forgotten and what remains is the taste and touch of him, reducing my awareness to a pinpoint focus, while drowning me in sensation.

"Ohmigod," I mumble on an exhale, when Nick finally releases my lips and outlines the second half of the bargain.

"And maybe after you could shave my head?"

Nick

When I said, "God, you make it hard," I didn't just mean leaving her.

Certain parts of my anatomy are screaming for attention, when I finally pull my truck away from her house, and I have to adjust myself several times, while driving up the mountain, a stoic Atsa in the seat beside me.

Before turning up the drive to the house, I decide to do a round of the campground. Make sure everything is kosher before I turn in. Other than a few lights illuminating the washrooms, the campground is dark and surprisingly quiet. I notice even fewer spots occupied than on Thursday.

When I get down to the water, I pull the truck off on the side of the trail, and let the dog out for a sniff.

I just step out on the dock when my phone rings.

"How's my sister doing?" Ben doesn't waste time with pleasantries. He's feeling guilt for not being here; this is the third time he's called since her surgery.

"She's doing okay. A bit sore, but she slept a good chunk this afternoon," I inform him.

"She awake now? Can I talk to her?"

"I'm not sure, I'm not with her. You should try her number."

"What do you mean you're not with her?" he barks.

"I'm just looking into a—"

"You were supposed to be looking after her," he spits out, cutting me off. "What kind of asshole move is that, to leave her alone? She just had fucking surgery."

I take a deep breath before answering; reminding myself it's his own guilt that is yelling at me.

"If you'd let me finish, I'd explain that we've had a couple of incidents up the mountain. My dad—"

"Incidents? What incidents?"

"Stop fucking interrupting so I can tell you," I finally snap, running a hand over my head. "Christ, Ben, calm the fuck down."

"Hey, Nick," Isla's voice comes over the line. "I'm putting you on speaker phone, since I just shoved Noah in Ben's hands so he won't be tempted to throw things." I chuckle at the mental picture I'm getting of a snarling beast, easily handled by his petite wife and even smaller baby son. "Can you hear me?"

"Loud and clear."

"So Stace is good?" Isla asks.

"She's fine. I left her on the couch with Mak, watching some kind of reality show."

"*The Amazing Race*, I was watching it, too. She got me hooked…"

"Are you gonna tell us what the fuck is going on there?" Ben barks impatiently.

"Language!"

"You kidding me? The kid can't even find his own mouth with his fist, you think he's gonna start cursing with it?" he says in response to his wife's admonishment, and I'm having a hard time not to laugh out loud.

"Thursday night Pops saw someone prowling around the campground, and then again up at the house." I barge right in without preamble. "He called me and gave chase, but whoever it was disappeared in the woods. This morning he found the chain on the shed cut and evidence someone had been trying to break in. A camper mentioned seeing someone run off and the sheriff's office was called."

"Why the fuck didn't you call me?"

"Because you asked me to look after the place for a reason. I assumed because you trusted me to do so, and that includes trusting my judgment about what constitutes enough reason to interrupt you when you're looking after your family during a time of loss." I've had it with this conversation. "Now as I said, your sister is fine—you can call her yourself to verify—and I'm sleeping in your house tonight, keeping an eye on the campground. I've got the dog with me." I take a deep breath as I turn my back on the water and walk back toward the truck. "If there is anything to report, I promise, I'll give you a call." With that I end the call, tuck my phone away, and open the passenger side door. "Come on, boy," I call out to Atsa. "Get in here."

The house is dark, and from what I can see, undisturbed, when I pull up and kill the engine. Atsa whines, and I let him out, grabbing my overnight bag off the seat. I take the fact that the dog is not barking, as a positive sign.

Once inside, I flip on only the light in the bathroom next to the spare bedroom, and strip down to grab a quick shower. It's not until I get out, and pick up my phone that I see a missed call and a text message.

Stacie: Ben is calm(er) now. Going to bed.

The message was sent just five minutes ago, so I figure it's safe to call back. I pad over to the bed, pull back the covers, and flop down on my back on the mattress, just as she answers the phone.

"You didn't have to call back," she says, the slightly husky quality of her voice wreaking instant havoc on my body. "I just wanted you to know everything is copacetic."

"You're the only person I know who can make big words sound sexy," I blurt out, resulting in a warm chuckle on the other end. She can't see my hand grabbing the base of my cock firmly. "And of course I had to call back. What self-respecting man would pass up on a clear come-on like '*going to bed*'?"

"It was not," she sputters, but I can hear a smile in her voice.

"Mak asleep?" I ask, letting her off the hook, for now.

"She is."

"So you're alone?"

"She insisted on sleeping in my room. She's just steps away on a mattress on the floor," she whispers, and unless I'm imagining it, there's a hint of regret in her tone.

"Not fair," I groan loudly, the sound of her voice making my dick even harder inside my fist. "Here I had plans to tell you exactly what I would do to you in that bed of yours. Describe in great detail how I would expose every inch of your body, tracing your skin with my fingers and lips. How I would drown myself in your scent until I couldn't resist getting your taste on my tongue…" I have to stop myself when I hear her deep gasp over my own heavy breath. "I'm so hard for you, it's painful," I confess, wondering if I have shocked her or turned her on, but unable to hold back the surge rushing through my body.

"Jesus, Nick." Her voice is thick with something dark and spicy, which has my balls draw tight against my body, and a groan escapes my lips as my release squirts over my hand and belly.

"Fuck me," I mutter to myself, when I hear a deep sigh on the other side of the line. "I'll make this up to you."

"Not fair," Stacie repeats back what I said to her just minutes ago.

CHAPTER 11

Son of a bitch!

First that old geezer nearly caught me up in the woods. I was getting away from him when I heard a dog bark and barely managed to get up that damn tree. I was floored when I spotted her walking up to the old man, with some big hairy mutt. Moments later they were joined by some tall bald dude. I had to sit there and watch them walk off, because of that damn dog.

Now it's a fucking camper. I'm losing my damn touch. How the hell am I gonna find out where that bitch lives, if I can't get inside that cabin?

I cut the chain on the shed; desperate to find anything that could help me get into that place on the cliff. I just about had the lock jimmied when those asshole hunters interrupted. Then this morning I saw a patrol car come driving past, that old man must've called in the sheriff.

Time to find a bed somewhere in town. The risk of getting caught up here, sleeping in the back of my pickup, is too big.

-

I could've grabbed the motel in town, it's not like I can't afford it, but it would be too visible. My comings and goings for anyone to see, my damn truck in the parking lot.

No, this is better. Some doped up chick, who is so eager for her next fix, she doesn't look too closely at who she invites in. A few dollar bills is all it takes to find a bed for a few nights. Never mind that it comes with that skank in it, or her damn kids in the other bedroom, but if I close my eyes, it doesn't matter what wet hole I stick my dick in.

Besides, for now, it's perfect for me. No one looks too closely in this place, and whatever they do see, they choose to forget.

It's also nice and close to the bitch's house.

Yeah, found it this morning when I was going to make another go at that damn cabin.

I spotted a truck parked outside and watched as the bald asshole put that dog in the cab and got in himself. I fucking ran all the way back to where I left my pickup, just in time to see his truck drive by on the road below.

I couldn't believe my luck when he fucking drove straight to a small house, right by the river. I pulled onto the street just moments after, watching him pull up in front. Some little girl came bounding off the porch of the house, running toward the truck.

The bitch's got a kid?

This is getting better and better.

Stacie

"Have fun!"

I wave back at my daughter who has her face pressed to the small back window of Nick's truck.

To say I was irritated with Nick's chipper greeting, when he walked in ten minutes ago, would be putting it mildly. I just spent most of the night tossing and turning in my bed, and when Mak woke up around seven, her mouth already running on about horses before her eyes were even open, I knew there wasn't a chance in hell I would get any more sleep.

Adding insult to injury, Nick felt the need to point out I looked tired. I'm sure he felt the heat of my glare, although I'm not so sure his interpretation was accurate.

I'm cranky, even as I am watching my daughter head off on her exciting adventure. My head is still tired, ready to catch up on some rest, but my body is buzzing with the hot and heavy kiss Nick planted on me. He sent Mak to grab her fishing tackle from the shed, and then cornered me against the fridge, making sure I couldn't miss the hard ridge in his jeans. I may have whimpered at the feel, given that I had to live off my imagination all damn night long. Feeling the real thing pressed against my hip was so much better than anything I could've dreamt up.

Fuck him.

I should be worrying about pain, given that I had surgery a couple of days ago, but instead I rush into my bedroom to rummage through my hiding spot. I have mentally crossed all my digits, hoping that the batteries haven't run out on the vibrator I haven't used since moving here. The familiar buzzing is music to my ears.

Sleep comes easy, after an intense, lightning fast orgasm that had been plaguing me since his call last night. The last thing I remember is turning off my toy.

-

Despite the throbbing in my face, I feel refreshed when I wake up a few hours later.

The loud bang of the screen door slamming on the other side of the house, followed by the hushed rumble of voices, has me sit upright in my bed.

"Let her sleep." I can hear Nick say. *"The better she sleeps, the faster she'll heal."*

"Can I help you cook, then?" My daughter, always looking for opportunity to hone her negotiating skills. As a fellow lawyer, I'm sure Nick will appreciate the irony.

I slip out of bed, straighten out the covers, and pad into the bathroom to freshen up before I join them in the kitchen. A quick glance in the mirror shows my hair a mess and most of my face covered, but the one blue eye looking back sparkles, more alive than I've seen it in a while. That, combined with the gentle heat between my legs, reminds me why.

I glance over my shoulder at the bed I just made, a feeling of unease taking hold. Walking back to the bed, I flip back the covers, run my hand between the sheets and lift both pillows, all without result. Nothing but dust bunnies under the bed when I drop down to my knees beside it.

In a near panic, I pull open the drawer of my nightstand and there, neatly back in its black satin pouch, is my top-of-the-line, dual-purpose vibrator.

I must've been really out of it, if I shoved it in my drawer. Mak often rummages through there in search of hair ties or ChapSticks I've been known to toss inside.

For personal items, I have an old lunch box in the bottom drawer of my dresser, where I keep my nighties and my winter socks. The box holds a few items that are not really meant for the eyes of a nine-year-old. That includes two raunchy books, which I should probably switch out for some newer material, a half-smoked joint and lighter, a sample-size tube of lube, a small butt plug I once thought would be fun to try out, and my battery-operated boyfriend, which I quickly return where it belongs.

By the time I walk into the kitchen, where I find my daughter shoulder to elbow with Nick at the counter cutting vegetables, the incident is all but forgotten.

-

"Good grief, I'm full," I exclaim, leaning back in my chair with my hands folded on my bloated belly.

"Wasn't that the best, Mom?" my daughter, supreme vegetable hater, gushes over the fabulous skewers we just ate.

Mushrooms, chunks of onion and peppers, slices of yellow squash, pieces of seasoned chicken, and finally cubes of some deliciously creamy cheese, all grilled, on a little propane grill Nick brought from home, on my porch.

I'd never heard of cheese you could grill, but that stuff is delicious and rich. Halloumi, Nick called it, apparently from Cyprus. Well, I don't care where it came from, but I want it as a staple in my fridge. I also want to buy a grill.

But when I suggest the latter, Mak shakes her head sharply.

"I don't think that's a good idea."

"Why not? This can't be that hard to make," I argue, immediately on the defensive when my culinary talents are questioned. "You cut a few things up and put it on a stick, how complicated is that?"

I'm shocked when I see big crocodile tears in my feisty girl's eyes. I immediately reach for her but she jumps up and out of reach. When she stops halfway through the room and swings around, I can see those same tears tracking down her cheeks.

"I don't want you to blow up again," she sobs, breaking my damn heart in the process, as she runs down the hall to her bedroom.

"Oh, baby..." I whisper, my throat closing on tears.

"That may have been my fault," Nick's voice startles me as he walks toward me from the kitchen, kneeling beside my chair so he's face-to-face.

"How so?"

"She wanted to know why she had to keep her distance when I was grilling, so I explained how dangerous it could be. It never occurred to me—"

"Of course not," I insist, cutting him off before he finishes that thought. "I wouldn't have either. Mak hasn't really reacted much at all. This whole time, she's been taking everything in stride, being the tough little trooper she is. I'm the one who should've known it couldn't be as simple as that. I'm her mother, I'm the one who should've—"

This time it's Nick who cuts me off, not with words, but with a kiss that has me almost forget my own name.

"Don't," he mutters against my lips. "When you get buried under a mountain of trouble, all you can do to stay breathing is tackle one issue at a time. There's no room to anticipate, to be preventative, when you barely have a chance to react to what is in front of you." I swallow hard when he gently cups my face, and stares into the single eye peeking out of my bandages. "You're doing fine, and so is she."

"I should go talk to her," I say, moving to get up.

"This one's on me," he insists, as he stands up instead. "Let me try first."

Nick

I'm not sure what I was expecting, but it sure wasn't the sobbing girl in my arms.

My foot was barely over the threshold of Mak's room, when she came flying at me, jumping up in my arms. As a lawyer, I can't help but wonder if I'm breaking any rules of conduct in handling her, but I can hardly drop her on the floor.

Making sure the door stays open; I carry Mak to the bed, sit her down, and crouch in front of her.

"Talk to me," I urge her, but the poor kid can barely get a full breath in, let alone speak. I realize there's more going on than the propane safety speech I gave her earlier.

"Okay, I'll talk to you," I suggest instead. "I imagine what happened to your mom must've been really scary for you." Her head stays down, but I don't miss the little nod of agreement. "And it can't have been easy to see your mom in pain." This time it's a little shake. "Did you know I knew your mom before you were even born?" That apparently piques enough of her curiosity to lift her red-rimmed eyes to mine, and I'm glad to see the tears have stopped. "I did," I confirm. "Just from seeing her around, though. She always came across as a strong person, someone who could take care of herself, of others. Am I right?"

"*Yes.*"

If I hadn't been watching her mouth move, I would probably have missed the whispered answer, but I'll take it.

"She was always here to take care of you, so it scared you—" I start, piecing together what caused her emotional outburst, but Mak surprises me.

"We're supposed to take care of each other," Mak interrupts vehemently, promptly bursting into tears again. "Mom always says that it's just the two of us and we have to look after each other. But she got hurt anyway."

"Hey…" I grab a handful of tissues from the box on her nightstand and mop at the wet mess on her face. "What happened to your mom," I hesitate for a moment, deciding on the spot to use straight talk. It seems too important to whitewash the brutal reality of what this kid feels with gentle euphemisms. "The explosion that burned your mom was not something you, or even she, could've stopped. How could you? You had no way of knowing she was in the wrong place at the wrong time. Accidents are like that: you can't see them coming." I give her a second to mull on that before I add, "And one more thing, I'm pretty sure when your mom suggested the two of you had to look out for each other, she didn't mean to leave out your Uncle Ben, or Isla, or even Uncle Al."

"He's right," Stacie says, walking into the room and sitting down beside Mak on the bed. "It turns out we have way more people looking out for us than I thought."

-

"I should kick my own ass," Stacie says when she finally comes out of Mak's bedroom, where I'd left them half an hour ago.

"Don't," I tell her, shifting over to make room on the couch for her. "Although it might be entertaining to watch you try," I add, biting my cheek.

"Be easier to kick yours," she fires back, sitting down, but not before she gives my ankle a firm nudge with her foot. "Do you think it's a professional reflex?" she muses, tucking her legs under her and resting her head back against the seat. "That we're so used to weighing, measuring, and distancing ourselves from every word out of our mouths, we forget how to be real? I tried to reassure my daughter, and in doing so, because of the words I chose, I accomplished the absolute opposite of what I set out to do."

The deep sigh that follows has me reach out and stroke a finger along her exposed collarbone. It gets her attention.

"Another professional hazard is analyzing everything to death," I offer, watching her raise an angry eyebrow, which I ignore. "Here's what I see: you have a precocious and sharp nine-year-old girl, who mirrors herself after her beautiful, intelligent, and responsible mother." I watch as Stacie fights the smile that wants to break through. "Your daughter has been stomping around in your grown-up shoes…and tonight the kid came out."

"I'm starting to dislike when you're making too much sense," she quips, and I grin in response.

"Maybe now would not be a good time to ask you to scrape a blade over my head, then?"

"You were serious?" she asks, surprised. "You had me so confused at first, but I ended up deciding you must've been joking."

"Dead serious," I admit, getting up and grabbing a plastic bag I'd left on the counter. I fish out a can of shaving cream and a sharp as hell, brand-new shaver. "Now should I be worried?" I ask at the glint in her only visible, bright blue eye.

"Grab towels from the linen closet in the hallway and gimme that," she orders, making a grabby motion with her hand and smiling much too gleefully.

By the time I get back with towels, there's a bowl of water sitting on the side table and a pillow on the floor between her feet.

"Take off your shirt."

It's a moment of truth for me. This is where old insecurities, belonging to someone I no longer am, come back to plague me. It's not a surprise, since the woman in front of me represents everything I've always wanted but never thought I could have. I look at perfection when I see her, and inside I still see the old me. I still don't measure up.

In one swift move, almost angrily, I whip off my shirt and wait defiantly for judgment that never comes.

"Aren't you gonna sit down?"

Mute, and feeling pretty fucking ridiculous, I sit down between her feet, as she indicates. I almost jump when I feel her hands land on either side of my neck, smoothing gently along my shoulders. Goosebumps break out over my skin and I have to focus not to shiver at her touch.

I feel almost bereft when she lifts her hands to drape one of the towels over my shoulders.

I don't trust myself to say anything, when she apologizes for rubbing cold shaving cream all over my head, or when she hums quietly under her breath as she makes long strokes with the blade over my scalp. I press my lips together when all I want to do is groan, as the soft soothing touch of her fingers follows every scrape along my skin.

"There," she says softly, wiping the remaining shaving cream off my head and neck. "All done."

When she runs a final cool hand over the smooth surface of my head, my barely held control snaps.

My cock has been painfully hard since the moment I sat down between her legs, and I've been able to smell her arousal since not long after she first put her hands on me.

I swing around and get up on my knees, my hands finding her hips.

"I believe I owe you an orgasm," I growl, her scent thick as syrup to my senses.

A sharp gasp is my only response when I find the waistband of the soft lounge pants she's wearing, and manage to strip them down to her ankles. With my hands behind her knees, I pull her to the edge of her seat and wide open. I only give my eyes a moment to take in the neatly trimmed dark blonde curls, framing her deep pink pussy, slick with arousal, before I let my craving take over.

"*Nicholas*," she hisses when I stroke her with my tongue, tasting her deeply. Her hands clasp the back of my head, her nails scraping the skin, pressing my face deeper.

I feast, sucking her small bundle of nerves between my lips before sliding my mouth down to her opening, and fucking her with my tongue. Her essence covers my face and still I can't get enough. If I couldn't draw another breath, I'd happily die here.

Her release comes on fast, her thighs clamp tight around my ears, as her hips buck to find more friction. The moment I insert two fingers and curve them up and latch onto her clit, she shatters under my touch.

I lift my head and rest my cheek on her belly, gasping for air much as she is.

Also, I'm pretty sure I just came in my pants.

CHAPTER 12

Stacie

"How's the face?"

Typical of Ben. No subtle or particularly tactful inquiries, not even a proper hello, but straight to the point.

"The face is fine, although it's a bit itchy, and I'm getting really tired of staring out one eye. How was today?"

Ginnie's funeral was this morning and I'd been sitting by the phone, waiting for his call. I'd talked to Isla over the weekend a couple of times and she sounded like she was doing okay, but I knew today would be tough.

"Sad," he says, sounding tired. "She went down for a nap with Noah, but I'm waiting for the wheels to come off at some point."

"Any idea when you guys will be home?"

"Isla's talking about staying for a bit, helping Al sort through Ginnie's things. He's been talking about selling his place. Coming back to stay in the trailer until he finds something in Dolores or maybe Cortez. Says he wants to be closer."

"Makes sense," I point out. "Isla's here, his grandnephew is here, he's got friends here—why wouldn't he?"

"It's fine by me. It'll make Isla happy," he says and I have to smile.

The change in my brother in the past year has been nothing short of shocking. I always had Mak to keep me anchored, but Ben, he moved through life rudderless. Whenever the wind would blow him in our direction, he seemed to soak up his niece's adoration. Like a recharging of his batteries before he took off again.

That restlessness is gone. I never thought I'd see him settled and held in place by the love of a fireball of a woman. The roles appear to have reversed, and I'm the one floundering now, while he is the North on my compass.

"Anyway," he concludes, breaking my train of thought. "I'm catching a flight on Thursday."

"I can come pick you up," I offer with a knee-jerk response, not quite considering I will still only have one eye to see. Ben has, judging by the snort on the other side.

"Left the SUV at the airport, Sis. I'll pop in when I get to town, say hi to Mak, before I head up the mountain. Your appointment Friday is at eleven?" he refers to my post-surgical, follow-up appointment with Dr. Ashrad in Durango.

"Yes, it is, but I've got a ride organized," I try to explain. Nick already assured me his day was clear and he fully expected taking me.

"Nonsense," my brother barks dismissively. "Why do you think I'm coming back Thursday? I'm driving."

I guess that's that, since he immediately hangs up after, not giving me a chance to argue.

Instead of diving back into the book I was attempting to read when he called, I glance outside, where I can just see the shimmer on the water of the Dolores River.

It's a nice day. A cool sixty-eight degrees out there, but with only a few clouds in the sky. My face may still be healing but my legs are fine, and I haven't been outside in days.

I grab my jean jacket off the peg in the hallway and my keys, slip my feet into a pair of Chucks, and head out.

The river is literally steps from my house, and when I sleep with my window open, I can hear the rush of the water. The noise is much louder when you're walking right alongside it, and drowns out any normal small-town sounds. It is truly an oasis where you can imagine yourself far removed from civilization. The trail along the water runs through brush and trees, blocking any view from the street just beyond. Something I appreciate even more now, with my head still swaddled in bandages.

Out here, with my feet moving, my arms swinging, and my heart pumping vigorously, I'm able to let my mind wander, and it has only one direction: Nicholas Flynn.

I haven't seen him since he left here Sunday night. I couldn't believe when he got up from the floor, looked down to where I was splayed out like a stranded jellyfish on the couch, where he'd just quite thoroughly devoured me, snagged his shirt, and pulled it over his head.

"I should go," he said, and I couldn't help feel rejection. He must've read that on my face. "Mak is just down the hall," he clarified. "I don't want anything holding us back the first time, but we would have to for her sake. Besides, if the way I feel now is any indication, I couldn't hold back even if I tried."

Now *that* I had liked. The idea that, even in my current state, I was able to cause him to lose control, made me feel pretty damn good.

I watched as he sadly pulled the shirt back over his torso, hiding the nice, solid chest covered with the perfect amount of chest hair, which narrowed as it trailed down, disappearing from sight behind his waistband. He was not sculpted, like some of the men I'd been with over the years. I could tell he worked out regularly, but he wasn't all hard planes and sharp angles.

The man is real, and the fact he's perhaps not perfect, makes him even more attractive to me. So much so, I find myself wondering what it would be like to be cuddled against a chest like that: strong but comfortable. Sadly, I never had a chance to find out Sunday night, or yesterday.

He called first thing yesterday morning to see how I'd slept, and if Mak had gone off to school okay. I found that unexpectedly endearing. Before he hung up, he made me promise I'd call him if I needed anything, but that he'd likely be tied up all day with work.

I'm not surprised, that's often the nature of our profession, the demands continue, even if you take a day off.

He called again last night, right after Jen had dropped off a lasagna and some Caesar salad, which he'd apparently ordered from her. I could hear the regret in his voice when he explained a merger he was involved with had hit some snags, and he'd be busy well into the night.

I haven't heard from him today, though.

I'm coming up to the edge of town where the path disappears, when I notice the trailer park, where we dropped off Mak's little friend, Becca, recently. There's a chain-link fence almost butting up to the path, and when I get close, I can make out Becca's trailer through the trees.

The woman who'd almost dragged Becca inside that day—her mother, I presume—is standing on the steps of the trailer, lips locked with some guy sporting a substantial beer gut, wearing a trucker hat. The guy steps back, tucks something down the front of the woman's shirt, and gets into the delivery truck parked out front.

I'm not sure what to make of the scene, and although it could well be simply a woman saying goodbye to her man, there is something unsavory in the way she plucks whatever he tucked there from between her boobs. I watch her shove it in her pocket as she watches the man drive off. Money for services rendered? Or maybe a drug deal? It might be my years in the DA's office that has me go straight for something shady, but the whole scene just makes me worry about Becca more.

The woman turns around to go inside, and I turn too, back toward home, when I feel the hair on the back of my neck stand on end. I look back over my shoulder at the trailer and find the woman still standing there. Her head turned this way, and despite the brush and trees between us, her eyes are zoomed in on me, with pinpoint precision. Even at this distance I can feel the venom in that stare.

It's enough to send a shiver down my back, and even though I watch as she finally steps inside and closes the door behind her, the feeling that I'm being watched follows me all the way home.

The feeling is so strong that I'm almost running by the time I finally unlock and push open my door. I slam it shut right behind me, and instantly turn the lock, something I haven't done since moving to Dolores. I peek out the small window beside the front door, but don't see anything, and already common sense returns.

That was stupid, judging from the throbbing in my face. I'm just jumpy from that woman's eyes on me. Besides, looking at the world through only one eye is a little unsettling. It can skew the way you see things, and maybe mistake one thing for another.

But when I turn and walk into my kitchen, there's no mistaking the bouquet of tiny little blue flowers sitting on the counter, in a vase from my own pantry.

Nick

"There's no card. Nothing. They're not even real, they're plastic."

I've got Stacie on hands-free as I rush down the road to Dolores.

I had just been saying goodbye to James Marx, who'd come in for an emergency meeting this morning to salvage his deal, when my phone rang. The panic in Stacie's voice was thick, and a cold fist closed around my heart as she asked me if I'd been by to drop off some flowers. I immediately grabbed the landline with my other hand and dialed the sheriff's direct line.

"Stay right where you are and stay on the line. I'm calling the sheriff," I told her when Drew answered his phone after the second ring. "Someone was in Stacie's house, left flowers inside in her kitchen."

"I'm actually just down the street at the high school. I'll be there in a couple of minutes."

I drop the landline in the cradle when he hangs up, and with my cell phone to my ear; I snag my keys off my desk, and beeline it out of my office.

"Just don't touch anything," I remind her, which is met with a loud snort.

"I'm the criminal lawyer here, remember?" she scolds me, which only makes me smile. That fire is a whole lot easier to take than the sheer panic I heard in her voice earlier.

"Is that Drew?" I ask when I can hear knocking in the background.

"Yeah, it is," she says, once again a little shakily. The bravado gone with the reminder of the gravity of her situation standing right outside her door.

"Okay, put him on the phone for me?"

I hear rustling when Drew's voice comes over the line. "I'm here, it's all good. I've got it," he says, instinctively knowing that that's the reassurance I was looking for.

"I'm on my way, tell her I'll be there shortly," I instruct him before I hang up and concentrate on driving.

-

There are two patrol vehicles from the sheriff's office parked in front, when I pull up outside Stacie's house. There's also a handful of gawkers on the street, drawn by the commotion.

I walk up the path to the front porch where I see Jen sitting on the rattan bench, her arm around Stacie. The moment Stacie sees me, she's on her feet and coming toward me. I'd be lying if I said I didn't feel my chest swell a bit when she reaches me and wraps herself in my arms.

Jen, who also got up, is standing at the top of the steps, her eyes locked on mine over Stacie's head. A small smile forms on her lips before she starts down the stairs.

"You'll stay?" Jen asks me when she gets close, and Stacie immediately steps out of my arms.

"Not going anywhere," I confirm, earning a nod of approval from Jen and a look of concern from Stacie.

"Good, because I came running the moment I found out something was up. I left the customer who told me standing at the counter," she says, starting to move down the path. "Keep your fingers crossed he didn't take off with all my damn pastries."

"Talk to me," I tell Stacie, grabbing her hand and walking her back to the bench on her porch.

"Nothing much to tell that I haven't told you already," she says, shrugging as she sits down. "I went for a walk, came back home, and found the flowers."

"Looks like someone came in the window in your daughter's room," Drew says, interrupting as he steps out the front door. "Unless your daughter wears a size eleven men's shoe and makes it a habit to climb out the window, I'm pretty sure he left a print on the window sill."

"I always keep a safety bar behind the sliding part on all the windows," Stacie pipes up, her back straightening. "We just use the vents at the top for circulation."

"I know. The bar is still there," Drew says. "But apparently the stationary panel can easily be removed when you pull away the stripping on the outside. Not the best construction, these windows."

"Why the hell would someone want to come in here just to put some fake flowers on the counter?" she wants to know.

"Is there anything else you can think of?" Drew asks Stacie, ignoring what was obviously a rhetorical question. "Anything else happen? Strange phone calls? Things out of place?"

I watch with curiosity as what is visible of her face first pales and then turns a fiery red, stark against the white dressings. Her eye flits between Drew and me before firmly settling on the sheriff.

"No phone calls, but now I'm thinking there was something that happened Sunday that I initially dismissed. An item I had taken out before I took a nap, had been placed neatly in my night table when I woke up." I see one of Drew's eyebrows jerk up ever so slightly, but the rest of his face stays impassive. "I thought perhaps I'd done it myself, but that never really sat well with me. You see, I never store it in my bedside drawer."

I have to give it to the man; he certainly keeps a straight face, when I realize both he and I know exactly what item she is referring to by now. Not so much by what she said, but by what she didn't say. Her vagueness speaks volumes, as does the bright blush on her one visible cheek.

It's not appropriate at all, but I still can't help wonder if it was me she was thinking of when she was playing with herself.

"Where do you normally store it?" Drew asks, dispassionately, and I have a renewed respect for the man. Any sign of emotion, of interest, or even of amusement on his part, and I think I would've planted a fist in his face.

"Bottom drawer, old metal lunch box," Stacie says, her gaze now focused on the floor at her feet. I put my hand on her knee and give it a little squeeze.

"I'll see if my deputy can get some prints off your nightstand. Just in case," Drew says, turning to go back inside.

"One more thing," Stacie says, stopping him in his tracks. "When I found the flowers, I'd just come back from a walk along the river. From the moment I turned back home, I swear it felt like I had eyes on me."

"See anything?" Drew asks.

"No. Just had the hair stand up on my skin."

"Anyone in recent memory who might hold a grudge? An ex-boyfriend? Someone you prosecuted?" I ask, looking first at Drew, who nods in agreement, and then at Stacie.

"I used to have many, it's par for the course when you make a living putting people in prison. No ex-anythings," she says pointedly, pausing briefly as she holds my gaze. "And you know I've not been involved in any cases since before last Christmas."

"Could be someone who simply hasn't been able to track you down. You did pick up stakes quite suddenly," Drew suggests. "I don't necessarily think it has to be recent"

"Why do you say that?" Stacie wants to know.

Drew throws me a concerned look, before he focuses on her.

"Because those flowers in there?" he says, waving his hand in the direction of the kitchen. "Whoever it was didn't leave you forget-me-nots by accident."

CHAPTER 13

Stacie

"You're coming home with me."

This has been going back and forth since the sheriff cleared out. Nick wants me to pack a bag and tag along with him, but I'm not about to tuck my tail and go running over some fake flowers.

I'm not sure why I'm so stubborn, but I'm sick and tired of being a victim. I've been dragging my ass since my accident and am just starting to feel some solid ground under my feet again. I'm not going to let myself disappear into the shadows again. What would that teach Mak? Someone says *boo* really loud and you scamper off? That's not what I want to impart on my daughter.

Drew and Nick already reinforced the strip on the window by nailing a board all along the bottom of it. A temporary fix, because no one could come out today. The earliest was tomorrow afternoon. We were lucky that the windows in the bedrooms are standard sized; otherwise it would have been longer.

"Nick, I'm tired, I'm sore, Mak is coming off the bus any minute, and I really don't want to traumatize her anymore than I absolutely have to," I plead my case this time, instead of just giving him attitude. "The kid's been through enough upheaval, and unless it is absolutely necessary, I really don't want her to worry about something that might turn out to be nothing."

"It's hardly nothing, Anastasia," he says, stepping into my space and placing his hands on my shoulders before he continues. "And I don't think Mak would object to staying at the farm for a few days."

"Maybe that's true, but not under these circumstances. We'll be fine, Nick. I'll keep my gun with me and I'll have Mak sleep in my room."

Nick drops his head between his shoulders and sighs deeply, before lifting up a fraction and looking at me from under his surprisingly thick lashes. I'd never noticed those before.

"Fine," he grumbles. "But I'm sleeping on your couch." He quickly raises his hand and presses a finger against my lips when I'm about to object. "No. No ifs, ands, or buts, Stacie. Work with me here. You want to stay here? Fine, then I'll be sleeping on your couch. Ben would fucking skin me alive if I left you alone."

A smile tugs at the corner of my mouth. He's not lying about Ben. He *would* probably tear a strip off him.

"Phfime..." I mumble against his finger, which he quickly removes. "Fine," I repeat.

I'm rewarded with a grateful smile that momentarily stuns me. Up close I can see his deep brown eyes warm, sprouting lines from the corners all the way to where his hairline would be, if he had any. Deep grooves run on either side of the tip of his rather broad nose, down to frame his smiling mouth. And an attractive mouth it is, with nice firm lips spreading wide over strong teeth. Instinctively I reach out, stroking a finger along the stubble of his five-o'clock shadow, to the middle of his chin, where a small dimple gets deeper when he smiles.

"Anastasia..." he warns with a growl, as the warmth in his eyes turns to heat. "Don't play with me when your daughter is about to come home, and there's no time for me to do all you make me want to do to you."

As if burned, I drop my hand from his face, but his words linger in the air like a promise. There is no lie in the desire he shows for me. No guise in the deep hunger his eyes betray when he looks at me.

There may have been times where a man has looked at me like that, but never quite with that intensity, and certainly not at this new version of me.

"Anastasia..." he warns again.

This time I heed his warning and turn away, just in time to see the bus stop in front of the house. I rush to the door to catch my girl, and watch from the porch as I spot Becca climbing off the bus behind Mak. She seems to hesitate, but my daughter grabs her by the hand and drags her along.

"Hey, girls," I call out as they come up the path. "I was just about to make some s'mores in the microwave. You guys interested?"

The whoops are loud as Mak storms past me into the house, a slightly more subdued Becca following behind, eyeing my bandaged face suspiciously as she passes. I can't help notice the way she seems to hold her left arm close to her body, barely moving it at all. Even when she takes off her backpack in the small entryway, she gingerly slides the strap down that arm.

Mak has already barged through to the kitchen, where I can hear her chattering at Nick. Becca, however, lingers in the doorway, and almost jumps a foot when I gently place a hand on her back.

"That's a friend of mine; his name is Nick," I tell her when she turns her large, frightened, brown eyes on me. Something is definitely not right with her. "Remember the scars on my face?" I ask her and she meekly nods, her eyes big in her face. "Well, I had surgery on Friday, to see if they could make them look a little better, make my face a little prettier. Nick's just here to help me out."

She lets me coax her into the kitchen. There I introduce her to Nick properly, before I sit her down on a stool at the counter, where she watches me pull out the necessary ingredients.

"What are we cooking?" Nick asks, leaning a hip against the counter and folding his arms over his chest.

"Zapped s'mores," Mak announces excitedly. "But don't worry," she adds. "Mom knows how to make these."

I drop the bag of giant marshmallows on the counter and let my mouth fall open, as I glare at my daughter. Nine flipping years old and already with the snide remarks. Puberty is going to be a long haul.

Mak is unimpressed, and just giggles at my expression, which draws a chuckle from Nick.

"Hey," I protest with an admonishing finger in his direction. "I'll have you know that I won a ribbon once for my zapped s'mores in college."

"Uncle Ben says that was a con…consild…consilderation prize," Mak feels the need to enlighten.

"Consolidation," Becca corrects her softly, and then throws a cautious glance in my direction, as if scared I might get angry.

Nick stifles a laugh. "I think you mean consolation prize, girls."

I narrow my eyes, but let a smile play on my lips when I look into Becca's worried eyes. Then I throw the full force of my ire at the others. Mak's still giggling, and only giggles harder when Nick snorts in an attempt to hold back his own laughter.

"I didn't know you were culinarily challenged," he jokes.

"Careful, buster," I threaten. "I might decide to get creative with my meatloaf on you someday."

"Oh no!" my daughter, who was never a fan, cries dramatically. "Not the meatloaf."

"Double serving for you next time," I threaten her teasingly, and this time I could hear a reaction from the other little girl.

A tiny little tinkle of sound, like the dainty peal of a wind chime in the summer breeze. She seems as surprised as the rest of us at her giggles, and I quickly give her a reassuring wink with my one visible eye, before turning to the serious business of zapped s'mores.

-

"Wash your hands, girls."

The milk and treats were inhaled, and not just by the two kids. Nick had come back for seconds, and was currently licking his fingers, which was not just a little distracting.

"You were already pretty."

I look down at Becca, who sidled up to me to get to the sink. Her soft voice was almost drowned out by the running water, but the message was firm. I have to swallow hard when I look into her earnest, upturned face.

"Thank you, sweetheart," I tell her gently. "Now wash your hands and then you can go play in Mak's room."

I turn to Nick, who's observing the interaction and make an *awww* face at him. He silently smiles before his attention is drawn to Becca, a frown on his face. I look and see her lift her left hand with her right to reach the stream of water.

"Did you hurt yourself?" I ask, and watch her little back straighten.

"I fell," she says quickly, her eyes staying fixed on the sink as she rinses the sticky residue off her hands.

"Can I see?" I ask carefully, handing her a towel to dry.

"It's okay," she says softly, taking a step back before she turns and rushes after Mak, who's already ensconced in her bedroom.

I was going to ask Nick if he noticed that, but one look at the way he stares after Becca, and I already know his suspicions match mine.

Nick

I don't know kids. I've never really been around them, but there'd been no mistaking that little girl's body language.

It's been two days since she followed Mak into Stacie's house, but I haven't been able to shake the glaze of fear in those big brown eyes.

-

I ended up driving Stacie's SUV when it was time to take Becca home, since she still only has the use of one eye. I was shocked to see where the girl lives. It didn't help that a tall, lanky kid with dark straggly hair—later identified by Mak as Becca's older brother—was sitting on the steps of the trailer when we pulled in and didn't look too impressed.

Stacie and I didn't have a chance to talk that night because she crashed at the same time Mak went to bed. Yesterday wasn't much better, since I ended up driving Mak to school in the morning. I had appointments in the office all day, but Jen promised to check in with Stacie, who'd all but pushed me out the door.

By the time I got back to her place last night, the bedroom windows had been replaced, and the sheriff was sitting at the kitchen island, chatting with Mak over what appeared to be dinner. The sight of that did not make me happy.

What also didn't make me happy was the knowing grin Drew tossed over his shoulder at me. *Fucker*.

Trying to stay on top of my cases, the worry about Mak and Stacie's safety, and now concern about Becca's wellbeing, had already drawn me in twenty directions. Good thing Pops was looking after the campground, or I would've had to add that to the list. As it was, I was wearing a little thin when I walked into that kitchen, and tipped right over the edge when I saw the resident playboy sheriff taking up what had been my stool just the night before.

Not even the surprised smile Stacie gave me was able to stave off my dark mood.

"Hey, you," she said. "I wasn't sure you'd come by. Drew came by with food, mentioned it was his turn to check on me, so I figured you guys had talked."

"Not that I can recall," I growled, shooting daggers at the asshole.

He just wiped his mouth on a napkin, got up, and deposited his plate in the sink, acting like he belonged here. It was all I could do not to deck him.

"I was just giving the guy a break," Drew said with a smile for Stacie, who looked confused between the two of us. "But I must head out. My shift is just starting, so it'll be easy for me to swing by a few times during the night." He bent down to kiss Stacie on the small patch of uncovered skin on the right side of her face, threw me a wink, and walked out the door, leaving me seething.

I've never been good with teasing. Most of the teasing I was subjected to at the hands of guys like Drew—I'm sure he was a jock in high school and college—felt more like ridicule and bullying. Besides, in all the years I've known him, I've never been the target of his jokes, or have I?

It's a question I've asked myself a few times since last night.

I fucked up. Big.

I was so pissed off; I ended up taking my insecurities out on Stacie. When she offered me something to eat, I threw out some snide remark, asking if she was sure she'd have enough and how many other guys she was planning on feeding tonight. Needless to say that wasn't received well, I'd pissed her off, and it wasn't long after that she suggested it might be better if I left.

Sometime during the course of the wee morning hours, after rolling around sleepless in my bed all night, I came to a conclusion: I need to come clean. There is no way I'll ever be able to get past the insecurities of the person I used to be, unless I tell Stacie who I am, the small part I played years ago at a crucial point in her life, and the connection between us that runs much deeper than she realizes.

-

No clue where to fucking start.

I never realized how out of my depth I am when it comes to relationships. It's one thing when all runs smoothly, but how to get back there after you've hit a bump, is another matter. At least I hope it's a bump and not an insurmountable roadblock.

I'd seen the concern in the look Stacie had thrown me over that little girl, Becca's head. I have to leave the investigation around the break-in at her house over to Drew, but I'll be damned if I can't find another way to ease Stacie's life a little.

Which is why I seek out Sheila the moment I walk into the office this morning. Since she works both for Doug, who handles family law, and me, I know she might have some suggestions.

"But what did you see? Did you actually see any injuries?" she asks, grilling me.

"She couldn't even lift up that arm, Sheila. And you should've seen her eyes. You can't be telling me it's normal for a little girl to regard the world with suspicion and fear?" I'm getting a little riled up at her questioning.

"Chill out, Nick," she admonishes me. "You're a lawyer, you know how this goes. Little or nothing can be done without tangible evidence; a witness, photographs, or a direct complaint from the child that someone is hurting her."

I do know, which is what is frustrating me, because I don't have any links to the child. Nothing I can pursue, not even via the school, since I have no business there. The only option left open would be either through Stacie, who I just screwed things up with, or through law enforcement, which means Drew would have another opportunity to come out the hero. *Son of a fucking bitch.*

Of course I'm going to talk to Drew—someone has to look into that girl's situation—but that doesn't mean I have to like it.

"Carmel," he answers on the first ring.

"Need to pick your brain," I jump right in, and I bristle when I hear his familiar chuckle.

"Want some advice on the ladies?" he jeers, making me grind my teeth. "Cause I gotta tell ya, friend, those vibes you were giving off last night aren't going to get you far."

"Don't be an ass," I grind out through clenched teeth. "I already fucked up last night, I'm not going to let you get the best of me again."

"You're kidding, right?" he laughs, and I almost throw the phone against my office wall. "The great, unflappable Nicholas Flynn crashed and burned? That's gotta be a first."

Those last remarks, and the tone they were imparted with, shock me.

"You know I'm just messing with you, right?" Drew says after a lengthy pause.

"Yeah, sure," I manage, shaking my head to clear it. "Look, for the record, *crash and burn* was one of my nicknames in high school, and I'm so far from unflappable when it comes to this woman…" I let my words drift off, wondering if I'm just opening myself up to a whole new world of hurt.

"No shit? Ben's little sister? Man, do I wanna be a fly on the wall when he finds out."

"Yeah, well, I didn't know she was his sister back when I first met her," I confess. "Although I'm not sure if knowing that would've made a lick of difference in college."

"College? But you would've been a good number of years ahead of her, no?" he points out, quite accurately, since I'm probably five or six years her senior.

"She was a student, I wasn't."

"You dog," Drew chuckles, surprised. "I bet she was a looker then."

"She's even more beautiful now," I tell him, and from the silence on the other side, I'm guessing that surprises him even more.

Feeling a bit uncomfortable with the amount of information I've shared, stuff that I haven't had a chance to tell Stacie yet, I steer the conversation back to the reason for my call.

By the time I get off the phone, I know that although the sheriff's office has never received any reports on possible child abuse, the trailer park in general, and Becca's brother and mother in particular, are no strangers to law enforcement. Not exactly encouraging news, but after hearing me describe the girl's behavior, Drew left no doubt that he'd be keeping a very close eye out for Becca.

I felt a lot better, both about the girl, but also about the stuff I shared. I actually feel encouraged enough to drive straight to Stacie's house when I get to Dolores. No time like the present to do some groveling first, and hopefully, she will give me a chance to explain a few things.

But the moment I pull up to her house, I can see that plan fly out of the window. Ben's big SUV is parked right behind Stacie's much smaller one, and the man himself is standing on the porch, watching me get out of the car, his arms folded over his chest and his face spelling thunder.

Shit. Forgot he was heading back today.

CHAPTER 14

Nick

He doesn't respond to my greeting, just moves aside so I can take the last step up to the porch.

"Trusted you to take care of her," he grinds out, even though I swear I didn't see his mouth move.

Ben makes for an imposing figure, but I'm prepared to take whatever he doles out to get to the woman inside.

"I know and I did." I cringe at how pathetically defensive that sounds, when I know I should've done better.

"Then how come I never got a call when shit went down here?" he barks, getting in my face, but I stand my ground. "First thing you should've fucking done was call me. That's my little sister in there."

"Your sister maybe, but not helpless. She's a grown-ass woman," I retort, getting a little steamed up myself. "If she'd wanted you to worry, she would've called you herself, but you had your hands full."

"I asked *you* to look after her," he repeats, poking a finger in my chest for emphasis. Now in a drag down fight, I'm pretty sure I'd get my ass handed to me, but that doesn't stop me from grabbing Ben's wrist firmly and deliberately moving his hand away.

"I fucking did," I growl. My turn to invade his space. "Not the way you would've: waltzing right over her like a caveman, but that's not me. The woman is just getting her sea legs—her strength—back. She doesn't need me making her feel powerless again." I watch as he steps back, the expression on his face evening out, but I'm not done. "And one more thing: you may not see it, being her brother and all, but that woman in there is a force in her own right."

My impassioned tirade feels a bit anticlimactic when Ben suddenly grins.

"Fuck me," he mutters. "Isla was right."

"What are you talking about?"

"Brushed her off when she said there was something building," he says, looking at me like a bug under a microscope. "Didn't see it then, but I see it now." One of his big paws lands on my shoulder, forcefully. "You're a goner."

"Sure, I like her," I start, a little uneasy at this turn around, but forging ahead anyway, despite the almost knee-buckling grip of his shovel-sized hand on my shoulder. "Respect her."

"Is that why she's in there, looking like someone ran over her puppy, wincing whenever your name is mentioned?" he asks, one eyebrow raised.

I should probably feel guilty at that information, but it makes me pleased instead. She cares.

"Something I could've fixed by now, if you weren't blocking my way," I fire back, not quite able to keep the smug grin off my face. Ben shakes his head and drops his hand from my shoulder, stepping aside to let me pass.

At that moment the door opens and Stacie sticks her head out.

"Are you guys about done pissing on my porch? Or do you need some more time? Dinner's getting cold and Mak's starting to chew on the couch, she's so hungry," she says, before stepping back inside.

All I have to go by is a single eye and a far too distracting mouth, and I've never been particularly talented in reading faces, but I'm guessing from what could be construed as a dinner invitation, I'm still in the game.

I follow Stacie's retreating form into the house. Stepping past Ben, he gives me an encouraging shove in the middle of my back.

A shove that feels more like a warning.

-

I don't have much of a chance to talk to Stacie until Ben leaves to go up the mountain to check on his own place.

She hasn't even made eye contact with me all night, but is glaring at me now. Ben just announced he'll be by to pick her up for her appointment in the morning and I jump in.

"Already taken care of," I announce, ignoring the evil eye I can see Stacie throwing me from the corner of my eye. I keep my focus on Ben, however, letting him know how dead serious I am. "I've got this; my day is clear and you've got stuff to take care of." A challenge, and he knows it.

"Why not let Stace decide?" he says, his eyes never leaving mine as he throws it back.

"Your call," I concede, turning to look in her now conflicted eyes.

173

I can see the internal struggle between wanting to assert herself against me, or standing up to her overbearing brother. Her gaze flicks back and forth between us when she finally stops, facing Ben with an apologetic sigh.

"He's right," she tells him reluctantly; I try not to gloat. "It would defeat the purpose for you to fly back to take care of business, and then end up sitting in a waiting room. Besides," she adds, turning a sharp glare in my direction. "A little time for contemplation while he's waiting for me might be good for Nick."

Ben barks out a laugh at my expense, but that doesn't keep the grin from my face.

I keep Mak, who is watching TV, company in the living room while Stacie sees Ben out.

"What are we watching?" I ask her, my attention drawn when a girl, not much older than Mak, perfectly sears a nice cut of beef. I can almost smell it over the lingering odor of our dinner. That had been spaghetti and meatballs, but not quite like any I've ever tasted before. Cooking is most definitely not one of Stacie's strong suits.

"*Junior Master Chef*," Mak replies, throwing a glance over her shoulder at the door, before leaning in to me and whispering conspiratorially, "Mom says when I'm ten I can help with the cooking, but I really don't want her to teach me."

"What are you two chuckling about?" Stacie says when she walks in, only making Mak laugh harder.

"Gordon Ramsay was funny," Mak lies with an innocent face. There's nothing funny about that man, and Stacie knows it, eyeing her daughter suspiciously.

"If you say so. Time to hit the sack, kiddo. Thank God it's Friday tomorrow, right?" She smiles at Mak's enthusiastic fist pump, as the girl gets up off the couch.

I get up and wander into the kitchen to tackle the disaster left by dinner, or rather the preparation of said dinner, while she looks after Mak. I'm still scraping the burned tomato sauce from the bottom of the pan when she walks in a little later.

"I was going to do that," she starts, quickly grabbing a tea towel to dry the dishes in the rack.

"Least I can do since you fed me," I say, glancing over to her. "Why don't you sit down for a bit?"

"I'm too restless."

"Nervous about tomorrow?" I ask, and she nods sharply.

"A little," she admits, falling silent again right away, but I don't push it. It doesn't take long before I hear her take a deep breath in. "I don't know why. It can't be any worse than it is now, right?" she asks, but she's not really expecting an answer. Not that I'd be able to give her one anyway. Truth is, I've been worried as well, not about the way she'll look, but her response to whatever the outcome is. "I can't help hoping that when the bandages come off, I'll be me again—like new—but I know that's impossible."

She reaches up to put a bowl on the top shelf, but comes up a little short, so I step up behind her, take the bowl from her hand and do it for her. I don't move away immediately, enjoying the feel of her body in front of me.

"Nicholas..." she whispers, when I rest my cheek against the top of her head. But she doesn't move.

"Beautiful...your eyes, the way you smell, the sound of your voice, the taste of your skin...just beautiful." I take in a deep breath when I feel her body lean back into me. I take it as an invitation to slip an arm around her waist, my hand spanning her stomach. "I'm an ass," I mumble in her hair. "That much is not news, but I've never been a jealous ass. Until a few days ago, when I walked in on Drew sitting here, and I realized that just like ten years ago, I might have missed my chance again."

Stacie slowly turns, and I take a step back to give her room.

"What do you mean? Missed your chance?"

Stacie

I lean back against the counter and wait for an answer.

He's good with his words, amazing even, melting my resolve like snow for the sun, but then he says something that gives me an unsettled feeling again. The feeling that I'm missing something. I know he mentioned seeing me around college, but with his specific reference to ten years ago, it almost implies it was more than that.

"I was the only child from a farming family, one that goes back generations, and going to law school was not something my parents had hoped for me. But I persisted, even though it was much harder than I expected. I didn't really fit in with the college crowd, being a farm boy and all, but it never bothered me much," he says, looking at me from under his lashes. The hint of vulnerability squeezes my heart. "Do you have anything to drink?" he asks suddenly, completely changing topic.

"Sure." I open the fridge and pull out the bottle of white wine. I grab a couple of glasses while I let him struggle with the cork.

"I graduated," he continues, taking a fortifying swig from his glass. "But wasn't quite sure which direction I wanted to go. I looked on, while others were being snapped up by law firms from all over. I had great marks, and one of my professors ended up offering me a position as a teaching assistant." He shrugs, as if he hadn't just exposed himself, concealed in the purposely-monotone narrative. "That's how I met you," he says, suddenly looking me straight in the eye.

"I'm sorry, I don't remember," I repeat what I recall telling him the first time he'd mentioned knowing me.

"I was pretty invisible back then."

"That's certainly not a problem now," I admit. "You're a hard man to miss." I really like the almost cocky smirk that puts on his face, but it doesn't linger long.

"I'd seen you around campus, and in a few lectures, but like I said, we didn't exactly run in the same circles." He pauses and lets his eyes roam over my bandaged face. "First thing I thought was how beautiful you were. Second thing I remember thinking, was that you might as well live on a different continent, you were so far out of my reach."

"Why would you say that? Was I —"

"No. Nothing you did," he interrupts, quickly reassuring me, before forging ahead. "I just never approached you at the time. Until that party…"

I see his mouth keep moving, but I'm not hearing a damn thing. My blood suddenly roars in my ears. My glass of wine drops to the floor, as I clap my hands over my mouth: he couldn't be…

Noticing my panic, he makes a move toward me, but I step further out of his reach.

"Anastasia, what's wrong? Stacie?"

I'm not sure what it is about his use of my full name that suddenly has goosebumps stand up all over my skin, but with it comes a deep feeling of dread in the pit of my stomach.

"Who told you my name?" I hiss; my whole body poised to bolt. "Who the hell are you?"

I watch suspiciously as his hand comes up and rubs over his smooth head. A head I carefully shaved not that long ago. That night I thought I'd found the beginning of something new, something hopeful.

My mind scans back to the sight of him taking his shirt off, exposing his torso…but I never saw his back.

"You told me your name," he says, lifting his hands up defensively. "Ten years ago. You were drunk out of your mind at a party, you needed help, and I brought you home in a taxi.

There's only one college party that stands out from all the rest, oddly because I can barely remember anything about it, but it netted me my precious daughter. All I can remember is laying in a bed, barely able to keep my head up as I watched someone walk out of the room, a large Celtic tattoo spanning his back.

"I can't remember you," I whisper confused, trying to match the man in front of me with the memory of a set of wide shoulders and narrow hips. "Take your shirt off"

I have to give it to him, he doesn't even hesitate as he wordlessly whips his shirt over his head and stands there, waiting, watching me take him in.

"Turn around," I order, and once again without objection, he does what I ask as I hold my breath.

Nothing. I approach, scrutinizing the skin on his back: no tattoo, no ink at all, and nothing else marring his skin.

"Can I put my shirt on now?" he asks. I realize he's turned around and I'm staring right at his chest. I wave my hand for him to go ahead.

"You were the guy who got me home?"

He pulls his shirt back over his head and looks me straight in the eye.

"That was me."

My knees buckle and I let myself slide down against the pantry door, dropping my head to my raised knees.

"Jesus…for a minute I thought…*Makenna.*"

"I know," he says softly, crouching in front of me, and this time I don't move away when he pulls me close.

-

I can't sleep.

After almost two hours of talking, I finally went to bed and left Nick to make himself at home on the couch. I was exhausted, both physically and emotionally, and was sure I'd pass right out. Not so.

I don't know how many hours later and my mind is still reeling with this information. The knowledge that Nick and I have a connection, which goes back as far as Makenna's conception, is bizarre, and that's putting it mildly. Anxiety around my appointment tomorrow is building too.

I finally start dozing off when a loud crash sounds from down the hall. My first thought is Makenna when I jump out of bed. I fly across the hall and into her bedroom, but she's still sound asleep in her bed. Her room undisturbed. I carefully close the door again and turn down the hallway.

That's when I hear the sound of the front door opening.

CHAPTER 15

Nick

It's my own damn fault.

I'm looking down at the remnants of Stacie's coffee table, which I literally flattened in my attempt to get up from the couch with a sheet tangled around my feet. By the time I got the front door open, whomever it was I saw standing outside the front window looking in, was long gone.

Sleep had been restless at best, and when I shot awake to a figure in the window, outlined against the single streetlight, I moved without thinking, the result in pieces at my feet.

"Come here," I invite Stacie, who'd come flying out of the house after me and is now fussing in the kitchen. I walk over to her and she turns right into my arms, leaning her forehead against my shoulder.

"Coffee should be done shortly," she mumbles, her voice as tight with tension as her body is.

"Sounds good." I rest my cheek on the top of her head, just holding her close. "Sorry about your table," I mumble in her hair.

"Don't worry. I wasn't crazy about it anyway. It gives me an excuse to shop for a new one," she announces, making me chuckle, but I sober instantly at her next words. "I'm glad you were here."

"Me too." I hold her a little tighter before adding: "I should call Drew, and probably Ben, as well."

"We should wait until Mak is on the bus." She leans back to look at me. "She'll be gone in a few hours and whoever it was is long gone anyway. I don't want to scare her."

"Tell you what," I negotiate. "Since your brother undoubtedly will barge in minutes after we call, we can hold off for a bit on him, but I do have to call Drew. See what he says."

"Fine." She sounds a little irritated, but resigned. "But when we get back from Durango, I'm diving into this. Someone is playing games and I'm not down with that."

"Not thinking this is a game, beautiful." Her eyes snap up to glare at me.

"Well aware of that, counselor," she says sharply, stepping out of the circle of my arms, to busy herself with cups and coffee. "My child was in the house this time, which is why I'm not going to sit around and wait for whoever is trying to yank my chain to get his jollies off."

"*Anastasia…*" I try softly, but she won't hear it.

"As much as my name sounds really fucking good from your lips, you're not going to convince me otherwise, *Nicholas*."

I can't help but grin at the way she mimics my tone. I like the sass on her. "Fair enough," I concede, pulling my phone from my jeans and taking a step toward the front door. "But I'm calling Drew," I tell her, showing her the phone in my hand when she turns to face me.

-

Drew showed up just as the school bus disappeared around the corner. Ben, whom I'd called as Stacie walked Mak to the bus stop, shortly after. I ignored his angry glare when he discovered we hadn't contacted him immediately, and gave them a detailed description of what went down, which wasn't much to begin with.

Ben hugged his sister tightly before she got in my truck, promising her he'd get to the bottom of it. Then he walked around to where I was standing by the driver's side door, talking to Drew.

"Never fucking thought I'd say this, but I'm glad you stayed here last night," he growled at me, drawing a chuckle from Drew, while I struggled to keep a straight face. "But don't let it get to your head and keep your damn eyes open."

I just gave him a nod, and with a chin lift at Drew, got behind the wheel, leaving the guys to look after the house. I had Stacie to look out for.

"I swear he thinks I'm still fourteen," Stacie grumbles in the passenger seat just as we pass Mancos. She's been stewing in her seat this whole time and has repeatedly avoided letting me grab her hand, but I have no trouble knowing whom she is referring to. "It's like he doesn't even acknowledge the work I've done in the past almost decade. I've had to deal with some crazy motherfuckers in those years and managed all right without him jumping in."

"It's a big brother's prerogative." I shrug, understanding Ben's need to protect her. What I'm feeling is not all that different. "Given what already happened to you this year, you can't fault him for freaking out a little. He almost lost you."

"I know," she says, softening a little as she turns to look at me. "How come you're not freaking out?" I bite down a grimace and give her a quick wink instead.

"Who says I'm not?" I pose to her. "I'd love nothing more than to lock you and Mak safely away at the farm, where no one can find you, but I figure that wouldn't go over too well with the woman I'm trying to impress."

"You're trying to impress me?"

"Fuck me." I roll my eyes dramatically. "I must not be doing it right if you have to ask." A quick glance over shows the tiniest of smiles playing on her lips.

This time when I reach over and take her hand in mine, she easily slips her fingers between mine.

Despite the stressful morning, I'm inwardly smiling the whole way into Durango.

Stacie

I'm nervous.

Damn, who the hell am I kidding? I'm petrified. Which is probably why I grab Nick's hand and drag him along into the doctor's office when my name is called. Credit to him, he doesn't say a word and calmly follows me inside, taking the seat next to me like he belongs.

Dr. Ashrad walks in and doesn't even blink when he sees Nick sitting beside me; he just nods at him before smiling at me and patting the paper covering the examination table.

"Let's have a look then, shall we?"

Reluctantly I let go of Nick's hand, who gives me a quick reassuring squeeze before releasing me, and I hop on the table, curling my hands tightly around the edge.

My eyes are firmly closed when I feel him pulling at the tape holding the bandages in place. Guess I don't want to risk seeing any flinching on Nick's face, because that would be almost as bad as looking into a mirror, which I'm not sure I'd be ready for.

Nice cool air brushes over my skin as Dr. Ashrad pulls away the last of the bandages, leaving only the smaller dressing covering my left eye.

"Hmmm," I hear him hum.

"Is that a good or a bad *hmmm*?" I want to know.

"Good," he simply says without elaboration. "This may stick a little."

"*Sonofabitch*," I hiss when he pulls the gauze back and both my eyes fly open.

"Sorry." I hear him mumble as I frantically blink against the sudden bright light flooding the retina in my left eye, after a week of total darkness.

With my eyes slowly adjusting to the light, I notice Nick, sitting on the edge of his seat, looking intently at me.

"That bad?" I can't help ask; still a little worried, despite the doctor's reassurances. He immediately shakes his head.

"Not at all. A little swollen and red, with some bruising around your eye, but the scar looks much smoother. You should have a look," Nick urges with an encouraging smile.

"The discoloration and the swelling will fade with time, as will most of the redness, although you should remain vigilant in avoiding direct sun," Dr. Ashrad informs me. "But before I get you a mirror, let me remove these few surface stitches."

I feel a slight pinch when he pulls the stitches free, but then he lifts a handheld mirror to my face. My left eye, albeit not exactly fresh looking right now, is no longer drooping. I don't even bother looking at the rest of my scar; I'm so engrossed at seeing symmetry in my face again. Even as my vision blurs with tears of relief, I can't look away.

I barely notice the click of the door latching, as Nick's arms are suddenly there, pulling me tight against his strong body.

"It looks good, right?" I finally manage, my ear pressed against the steady thump of his heart.

"It does. I'm glad for you," he mumbles quietly and I lift my head away, tilting it up to look into his warm eyes. "You've always been beautiful to me, but it makes me happy that this might help you believe it."

With infinite tenderness, he presses his lips on mine, before brushing them ever so lightly over the scar on my face. I'm about to dissolve in tears again at the sweet gesture, when the door opens and Dr. Ashrad is back, with some papers and a tube of something in his hand.

"These are aftercare instructions and this is a medicated ointment you should apply twice a day," he says, handing them to me. "Make sure your hands are washed before application and massage it into the scar gently. It should help to keep the skin stay supple as it completely heals. Avoid rubbing your eye or crying," he says with a sharp, warning look in Nick's direction that makes me chuckle. "And check in with Linda on your way out. I'd like to see you again in about six weeks, to see how you've healed. If you decide you want me to see if we can improve on some of the other scars on your torso or limbs, let me know."

I shoot a look at Nick at the reference to the scars he hasn't really seen yet, but he doesn't react at all. Dr. Ashrad shakes my hand and then Nick's, before opening the door for us.

"Want to grab a quick bite?" Nick asks as we walk out of the hospital. When he senses my hesitation he quickly adds, "We don't have to get out of the car, we can hit a drive-thru or I can grab something and we can park by the river?"

"That sounds good," I concede, liking that last idea. "As long as we're back in time to get Mak off the bus, I'm good."

-

My phone rings just as I'm wiping some lingering crumbs from the front of my shirt. I'm clearly a messy eater, especially eating that amazing sandwich from Oscar's Cafe Nick recommended.

We found a quiet spot along the Animas River not too far from downtown, but the rush of the fast-moving water drowns out the city noises quite effectively. I could almost imagine myself in the middle of nowhere, Nick's solid thigh pressing against my leg making for a delicious daydream where we become one with nature, so to speak—but my ringtone spoils the fantasy.

"Hey, Ben," I answer, after a quick peek at my screen reveals the caller.

"How is it?" he barges right in, as is typical of my big brother.

"Good. I think…the doc seemed pleased. My eye looks much better. A little less Quasimodo."

"Knock it off," Ben gruffly scolds me for joking. "You've never been anything but gorgeous."

Gah…I have to swallow hard; my brother sweet is threatening to get me sloppy.

"Nick said something similar," I say, lifting my eyes to find the man in question studying me intently.

"He did?" Ben sounds pleasantly surprised.

"Absolutely, but you guys have to stop being nice, or I'm gonna cry, and you know you hate me emotional," I warn them both. "Besides, Dr. Ashrad said to avoid crying."

"So noted," he says brusquely. "Now, next reason I called; I have Mak. Now don't get your knickers in a twist," he says right away when I start to protest. "I happened to be driving by the school and saw the kids being rushed out of the building and went to check it out. Apparently the school received a bomb threat."

"In Dolores?" I question incredulously.

"Probably a hoax. They can't take any chances, though. All the kids were sent home so Drew and his guys can check it out."

"We're just finishing up lunch, we'll head back right away," I tell him, already getting to my feet.

"Actually, I thought I'd keep Mak with me. I have to go into Cortez to pick up a few things, and she needs a new reel for her rod. The trip'll likely include a stop at Sonic." He pauses for a moment, but before I can launch an objection to the junk food, he continues, "It's been a while since I took her fishing, so I thought I'd take her down to the reservoir. She can just crash here with me. You both can. Or I can drop her off at home tomorrow."

The last is posed more as a question than a statement. I'm not sure why I sneak a peek from under my lashes in Nick's direction, but I can feel a blush crawling up my face as I consider the possibilities of an empty house.

"I'm sure she'd love that," I respond, trying to keep my voice level. "I think I'll just stay home. I have some laundry I've been ignoring and an episode of *Live PD* I don't want to miss. Be nice to have a quiet evening, alone."

Not surprisingly, my attempts at playing it cool fail miserably.

"Right," Ben says mockingly.

"Can I talk to Mak?" I ask in an attempt to distract, as I try not to look in Nick's direction.

My daughter sounds excited to be spending some time with her uncle, which goes a long way to alleviating any guilt I might feel at my own excitement over a night *minus* kid.

By the time I tell Mak I'll see her tomorrow and hang up, Nick has cleared away the remnants of our lunch and is looking at me with barely contained heat.

"You know that's not going to happen."

"What?" I look at him confused.

"Any of it," he clarifies as he closes the space between us. "Laundry, TV, alone, or quiet—none of that is going down."

"Is that so?"

I tilt my head back as his arms slip around the small of my back and tug me close. His normally warm brown eyes are like hot coal, almost glowing with intensity as he looks into mine.

"Fuck yeah…I have ten years of pent-up fantasies to live out. I wouldn't survive trying to tackle them all in one night, but I'm sure as hell going to make a dent."

I don't know whether to swoon, laugh hysterically, or kick him in the nuts, but there's no denying the warm heat pooling between my thighs—or the nerves churning in my stomach.

Sonofabitch!

What are the fucking odds?

Thought it was a good plan, for an easy twenty bucks the kid agreed to call the school at a set time. Little shit even thought it was funny.

I'm waiting at the far end of the parking lot, watching the main school doors open and kids come filing out. I'm all geared up to snatch the bitch's little spawn the moment I see her walking out, when a black SUV pulls in, blocking my view.

Move, asshole!

When it's clear that's not happening, I move my truck where I can see better.

I tense as I watch the driver, some tough-looking, older dude, get out and walk over to a sheriff's cruiser just pulling up. I'd hoped to be out of here before they showed. Last thing I want is to draw attention to myself, so I can't do anything but watch as the older guy ends up loading the object of my attention in his shiny SUV, and drives off.

I slam a fist on the steering wheel, furious my plan failed, when I spot a familiar face in the crowd of kids. That hooker's dorky little kid. Not only red hair, freckles, and glasses, but also a doped up, drunk skank of a mother and a delinquent big brother. If a God exists, he's a cruel motherfucker.

No wonder she's staring longingly after that SUV. I watch as she raises her arm and waves at it, a hesitant smile on her face, and I wonder if she knows my target.

A new plan forms almost immediately, and when I quietly drive out of the parking lot, over to my temporary lodgings at the trailer park, I'm smiling broadly.

CHAPTER 16

Nick

"Jesus, just get down on the ground, you moron!"

I chuckle, watching as Stacie gets all worked up over some idiot who just got caught trying to steal a car, and is refusing to back down to the police.

We're watching that show of hers. Not exactly my choice, I'd rather be doing something else right now, but things just kept getting in the way.

It started with the stop we made at Walgreens in Cortez, at Stacie's request. She insisted I stay in the car while she picked up a few things inside. I did at first, until I remembered that if things would run their course, the way I imagined they would, I might need to get a few supplies of my own.

I walked in, just in time to catch two employees gossiping loudly about Stacie who was standing in line for the checkout, trying to pretend she didn't hear every word. They noticed me, but barely spared me a glance, until I stepped in their space.

"Tell me," I started, looking from one shocked face to the other. "Does it make you feel better about yourself to harass customers? I sure hope it's worth it once I'm done talking to—"

"Let's go," Stacie hissed as she pulled me outside by the arm. "It's not worth it."

"Like hell," I countered, swinging around to face her. "I'm not going to stand by and let them talk about you like that."

"No?" she fired back, planting her fists on her hips as she glared at me. "You think making a scene, dragging out the manager, and creating God knows what kind of drama is going to make me feel better? What are just two bitchy cows, I can easily ignore, quickly becomes a circus I can't avoid. How is that going to help me?"

"*Fuck*," I swore under my breath, recognizing her point. I'd been so eager in my quest to jump in the fray, to exert myself as her hero, that I lost sight of her best interests.

It was a humbling lesson.

One that carried through the remainder of the afternoon that included picking up some groceries for the weekend, and making a quick stop to drop some things off for Pops. We weren't able to get out of there until we tried some of his homemade chicken noodle soup and a chunk of his fresh bread. The bread is something new he's been trying, and is getting quite good at, but the soup I can remember him making when I was still a little boy.

I made the mistake of saying something to that effect, which resulted in Pops pulling out an old album he'd been looking through. For an hour, he sat beside Stacie on the couch, flipping through the old pictures, a lot of them embarrassing for me. I'd grown from a chubby child into a large man before I lost all the weight. I wasn't about to say anything though, it had been a long time since I'd heard Pops talk about my mom. I sat and listened, occasionally catching a sweet smile Stacie would send in my direction.

It had turned out to be a much different afternoon than anticipated, but a good one nonetheless.

After we got back to Stacie's and put the groceries away, I offered to make us a simple omelet for dinner, while she took a shower.

Right now, sitting beside Stacie on her couch with my feet up on her table, and her feet in my lap, as I listen to her argue with the TV, I can feel the heat building again. My fingers softly stroke the exposed skin of her ankle, and despite her focus on the events playing out on the screen, her reclined body is responding to my touch. That's where *my* eyes have been, zoomed in on the tight puckering of her nipples under the thin tank top.

Any self-consciousness around the scarring on her face and left arm seems to have disappeared around me. I don't think the remaining insecurities have much, if anything, to do with me necessarily, but more with her. She is starting to believe the way I see her.

Good, since I'm planning to see all of her tonight.

I slide my hand on her left ankle up and under her pant leg. Slowly, so she doesn't pay much attention at first, but when I reach her knee, she turns her head away from the TV and looks me in the eye.

I hold her gaze as I stroke my hand higher and encounter the puckered skin halfway up the outside of her thigh. She draws her bottom lip between her teeth, pulling at it. A soft hiss escapes her mouth as I run my entire palm up and slide it over to squeeze her butt cheek in my hand. *Thank fuck for yoga pants.*

"These are coming off," I warn her.

The sounds of her TV program still run in the background but her focus is completely on me. I quickly pull my hand clear and with a firm grip on her elastic waistband, and my eyes firmly holding hers, I slide her yoga pants down her legs, taking her panties along.

"Beautiful," I mumble without looking away from her face. I lean over to kiss her slightly-parted lips, my palm purposely sliding up from her hip, following the scar under her top.

"You haven't even looked," she points out, her voice muffled and slightly tremulous against my mouth. I lift away and sit up straight.

"I don't need to, to know that," I tell her. "But I will if you want me to."

Accepting her nod as confirmation, I turn my gaze to her feet still in my lap and slowly run up her legs. I take in everything: the smooth, silky pale skin, in sharp contrast to the hard ridges of the purplish, red scarring. Mostly though, I'm drawn to the trimmed nest of ruddy blonde curls at the apex of her legs, and distractedly run my fingertips through.

My cock, rock hard by now, is straining against my fly. It's unbelievably erotic, sitting here fully dressed, with the gorgeous, half nude, subject of my dreams in my lap. I have to squeeze my eyes closed and go over balance sheets in my head so I won't blow a load in my jeans.

A sharp inhale has me snap open my eyes on Stacie, who looks pained.

"It's okay," she mutters, starting to lift her feet from my lap. I grab them and hold them firmly in place, letting her feel my erection.

"No," I disagree. "You don't get it. I'm trying hard not to erupt in my pants, here."

The stressed look on her face slowly morphs into a mischievous smirk, lifting one side of her mouth, and as I watch, she grabs the hem of her tank top and lifts it up and over her head. "Not helping," I groan.

Like a fucking homing beacon, my eyes zoom in on the dark rose tips on the creamy white globes of her breasts. Like a goddamn cherry on top. My mouth literally waters and I bend over to have a taste.

I love the way her body arches off the couch when I suck her nipple deep into my mouth, her other one pleading for attention. Much different than its twin, burns have eaten away at her left breast. The outside of the mound is scarred, right up to the nipple, but on the inside; the skin of her cleavage is smooth and unmarred.

It doesn't matter. I slide my open mouth from one breast to the other, tasting every inch of her skin before laving attention on her left side.

My senses are overwhelmed with her scent, her taste, and the feel of her fingers on the back of my head where she holds me to her. She's giving me all of her, and suddenly having all my clothes still on, while she has stripped herself bare in every way, feels cowardly.

Abruptly, albeit reluctantly, I straighten, lift her feet from my lap and stand up.

"Stay," I order her when she tries to move.

I toe off my shoes, peel off my socks, and open the buttons of my fly. I reach my arms behind me and grab my shirt, yanking it over my head. Stacie watches my every move, and I can almost feel the touch of her eyes on my body. My hands pause at the top of my waistband, but then I see her tongue peek out and leisurely lick along her plump bottom lip, and I can't get out of these damn jeans fast enough.

My cock bounces against my stomach as I struggle to get my feet out of my pants. It doesn't help that Stacie slowly opens her legs, exposing the swollen pink lips of her pussy, already slick with her need.

"*Jesus.*"

Stacie

God, he's phenomenal.

I'd had opportunity to check out his chest before, but not the rest of him. Long legs with solid thighs dusted with sparse dark hair. An impressive package, balls high and tight to his groin, his cock deeply flushed and jutting almost straight up, the bulbous head weeping drops of precum.

Nick stands dead still, watching me take all of him in, a hint of hesitation about him. That glimpse of insecurity is enough to have me sit up, without any thought to my own hang-ups, and put my hands on those solid thighs. His eyes burn hot as he looks into my upturned face. His mouth falls open as I slowly lean in and run the flat of my tongue along the underside of his cock, tracing the thick vein all the way to the crown.

"Oh *fuck*," he exclaims, when I wrap a hand around the base of his length, bringing the head closer to my mouth so I can slide him between my lips.

The taste of him is heady, but more than that, the effect I have on him floods me with a sense of power I thought I'd lost. The muscles of his thighs tremble. He stares down at me reverently as his hand comes down to cup my face, while I work him gently, but firmly with my mouth and fist.

He can't take much, before he braces my head in both his hands and carefully pulls himself free of my mouth.

"I want inside you, Anastasia. I want the heat of your touch on my skin, so I'm reminded this is not a fucking fantasy, but real."

He sits down on the couch and pulls me on his lap, lifting my leg so I'm straddling him.

"*Shit*," he swears, dropping his forehead between my breasts. "I never got around to picking up those condoms at Walgreens." I don't know whether to laugh or cry at his defeated tone.

I end up doing neither; instead I reach over between the pillow and the couch, and fish out a familiar foil packet.

"You didn't, but I did," I admit, smiling into his surprised face.

Instead of handing over the packet, I rip it open with my teeth, and carefully roll the condom down his length myself.

"You own me," he whispers, leaning in to brush my lips with his.

His fingers play through my slick heat before he slides two hands under my butt and lifts me up. I place both of my hands on his shoulders and brace myself as he positions me over his straining cock.

"Take me," he orders, waiting for me to claim him.

I slowly let myself sink down on him, watching the expression of sheer rapture on his face as he fills me so deep, I can't tell where he ends and I begin.

I get so lost in the sensation of riding this powerful man; I don't even realize I'm crying until he lifts a hand and brushes at my tears. He doesn't say anything though, seeming to understand these are tears of an emotional release other than sadness or pain.

"Hold on, I'm taking over," he suddenly growls, as he surges up.

With one arm under my ass and one across my back, he flips me down on the couch and drops in the cradle of my thighs, his body now covering mine. One of his hands slips between our bodies and effortlessly finds my clit as the head of his cock presses deep inside me, hitting the mark with every surge of his hips.

"I'm coming," I warn him when I feel the tension coil tightly before it snaps into wave after wave of my climax.

"*Beautiful,*" he groans in my neck as his hips buck his release.

It takes a while to regain our respective breaths, but when Nick lifts his weight off me, I groan at the loss of him. I fold my arms behind my head and watch as he ties off the end of the condom he removed.

"Hope to God you bought more of these," he remarks when he catches me looking. "I'm not done with you yet. Although, I think we should move this party to your bed."

I giggle like a damn schoolgirl when he pulls me up from the couch and guides me in front of him, down the hall to my bedroom. I can't remember if I've ever traipsed around the house naked. I went from living with roommates to living with a baby; I don't think I've ever had the opportunity. It feels liberating.

Beside the bed, Nick pulls me into a one-armed hold, kissing me deeply before he unceremoniously dumps me on the mattress. He disappears into the bathroom and returns with a wet washcloth, just minutes later.

"What are you doing?" I yelp, when he spreads my legs wide and lays the icy cold cloth between my legs. "That's cold!"

"I know," he grins. "No worries. I'll take great pleasure in warming you up again."

The cold is bordering on painful, but when just moments later, Nick's warm tongue slicks between my legs, from back to front, the flush of heat is instant. I have only a second to consider myself lucky I had a shower earlier, before any rational thought evaporates at his touch. His hands press against the inside of my knees, spreading me even wider before his head disappears again, the flat of his tongue trailing a wet path from my ass to the tight bundle of nerves at the top of my folds. A deep, long shiver runs the length of my body at the slightly illicit sensation.

"Not now," his voice vibrates against my sensitive flesh, as a digit firmly massages the tight ring of what thus far has been uncharted territory. "But one day, I will have explored *all* of you."

His meaning is clear, and rather than being threatening, it feels more like a promise.

One I'm afraid I won't be able to resist: I am clearly putty in his hands.

Dammit!

First it was the tough-looking dude taking off with her kid. Then I got to the trailer and the hag was screaming her head off over some dumbass shit. After I got her ass settled down, I told her I was going out for smokes; little did she know where I was really headed.

Hmmm…

Interesting—looks like Ms. ADA has herself a little action going on tonight.

CHAPTER 17

Stacie

"It was huge!"

Mak spreads her arms as wide as she can in illustration.

"That big, huh?" Nick asks, a smile on his face.

"Yup. It's a Ka...what was it called again, Uncle Ben?" she asks my brother, who is busy scowling at Nick.

He's been glaring at Nick since he and Mak walked in twenty minutes ago, catching us in the middle of breakfast prep. Still in our PJs. Well, I was in PJs; Nick had just pulled on his jeans, which hung precariously low on his hips.

Mak was too distracted, checking out my face, to notice the silent interaction between the two men in my life, which resulted in Nick tagging his shirt. He found it on the floor by the newly delivered coffee table, which also did not go unnoticed by Ben.

I ignored all of them and focused my attention on stretching breakfast for two, to four.

My daughter, who is seldom at a loss for words, provided a wonderful diversion with her excited recounting of her fishing adventures.

"Kokanee salmon." There's no mistaking the soft tone to his voice when my brother answers Mak. He loves her to distraction, and vice versa.

Part of me wonders if perhaps Ben doesn't also feel a little put out by his niece. She's had him as the only man in her life, but now has to share that spot with Nick who, since taking Mak to his ranch, seems to have gained her favor.

I slide a plate with a stack of pancakes on the counter, and turn around to grab the bacon I kept warm in the oven. By the time I turn back, there are two pancakes left on the plate, and the three of them are already stuffing their faces.

"Hey," I protest feebly, setting the bacon down and quickly grabbing for a piece or two before that is decimated by grabbing hands as well. "You'd think you guys are never fed."

"Strenuous activity always makes me hungry," Nick says with a wink, and I have to turn away when I feel myself blush. Most of our night, and all of our morning, had been spent burning huge amounts of energy in the most pleasurable of ways.

Ben clears his throat loudly and I quickly grab the coffee pot.

"More?" I ask Ben, blatantly ignoring the undercurrents in the room. Bless Mak, who continues to stuff her face, undeterred by any tension.

"Half," Ben says after a pregnant pause that causes Nick to look up from his plate. "I've gotta get back to the campground shortly. Large group of hunters coming in."

"What's the latest on Isla and the baby? How long are they staying in Arizona?"

Ben's expression softens instantly at the mention of his family.

"They've got most of Al's house packed up and are moving it bit by bit to a storage unit. One of his buddies there is going to ship it once Al's found a place here in Dolores. Until then, he's staying with us. Isla says once they have his house empty and on the market in another week or two, they'll rent a trailer for the rest of his stuff and start driving." Ben gets up and walks over to where Mak is sitting, pressing a kiss to the top of her head. "I should head out. I've got stuff to do. Thanks for keeping me company, kiddo," he says to Mak, who looks up at him adoringly, with her mouth full of pancake.

"Later, Uncle Ben," she manages, but not without spraying him with crumbs.

"Don't talk with your mouth full," I admonish, following my brother to the front door where he turns to face me.

"You good, Sis?" he asks, touching his fingers carefully to the scar on my face, but I know he's asking about more than just that.

"I'm good." I smile reassuringly, as he tosses one last glare over my shoulder, undoubtedly directed at Nick who's been quietly eating and listening. "Why don't you come by for dinner tomorrow?"

"That depends…are you cooking?" he asks with a smirk.

"Kiss my ass, Ben," I fire back, which only makes him grin wider. With a peck on my cheek, he walks out.

"Mom," Mak calls out as I close the door behind him and turn back to the kitchen. "Can I go fishing?"

"First, clean your room," I instruct her firmly. "I checked this morning and it looks like a bomb exploded in there."

"I was packing an overnight bag," she snaps, as if that should explain the state of her floor.

"Not sure how stuffing some clean underwear and a toothbrush in a backpack needs to result in half your closet on your floor, but you need to pick it up before you do anything else."

"Fine," my moody girl spits out, before stomping off down the hall with attitude that can't be missed.

"Holy hell," Nick mutters, looking after her in shock. "How did she go from sweet to snarling like that?"

Before I can explain the pitfalls of early onset puberty, there's a rap on the door.

-

"In the last six months, three guys you prosecuted were released on parole, and all of them have been checking in with their PO on schedule," Drew says.

He popped in to see if we'd had any disturbances last night, and to let us know that they didn't get any help from the few prints they collected from Mak's window. I quickly hopped in the shower and put some clothes on, while Nick played host and put on a fresh pot of coffee. I didn't want to leave those two alone together for too long.

I just walked in to overhear Drew.

"So what then?" I ask, pulling up a stool and smiling at Nick when he slides a fresh cup of coffee in front of me. "I mean someone clearly wants to mess with my head, at the very least," I offer.

"Well," Drew drawls out. "I've been doing some digging into that girl's family. The one Nick alerted me on?" he clarifies when he sees my questioning expression.

"Becca?" I ask, turning to Nick, who's looking a little sheepish. "You talked to the sheriff about her?" His only response is a self-conscious shrug of his shoulders. It only melts me a little bit more. Somehow the fact that a single guy, who by his own admission has no experience with kids whatsoever, would display such concern for a little girl, he's met only once, is heartwarming.

"The family moved here last year from Grand Junction," Drew continues. "Mom's records show she'd been picked up for soliciting a few times. I spoke with a vice officer who dealt with her, and he tells me that CPS had just opened an investigation when the family suddenly up and left. I've contacted CPS, but they had little to add, just that a neighbor had been concerned about the little girl and had called them in. They were interested in the family's whereabouts though, and plan to forward the file to someone local. Chances are they'll contact the school here, and I've given them your name," Drew says to Nick. "Since you alerted me."

"Feel free to give them my number too," I tell him.

"If you're sure," the sheriff asks. "Because that neighbor who called the CPS on them in Grand Junction? His trailer burned to the ground, not days after. It was arson and the old guy barely escaped with his life. Swears it was the boy, but the family was gone the morning after."

Nick

Stacie cooked, so I'm doing dishes while she shows Drew the door.

What was supposed to be a quiet morning, turned out to be rather hectic. I could've done without the blatant hostility from Ben, and certainly without the antagonizing smirks and grins from Drew, both men I considered friends. I would've rather had breakfast in bed, as we'd planned before everyone came barging in.

"I have a dishwasher, you know?" Stacie teases when she slides her arms around my waist from behind and rests her head against my back.

"Faster this way," I tell her, putting the last of the plates in the rack and wiping my hands on a towel. I turn to take her in my arms. "Can I quickly hop in your shower?"

"Sure." She smiles up at me with her head tilted back. "There are towels in the linen closet in the hall. I should check my emails, I haven't been online since Wednesday, and I'd like to make sure my last research passed muster before I close out that case. I'd like to come into the office on Monday, if that's okay with you?"

"If you feel you're ready, then of course it's okay." I drop a brief hard kiss on her lips before turning down the hallway.

I'm just rinsing off the fruity soap I found in the shower, when the bathroom door flies open.

"Nick? Where's Mak?" Stacie says, pulling open the shower curtain.

"Fishing," I tell her, turning off the water and grabbing for the towel. "When you were in the shower earlier? She said you okayed it when you checked on her room."

When I see the expressions on Stacie's face morph from shock to stark fear, I am instantly nauseated at the strong feeling of dread rushing through me.

"I didn't," she whispers, but I'd already gathered that from her reaction.

I'm tugging my jeans over my wet legs and rush down the hall, pulling my shirt on over my head. With bare feet shoved in my boots, I run out the door, eyes already scanning the river across the street. I hear the crunch of gravel behind me as I come to a stop on the riverside path, and feel Stacie's small hand grab onto the back of my shirt as she catches up.

"Where is she?"

"Mak!" I yell over the rush of the water.

"Makenna!" Stacie tries, stepping up beside me as we scan the riverside as far as we can see.

I spot a lone fisherman, a few hundred feet upriver, and start walking toward him, Stacie still hanging onto my back.

"Excuse me," I start, drawing the man's attention. "Have you seen a little girl with a fishing rod out here in the past thirty minutes or so?"

"You're looking for just one?" the older man asks. "Because there were two girls coming down the path earlier, but only one with a fishing rod. They went up river not that long ago." He points further up the path and Stacie shoots past me, running.

"Thanks," I manage before taking off after her.

I quickly lose sight of her when she disappears around a corner, but run harder when I hear her call out, "Mak!"

By the time I catch up, Stacie is already reading her daughter the riot act. Her little friend, Becca, is standing off to the side, her eyes darting around, as if looking for an escape route.

"You are grounded for life, young lady," Stacie scolds Mak, an admonishing finger waving in her face. "What were you thinking?"

"You said I could go after I cleaned my room. My room is clean," the spunky little mite fires back with some serious attitude.

"I said *first* clean your room, implying we'd talk after. And we didn't. I certainly didn't check your room and tell you that you could, like you told Nick. You lied." At those last words, Mak turns a guilty look to me. I try to keep my face impassive, but it's hard not to melt at the tears gathering in her eyes. "And what are you doing all the way over here? You know you're supposed to stay in sight of the house at all times. I was scared out of my mind." Stacie's voice cracks.

"Becca said her line was stuck. I was just coming to help," Mak says, her bottom lip starting to wobble at the sight of her mother's distress. "I'm sorry."

She points at a discarded rod at the edge of the river and I walk over to pick it up. One firm tug pulls the line free from whatever was holding it captive, and I quickly reel it in. I hand the rod over to Becca, who is still looking around worriedly.

"You should probably head home too," I tell the little girl.

"I'm sorry too," she whispers, before sending one last concerned look at Mak and Stacie, and rushing up the path.

I pick up Mak's discarded rod and tackle and turn away from the water to find mother and daughter with their arms around each other, hugging it out.

"Why don't we take this inside?" I suggest carefully, and lead the way back down the trail, checking occasionally to make sure they're following behind.

"Go to your room, Makenna," Stacie says when we walk in the door.

"But, Mom…"

"No arguments, Mak. I need a moment to cool off before I deal with you."

"This is *so* not fair," the defiant girl says, folding her arms over her chest, exactly as I've seen her mother do in an argument. However, this is not the time to wave a red flag in front of Stacie, who pulls her shoulders almost up to her ears. I insert myself between them before she explodes.

"You heard your mother," I intervene in a low voice. I'm probably overstepping all kinds of lines here, but I'll deal with that later. For now all I'm interested in is disarming this explosive situation.

Mak looks at me through squinted eyes, but I don't even blink. I can see her trying to come up with a retort, but she eventually gives up, turns on her heels, and stomps down the hallway.

The loud slam of her door seems to break something in Stacie, whom I'm just able to catch as she tries to get past me to get to her daughter. She only struggles for a second before she collapses, sobbing against my chest.

"She's gonna be the death of me."

I firmly close my mouth, and just hold her, no matter how much it's on my lips to say: "The apple doesn't fall far from the tree."

Somehow I get the sense that observation may not go over well.

So fucking close!

I caught the little brat this morning as her mom was still snoring off the dope I supplied her with last night. Anything to keep the bitch quiet so I could execute my plan. I was frustrated as all hell to find the kid's bedroom door locked, and I didn't want to kick in the door with her asshole brother next door. So far he's been manageable, but I don't know how far I can push it when it comes to his little brat sister.

So I'd lain in wait until I heard someone scurrying around the kitchen. She was just trying to disappear back into her room with some cereal when I snuck up behind her. It didn't take much to get her to open up about her little friend. Especially when I told her in detail what I'd do to her if she held out on me.

The odds were long, timing it so I could get at the little bitch while fishing, but other than at school, which already fucking failed, it was the best way to try and catch her alone.

I couldn't believe my luck when I saw her coming out of the house with her rod. Using the little brat to lure her friend had been a stroke of genius. It would've worked, if not for that same bald guy I'd seen sticking it to the ADA bitch through the window last night, barreling out of the house and yelling the kid's name. The bitch was close on his heels.

I'm fucking beside myself with frustration, watching them run up to the girls, just moments before I have a chance to grab her.

The hooker's kid keeps looking over at me, almost fucking giving me away, and it takes everything out of me not to move from where I'm hiding and show myself. She's gonna get it later.

They're all gonna fucking get it later.

CHAPTER 18

Stacie

"This one is Maisy, Mom. Come pet her."

Mak is getting a little too close to the massive head of the horse, in my opinion. How can you even tell if a horse is going to bite? I about have a spontaneous bowel movement when Mak almost sticks her hand in its massive mouth.

"She's friendly. See?" Nick says, looking up from where he's checking the bandages on the injured horse's leg. He must've noticed the death grip I have on Mak's other arm, ready to yank her out of the jaws of the large animal.

"If you say so."

Yesterday we mostly stayed indoors, with the exception of a quick trip to the grocery store. Mak had been moody and not very happy with her house arrest, which made for a tense atmosphere in the house, despite Nick's attempts at diffusing when he was there.

After helping with the groceries, he'd left to check on his dad and the ranch, but he was back in the evening.

I would've loved a repeat of the night before, when he managed to make my body sing, but he insisted on staying on the couch, with Mak in the house. Given my daughter's questionable mood, I agreed the timing might not be right for that. Besides, I'm not really sure what it is we're doing here, but if I've learned anything, it's that you grab what you can, while you can. So I plan to have that talk with Mak—soon.

This morning it had been Nick who suggested checking out the farm and having lunch with his dad. Mak of course was all over that, and I gave in, mostly because I hoped his father had some more of Nick's childhood secrets to share. With his promise that we'd be back in time to prep dinner for Ben tonight, I got dressed in the jeans and sneakers Nick suggested.

It's beautiful, this spot. Nestled against the mountains in the back, the large two-level ranch house, with an old-fashioned wraparound porch, had been a surprise the first time I saw it. I don't know why I'd pictured some kind of utilitarian bungalow, but the rustic and well-tended family home, complete with window boxes and flowerbeds was far from it.

The driveway leading up to the house is lined with fruit trees that must look spectacular in the spring. This visit, Nick took the time to explain that the wheat fields closest to the road were leased by a farmer on the other side of Dolores, but the fruit trees and the horse meadows closer to the house were theirs to tend.

"Pops wasn't ready to give up farming altogether," he explained as we were driving up to the house. "But this is for fun, as long as he can manage."

"I love it," I admitted with a smile.

Nick's father was having a coffee on the porch, sitting in an old rocker that looked like it had seen better days, when we drove up. He got to his feet as soon as we got out of Nick's truck. The big smile on his face when my daughter bounded up the steps and greeted him, with a big hug, was enough to firmly cement the old man in my heart.

We ate the lunch we picked up at the Depot outside on the porch, but pretty soon Mak got restless and wanted to go see the animals. I slowly followed behind an animatedly chattering Mak and a much more subdued Nick, observing his easygoing manner with her. Even though I wanted to pull her back to safety when she confidently approached the large animal, Nick simply stood back. Sure, he was close enough to intervene in case, but he let my daughter take the lead.

Mak hasn't had much male influence in her life—in large part by my choice—but it's becoming clear to me that I've done my daughter a great disservice. With every new man who finds a place in our life—Ben, Isla's Uncle Al, and now Nick, and his father as well—Mak seems to bloom a little more.

Taking a page from my daughter's book, I let Nick's confident grin lead me, and hold out my hand flat, like I saw Mak do. The horse's lips, surprisingly soft, skim restlessly over my palm, as if looking for something. She lifts her head a little and I'm about to pull back my hand, a proud smile on my face, when suddenly the horse sneezes, leaving me with a handful of horse snot.

"Ewwww!" I blurt out, to Mak's great hilarity.

"Here," Nick says, taking my sticky hand and leading me to a water trough at the edge of the pen. "You really are a city girl, aren't you?' he mumbles, barely able to contain his grin as he carefully rinses my hand in the murky water.

"I've been camping," I offer defensively, but that just seems to amuse him more.

"Yeah? You know how to pitch a tent? I'll have to take you up near Telluride then," he says, carefully wiping my hand on his shirt. "Some beautiful backcountry spots there." He must've seen the panic on my face because suddenly he busts out laughing. "When was the last time you were in a tent?"

"College," I admit grudgingly, walking away to try and avoid going into detail, but like a tenacious lawyer, Nick won't let go.

"Where'd you go?" he digs, and I look down at my sneakers as I mumble a barely intelligible response. "Sorry, what?" he asks, stopping me with a hand on my shoulder. I turn and look at him defiantly.

"Albuquerque Best Buy parking lot, waiting for the doors to open on Black Friday," I admit, seeing the humor dance in his warm eyes, before I quickly add by way of explanation, "they had a great deal on the Wii Fit."

I can hear him laugh behind me as I march back to the house.

-

"You made this?" Ben asks with his mouth full, disbelief in his voice.

"I did," I answer, trying to hide the pleased grin on my face. It's not often my attempts at feeding my family is appreciated, especially not when my sister-in-law is a wizard in the kitchen and impossible to live up to. So the simple fact that everyone at the table, including Mak, who can be fussy, is wolfing down their dinner, is a boost to my culinary confidence.

When I'd mentioned trying this stuffed chicken recipe and risotto for dinner tonight, Nick gently intervened. He suggested it might make more sense to keep it simple, but do it well, as opposed to going all fancy, but half-assed. It took a bit of restraint on my part, being automatically defensive, but his words resonated.

The taco salad he suggested instead, had been easy to make, was fun to prepare, and looked fabulous once put together. I'd been dubious about the bag of Doritos, but the added crunch makes the salad amazing. The only cooking required was the ground beef with taco spices, the rest was chopping and slicing.

"'S good," he mumbles, as he shovels another forkful in.

I look over at Nick, who winks at me, and I throw him a grateful smile. I've had a bitch of a year, and to top it off had some creep break into my house; despite all that I can feel the ground start to level out under my feet.

I look around my dining table at the people who are important to me, eating food I prepared for them, and I feel a deep satisfaction settle over me.

Nick

"How long are you planning on staying here?"

Ben's question last night when he cornered me alone outside Stacie's house, putting out the garbage, is still playing through my head this morning. Oh, I quickly responded with, "However long it takes," but I recognize the concern in his question. He's felt responsible for his sister his whole life, and clearly it's not easy to hand over, or even share, responsibility for her safety.

Although he'd seemed satisfied with my answer, I still felt the need to add, "I care about her a lot."

"It's obvious, and I'm glad for her," he said, nodding as he looked down at his boots. "I'd be fucking ecstatic if we didn't have some lowlife out there, playing games with her. I don't have a good feeling about this." He looked me straight in the eye and I saw anger burning there.

This morning, after another night on Stacie's couch, the brief conversation still plays in my head. Ben is uneasy, and from someone who's spent his entire career working on instinct, that fucking means something. It makes me very worried.

I pull into my parking spot at the office. Stacie is dropping Mak off at school and plans to be here around nine for her first day, so that gives me time to give our good sheriff a quick call.

"I've got nothing for you," Drew answers, clearly recognizing my number.

"What about—"

"Nick, my man," he interrupts. "I'm digging, but we've got little to go on. I've contacted local law enforcement to check in on the guys that were released recently, but it's not high on their priority lists. All I can tell you is to stay vigilant and let me know if anything, however small, catches your attention."

"Fine. She's starting here today, so it's not hard to keep an eye out."

"Your office?" he wants to know. "She have any cases lined up?"

"Sheila was looking into that. I'm sure she'll be busy soon enough."

I end the call shortly after, when Sheila walks into my office, a pile of file folders in her arms, and I'm quickly drowning in work. All stuff that piled up after taking time off last week.

It's after noon by the time I look at the clock and realize I never saw Stacie come in. Dropping the folder I was reading, I get up, and go in search of Sheila, who is nowhere to be found. Doug's office is empty, but Mondays he's usually in court. The hallway on the other side of the reception desk is quiet, and the door to Stacie's new office is closed.

There's no answer when I knock, so I push open the door, only to find the office empty. What worries me is that it looks like no one's been in here. No files, no paperwork, no empty coffee cups. Nothing.

Slightly panicked, I stop at the door to the ladies' room, pushing it open.

"Anyone in here? Stacie?" My voice bounces off the tile walls, but there's no answer. Now I'm worried.

Back at the reception desk, I grab the phone and start dialing Drew's number, when I hear the front door open behind me.

"I got you pastrami on rye," Sheila says, carrying a take out bag from the Spruce Tree coffee place.

"Have you seen Stacie?" I quickly replace the receiver on the phone and automatically grab for the sandwich Sheila holds out.

"She's in court," Sheila explains, and my confusion clearly shows, because she rolls her eyes before explaining, "I didn't think you wanted to be disturbed so I sent you a text. Sheriff Carmel called looking for her earlier. Wanted her to meet him on a case."

I vaguely remember hearing a ding, but I generally ignore those when I'm working. Drew sure as hell didn't waste any time. To say I'm cool with the idea of him ingratiating himself with her would be a lie, but I still manage to head back to my office, eat my lunch, and concentrate on my case. I may not be able to trust our sheriff any further than I can toss him, but I trust Stacie.

I look up when there's a knock at my door.

"Hey, you." I smile when Stacie pushes open my door.

"Hi," she says, throwing a quick glance over her shoulder before closing the door behind her, leaning back against it. "I just got my first client off." Her smile is big as she saunters over to my desk, leaning forward, bracing her hands on the edge. After a day of digging through libido deadening, dry legal jargon, my cock jumps to attention at her seductive pose.

"You didn't waste any time," I compliment her, folding my hands behind my head as I lean back in my chair.

"I know," she jokes, pursing her lips and blowing on her nails. "I don't think Drew was all that pleased. He's the one who suggested my name to this guy they had on distribution charges, but I have a sneaky suspicion he thought he was throwing me a harmless bone. He certainly wasn't expecting me to get his case thrown out on a technicality."

"Come here."

I see the little hitch in her breathing at the sound of my commanding tone, and that tiny visible reaction has synapses firing off all over my body. Immediately the atmosphere in the room becomes so thick with sexual tension, I can taste it.

The restraint of the past few nights, knowing she was sleeping just steps away, but unable to get near her, was a challenge. Which is probably why my heart is about to pound out of my chest at the sight of Stacie slowly rounding my desk at my order.

I swivel my chair in her direction and the moment she's within reach, I grab her by the hips and pull her between my spread legs. I wrap my arms tightly around her hips, bury my face in her soft belly, and inhale her scent. I may enjoy exerting my will, but the truth is; this woman owns me.

The words burn on my lips, eager to escape, but before I can give them voice, I hear the door open.

"Oh, I'm sorry…" I hear Sheila's voice as Stacie jerks out of my hold. "I knocked. There was a phone call for Ms. Gustafson."

"Stacie, please," Stacie says softly, her face flushed in embarrassment.

"Right," the other woman answers, looking no less uncomfortable.

I can't do much. I can't even stand up, since that would only add to the embarrassment. My dick hasn't quite caught up to the interruption, and is still eagerly tenting my slacks.

"Sheila," I start, breaking through the awkward standoff and drawing her attention. "The phone call?"

"Right," she says again, turning to Stacie. "Dolores Elementary called. You left this number with the secretary? She wasn't able to reach you on your cell." Stacie immediately digs through her pockets and pulls out her cell.

"Damn, turned it off for court and forgot to turn it back on. What did she call for? Makenna okay?"

"She didn't say, she just mentioned hoping to speak with you about a missing student?" She's barely finished her sentence and Stacie is already dialing what I presume is the school.

I'm itching to take the phone from her hands, eager to take over, but it's not my place. Not yet anyway.

"Hi, it's Stacie Gustafson? Makenna's mom? Is she okay?—Becca? No, I haven't seen her since Saturday morning, why?"

I nod at Sheila, gently dismissing her as I get up from behind the desk and walk over to where Stacie's staring out the window. Her shoulders are drawn up and her body language is tense, distressed, so I put my hands on her upper arms, trying to soothe with my touch.

"All right, I will," she says to the person on the other side. "Keep her in the office, please? I'm on my way. I'll be there as soon as I can."

"Talk to me," I urge her when she turns around, her pale complexion stark against the healing skin of her scar.

"Becca didn't show for classes this morning, and there was no answer when they tried calling her mom's phone. The girls' teacher thought perhaps Mak might know something, since the two are close, but she says she doesn't. They called me because Mak apparently got very upset when she overheard them talk about calling the sheriff. I should go."

She grabs her purse, tucks her phone inside, and heads for the door.

"Wait," I call out, grabbing my own phone and a stack of files, before following her into the hallway. "Give me your keys, I'll drive."

"But what about your truck?"

"It'll be here tomorrow," I dismiss, shrugging.

For a moment, I think she's going to object, but then she nods once, sharply, and proceeds to hand me the keys.

"Taking the files home," I call out to Sheila, who's standing by the filing cabinet, her back turned.

"Everything okay?" she wants to know, swirling around.

"Makenna is fine," I answer, since Stacie is already out the door.

Mak may be all right, but my gut churns when I start thinking about what may be wrong with Becca.

CHAPTER 19

Nick

"Is she asleep?"

"Not yet," Stacie says as she plops down on the couch beside me, her face shiny from the cream she rubs into her skin a few times a day. "She's trying to read. She still says she thinks something happened to Becca. That she wouldn't have left without saying goodbye."

Drew had popped by not long after we got Mak home from school. The girls' teacher had contacted the sheriff's office, and although a truant child is not normally something he'd respond to, he'd already been keeping an eye on the girl. He admitted to me that he'd driven by the trailer, but no one was home. A neighbor mentioned seeing the boy get behind the wheel of the family car, a rusty Dodge Shadow, but he couldn't tell if anyone else had been in the vehicle, and he couldn't remember what time of the morning it had been. Drew wanted to see if perhaps Becca had mentioned anything to Mak about visiting family.

He'd been careful with his questioning, and suggested to Mak that perhaps there'd been a family emergency and there hadn't been time to say goodbye.

Clearly she wasn't buying that explanation.

"Some kind of family emergency seems the most likely explanation, though," I suggest, throwing my arm over her shoulder and pulling her close. "Why else would the whole family be gone?"

"You're probably right," she says, scooting out from under my arm. "I need a drink. You want a glass of wine?"

I nod and watch as she expertly uncorks a bottle from the wine rack and pours a couple of stiff drinks.

"To your first day and your first win," I toast, holding up the glass she hands me. "And to what I hope is a long and fruitful collaboration."

She clinks her glass to mine, a teasing glint in her eyes.

"Are we still talking about the firm?" she asks, grabbing the remote and flicking on the TV.

I grin. "The two aren't mutually exclusive, counselor."

"That's what I thought," she says smugly, curling up beside me.

-

Long after Stacie's gone to bed—after a heavy make out session on the couch with the evening news drowning out the soft moans and groans—I'm still staring up at the ceiling, wide-awake.

So many things are vying for attention in my mind and I just can't seem to shut it down. The past month or so has completely thrown my life into a tailspin.

I may be a slick and smooth operator when it comes to my work, but not so much in my personal life. Much more quiet and unassuming, and most definitely not a priority. That has changed. I'm almost concerned at how little I care about the files I brought home that are still lying unopened on the dining room table. I've always been the consummate professional, but my focus has definitely shifted to the two females down the hall from me.

I love Anastasia. I've known that since the first time she actually kissed me. Whatever I felt before was amplified by the fact that she was unattainable, a fantasy that was far beyond my reach, but the reality of her is so much more.

It's a weird experience, being in love. It's both terrifying and awesome. All-encompassing in a way that makes you *forget* yourself, and liberating in a way that allows you to *be* yourself. It's like your entire being is exposed and unguarded to this one person, which is scary as fuck, except you're getting the same in response, and that is a beautiful feeling.

A soft click and a rustle alerts me, and I squint to look down the dark hallway.

My first reaction is that Stacie has come looking for me, which I would welcome, but the much shorter shadow coming this way tells me it's her daughter. I wait until she's almost at the front door, where she's more visible by the streetlights outside, before I speak.

"Mak?" I whisper carefully, but it still makes her jump.

"Nick? I thought you'd be sleeping," she says, whipping around, making it clear she'd not only been thinking it, but she'd counted on it.

"What are you doing?"

The pause is heavy as I see a myriad of emotions play out on her face before she settles on resigned.

"Becca is outside and I can't get my window open."

"What?" I try not to raise my voice as I swing my legs over the side of the couch and grab for my jeans. "Wait," I tell her when she starts turning the locks on the door. "You don't know what's out there. I'll look."

"You're gonna scare her." Mak turns her back to the door, blocking it.

"Honey," I plead as I tug a shirt over my head. "I promise she's got nothing to worry about from me."

"Duh, *I* know that," she says, rolling her eyes with attitude. "But Becca doesn't know you."

It's probably not the right moment to smile, but Mak's words make me do just that.

"Then you'll just have to vouch for me," I insist, gently taking Mak by the upper arms and moving her to the side, before I turn the locks and carefully open the door.

The night air is crisp, bordering on cold and it's quiet. The only thing I hear is the rush of the river.

Mak tries to squeeze past me, but I grab her hand at the last minute and hold on tight.

"Stick by me, honey. Don't want you going off on your own."

Her only response is a tightening of her little hand around my fingers, and a slight tug to follow her, down the steps and around the side of the house. It's much darker here than it is out front and it's difficult to even make out the trees on the edge of the property.

"Becca?" Mak whisper calls for her friend, who is nowhere to be seen. At least not until a shadow that looked to be part of the tree line suddenly starts moving toward us. I quickly tug Mak behind me, trying to identify who it is first.

"H-hi…," a very bedraggled, pale and wide-eyed Becca whispers back.

Stacie

Not sure what wakes me up, but when I sit up in bed, I can feel a cold draft against my skin.

I grab the old, flannel men's shirt I use as a housecoat, and pull open the bedroom door. I notice right away Mak's door is still closed, but the cold seems to be coming from down the hall. I'm surprised to find the front door open and the couch empty. Shoving my feet in a pair of flip-flops I left by the door, I slip outside, tugging my shirt closed against the cold.

"Nick?" I call out, making my way down the steps.

His truck is not parked out front, and for a moment I think he's left, but then I remember: he drove us back to Dolores in my SUV. His truck should still be at the office. He also would never leave the door wide open, unless he was somewhere near.

Unable to see where I'm putting my feet, I carefully make my way around to the side of the house. With the light from the streetlamp behind me, it's virtually impossible to see anything when I stare into the inky darkness in front of me.

I'm about to turn around and head back in, when a body slams into me and a pair of arms band around my body.

Nick

"It's okay," I tell Becca, who looks like she's about to run back into the trees.

To make myself less threatening, I crouch down on one knee, bringing me to almost eye level with the girl. Mak steps up beside me and puts her hand on my shoulder. The touch is likely for her own security, but it has a similar effect on Becca, telling her I can be trusted.

The girl is visibly shivering, and I have to restrain myself not to wrap my arms around her small body and warm her. Her face is dirty, and streaked with tears, her bright red hair is a wild tangle and her knobby knees look scraped.

"It's okay," I repeat, softening my tone even more.

"H-he…h-he…" Her eyes dart around us as she tries to speak, her teeth chattering from cold or perhaps fear. "He k-k-killed h-her…"

Before I even have a chance to open my arms for her, Becca flings her little body against me, nearly knocking me to my ass. I manage to stay upright and wrap an arm around the quietly sobbing girl, while reaching for Mak beside me with the other.

So many questions I want to ask. Who is *he*? Is she talking about her mother? Where has she been? But instead, I concentrate on calming her as best as I can and getting both girls safely inside the house.

But before I can move, Mak breaks free from my hold and takes off. I jump to my feet, lift Becca up in my arms and run after her.

Stacie

"How are you holding up?"

I turn around from the kitchen sink to find Nick right behind me. Beyond him, I can just see Drew sitting on the coffee table, facing Becca, who is cowered in the corner of the couch, my daughter right beside her like a little sentry.

"How are they holding up?" I return with a nod in the girls' direction.

I almost had a heart attack when Mak slammed into me outside. I had no idea she was even out there. I barely opened my mouth to question her when I could make out Nick approaching holding Becca in his arms. I can't tell you how relieved I felt at seeing her. I'd been telling myself all night that she was off somewhere with her family, like Drew suggested, but I never really believed it.

The next half hour had been heart-wrenching as we waited for Drew to get here from Macos, listening to Becca's incoherent sobbing, and Mak's sympathetic tears. The moment he walked in, however, both girls seemed to calm down. I'd been keeping a stiff upper lip, trying hard not to show how shaken I was for fear it would just scare the kids more. But when Drew sat down with the girls, and Nick kept vigilance beside Mak on the couch, I came into the kitchen. Purportedly to make a pot of coffee, but in reality I needed space to have a mini breakdown.

"They're doing fine. Who knew our sheriff had a way with kids."

He cups my face in his large hands and brushes at my wet cheeks with his thumbs. I grab onto his wrists for security.

"Has she said anything?"

"He's got the patience of a saint. For now he's simply building rapport, asking about her likes and dislikes, school, anything but what he's gotta be itching to know."

"He's waiting for CPS to get here, I'm sure," I offer. It's the first thing Drew mentioned doing on his way here. I know Nick had talked to him about Becca, and he'd been waiting for an excuse to call someone in.

"I just called Ben," Nick says softly.

"I never even thought of that," I admit, feeling guilty.

"I wouldn't have either, if Drew hadn't asked who made the girls feel safe. Mak didn't even hesitate; she named Ben instantly. I figured she needs to feel as safe as possible right now, so I called. I'm sorry if I overstepped."

I can't hold back the tears. He didn't overstep—he stepped in. For my daughter—for me. If anyone had asked me in that moment who made me feel safe, I wouldn't have hesitated; I would've answered with *Nick*.

"Not at all." I smile at him through my tears. "It's perfect."

He bends down and brushes a kiss over my lips, briefly leaning his forehead against mine, before straightening up.

"How about that coffee?" he asks. "I don't think we'll be doing much sleeping anyway."

I start pulling down mugs from the cupboard when something occurs to me.

"What was Becca's answer?"

"To what?" Nick's expression is puzzled.

"Who makes Becca feel safe?" I turn my head to see sadness in Nick's eyes.

"No one. She said no one."

I swallow hard. The poor little thing. *I wish I could…*

"We're going to change that, if it's the last thing we do," I find myself stating firmly, throwing a challenging look at Nick, but he doesn't look like he's going to argue. A slight tilt at the corner of his mouth and a sharp nod of acknowledgement tells me he's on board. *Good*. Because with or without his help, that little girl will learn what it feels like to be cared for.

-

"We've got a problem," Drew says as he walks into the kitchen.

Ben finally left with Mak when the social worker from CPS showed at about three this morning. It hadn't been easy to convince Mak to leave her friend, but when exhaustion set in, and she could barely keep her eyes open anymore, Ben simply lifted her off the couch and took her.

Not that he'd been thrilled about leaving, he'd wanted me to come as well, but one look at Becca was enough to make him realize I was needed here. That was not an understatement either.

Drew had taken off earlier with one of his deputies to have a closer look at the trailer, and Becca had clung to me since he left. Ben freaked her out at first, with his menacing looks, but she watched him interact with Mak and that calmed her down. Then when the social worker walked in and started asking her questions, she completely dismissed the woman and would only make eye contact with Nick or me. He had thrown up as mediator and with Becca safely tucked under his arm, coaxed her into answering the woman's questions.

I'm back in the kitchen, taking a sanity break in this clusterfuck of a night, when the sheriff walks in.

"What kind of problem?" I ask, in the same quiet tone he used.

"I'm going to have to question the little girl," he says solemnly. "We found her mother dead on the floor of the bathroom. Brutally beaten." I clap my hands over my mouth to hold back any noise. I'm not an idiot, I knew this was a possibility, but part of me hoped... "That's not all," Drew whispers, and I catch Nick's questioning glance over the sheriff's shoulder. I give him a sharp shake, to which he closes his eyes. "It looks like the girl was there. Was a lot of blood on the floor, and some of it was trampled through the house—by little feet. I fucking hate this, but I have to get as much information as I can from her, Stacie."

He looks pained, and I'm sure he hates it as much as he claims, but I also know how important it is in any investigation, to move as fast as possible.

"Give me ten minutes to try and get some food into her, while you go distract that battle-ax from CPS. Put in a good word for me, because I want Becca to stay here with us. Then I'll help you tell her."

I turn back to my pancakes, my knees shaking, as I dismiss him.

I've been in this situation before, present when a child is informed of a parent's passing, but goddammit if it doesn't rip me apart every fucking time. I was only a little older when I was told I would never see my parents again, and every time I see another child's devastation, my own becomes as sharp as the moment I heard those words coming at me.

So I need a goddamn minute.

She saw.

The little bitch saw and took off.

I should've taken care of her, but I was too freaked out and bailed.

It's all that damn cunt's fault.

I caught her with her hands in my fucking pockets. Cracked my eyes and there she was, sitting on the ground beside the bed, fishing my wallet from my jeans. Said she just needed a few bucks to give her brat some school money, but I could see the shaking of her hands and the wild look of need in her eyes. She needed a fix.

I didn't think, I reacted, grabbing the lamp from the nightstand and hitting her over the head with it. Crazy bitch didn't even go down, despite the gash that opened up on the side of her head. She held on tight to the wallet and started crab walking toward the bathroom door.

She could've stopped it right there. Could've dropped my fucking wallet and walked away, but her need for a fix was bigger. She left me no fucking choice.

Skank damn near broke my foot when I stuck it in the door she was trying to slam in my face. That only pissed me off more.

She never let go of my wallet. Not even when I'd broken the skin on my knuckles against her teeth, or cracked her skull against the bathtub. I knew she was fucking dead before I let her body slip from my hold, but her hand still held my wallet in a death grip. Stupid crazy bitch.

I had to bend her fingers back to get at it. All covered in blood, I stuck it under the tap, looking at my face in the mirror over the sink. Freaked me the fuck out, when it took me a minute to recognize the guy in my reflection.

Sonofabitch.

It wasn't until I was pulling on my shoes that I remembered the damn wallet on the side of the sink. I tried not to look at the mess on the floor as I stepped over the threshold—and that's when I saw her.

The door into the narrow hallway was open a crack and I could see the flash of red hair whipping by. By the time I got through the door, I could hear the storm door slam.

Instead of going after her, I grabbed my stuff, wiped my fingerprints off as much as I could remember, jumped in my truck and took off.

Back to Albuquerque to make my weekly meeting with my parole officer.

I'll get her later.

CHAPTER 20

Nick

This is fucking brutal.

I'm not sure if it's a protective instinct or the serious lack of sleep that is making me want to whale on our good sheriff, but the only thing holding me back is that Becca doesn't need more violence in her life.

The girl is wedged between Stacie and myself, a choice she voiced when she was asked where she'd be most comfortable. At this point, the social worker is merely here as observer, because it's clear that the girl is barely hanging on.

"I'm sorry, darlin'," Drew drawls, leaning forward and tapping his index finger on the top of Becca's dirty sneaker. A seemingly innocuous touch, but still establishing a connection and conveying the message without being invasive.

He just told her they found her mother dead, and although she already knew, or at least suspected, I imagine hearing it confirmed makes it so much more real.

"Do you remember what happened?"

The little girl stiffens beside me, and I notice Stacie bending down to talk softly in her ear. Becca gives Drew a little nod.

"Were you at home?" Another little nod. "In your bedroom?" Drew keeps guessing, and she gives him another nod. "Were you sleeping?" This time he gets a shake and an answer.

"Getting dressed. For school."

"Of course," Drew answers easily, while scribbling on a notepad. "Do you have an alarm or did someone wake you?"

"Jay's alarm. It's loud."

"Who's Jay?"

"My brother. He has to get up first, 'cause he goes to school in Cortez, so he gets the alarm clock."

That's more than she's said all night. Drew is distracting her with details, and it seems to be working, but eventually the hard questions will come.

"That makes sense," Drew answers her, nodding in understanding. "So you were up, I guess your brother was up, and was anyone else up? Who else was in your house?"

"Momma…and h-him."

Fear pours off her in thick waves, cloying the air. Stacie feels it too, because she pulls the girl on her lap and I wrap my arms around them both.

"Nothing's going to happen to you here," I promise, looking her in the eye.

"So your Momma woke up as well?" Becca turns her watery gaze back to Drew, who skillfully avoids talking about *him,* and nods.

"I think when Jay left. He slammed the screen door. Momma came into my room."

"To see if you were up?"

"No," she replies, shaking her head. "She was looking for my piggy bank."

"Why?"

"Money." The matter-of-fact way she says that, accompanied by a shoulder shrug, gets me steamed. "That's why I always carry it with me in my backpack."

I can't even begin to express how furious that makes me, but I see the same anger reflected in Stacie's eyes, over the top of Becca's head.

"She was mad," the little girl continues. "Went back in her bedroom and that's when I heard him."

"Is he your momma's boyfriend?" Drew probes, and she shrugs her shoulders again.

"One of 'em, but the others don't usually sleep over."

Fucking unbelievable. I'm pressing my lips together so the indignant anger I feel on her behalf doesn't come flying out, but it's damn hard.

Now that Drew has her talking, he carefully guides her step-by-step through the events of yesterday morning. Mom and the boyfriend got into an argument, which clearly escalated. Becca hid in the closet, until she couldn't hear any noises and thought maybe he'd left. The poor kid found her mom in the bathroom, blood everywhere. That's when she heard the guy in the next room, and she bailed it out the door.

She'd been hiding in the brush along the river, until the cold drove her here.

"Becca? The man in your house, can you tell me anything else about him?"

The girl mumbles something unintelligible at Drew's question.

"I can't hear you," Stacie tells her gently.

"He has a white, rusty old pickup truck and his name is Kevin, that's all I know."

-

"You try and get some sleep, too."

I didn't learn the social worker's name until just twenty minutes ago. Rita Mayers, and she's actually quite a nice lady, despite my initial aversion to her. That probably had more to do with Becca's reaction to the woman than anything else.

She had Stacie sign some forms, so that Becca could stay with her for the short-term. The girls just went to lay down for a bit. Maybe catch some sleep. I'm just showing Rita out before calling the office.

"I might."

"Give me a call later today," she said, handing me her card. "Especially these first few days, it'll be tough, so rather than having me disrupt whatever routine you guys are building with her, I prefer staying in touch by phone for now. Give her a chance to adjust."

I tuck her card in my pocket and close the door, locking it.

Drew left earlier after he'd gotten all the information he was going to get out of the tired little girl. He has a description of the vehicle and a first name. Not a whole lot to go by, but it would have to do. He was hoping to find out more from her older brother, but when he asked her where she thought her brother could be, she shrugged and said he often disappeared for days at a time, sometimes staying with friends in Cortez.

Jay—or Jason, as Drew quietly told me when he called me out on the porch—is a seventeen-year-old schoolyard drug dealer. Small time, Drew said, but known to the cops. He was going to see if he could get some help from the Cortez PD to pick the boy up.

I can barely keep my eyes open until eight o'clock, when I know Sheila will be at the office.

"Morning," I say, when she answers the phone on the third ring.

"You have an eleven o'clock with George Bond at First National, and then lunch with—"

"*Sheila*," I cut her off before she recites my whole goddamn schedule for the week. "Something's come up. I'm going to need you to cancel those appointments."

"You absolutely cannot," she says with a vehemence that surprises me. "This would constitute the third time you cancel with George, and after trying to soothe his ruffled feathers the last time you ditched him, I'm betting this time you will lose any goodwill you've managed to build over the years. I don't know what has gotten into you, but for someone who has always been an example of professionalism, you sure as hell haven't acted very professional lately."

"Sheila…" I plead in a more conciliatory tone.

"Don't *Sheila* me. I haven't spent eight years of my life helping to build your vision for this firm, only to have you lose your focus because of that woman."

"That *woman*," I snap, "is not only someone I plan to have in my life for as long as I can keep her, she also happens to be one of your bosses, as of yesterday." Frustration has made me loud, so I rein it in before I wake up the girls.

"So noted," Sheila comments tersely, and I feel bad for tearing a strip off her when she's just trying to look out for me.

"Look—here's what I'll do. I'll go straight to First National to see Bond at eleven, but cancel my lunch. I'm coming straight back to the office after that. Not for long though, just to pick up anything I need to handle for the next few days. And…" I add when she starts voicing a protest. "I'll fill you in on what's going on when I get there."

A quick glance at the clock, when I hang up, has me groan out loud. Eight twenty. All I have for work clothes is the suit I was wearing yesterday. I briefly contemplate driving out to the farm to get a clean dress shirt, but quickly dismiss that option. Not only do I not want to leave Stacie and Becca here alone, but if I allow myself half an hour to get dressed, get my dad over here to keep an eye out, and make it into Cortez for my appointment, it gives me less than two hours of sleep as it is.

I have every intention of sleeping on the couch, but when I go take a peek around the bedroom door to find them both sleeping, I change my mind.

Without bothering to get undressed, I curve myself around Stacie's back, who in turn is curved around Becca's. Like spoons in a drawer, each protecting the next.

―――――――――∞―――――――――

Stacie

Phoning his father had been a good call.

Just like he'd done with Mak, with his straightforward and no-nonsense manner, it took Henry no time at all to get Becca to relax in his presence.

He'd already been there when Nick woke me up with a soft kiss on my cheek. I quickly hushed him when he started to apologize for needing to keep an appointment. I'm not only a big girl; I'm a lawyer as well, so I get it. I carefully slid out of bed, letting Becca sleep, and followed Nick out of the room.

Nick left it to me to explain the situation to his father, who was such a wonderful listener, I talked much more than I'd intended. I let down my guard, and even cried, as I explained how this situation brought back some difficult memories for me.

"That's understandable," he'd said, before bringing a healthy dose of reality to the table, which dried my tears faster than they appeared. "Good thing you're no longer a lost and lonely child, but a capable adult now. One who has her family by her side, with a good man at her back, and has an opportunity to help that girl get to a point where she might hope for the same one day. It's a blessing."

Talk about getting things put into perspective for you. A side of me wants to be defensive, but that's just a knee-jerk reaction. I can't deny that I allow myself to get lost in those painful memories at times. Using the pain of their loss like some kind of tribute. But in a very plain and direct way, I've just been told that this is not about me, but about Becca. That my role is not to grieve with her, but to allow her to.

"You're a wise man, Henry," I told him, patting his arm with my hand.

He'd been out on the porch with Becca for the past half hour.

She woke up, a little disoriented, and had been suspicious of Nick's father at first. Within minutes he had her smiling at his description of Maisy blowing snot all over me. He was smart in his approach. Following what he must've learned from Mak's interests, he banked on it that Becca's ran along the same lines.

From horses to dogs, and finally to fishing, but no matter how hard he tried, he couldn't convince her to leave the safety of the house to try a line in the river. Finally he got her to settle for a game of Go Fish on the porch, giving me a chance to give my brother a quick call, outside of Becca's earshot.

"Talk to me," he says. His preferred way to answer the phone, since he doesn't like talking on it.

"She's good. Nick's father is here doing a fantastic job of distracting her. How's Mak?"

"Where's Nick?" he asks instead.

"He'll be back. He's just picking up some work from the office."

"He left you alone?"

I knew it was coming, but I wasn't about to let Ben attack Nick.

"Yes, he did, and with my blessing. For your information," I spit out, building up steam. "That man sat or stood beside me all damn night. Looking after us. He's the one who handled the sheriff and the CPS, and he's the one who finally tucked us in bed this morning, barely getting any rest himself. He's also the one who made sure we weren't alone while he's off to arrange working from home the next couple of days."

"He shouldn't have left you," my stubborn brother persists. "At the very least he should've called me."

"He knows you have Mak, for Christ's sake! He left it up to me, and I'm calling you now."

"Not good enough," he snaps, and I lose it on him.

"Didn't you leave your wife and son behind in Arizona to take care of business here?"

I know I'm hitting a sore spot, but dammit…

"That's not the fucking same," he barks, clearly upset. "I trust her to tell me if she needs me. I'd drop every fucking damn thing in a heartbeat. She knows that."

"And there it is," I snap back, angry tears blurring my vision. "The difference between you and him? Is that where you still don't trust me to know what's best for me, he does. He listens. You're a hypocrite, because for years I didn't even know where you were while I handled my life on my own, but now that someone else has stepped up to the plate, you think you can criticize him? Hell no, Ben. Just, hell no." I take a deep breath, trying to bring my heart rate back down and checking to make sure Becca hasn't heard my rant. Even though Henry's concerned eyes meet mine through the window, Becca's are firmly on the card game. I turn my attention to a surprisingly quiet Ben. "Now please tell me how my daughter is doing."

After a very pregnant pause, during which I wonder if he's hung up on me, he finally answers.

"I kept her home from school. Let me get her."

Two seconds later, my Makenna's voice comes over the phone, peppering me with questions and telling me excitedly about the little camera her uncle bought her this morning. I smile at the knowledge my little girl is safe with Ben, even though I'm sad we argued. I talk with her for a bit, confirming that yes, Becca is sad, and letting her know that I'm sure her friend would love to see pictures of Atsa, who she's apparently been following around with her camera.

"Uncle Ben wants to talk to you," Mak announces, and true to form, I don't even get a chance to say goodbye before my brother's voice comes over the line.

"Sis?"

"Still here," I confirm in a soft voice, matching his.

"You good if we pop in later? I'll bring dinner for all of us." It may not sound like it to outside ears, but I love Ben enough to know this is his way of apologizing. Perhaps not so much in words, but definitely in tone and in gesture. Something he confirms seconds later.

"Bring the dog," I say smiling, giving him my version of absolution. "But make dinner for—"

"Six," he cuts me off. "I know. I can count."

"Smartass." My grin is wide, and only gets wider when I hear his mutter before the line goes dead.

"All day, every day."

CHAPTER 21

Nick

"She thinks I'm too protective."

I look over at Ben, who'd insisted on stepping outside on the porch with a beer. I know he's talking about Stacie.

She is inside, putzing around the kitchen, while the girls watch some kind of kids' movie on the small TV in the living room. I can see Becca, whose eyes flit over to the window every so often, to make sure I'm still there. I smile at her before turning my attention back to Ben.

"I get it," I tell him. "And given what all happened to her, I can't blame you."

"Tore a strip off me earlier," he says staring into the darkness, almost as if I hadn't spoken. "Pissed she was. More pissed than I've ever seen from her; because of you."

"Me?"

I watch as his head slowly turns around and his eyes focus on me.

"You love her."

It's more a statement than a question, but I answer anyway.

"I do."

"Yeah," he says, dropping his gaze to his shoes and rubbing a hand through his silver hair. "Figured as much."

He pauses to take a long tug from his beer before continuing. "Pretty sure the feeling is mutual."

Though not as good as hearing it from the horse's mouth, so to speak, I do a virtual fist pump at his words, and I have to work to keep my face impassive.

"It's hard to stand back when I'm so used to stepping up. Your job now. I get it. Fuck, I was in your shoes not that long ago when Al got in my face about Isla."

I've been quiet, letting him talk because I know it's leading up to something. A moment later that thought is confirmed when he turns to face me.

"I know you've got her back," he starts. "And I'm grateful, but don't leave me out of the loop. It fucking messes with my head."

I almost laugh at the frustrated scowl on his face.

"Never intended to," I assure him. "Since when is this a fucking competition?"

"What competition?" Stacie walks out on the deck, coming straight to my side with a questioning smile on her face.

For a moment Ben and I stare at each other over her head, before I break away and look down at her.

"None. We're just coming to the conclusion that we're all in this." I curl my arm around her waist and tug her close. "All of us," I emphasize, giving her a squeeze.

"Right," Ben mutters. "So I should probably tell you that I called Neil this afternoon."

I remember Neil is one of the guys with GFI Investigations, a company Ben works with on occasion, and the same guys who helped out earlier this year, when Stacie was hurt.

"The techie?" The answer is a confirming nod.

"I spoke to Drew before I got here and he doesn't have much to go on. Just that first name and a truck description but nothing concrete. Nothing to tie the guy in with anyone or anything else. I asked him to run everything through this program he has. Any information on Becca's family, her brother and mother's run-ins with the police, prior addresses, any information from neighbors—everything we know." He looks at his sister, who is listening intently. "Even told him to put in your information, including all of your old cases. I want to see if this incident ties in with what's happening with you these last weeks. See if we can find a connection. Any connection," he says, glancing at me. "Because my gut says this is all connected."

"Thanks for telling us," Stacie says, almost sarcastically.

"Look," Ben snaps, and I brace for another confrontation. "You made your point earlier, which is why I'm here now. But I won't hold off on doing what can be done to keep you safe, just so I can run it by you first. That's the difference between us; your profession requires you to examine things carefully before you act, but in my line of work; I have to make decisions on the spot—or lives could be lost."

I stay quiet, sensing that this is more between those two than it involves me. I note how Stacie presses her lips together and casts a glance through the window to the girls inside.

"Point taken," she finally says, giving her brother a small nod before she untangles herself from my hold and walks up to him, pulling him into a hug. "There's too much at stake."

Giving them a moment, I head inside to use the washroom, passing the girls on the couch, but just Becca looks up at me. I give her a little wink before disappearing down the hallway.

My business done, I wash my hands and glance in the mirror. Not something I do often. In an almost abstract way I notice how the vertical scowl lines, that normally deeply bisect my eyebrows, are much less notable. Even my mouth seems more relaxed than my usual tightly pressed lips. It feels a little like finally being at ease in my skin, after years of forcing the fit.

Funny how amid this fucked up situation, I seem to be finding my sweet spot.

The smile on my face as I pull open the bathroom door drops immediately when I find Becca waiting on the other side, worry on her face.

"What's wrong?" I go down on one knee so I can look her straight in the eye.

"It's just…" She hesitates, looking over her shoulder to the living room.

"You can tell me."

"You shouldn't be out there," she whispers, confusing me.

"Out where? On the porch?" She nods almost eagerly. "Why?" I want to know.

"He's watching. I know he is."

"How do you know that, Becca?"

"Because he was there that day…"

Stacie

"He *what?*"

Ben's loud reaction has me jumping out of my skin. One glance at the girls shows me he certainly startled them. Becca looks like she'll bolt any second.

"Would you keep it down?" I hiss at him, poking a finger in his chest. "You're freaking the kids out." He grabs my offending hand and leans close.

"He's been watching you, Stacie," he hisses back. "He used that little girl to lure our Mak to him, for fuck's sake!" He steps in closer and adds in a whisper, "And after that, he killed her mother."

Nick just finished telling us how the same man, this Kevin, had apparently enlisted Becca's help to snatch my daughter. He'd threatened to hurt her, hurt her mom, if she didn't comply. Poor kid.

The implications are pretty clear; as Ben suggested earlier, what happened to us, and what happened to Becca's mother is all connected.

"Drew needs to know," Nick suggests from behind me, and I turn to lean my head against his chest. As if by rote, his arms slide protectively around me. "You wanna call him?" he directs at my brother over my head.

I hide my face in his shirt, but I can hear Ben's footsteps as he heads down the hall, presumably to make that call in the privacy of my bedroom.

"Pack a bag," Ben instructs a few minutes later when he walks back into the kitchen.

"Why?"

"Because we need a chance to find him before he can get to you." The brutally fierce way he tells me has a cold fist of fear squeeze my heart.

"*Fuck*," I hear Nick mutter.

"You can't stay here, and I don't think taking you up the mountain is safe. It would be too much of a coincidence to assume the break-in is unrelated. I'm not willing to take that chance," Ben says.

"The farm," Nick offers. "It's removed from the road. Has a long exposed driveway. I doubt it's been on his radar."

"And it has your dad," Stacie adds, making me smile.

"And it has my pops," I echo. "Along with the double-barreled shotgun he would have no compunction to use on anyone threatening these girls."

"Call your father," Ben rumbles, nodding at Nick.

I'm already making mental lists: the school needs to be notified the girls won't be there, the call to CPS I'll be making first thing in the morning, and the clothes I'll need to pack for the girls. For now, Becca will need to share Mak's stuff, until I have a chance to ask Drew about her things. Another thing to add to my list.

This is what I'm good at. It's like getting a new case to process; you break it apart and start dealing with each of the individual pieces until it all fits together. Except of course, this time is much closer to home.

-

"Why don't you step away from the stove and hand me that spatula."

I swing around at Henry's voice behind me.

Last night I wanted to wait until morning to pack up the kids and head out to the farm, but Nick made a good point. He proposed moving under the guise of night would be much likelier to go undetected than during the day. If this Kevin guy was still around, keeping an eye out, he's less likely to do so after ten at night, when most people are heading for bed.

By the time we got to the farm, Ben behind us to make sure we weren't being tailed, it was close to midnight. The girls had both fallen asleep in the back seat before we turned onto Main Street. Henry was waiting on the porch steps and after a brief introduction to Ben, came to fetch Mak from the car and carried her into the house, while Nick followed behind with Becca in his arms. That left Ben and me to deal with the bags.

With the girls safely tucked in the queen-sized bed in the spare bedroom, and Ben on his way home, I crawl into Nick's bed, not even taking a glance at his domain before my eyes drift shut. I never even noticed Nick slipping in behind me.

I thought I'd surprise everyone with breakfast this morning. I woke up early and found to my delight that the kitchen was equipped with a Keurig, the pods neatly aligned in the little rack beside it.

At six in the morning, everyone was still sleeping, so I went about to make myself a coffee, while checking the cupboards and fridge for supplies. The two things they had plenty of were bread and eggs. French toast seemed the logical choice, even though my previous attempts at recreating the sweet fluffy delicacies Isla whipped up with a mere flick of her wrist, had failed dramatically. It was still early, and there were plenty of supplies for me to have a few trial runs if need be.

I didn't count on Henry getting up.

"I'm not kidding, girl. Step away before you set fire to my kitchen."

"You're up early. I thought you'd sleep in," I observe, stepping back as he muscles his way in front of the stove.

"I did," he fires back, picking the pan off the stove. "Half the blooming day is already gone."

I glance at the clock showing barely seven in the morning, when the old man bumps me out of the way and moves in front of the sink, the pan in his hand.

The "Hey!" that flies from my mouth is too late. My French toast is already being ground to pulp in the garborator.

"That was my surprise breakfast," I protest indignantly.

"It certainly was a surprise," he fires back. "I could barely make out what on God's green earth it started as, let alone what it was meant to become." I watch as he grabs a large bowl from the cupboard and pulls the fridge door open, pulling out ingredients so fast I can barely keep up. All the while continuing to mutter under his breath. "Whatever that was went from crispy to carcinogenic ten minutes ago, girl."

My mouth opens and closes like a fish as I listen to Henry's tirade. The only thing keeping me from having my good intentions crushed, is the playful glint in his eyes as he throws me a wink.

"I'll whip us up some proper breakfast. It needs a bit in the oven, you've got some time to catch a bit more sleep," he says, looking at me as he tips his head to the door. "It'll take me a while to tend to the animals."

I'm still smiling when I carefully try to slip under the sheet without waking Nick.

"What are you smiling at?"

I look up and see his eyes shimmer between half-closed lids.

"Your dad. He totally foiled my plans for French toast and basically sent me back to bed. I wouldn't be surprised if he didn't mean to sleep. He let me know in no uncertain terms that he'd be outside for a while." I grin at the single eyebrow Nick pulls up high.

"Pops may be an old coot, but he still has some good ideas left in him," Nick growls, as he lifts the sheet over top of our heads and dives on top of me.

His hard deep kiss, combined with his solid thigh pressed up between my legs, is enough to have me writhing against him.

"God," I blurt out when his lips leave mine to trail down my jaw, to my neck where he licks and nibbles at the soft skin. "I swear you could make me come just by kissing me like that."

"Not today," he mumbles, as he pulls at the neck of my shirt down exposing my breasts. "Today I have other plans." Plumping my breasts with his hands, he leans down sucking first one, and then the other nipple into his mouth, releasing each with a plop. "Morning, my beauties," he whispers, burying his face between them.

My hand finds its way to the back of his head as my heart swells. Knowing that, as different as one side is from the other, he doesn't see them as different. He doesn't see *me* as different, and that makes me *feel* beautiful—no matter what the mirror says.

Despite the fact we are in the middle of a fucked up situation, or perhaps even because of it, I don't want to hold back. With both my hands bracketing his head, I carefully lift his face, his gaze immediately seeking out mine.

"I love you," I murmur, watching a light go on in his eyes. He rises up on his knees and his hands find the waistband of my panties, tugging them down my legs without ever looking away.

"Say it again," he whispers, his voice hoarse from sleep or perhaps emotion, as he reaches for the nightstand.

"I love you."

I'm only partially aware of the condom he rolls on after pulling his cock from his boxers. All I can see is the wonder in his eyes, and all I feel is his body as he settles his hips in the cradle of mine.

"With all my heart," I hear him whisper as he surges forward, filling my body and my heart completely.

-

By the time we follow Mak's chatter in the direction of the kitchen, my hair still wet from the lightning fast shower, something has fundamentally changed.

For the first time, I feel part of a whole.

I don't really think it has anything to do with the feelings expressed, or the mind-blowing orgasm that followed. It's just a slight shift of perspective; where one moment we are sharing our respective lives with the other, and the next we are sharing a life. Period.

There isn't much time to ponder on that, because the kids are already sitting at the kitchen table, starving, I'm sure. Henry stands behind the counter in the kitchen, wielding a pot of fresh coffee, and wearing a smile. A rarity I take as the kindness with which it is intended.

Of all the fucking luck—is this shitshow ever going to go my way?

I finally get my ass to Albuquerque, in my piece of shit truck, to meet my PO, and the motherfucker is out of town for a funeral. He's supposed to be back in his office tomorrow, so I reschedule with his receptionist for tomorrow afternoon.

Guess there's nothing left to do but find a willing hole to shack up with for the night. I head to my favorite bar in town, where I grab a beer and a corner booth. It isn't long before a tall, lanky woman sidles over and introduces herself. What the hell kind of name is Vyanne? At least she doesn't reek of drugs and desperation, which is a damn sight better than that strung out skank in Dolores.

This night I'm sleeping in clean sheets.

-

After waiting most of the afternoon, I play the reformed convict for my douchebag parole officer.

Stepping out of his office, I notice the sun is setting. Looks like a night trip back to my target. I hop in my ride to head back to Colorado and turn the key.

Nothing.

Fuck! I thought it was running like shit on the way into town. I pop the hood, only to see the damn coil wire burned in half. Not a chance in hell I'll get the damn thing fixed tonight.

CHAPTER 22

Nick

"I'll try to get out of going to the game and fly back tonight."

I hate having to leave the girls, but this meeting in Denver is the final step in the Marx deal. After this is done, the rest of my caseload is relatively easy in comparison. At least nothing that involves the kind of hours I've docked on this merger, or traveling to Denver. But Marx has a private box arranged for the Colorado Rockies' game tonight to celebrate, which means staying overnight, but I'd much rather sleep in my own bed, with Stacie beside me.

"We'll be fine," she murmurs sleepily as she snuggles in my neck, wrapping her long limbs around me. She pulls up a knee, rubbing it along my leg, giving my cock all kinds of ideas. "Your pops is here, Ben was planning to take the girls fishing today. We'll be fine," she repeats.

I shift her so she's on top of me and pull her knees to bracket me by my hips. She moans lightly when she feels the evidence of my current mindset between our bodies. With my hands on her ass, I press her already wet sex against the base of my cock, as I flex my hips underneath. This time she moans louder.

"Shhh." I silence her with my mouth, catching all the little sounds she makes as she rocks herself against me.

"You'll be late," she whispers with her lips brushing mine.

"Don't care."

I don't. It's five in the morning, Pops and the girls are still asleep, and I'm living my fucking fantasy with Stacie in my bed every night these past days.

"I'll be fast," she promises.

I hiss sharply when she lifts her hips and with one hand positions the head of my cock at her entrance. Warm, wet heat engulfs me as she eases herself down, and I press my head back in the pillow, emitting a deep groan. So fucking good. Every time I'm buried deep inside her is like coming home.

She does a swirl, this little gyration of her hips, when she slides back down. Just at the end, a subtle torque of my cock that sends an electric current the length of my body and makes my toes curl. The third time she lights me up like that, I've reached my limit.

With one arm around her lower back to keep us attached, and the other used as leverage to flip us, I take over.

"Eyes on me."

Her eyes immediately find mine as I lift my body off her, place my hands behind her knees, and spread her up and wide. My hips piston, and my balls slap against her ass, as I drive into her at a furious pace, using my hold on her as leverage. With the deep groan of her climax, and her nails digging into my ass as encouragement, I come inside her in long, jerky spurts.

It's not until I drop her legs and lean over to kiss her sweetly, that I notice the lack of a condom.

"Anastasia..." I lift up and look down at her.

"I know," she whispers, her eyes wide in shock before she shakes it off, and a tentative smile pulls at her mouth. "Not now; we have enough to worry about."

"I'm sorry."

She shakes her head sharply at my apology.

"Two in this bed, Nick, but we're not doing this now. You need to get ready or you'll miss your flight."

By the time I come out of the bathroom and tuck my shaving kit in the overnight bag, I hope I won't need, Stacie is already drifting off again. I grab my bag in one hand and with the other brace myself in the bed; so I can lean down to kiss her.

"I'll call," I promise softly, pressing my lips against hers.

"Mmmm. Be safe," she mumbles half asleep when I straighten and walk for the door, where I stop to have one last look at her. Blonde hair spread out on my pillow, the curve of her ass under the sheets, and my seed slowly slipping from her body.

"Love you, Anastasia." My voice is barely loud enough for the naked ear, but when the corners of her mouth turn up, I wonder if she heard me.

-

"No thanks."

I smile at the flight attendant who offered me a *Denver Post* the moment I sat down in my first-class seat on the small plane. Silly expense really, for a one-hour flight, but the arrangements were made by Marx's assistant, so I wasn't about to object. His money to waste if that's what he chooses. I'm just glad I made it to the airport in time.

It had been fucking tough walking out of the house this morning. Pops had been up when I walked into the kitchen, shoving a travel mug of steaming coffee and a toasted bagel in my hand.

"Can't think on an empty stomach, boy," he said, like I was twelve years old again. It had been his favorite saying every morning when he made me sit until I ate all my mom's lumpy oatmeal. She wasn't a great cook either, much like Stacie. She could do the essentials, but she just didn't have that touch. Pops has it; he can turn anything into a meal and make it taste great. I'm no slouch in the kitchen either, but I barely get a chance to cook. That's my father's domain.

"I'll keep an eye out," he assured me as he ushered me out the door, not even giving me a chance to thank him.

The flight attendant was back just minutes later offering coffee, which I gladly accepted, since I left Pops's travel mug in the car, barely touched in my hurry to get here. I'd need copious amounts of caffeine to get me through this day to keep my focus sharp. I can already tell that will be an issue, since my mind insists on replaying every second of this morning's feverish tangle.

I realize too late I should probably have accepted the fucking newspaper.

I need it to cover my lap.

Stacie

"Does the name Kevin Borland mean anything to you?"

I just sat the girls down with a sheet of math questions I printed off when the phone rang.

Their teacher sent me their scheduled classwork when I spoke to her earlier this week. I didn't go into specifics about the police investigation—I'm sure the rumor mill will take care of that in a place as small as Dolores—but I did tell her that Becca was with us for now. She easily accepted my wish to shield the girls for a bit, until everything settles down, and was happy to send me some work so they wouldn't fall too far behind.

The last few mornings we've eaten a hearty breakfast—thanks to Henry—and sat at the dining table where the girls would do a few hours of schoolwork.

I took the phone and slipped into the kitchen, where I could still keep an eye on Mak and Becca, but they couldn't hear my conversation.

"Criminal Sexual Penetration was the official charge. Happened at a bachelor party, his party, if I remember correctly. My office asked for nine years and got them. The guy was a creep and didn't bother hiding it. The judge saw right through his defense." I fire off the particulars for Drew without hesitation.

I'm not sure why, but something about that case stuck with me. Maybe it was because it dropped in my lap right before the start of the trial and I was scrambling to catch up. One of the other ADAs, who handled the case up to that point, had to go out of state for a family emergency.

Rather than delay the trial until his return, it was handed to me.

"That's the one," Drew confirms. "He was released on parole six months ago, but the case wasn't listed as one of yours. Neil found it when he broadened his search to include every convict the Albuquerque DA's office put away, who was released in the past year."

"So you think it was him?"

"Can't say for certain. Only one way to know for sure, which is why I'm calling." He takes a minute to clear his throat, and I use it to check around the corner to find the girls still bent over their papers. As usual, the tip of Mak's tongue sticks out in concentration, something Ben does on occasion as well. "I know Nick's not there. I just got off the phone with Ben, and he mentioned Nick is out of town. Ben said he's heading your way shortly, but told me I'd have to call you myself and ask."

"Ask me what?"

"With your permission, I'd like to show Becca a photo lineup." It's clear from the tone of his voice that this is the last thing he wants to put the little girl through.

"What about her brother?" I ask immediately. "Why not ask him?" Drew's deep sigh does not escape me.

"Cortez PD can't locate him. We've got the state patrol keeping an eye out for the vehicle, but so far no luck on Jason. Look," he says in a conciliatory voice. "I don't want to put that little girl through this either, Stacie, but you know as well as I do, that time is of the essence, and it's the only potential lead we have on the guy."

Instead of firing off the knee-jerk refusal that wants to escape, I take a deep breath and think it through. In my experience, victims and witnesses of crimes, some even as young as Becca, often find strength in pointing a finger at the person they perhaps fear most. In a way, it's taking back control, and I think perhaps it's time Becca was given the chance to learn she can make a difference in her own life.

"Okay," I therefore say, after a pregnant pause.

"You sure?"

"Just give me half an hour so I can prep her."

This too is familiar territory for me. Witness preparation is something I was often involved in.

I toss a fresh pod in the Keurig and plan my approach as I wait for my coffee to percolate. I'm just adding some creamer when Henry walks into the kitchen.

"They think they might know who *Kevin* is," I tell him, making room for him at the coffee machine, where he refills his mug. He turns his head to look at me.

"The guy? That guy?" He jerks his thumb in the direction of the dining room table.

I quickly fill him in, and he agrees to stay close to keep an eye on Mak, while I deal with Becca.

"Girls," I say, walking up to them, setting the coffee in my hand on the table. "Put your pencils down for a sec, I have to talk to you."

I purposely don't single Becca out right away, giving me a chance to rest my hand on the back of her neck first. Still she looks up at me warily.

"Uncle Ben will be here shortly," I start, but am immediately interrupted by an excited Mak.

"Yay!" she cries out. "We're going fishing!"

Throughout Mak's outburst, I watch Becca, who continues to keep her focus on me. It's heart-wrenching to see the difference between the girls; Mak instantly jumping to the best possible conclusion, while Becca appears to be waiting for that other shoe she just knows is going to drop. It only makes me more determined that this girl's life will get a whole lot better, if I have anything to do with it.

"The sheriff, too. He has some pictures he wants to show you, sweets," I address Becca directly. "He's going to ask you if you know anyone in those pictures." I crouch down by the side of her chair so I'm at eye level. "Becca, honey? Do you think you can do that?"

"Is it like *Where's Waldo*?" Mak pipes up, and I have to bite back a grin. She draws Becca's attention, who lifts her gaze to her friend, and a little smile tugs at her mouth.

"More like *Memory*, silly," Becca returns, and the two of them burst out in little girl giggles I don't understand, but am thrilled to hear.

-

Half an hour later, Ben has Mak in the kitchen, the low mumble of their voices comfortable in the background. Henry is back outside doing whatever it is he does, and I'm sitting at the dining table, at a bit of a distance from Becca and Drew.

Luckily she remembered Drew and seemed reasonably at ease with him, until I was about to leave. Then she looked at me with panic in her eyes. Something that Drew picked up on immediately and he indicated for me to stay. I purposely am not sitting too close, because I don't want any reaction I might have to influence Becca.

Drew pushes a button on the small voice recorder, puts it down on the table between him and the girl, and states the date, the location, and all three of our names. Then he turns toward Becca.

"Just start flipping them over, honey," he says, tapping his finger on the stack of upside down photos in front of her. "When you find someone you know, put them aside."

Very slowly, as if whoever is in the picture could jump out and grab her, Becca flips the first picture over. I make it a point not to look at the picture, but at her reaction. There is none for the first picture, or for the second, or even the third.

All the blood literally drains from the little girl's face when she flips over the fourth sheet and shoves the paper as far away from her as she can.

"Becca?" Drew prompts her, carefully touching her arm. She flinches as if someone hit her, and keeps her eyes closed after that.

"Honey?" I try, hoping to God I'm not responsible for scarring that poor thing even further.

"Do I gotta look at the rest?" she asks in a shaky voice.

"No, sweetheart," I jump in before Drew has a chance to answer. "You don't have to." My eyes find Drew's over her head.

"You don't," he confirms. "But do you think you could tell me why you put picture number four aside?"

I glare at him. Sure, I know he's got a job to do and it's in all of our best interest, but I really, really hate seeing that little girl trying to pull herself together. She slowly opens her eyes and looks directly at Drew.

"'Cause that's him," she whispers.

"That's who, Becca?" Drew pushes some more, and I'm about to launch myself over the table when she answers in a much clearer voice.

"Kevin. He hurt my momma."

The thick silent tears that run down her cheeks as she continues to look straight in Drew's eyes almost rip my heart from my chest. I'm about to get up and go to her when I hear Ben call out.

"Mak! Stay here!"

"Can I see now?"

My daughter, who was supposed to stay in the kitchen, is apparently tired of waiting and rushes over before Ben can grab hold of her.

"Hey," she says, staring at the picture on the table. "I know him. I've seen him before."

I'd been too preoccupied with Becca to even glance at the picture but now my eyes drop down.

"You saw him? Where was that?" I hear Drew ask, as my eyes register the familiar face in the picture. Becca picked out the Kevin Borland I remember.

"At the school," Mak says, and suddenly I shoot up straight. "It was when Uncle Ben was at the school to pick me up, Mom. Remember?"

"The day school was out early?" I ask her and she nods her head.

The day of the bomb threat.

-

Drew left almost right away, eager to hunt down his lead, and Ben and the girls had gone fishing.

I wanted to keep them home, but Ben convinced me it would be much better to give them something normal and fun to do. I wasn't too sure I was on board with his idea of fun, but the girls sure were.

By the time Henry came in to start on dinner, something he refused to allow me to even attempt, I had all the laundry done, every sheet in the house washed, the two bathrooms scrubbed, and the floors mopped.

"Christ, it smells like a laundromat in here," he says, pulling what looks to me like random supplies from the fridge and cupboards and dumping them on the counter.

"I did laundry," I offer, adding as an afterthought, "And I cleaned." He turns to look at me with an eyebrow raised.

"No shit. Going a little stir crazy, are we?"

"You have no idea," I sigh dramatically, making him chuckle. "I'll be so glad when this is over and I can start earning my keep again."

"I hear ya," Henry commiserates, before handing me a bowl. "In the meantime though, I'm gonna teach you to cook."

I put the bowl down on the counter and back away, my hands raised defensively.

"I appreciate the thought, but you're not the first one to try. I've even taken classes, but I just don't have the touch."

"Bullshit," he spits out, picking up the bowl and shoving it in my midriff, so I have no choice but to grab hold. "You need talent to be a gourmet chef, which is what you're lacking."

"Thanks," I scoff, rolling my eyes.

"Don't give me that," he warns me, but with a sparkle in his eyes. "You've been aiming too high. I'm not interested in turning you into a gourmet chef, but I'll teach you to cook, because that just requires skill, and skills you can learn."

I'm covered in flour by the time the girls walk in, followed by my brother, carrying a tray.

"I could kiss you," I tell him, snatching the cup marked *Stacie* from the cardboard holder. "You went to Jen's." I take a long sip from the pure nectar Jen makes me.

"We did," Mak answers for him. "And we got hot chocolate with whipped cream."

"Before dinner?" Henry points out sternly. This time it's Becca who pipes up.

"Yup," she says, smiling bigger than I've ever seen her smile. "Because we catched a fish."

"That so?" The old man makes a big show of searching around for said fish, making the girls giggle. "I don't see it."

"We set it free," Mak offers, making Ben chuckle with her choice of terminology. "Uncle Ben said it still had some growing to do."

"Good thing your mom made us a chicken pot pie then," he says, smiling at Mak's scrunched face.

"Not so sure about that," my brother adds to the mix. He's fast losing any goodwill the caramel macchiato bought him. "Looks like she's wearing most of it."

In the end, he stayed for dinner and liked it. I figure it'll take me a while to outlive the bad rap I gave myself over the years.

> **Nick:** I won't make it home tonight. Couldn't change tomorrow's 2 pm flight to earlier.
> Miss you.

I didn't see the message until I slipped between the clean sheets on Nick's bed, after tucking in the girls. I turned off the sound when Drew came by and never bothered turning it back on.

One glance tells me I missed a few calls as well.

I miss him too. I've been spoiled sharing a bed with him all this time and it feels empty now.

> **Stacie:** I miss you too. Sorry I missed your calls.
> Phone was off.
> Have much to tell you.
> Can't wait to see you tomorrow. ILU

It took a while for the response to come but when it did, it left a smile on my face as I drifted off to sleep.

> **Nick:** Tomorrow. With all my heart.

CHAPTER 23

Nick

Amazing how time crawls when you have to wait to get where you want to be.

It's noon on Saturday, and for some reason, it's an absolute zoo at Denver airport. I know I'm early, my flight doesn't leave until two, but I had to be checked out of the hotel at eleven. I didn't really want to go anywhere except home, so I came straight here.

Marx had been pleasantly surprised when I ended up showing at the ballpark after all. That afternoon, I'd explained that although I really appreciated the gesture, I had some pressing issues at home to take care of and wanted to try and catch a flight that night. Of course that didn't happen, since whatever flights were heading into Durango were already overbooked. Weekend commuters, the woman at United called them.

I finally talked to Stacie this morning, when I couldn't wait any longer to hear her voice, and ended up waking her. She didn't seem to mind, though. Last night she'd messaged that she had a lot to tell me, and she wasn't lying.

Sounds like they had quite the day. She told me about Drew's call and the photo lineup. I ground my teeth when she mentioned Becca's distress, but Stacie was adamant that once it was done, the little girl seemed to have an extra bounce in her step. I sure as fuck hope so, or I'll have a word with our good sheriff for springing that on her.

Despite my concern, her sleepy rendition of Pops when she told me about the cooking lesson had me chuckling. She was dead on with her intonation. So by the time I reluctantly got off the phone, after promising her I'd be home soon, I was smiling.

"Boarding of Premier Class passengers flying United Airlines flight 4584 at gate B81 will commence shortly. All other passengers please remain seated until your section is called."

I smile at the attendant when she scans my boarding pass, hands it back, and waves me through. Luckily, I have a single seat by the window, with no one beside me. I pull out my phone and turn it to airplane mode, before I lean back in my seat. Not a fan of casual airplane chats. I'd rather sit with my eyes closed, lost in my own thoughts, and those travel inevitably to the girls.

Even last night, while enjoying a couple of beers and some appetizers in a glitzy private box, all I could think about was how the girls would really get a kick out of that. I even mentioned it out loud to Marx, who smiled and told me to call him anytime I wanted to bring them to Denver and take in a game.

"Newspaper?"

I open my eyes to find the flight attendant standing beside me with the *Denver Post* in her hand. Smarter this time around, I gratefully accept and fold it over my lap, just in case. Leaning my head back and closing my eyes, I let my thoughts drift back to Stacie, the sound of her sexy, raspy, sleep-tainted voice this morning, and how I can't wait to be home to wake up to that tomorrow morning.

"Business or pleasure?"

The woman seated on the other side leans slightly into the aisle. Her gaze is open, friendly, and definitely interested. I wonder what it is she sees.

"Business," I answer politely.

"Are you staying in town?" she asks, and I realize she thinks my business is in Durango.

"Actually, my business was in Denver. I'm heading home."

"Oh? Lovely place, Durango. One of my boutiques is on Main and Eighth, just a block from the Strater Hotel, so I'm there often," she says, a small suggestive smile on her carefully painted lips.

The woman is probably in her late thirties and well put together. If I wasn't already living my dream, I might have considered taking her up on what she was offering. It's the kind of uncomplicated, no-ties encounter I used to prefer. Interestingly enough, everything about Stacie has been complicated from the get-go, and I wouldn't trade it for the world.

"Actually, I just fly in to Durango, I don't actually live there," I explain, trying not to be too obvious with my rejection, but I'm clearly still too obtuse.

"I hear it's beautiful," she says, reaching out semi-casually to brush my sleeve with her long fingers. "I've always wanted to explore but haven't had the chance. Perhaps you could tell me what places I should visit—over a drink at the Strater?"

Bold. I clearly have to shut this down.

"Nice hotel. Was there not too long ago with my girls for a charity gala."

She doesn't need to know that we barely knew each other then.

"Your girls?" she echoes, pulling her hand back as if it is burned.

"Makenna is nine."

I'm well aware that I am purposely misleading her, but I haven't lied. Plus, it seems to do the trick. She sits back in her seat and pretty soon is engaged in conversation with someone on her other side.

I lean my head back again and close my eyes, letting my mind drift. I do think of them as *my* girls, even if they aren't. Not yet anyway, but I'm going to change that.

Soon.

-

It's well after three by the time we land. I pull my phone from the pouch on the back of the seat in front of me and tuck it in my pocket, grab my bag from the overhead compartment, and rush off the plane.

Durango is one of those airports where you literally walk from the plane to the terminal over the tarmac, and my long legs are eating up the distance. I'm eager to get home and I walk right through the terminal, straight out the other side to the parking lot.

My father's car is exactly where I left it. Made more sense to leave the truck at home for him to use. I climb behind the wheel and figure I'll make it home by five, hopefully in time for dinner.

Stacie mentioned this morning that Pops taught her to make chicken pot pie last night. Today they had plans to process some of the apples weighing down the fruit trees along the driveway. Pops makes apple jelly, apple chutney, apple pie, and fresh applesauce every year. The cold storage in the basement holds years' worth of canning, and still every year he adds.

The pies and applesauce never last, though. He tries to freeze some, but inevitably by the time we leave Christmas behind, the last of the pies and applesauce are gone.

I'm hoping whatever is for dinner—it comes with apple pie for dessert.

Stacie

"What did you do?"

I take one look at Henry, stumbling in the backdoor, and drop the towel I was drying dishes with, rushing to his side. I help him over to a kitchen chair, where he sits down heavily.

"Well?" I push, because he hasn't answered me yet.

"It's nothing," the stubborn old coot bites off, but I clearly saw him wince every time he put weight on his right foot.

"Bullocks, it's nothing," I fire back, kneeling down and carefully pulling off his boot.

"*Doggone it. Son of a pup!*" His yelp brings the girls running from the living room, where they'd been watching Saturday cartoons.

"What happened?" Becca asks sweetly.

Henry looks up at her and the grimace he was wearing instantly smoothes out.

"Just twisted my ankle, little one. Saw the prettiest apple on a top branch and reached a little too far. Toppled that stepladder right over."

"You went apple picking without us?" Mak accuses, less concerned about his injury than she was about his perceived betrayal. "You said we could help."

Letting Henry deal with the girls is a great distraction, I have his boot and sock off with only one dirty glare in my direction.

"That may need an X-ray," I point out. His ankle is already swelling and turning color.

"No way. In my almost eighty years, I've had enough sprains to know that's just what this is. Don't need no expensive tests to tell me that. Ice and elevation, that's all I need," he grumbles.

I don't bother arguing, knowing it would be a moot point. Instead I decide to wait for Nick to come home, so he can try and strong-arm his father.

With the girls' help, I get Henry settled on the couch, his foot on a throw pillow on the coffee table. Mak shoves the remote in his hand.

"We were done watching anyway," she says magnanimously, and in the brief moment where my eyes meet Henry's over Mak's head, I see humor light his eyes.

"I'll get the ice," I announce, leaving him in the care of the girls.

In the kitchen, I wrap a bag of frozen corn in a tea towel and glance out the window. The ladder is lying sideways, partially in the driveway, not too far from the house, the abandoned bushel basket still by the tree.

In the living room, Henry has found something to watch and only hisses lightly when I put the ice pack on his ankle.

"Is it hurting? Can I get you some ibuprofen?" I offer him quietly, but he declines with a sharp shake and a dismissive wave of his hand.

"That won't do a damn thing," he gripes. "Medicine cabinet in my bathroom. Bring me the prescription bottle."

"Sure thing."

There's only one prescription bottle in his cabinet and I check the label. *Percocet*. The date of issue on the label is eight months ago, and there's only two tablets left, so I figure it can do no harm.

I hand him a glass of water and the bottle, before I look over to the girls who are piled into the large club chair, leaving the entire couch for Henry.

"How about you girls help me get some of those apples picked?" I ask them.

Loud cheers and a mad scramble for the door; I turn to rush after them before they disappear outside, when Henry grabs my hand.

"Listen, it's cold out, so bundle up. Also, someone from Our Lady Of Victory is supposed to come pick some apples this afternoon for their annual bake sale, so keep your eye out. They do that every year."

I look down in the old man's face, seeing the warmth in his eyes, and recognize the veiled apology for his earlier grump. Already forgiven, I lean down and kiss his cheek to convey this, before rushing to intercept the kids.

Ignoring their protests, I herd them down the hallway to their bedroom and instruct them to dress in the sweaters I had the foresight to pack.

Apparently, I didn't think to pack myself anything resembling a sweater, so I open the door to Nick's walk-in closet to see what of his I can pilfer. I spot a hoodie and pull it off the hanger, accidentally knocking the hanger off the rail. I bend over to pick it up, and that's when I see it: the edge of a large frame and the bottom half of a familiar image. Before I can have a closer look, Mak's head pokes into the closet.

"Are you ready yet?"

-

I glance over at where the kids are picking up the good apples that have fallen and putting them in one basket, and tossing the rotting ones in a big bucket for the horses. I'm on the ladder on the other side of the driveway, trying very hard not to do what Henry did and reach for that perfect apple that always seems just out of reach.

We've been out here for a while, and Henry wasn't kidding, there's a very distinct chill in the air. I'm used to the Albuquerque weather, which at this time of year is still in the very comfortable high sixties to mid-seventies. I'd be surprised if the thermometer reached forty here today.

I climb down and toss the apples, I gathered in the pouch of Nick's hoodie, into the basket. We've already filled one bushel, and set that aside for when the church person comes. Saves them having to pick them and the girls are still having fun. I, on the other hand, am losing feeling in my fingers. I'm just considering calling the girls in for some hot chocolate, when I notice a white van turn into the driveway. I assume it's whomever is coming from Our Lady Of Victory, and call to the girls to stay on their side of the road before I turn to grab the bushel I put aside for them.

Behind me a door slides open, as I bend over to lift the basket and promptly drop it when I hear Mak's high-pitched voice call out in warning—but I don't even have a chance to turn around before my world goes black.

Nick

That's odd.

I pull into the driveway and immediately notice a bushel basket on its side, apples spilling out all over the road. A little further down is my dad's stepladder, sitting under a tree. On the opposite side, I see another basket and a bucket.

That's not like Pops, to leave his stuff out here.

I pull up beside the truck, grab my bag from the passenger seat and get out. All I can hear is the TV when I walk into the house, and I know right away something is off. I drop my bag just inside the door and walk into the living room. The TV is turned to the Discovery Channel and Pops is asleep on the couch.

"Pops? " I gently shake his shoulder to wake him up. "Where are the girls?" I ask him when he blinks his eyes open, looking confused.

"What?" he mumbles, clearly disoriented, as I impatiently walk past him to check the bedrooms down the hall. Empty, the only thing out of place is the picture of Stacie I bought at the charity auction, laying on my bed. I'd tucked it away the first night I found her fast asleep in my room. She clearly missed seeing it or she would've said something. I was afraid that seeing it might be insensitive, since it depicts her scars before she had the surgery, so I tucked it away until I could broach it with her. She must've bumped into it.

Fuck.

What if the fact I hid it from her freaked her out? I'd like to think there's enough trust built up that she wouldn't walk away without confronting me, but what the fuck do I know? Wouldn't be the first, and likely not the last time, I put my foot in.

When I get back to the living room, the TV is turned off, Dad's sitting up and is looking much more coherent.

"Where's Stacie?" he asks right away, and that feeling when you know something is off is suddenly so overwhelming, it's making it hard to breathe.

"Not here," I manage in a strangled voice. "Pops, where did they go?"

I watch as the blood drains from his face as he looks around the room.

"They're not outside? They were picking apples," he mumbles and I'm only half listening, already dialing Ben's number. "I fell asleep," is the last thing I hear him say before I walk into the kitchen and turn my attention to the call.

"Talk to me," Ben answers in his usual manner.

"Are they with you?"

I don't need an answer; I can feel the thick waves of dread in the silence. Without warning, the contents of my stomach surge up and I just make it to the sink, dropping the phone on the counter.

I'm retching so hard; tears are running down my face when I finally come up for air. I never noticed Pops following me into the kitchen, but he's right there, handing me a towel with my phone to his ear.

"About one? Maybe two. I fell off a ladder picking apples and the girls offered to finish it. Those dang pills must've put me to sleep." I watch my father turn his eyes on me. "I'm sorry, Son," he says into the phone, but he does it while looking straight at me. Then he hands the phone to me.

"Nick?"

"Yeah," I answer, my voice raw.

"Fucking pull yourself together," he barks roughly. "Sit your father down with a pen and paper and tell him to write down everything he remembers. Then go out there and check if you see anything out of place. Any damn thing you find, you do not touch—you call me right away. Got it?"

"Got it," I answer weakly.

"Nick?"

"Yeah?"

"We'll find them. I swear to fucking God we'll get our girls back."

CHAPTER 24

Nick

Dad manages to shove a flashlight in my hands as I aim for the door.

I'm barely outside and already regret I didn't grab a jacket; it's fucking cold out. A quick glance at my watch shows twenty past five. Last time Pops saw them was two at best; that's three and a half hours missing, for fuck's sake. Enough time to…

I clench my teeth and shake my head sharply as I make my way over to where the overturned basket is lying on the road. I can't think like that—I'll go nuts.

There's nothing obviously amiss, other than the basket and the apples spread over the ground. I'm not a goddamn investigator, how am I supposed to know what the fuck constitutes *out of place* in this situation? We're outside for chrissakes.

Taking in a deep breath, I look again: in the grass, on the side of the road, I check the ditch along the fencing. I even look up in the damn trees before glancing back at the ground underneath. There I see it—two parallel marks in the dirt that stop abruptly at the side of the road, like someone's been dragged. A cluster of footprints I can't quite all make out, but it looks like there are some prints that are much smaller than the rest. Now that I'm focusing on the ground, I can make out tire tracks as well. Very faintly. Not that it tells me much—it's a fucking driveway.

I make my way over to the other side of the road, where the second basket and a bucket still stand upright in the middle of a pile of apples.

"Goddammit girls, where are you?" I mutter at no one.

My head shoots up at a faint sound that seems to come from the other side of the fence on this side of the lane. I stand perfectly still and let my eyes scan the fence line. I don't see a thing at first, but then I hear it again…like a whimper. Then I see it: a pink shoelace sticking out of a pile of branches and debris in the ditch, slightly to my left. When I focus closely, I notice some of the dead leaves vibrating.

"Makenna?" I call out softly, inching closer. "Sweetheart?"

The only answer I get is a louder whimper and a now violent shaking of the brush pile.

"It's okay. It's Nick, baby," I coo, lifting the branches away to find bright red hair instead of Mak's dark head. "Becca, honey, it's me."

The little girl is curled up in a tight ball, her knees high and her face pressed down in the ditch, her arms covering her head. I carefully pick some sticks and leaves off her back before leaving my hand there. I can feel her little body shaking.

"It's okay, Becca. I've got you now," I murmur, lifting her gently with my hands under her arms.

The moment I start turning her toward me, she flings herself around my neck, her little arms so tight it's hard to breathe. The only sound is the soft whimpers that slowly turn into keening.

Jesus.

I've got to get her inside, her little body is freezing.

"I've got you, baby. Let's go see if we can get Pops to make us some of that hot chocolate, okay?"

I tuck the flashlight in my back pocket and with one hand keeping her head pressed in my neck, and the other under her butt to hold her up. I walk as fast as I can back to the house.

Ben arrives not long after I walked in the door to a waiting Pops, holding up a blanket, which I wrap her in. I sit down on the couch with her, since she's clearly not ready to let go of me.

"She say anything?" Ben asks me and I shake my head.

"Found her hiding under a brush pile, on the other side of the road, in the ditch. She's freezing. We'll get something warm inside her first."

"Drew's on the way. Flemming and Neil are on their way, too. We need to know what she saw."

"Don't you think I know that?" I snap, hanging onto my sanity by a thin thread. "What do you want me to do, man?"

"All right, that's enough," Pops warns, hobbling in with a mug in his hand. "I'll get Becca here warmed up," he says, putting the mug on the table and sitting down next to me. "You two go duke it out on the damn porch. I'll take the girl." He reaches over and pries her clinging body from me, setting her firmly on his lap, her back against his front, both his arms wrapped tightly around her. "Go on," he orders. "We'll be just fine. Won't we, little one?"

Ben immediately moves toward the door, but I follow slower, keeping half an eye on the girl's stark white face. My father's head is bent close to hers, and I can hear him talk to her.

"You're a tough one, aren't you, Becca? You did real good, hiding out so you can help us find them. Real good. Now I need you to drink some of this hot cocoa, it'll help you warm up. I even put some of those little marshmallows in you liked last time. Remember that?"

The last thing I see before I step out the door is Becca's red hair bouncing as she nods at Pops.

What are the fucking odds?

This week has been a clusterfuck of epic proportions. Didn't get in to see my PO until Tuesday when the damn truck broke down. Luckily, I had that chick's number, Vyanne or something, and she was apparently ready for a repeat performance and picked me up. I kinda lost track when the bitch pulled out some high-grade coke that went nicely with the bottle of Jack.

Before I knew it, it was fucking Friday morning. I considered taking the bitch's car, but that would mean I'd have to off her, since she'd be able to make me to the cops, no problem. Instead, I waited till she headed out to pick up some milk, grabbed my bag and beelined it out of there, only to find my truck gone. Some fucktard either towed it or managed to get it fucking going, but she was no longer there.

I started walking, when I spotted that panel van parked beside the dumpster behind a strip mall. Jimmying the door was a piece of cake. I tossed my bag on the passenger seat and climbed behind the wheel. Jail is good for something. I came away knowing how to do more illegal shit than when I went in. Hot-wiring a car being one of them.

I thought the luck was short-lived when I got back to Dolores and drove by that cunt's house, hoping to pick up where I left off, and found it dark and empty. But that changed when I drove around the block a second time, to make sure, and spotted her little brat getting in the back seat of a big SUV in the parking lot of that coffee place. I was surprised to see it go in the opposite direction from her house and decided to trail a few cars behind.

I pulled off to the side when it pulled into a long driveway to a farmhouse, set back quite a ways from the road. From that distance I wasn't able to see who got out, but I did recognize the big bald dude's pickup truck parked out front. Pretty fucking sure that was not a coincidence. Looks like the bitch and her spawn are slumming with her fuck buddy.

I was parked on the shoulder and took off when the SUV pulled out again, to avoid being seen, and parked a little further on at the end of a dirt road by the river. The back of that van is a fuckload more comfortable than the bed of my truck for sleeping.

This morning I was back, but this time I parked at the same side of the road as the farm, hoping to have a better view. All fucking morning I sat there, planning and plotting. An old geezer came out of a shed on the side of the house, carrying a ladder and there wasn't a fucking thing I could do to get closer to the house without being seen.

I must've dozed off at some point, because next thing I know, it's not the old man, but that bitch, clear as day, on that same damn ladder.

My patience thin—I didn't stop to think, but acted.

Stacie

"Mom? Mommy…"

God my head hurts. Is that Mak?

I gingerly crack my eyelids, and get a quick glimpse of familiar surroundings, before a stabbing pain has me squeeze my eyes shut again.

My mind is foggy and not quite processing.

"Mommy?" My daughter's voice for sure, and she sounds upset.

I force my eyes open again and this time ride out the surge of pain when the sparse light hits my retinas.

"Makenna?" I try to call back, but my voice is raspy with lack of use, as I take in my surroundings.

Why am I sitting on the kitchen floor?

I try to pull a leg underneath me so I can get up, but my legs won't move independently. They're tied, as are my arms, behind my back.

"Mak?" I call again, a little firmer and this time I hear a responding sob as I tug restlessly on my restraints. I can't see her, but she's somewhere on the other side of the island.

Without thinking, I try to move in that direction but only manage to fall over, landing hard on my shoulder. Right. I'm bound. My senses are so scrambled; it's hard to think.

Shaking my head to clear the fog, I try my hands behind my back. Whatever is tied around my wrists is damp and only seems to get tighter as I try to wiggle my hands. I'm like a turtle on its back: immobile, exposed, and vulnerable.

"You have to wake up, Mommy. He's coming back."

I freeze.

"Who, baby?" I manage through the paralyzing fear that finally registers. Sharp and clear, cutting a straight path through the confusing fog.

"That man I saw in the parking lot at school, the one from the picture," she sniffles.

"Can you come to me? I'm tied up, baby," I call out, already on the move myself; wiggling like a worm along the tile floor. "Where are you?"

"He tied me to the table."

The dining room table is just on the other side of the kitchen island. A solid oak table on a single heavy column. She wouldn't be able to move it if she tried.

"I'm coming."

I hear the determination in my own voice, but that doesn't help me move any faster. It's hard to find purchase on the slick floor with my feet tied together, and every move results in a sharp pain in my head. Still I persist, my girl is on the other side.

"Where did he go?" I ask, biting down the bile that surges up in my throat, as I slowly crawl into the small passage between the counter and the fridge.

"I don't know!" Mak sobs.

"Hang on, baby. I'm on my way."

"He just said he'd be back. You were moaning, Mommy. I'm scared."

"I'm fine, sweetie, we'll both be fine."

Finally, I see her in the faint light coming in from the street. She's sitting under the table with her back against the base, her face a lighter orb. I only now register it's already dark outside. Somewhere along the way, I've lost a chunk of time.

"I can see you, baby, can you see me?"

She looks up and immediately her face crumbles, as another bout of tears floods her eyes.

"Keep talking to me, Makenna," I urge her. "Keep your eyes on me and keep talking. I'm coming."

"I didn't know it was him at first, I thought it was the church people. I came around the van and saw him behind you with his arm up. I tried to warn you, but he hit you over the head with something. I thought…" She dissolves in tears again.

"Baby? I'm okay, look at me. I'm all right. Almost there."

And I am. I'm so close that if I could stretch my arms, I'd almost be able to touch her feet.

"Hurry," Mak suddenly hisses, her head tilted and her eyes on the back door of the kitchen. A light crunch and then another. Someone is coming up the gravel path from the back shed. "He's coming."

With renewed urgency, and a singular focus at getting to my daughter, I scramble along the floor. With one last surge of energy, I launch myself forward, landing with my face inches from her hip, just as the back door opens.

CHAPTER 25

Nick

Drew is just driving up when I step out on the porch, leaving Pops to tend to Becca.

"What do you know?" he asks, getting out of his patrol car and walking up the steps, a folder in his hands.

"Nothing," Ben growls. "Girl is near catatonic."

"Pops will get her to talk," I suggest, feeling an almost childlike faith in my father's abilities. Or maybe I'm just that desperate.

"I was just fucking here yesterday," Drew says. "The kid did good, picking the guy's mug shot out of a lineup. Name is Kevin Borland. I contacted his PO earlier today and he confirmed that Borland hasn't missed an appointment yet. Including one he had on Tuesday. So before we jump to any fucking conclusions, we need more information."

"They've been fucking gone for hours," I protest, just as Ben pipes up.

"That's my sister out there," he bites off. "And my goddamn niece."

Drew holds up a hand when Ben takes a step toward him.

"Exactly the reason why we can't fucking go off half-cocked and miss something important, you jackassess." Drew slaps the file he's holding on his leg a few times. "I brought a file on Borland. A bit more background info, a few more pictures. I'm hoping it'll help. And just so you know, I'm not fucking twiddling my thumbs here, I've got one unit finishing up a deadly crash investigation, just south of Cortez, and then they'll come straight here. Two other patrol units are on standby, awaiting further notice."

"I've got Gus and Neil on the way," Ben offers, and Drew nods his head. I'm sure this doesn't come as a surprise to him. From what I remember, GFI Investigations worked closely together with the Montezuma Sheriff's Office on more than one occasion. The last time was when Ben, and his then fiancée, were dealing with a stalker who turned violent.

"Makes sense if we set up shop here, if that's okay with you?" Drew asks me, and I just glare. "Right," he continues. "Now, how about we see how your dad is faring with the little one?"

Pops looks up and winks when he sees me come in, leading the way. Becca is still on his lap, but sitting up straight, the mug of hot chocolate clamped in her hands, and her eyes peeking apprehensively over the rim.

"Hey, sweetie," I start, drawing her attention from the men behind me as I sit down on the coffee table in front of her. "You getting warm?" I reach out and brush a red curl from her forehead. At least the kid has some color back in her face.

I'm rewarded with a barely perceptible nod. Small, but I'll take it.

"You remember the sheriff, right?" Another little nod as her eyes drift over my shoulder to the man in question. "And Mak's Uncle Ben?"

I realize my mistake when her eyes pool with tears on hearing her friend's name.

"Take a deep breath, little one," Pops mumbles in her ear, while his eyes plead for caution over her head. I nod my understanding.

"We're going to try and find them, Becca. All of us. The sheriff has deputies who are ready to help, and Uncle Ben has really good friends who helped him before. They're going to be here soon, too. A lot of people want to help, but we need your help first."

Becca looks at me wide-eyed as she slowly lowers the mug, tilting it precariously in the process.

"Here, let me hold on to that for you," Pops intervenes, taking the mug from her hands, but his movements still when she suddenly speaks.

"We thought it was the church people. The white van. It looked like a church van, but it wasn't." I can see the fear return to her eyes as she remembers, and I quickly grab her little hands to anchor her. It seems to work, because she takes in a deep breath before she continues. "He was wearing a ball cap but I know it was him. I saw through the window. I tried to grab Mak's hand, but she was already crossing the road, so I hid in the ditch." Her last words end in a sob, and I act on instinct, reaching out and pulling her onto my own lap, where her arms curl their way around my neck once again. "H-he took them. He h-hurt Stacie and then…h-he grabbed Mak and put both of them in the van. I'm sorry," she mutters, as I stifle a sob of my own.

"You were smart," I tell her, stroking her hair as I fight to hold onto my composure. "You did the right thing, sweetheart. We wouldn't know where to start looking if you hadn't hid, so you could tell us."

"He's right, you know?" Drew says, sitting down beside me on the coffee table and bending his head so he can look her in the eye. "Thank you. You helped me once before, and now you're helping again—telling us about the white van. Did you happen to see if there were windows all along the side of the van?" he probes.

Part of me wants to shield her, but I'm well aware she's the best shot we've got. I hear the door open behind me, and the sound of lowered voices, but I keep my focus on the girl, who's shaking her head.

"No windows on the back, just on the front."

"Panel van," Pops mumbles, before he struggles to his feet and adds, "I'm gonna get some coffee going."

"That's really good," Drew confirms. "Now, did you notice any writing on the side? Any words?" Becca sits up a little straighter and lets go of my neck, nodding her head at the sheriff.

"Two," she says, holding up her fingers to illustrate. "*Carpet* and another *C*-word, but I couldn't see the rest that well."

"Cleaning?"

This time I turn my head to see Neil James, the youngest GFI member, saunter into the room. His big disarming smile is directed at Becca, who startles, and I tighten my grip on her. But the pretty boy looks and the bright smile work as well on her, as I'm sure it does on the slightly older female population.

"I think that's what it said," she says.

"Good," Neil says, sitting down on the couch across from us, opening a laptop, and perching it on his knees. "Let's see if we can find it. Wanna help?" he asks. Before I know it, she's sliding off my lap and taking a seat next to the smugly smiling investigator.

"Always with the damn charm," Ben grumbles behind me.

Leaving Becca in the apparently very capable hands of the younger man, I follow the scent of coffee into the kitchen. Drew close behind me.

Pops is pulling the first steaming mug out of the Keurig and hands it off to the sheriff, who plops his file on the counter as he doctors his coffee with the sugar and cream Pops has put out. I pull the file toward me, and start flipping through it, while waiting for the next cup, when my breath catches in my throat.

Between a bunch of sheets of paper are a few photographs, and although the face staring back at me in the first few is somewhat familiar, it's not until I flip over the last one, obviously dated much further back, that I connect the dots.

The reality of what is staring back at me is almost too much to stomach.

―――――⟨⟩―――――

Stacie

"I was going to dump you in the fucking river first," he says, a smile on his face as he empties a bottle of alcohol around the kitchen island, immediately reaching for another. "But that seemed too fast, too easy. I spent eight fucking years forced to stare at the walls, knowing that my life was over. Only fair I give you a little taste of what that feels like."

He'd walked into the kitchen as if he belonged there, all but ignoring the fact I was no longer on the kitchen floor where he left me. The two brown bags he carried were set on the counter before he even scanned the room; easily finding me huddled against Mak under the table. Almost casually, he mentioned how he had to drive to Cortez to hit up a few stores for the supplies he needed. He matter-of-factly explained buying too many bottles in one place, would make people remember, and he didn't want to be remembered.

He'd been as cool as a cucumber, until now, with some of his seething anger rising to the surface.

"Your life isn't over," I point out, pressing closer to Mak, who is now shivering uncontrollably and watching him empty the second bottle along the floor to the living room.

"No?" he sneers, turning furious eyes on me. "You fucking know it is. You ended it just as surely as I'm ending yours."

"*Shhh*," I soothe Mak, who starts whimpering at his words. I manage to scoot up a little against the table base, so she can press her face against my shoulder. I continue to mumble softly in her hair, hoping the nonsense I spout is drowning out the insane vitriol he's unleashing.

"But first I'm going to have some fun with you. I'll have to pull a fucking bag over that ugly mug of yours first. Maybe I'll do your fucking spawn instead," he spits, a lecherous grin on his face that has the blood freeze in my veins. "Pretty little thing. I'll have my way with her just like they did with me, the first time I turned my back in the showers." He grabs a third bottle from the counter and splashes the alcohol liberally around and on top of the dining room table. "I'm fucking taking back everything you took from me, you evil cunt!"

Mak stiffens against me at the violently hissed profanity, and powerless to do anything else, I start softly singing old nursery rhymes in an attempt to comfort her, all the while frantically going over my options. I'd die first before I'd let him put his sick hands on my baby.

Surely they're looking for us. Henry would've come looking and Nick should be home by now. I have to trust they'll be looking. And Ben…my God, he's been through so much.

So much time has passed though; they may not realize we're still here right under their nose.

"And don't bother trying to undo those," Kevin taunts, dragging me from my thoughts as he apparently catches my continuous attempts to loosen the binds around my wrists and ankles. "Another thing I learned in the slammer. Damp tea towels are much harder to undo than rope and the more you try, the tighter they get." He cackles wildly before adding, "The added benefit is that they burn up easy."

I'm not an idiot. I'd figured he was preparing to set a fire. I fight hard to keep the absolute terror from my face at the thought of, once again, feeling the intense heat eating at my flesh—at my daughter, God forbid. I'm sure he picked a fire for that reason; he wants to feed off my fear.

I'll be damned if I give that to him.

When he comes close, passing with a new, full bottle once again, I pull up my legs and kick out as hard as I can against his legs, setting him stumbling.

"What the...*fuck you, bitch!*"

Before I have a chance to kick out with my legs again, he has hold of my ankles, dragging me out from under the table. I watch his face, contorted with rage, as he hauls back with his fist and knocks my head back. Mak screams once behind me, before she dissolves into an anguished mewling.

"Making you suffer for that, you revolting piece of shit." Spittle flies from his mouth, hitting my face as he leans close, his hand fisted in the front of my shirt, pulling me half off the floor before slamming me back down. "Taking the little bitch with me. Gonna use her up good before I ditch her. I'll make sure you die knowing the suffering I'll put her through is all on you."

I hold on to the piercing pain where his fist slammed into my face, to keep from sinking under, and scream.

Next thing I know, something is forcefully shoved in my mouth. Through the blur of tears, I see he's taken off his shirt and used it as a gag. The pungent stink of sweat and alcohol is thick, and I feel the bile rise. I close my eyes and focus on breathing through my nose, without choking on the stench.

Hearing a rustle behind me, I turn my head and watch through clouded eyes as my daughter is pulled from under the table. She looks in shock, quiet as her hands are bound behind her once again. He props her up against the back door, like a bag of garbage to be taken out.

I try to make eye contact, but Mak's eyes stare unseeingly in the distance. So focused on my little girl, I don't notice him moving around until he sets the brown paper bags with empty bottles beside Mak by the back door.

"Did you know most accidents happen inside the house?" he asks, as he rifles through the kitchen cupboards, pulling out a frying pan and a bottle of oil. I try to move, but my limbs are not cooperating, I can't seem to make any headway. "A lot of them in the kitchen. People carelessly leaving pans unattended on the stove, or leaving the gas on. Sometimes both," he snickers.

I hear the whoosh of a flame and then his boots appear in my view. I look up, pleading with my eyes and the muffled sounds I can make behind my gag, for him to spare my daughter. I already know when I look in those cold eyes; those pleas will go unheard.

"Vindictive little cunt, you are," he hisses, so close a waft of rancid breath hits my face. "Couldn't believe it was you when I saw you in that courtroom. You're good, pretending you didn't know who I was, but you got me good, didn't you?" I'm not sure if it's the hit over my head, but I don't get what he's talking about. "You got me double, really; first when you got me convicted of rape and stuck me in that cage, and second, when as a result; the woman I was scheduled to marry—the same woman who was carrying my *child*—gave up on me. On my baby. The bitch offed herself. My baby never had a fucking chance because of you." He pokes a dirty finger to my forehead. "Just like your baby doesn't stance a chance…because of you."

I force my eyes to stay open, even though I want to close them and shut down. I need to fight for my Makenna, but there is no way my pathetic attempts will get to her before he does. I'm helpless as I watch him pick her up, and toss her over his shoulder. Then, with one arm around her legs and holding the paper bags, he opens the door and steps out.

Straining for a last glimpse of my daughter, all I can see—just before he pulls the door shut behind him—is a large tattoo of a Celtic cross, spanning his shoulder blades.

I swear my heart stops as I listen to the steady hiss of gas filling my kitchen.

CHAPTER 26

Nick

"You look like you've seen a ghost."

Rubbing both hands over my face, I look through my fingers at Ben walking into the kitchen, wearing a look of concern. Noticing the file folder open in front of me, he pulls it toward him and starts flipping through.

"Understatement of the fucking century," I mumble, my earlier nausea back with a vengeance.

"You know him?" Ben asks suspiciously, tapping his index finger on the photograph and eyeing me with intensity. The air in the kitchen crackles as both Drew and my father's heads swivel around at the sharp tone of Ben's voice.

"Years ago. Didn't know him exactly, but saw him around."

God, what a fucked up situation. I don't even know how much detail I should share. I would in an instant if I thought it would help Stacie and Mak, but all I can see is heartbreak.

Ben hammers me with questions, most of which I can't answer, so I confess I saw him only the once.

"It was at a college party. Let's just say the guy made an impression. I've never seen him since."

He knows. The way Ben is looking at me through slitted eyes, he fucking knows the significance of what I just revealed.

The ringing of a phone cuts through the thick tension, and Drew steps out the back door to take the call.

"Found it!" Neil calls from the living room, where he and Becca have been bent over his laptop. Ben's already on the move and I follow him inside.

"Discount Carpet Cleaning, a company in Albuquerque, filed a report for a white panel van stolen from behind their shop," he reads from his screen. "The report indicates the company name is displayed on the side, but some of it's peeled off."

Drew, who walked in during Neil's description, starts barking instructions into the phone before ending the call.

"Roadblocks are up both sides of Dolores. Cortez PD is on the lookout and so is the state patrol."

"Isn't that closing the gate after the horse is gone?"

With a pointed look at Becca, Drew nudges his head to the door.

"I've got her," Pops says, taking Neil's spot on the couch and grabbing the remote from the table.

We follow Drew outside, where Neil puts his fingers to his mouth with an ear-piercing whistle. A large man jogs up the driveway and comes straight up the steps.

"What've you got, Gus?" Drew asks him, after a round of monosyllabic greetings.

"Bupkis. Nothing that'll help us quick. Whatever there is, your guys are collecting," he directs at the sheriff.

Neil fills him in on the white van, and I repeat my question when the roadblocks are brought up.

"This was not a well-planned grab," Drew explains. "All the signs are that Borland saw an opportunity and went with it. First off, stealing a van with identifying markings is obviously an impulsive move. Next, there was no way for him to anticipate the girls to be out there apple picking, so he saw an opportunity and took it. All indicators—he didn't go far. He's familiar with Dolores. My bet is he's here somewhere."

"Agreed," Gus rumbles. "We need to check out empty lots, storefronts, warehouses."

"Trailer park," I blurt out.

"That trailer is still a crime scene," Drew says. "Plus, he wouldn't go where neighbors might recognize him."

"What about that lot on the other side of the rec center?" I counter. "Full of old trailers."

In the next five minutes, we come up with a list of possible locations to start with and divide it between us. Neil is going to stay behind and see if he can get an *eye in the sky*. I have no idea what he's referring to but Gus quietly explains.

"Satellite; kid's good at getting into places with the touch of a button." When I nod my understanding, he turns to the other two. "Back of my truck, grab a radio. Let's go."

Armed with a radio Ben showed me how to use, and instructions to check out the southwest quadrant, south of the highway between the library and the bridge coming into town on the west side, I hop into my truck and follow the others into town.

It's close to eight and almost completely dark by the time I pull into the library parking lot. The girls have been missing for fucking hours, and I struggle not to imagine what he could've done to them in that time.

The library lot is deep, stretching all the way to the river's edge, but other than a car someone left behind, the place is abandoned. Before hitting all the streets in the predominantly residential neighborhood, it makes more sense to check all the major businesses and parking lots along the south side of the highway.

Nothing. Not a damn thing. I haven't heard anything over the radio either.

I turn back into town, but instead of sticking to the main drag, I take the first right that'll get me to Riverside Avenue. It runs parallel to the highway but along the water and has much less traffic. Every block in this neighborhood has an alley that runs behind the yards. I check every one of those, as well as the streets as I slowly roll east along Riverside.

Realizing I'm heading straight for Stacie's house, just as I'm passing Fifth, I inadvertently speed up. Crazy to think that would even be a possibility, but still.

My hand immediately reaches for the radio on the seat beside me when I see the back of a white cargo van, parked in the alley behind her house. I quickly look behind me, and seeing no one, I back up a little and pull off on the side of the road. Keeping the shed between me and the house.

"*Found it*," I call in, throwing all radio protocol out the window. "*Behind Stacie's house.*"

"*Stay put. Don't make a move,*" Drew barks.

"*Need a fucking address.*"

"*Seventh and Riverside, west corner,*" Ben responds to Gus' question, before addressing me. "*Do not fucking move from where you are. Tell me you understand.*"

"*Got it.*"

But even as I'm confirming, I'm getting out of the truck. Fuck it! I need to do something.

I duck and run maybe fifty feet down an exposed part of the trail along the river, to where a copse of trees and thick brush gives me some shelter. I have a better view from this angle, with most of the front and all of the side and back yards in my sights.

There's no light visible through the windows, and with time crawling by, I have second thoughts. It doesn't look like anyone is there, and I should probably have checked to make sure it's even the right van before I radioed it in. Is it possible I've just sent everyone on a wild-goose chase?

Just as I've convinced myself I may have made a mistake, I see a man coming out of the house. The light from the streetlamp on Seventh hits him, just for a moment, before he walks into the shadows, but I can tell he's not wearing a shirt, and he's got something tossed over his shoulder.

Scratch that. He's got *someone* tossed over his shoulder.

All rational thought is gone as I come out from my hiding place and cross Riverside, just as I see him step into the alleyway.

"*Hey!*" I yell out as I turn into the alley and see him opening the back door of the van. He whirls around at the sound of my voice and lowers the small form in front of him. Shielding himself with Mak's little body, one hand curved around her chin and the other on top of her head. Even at this distance, I see the tips of his fingers digging into her cheeks. Something about the hold he has on her freezes the blood in my veins.

"I'll kill her," he says, a smirk on his face. "If you don't stop right where you are, I swear to God I'll snap her scrawny little neck. Amazing the shit you can learn in the slammer."

I stop immediately, my hands up, palms out. I'm close enough so I can see Mak staring at me; the look in her eyes almost vacant. I hope to God she's in shock and not hearing any of this.

A car door slams and running feet crunch on the gravel. I stick my arm out to the side in an attempt to warn whoever is closing in behind me.

"Stay back. He's got Mak."

The footsteps come to an immediate halt and I hear Ben's deep voice behind me.

"Ten-four. Stay cool, I'll take care of this," he says quietly, but I ignore him. I hold perhaps the only weapon that can stop him and negotiating is *my* fucking field of expertise.

"You don't want to hurt her," I tell him, my hands spread out at my side as I take a careful step forward.

"*Fucking stay put*," Ben hisses. I don't listen.

"That's where you're wrong," the man says, chuckling like it's the funniest thing he's heard all day. "I do wanna hurt her. Like I told her vindictive cunt mother, an eye for an eye. She killed my baby, I'm gonna take hers."

"Vindictive?" I pick up on the word that seems out of place in his tirade, inching another step closer.

"Bitch had it in for me the moment she saw me in that courtroom. Went after me like a fucking rabid dog, slapping me with that rape shit." He starts laughing, more like cackling. "Must've thought it was her lucky day, she'd have a chance to get back at me."

"For what?" I ask, knowing full well what he's referring to, but wanting him to lead the way.

"She was a wild bitch at a party, and I tamed her. Nothing me, my cock, and a drop in her drink couldn't handle," he snickers, shrugging his shoulders, but never letting go of Mak's head.

I hear Ben growl behind me as he clues in, but I wave him back with a hand. I've got him right where I want him, like a key witness, lead carefully to a single possible conclusion.

"How long ago?" He looks at me, clearly confused at the question.

"What the fuck difference does that make?" he blusters, shuffling impatiently and taking a quick peek over his shoulder, where Drew and Gus are blocking his exit on the other side of his van. "Nine, maybe ten years?"

Got him.

"Do you know how old she is?" I gesture at Makenna, who hangs limply in his hold.

Stacie

I wonder if I'm pregnant.

Funny, the stuff you think about when your life is hissing away.

It's only a matter of seconds before the oil flames in the pan will ignite the gas, and yet my mind has jumped to the last time I saw Nick. Why does it feel so long ago? I remember feeling him slide out of me; I remember his words. Unlike the only other time I had unprotected sex.

That's the jump my mind made; from the shock of seeing the only memory I have of another night long ago when my mind was not in charge—to Nick, and a baby.

A sad thought: I'd not only failed to protect the one I had, but wouldn't be able to save even the promise of another.

In a sudden burst of adrenaline, I surge up, using every little muscle I have at my disposal, while ignoring the screaming pain of my body. Pulling my knees up, I plant my heels in the sopping rug and shove my butt back. I do it again. And again. As far away from the stove as I can get.

Tears stream down my face with the strain, or perhaps it's with the realization that my final effort to at least try to save myself is futile. But anything is better than not doing something while death is coming at you hard.

Too many regrets.

If by some miracle I survive—my little girl survives—I vow never to live a life filled with regrets. No opportunity will be left untested. Every moment will be lived and celebrated, treasured for the beautiful gift it is. I won't be hiding anymore. Not my face and not my heart. Not from Nick, not from anyone.

With the dining table between me and the kitchen, I scurry around to where my back is against the base and my head is braced underneath the tabletop.

This moment right here is a choice; to cower here, waiting for the inevitable—or to fucking live and fight, until there is nothing left.

With the last bit of strength I have, I heave up, toppling the table on its side, and I collapse, spent, behind it.

I don't have time to draw a breath when all air is sucked from around me. A chaotic flash of sound and light erupts before I slip into a painless dark.

Nick

"The fuck you say," he mumbles, his eyes wide in disbelief. "The fuck…"

I watch as he slowly releases his hold on the little girl, letting her slide down the front of his body, and collapse at his feet.

The next moment—a loud explosion, followed by a spray of debris, shakes me to the core. I immediately crouch and turn to the house, as smoke pours from a massive hole in the back wall where the kitchen window and door used to be.

Without hesitation, I am on my feet and running with the rattle of falling glass around me. Straight toward the house where flames are shooting from the opening.

"*Anastasia!*"

There is absolutely no doubt in my heart that she is in there, somewhere in that infernal devastation is the woman whose mere existence is my reason for breathing.

I don't register the chaos of voices and screams behind me, as I catapult myself through the thick smoke and flames, right into the pits of hell.

Scrambling for purchase with my feet on the rubble, I squint against the smoke and look for something, anything, recognizable. Flames shoot up from everywhere. I instantly know an accelerant was used.

"Stacie!" I yell, but am punished immediately by the astringent burn of smoke down my airway.

Coughing, I pull the neck of my shirt over my mouth—for all the good it will do—and focus on the one recognizable thing on this side of the house; the dining room table. It's on its side, the tabletop on fire, but I can still see the gouges and divots from flying debris.

"*Fucking hell*," I hear Ben swear behind me, before he too bursts out coughing.

The sounds of the fire is something I've never experienced before. Crackling, hissing, moaning, and whenever she finds a new source of air, or combustible element to feed her, her roar is deafening.

That's why I don't hear what Ben is yelling, until he gives my shoulder a firm shake and points at the dining table.

"We've gotta lift it. Something's moving."

Moving means alive, and I don't even waver, I grab onto the burning surface on one side, Ben on the other, and together we heave it over.

"*Jesus*," Ben hisses, but all words are stuck in my throat as I recognize Stacie's blonde hair under the blood and the dirt.

Immediately I clear her body of debris, slide my arms underneath her, and lift her up. There's no waiting for backboards when the fucking house is burning down around you.

Ignoring Ben, who seems frozen, I hurry away from the flames and out the front door, the woman who holds all of my heart in my arms.

CHAPTER 27

Stacie

"Can I come in?"

Drew's head pokes in the door.

"*Yes,*" I answer, more of a rasp than an actual sound, but he gets the gist and sits down on the chair beside my hospital bed.

He's the first familiar face I've seen since I woke up in this bed a short while ago. Medical personnel have been in and out, poking and prodding, and I let them after the nurse assured me my daughter was fine.

From what I gather, I was knocked out, have a large laceration on the back of my head, a fractured orbital bone, suffered some smoke inhalation, and other than that: bruises, cuts, and scrapes. The first was stitched, the last were cleaned and bandaged, and the rest of my injuries have to heal on their own. The irony is, other than singed hair, I did not sustain any burns.

"*Where is everyone? Have you seen Mak? Is she okay?*" I pepper Drew with questions, which only results in a coughing fit that hurts enough to fill my eyes with tears.

"Do I need to get a nurse?" Drew asks, worried. I shake my head as I try to get some air. "Let me do the talking, okay? Your daughter is with Nick's father and Becca in the cafeteria. Neil drove him and the girl here, because Nick refused medical treatment until there was someone familiar who could look after Mak."

"*He's hurt?*" I manage, without dissolving in more coughing.

"He pulled you out of a burning house," Drew says. "His soft manicured hands won't look the same." I open my mouth in Nick's defense, when I notice the smirk on his face. *Tease.* "He and Ben went right through the flames to get to you," he continues more solemnly.

"*Ben?*"

"Saw him walk out, so he's fine, but I'm not sure where he's off to." It's out of character and I scrutinize Drew's face for answers, but he looks away, glancing out the window instead. "Borland is in custody," he informs me. "I'm about to head over to question him, but he's tucked away safely. You can breathe easy now."

"*Good.*" I blink furiously to keep the tears of relief at bay. A warm hand covers mine and gives it a squeeze.

"I wish we could've grabbed him before he hurt you, Stacie—before he was able to do all this damage. Your house…Jesus."

I lift my hand up, palm out, to stop him.

"*Doesn't matter,*" I rasp, remembering the last thoughts I had when I was sure my time had come. "*Things don't matter.*"

Drew nods once, sharply, before he gets up, leans over the bed and kisses me on the forehead.

"I'll be in touch."

I watch his broad back disappear out the door and close my eyes.

-

"Hey, beautiful."

I blink a few times to find Nick beside my bed, his voice not much better than mine. I notice both his hands are bandaged up. He sees and shrugs.

"Your hands."

"It's not too bad. They'll heal," he assures me. "Will it hurt if I kiss you?"

I smile and shake my head, as he's already lowering his mouth to mine, pressing gently against my lips.

"*Love you,*" he whispers, never losing contact, so I can feel his words brush my skin.

"With all my heart," I respond, and his gaze, just inches from mine, goes liquid.

"You okay?"

"I'll be fine," I assure him and watch as his eyes close.

We stay like that for a bit. Staying as close as our injuries will allow, breathing in each other's air. Communicating everything with just the slightest touch. No words are needed.

"Mak?" I finally ask, and he pulls back a little.

"She has some bruising where he held her." A dark shadow passes over his face, and he looks away. "They'll heal."

"Nick?" I wait until his eyes meet mine again. "Tell me, what's wrong with my baby? Why isn't she here?"

He swallows hard; I watch his Adam's apple move and brace myself.

"It was hard on her. The whole situation was so fucked up. By the time I got to them, she looked like she'd checked out—like there was no one home."

My poor baby. Such a tough little cookie she'd seemed the first time I ended up in the hospital. While everyone else had still been struggling to process what happened, my little girl seemed to take it all in stride. I thought it had been such a blessing, that she moved right along, never showing any adverse effects. Fuck, even as recently as the first time we met Henry, she'd talked about me almost dying as if she was discussing homework. I should've known the other shoe would drop. I just wish she hadn't had to go through the additional trauma.

"Bring her to me," I urge Nick, who slowly shakes his head. "I mean it. She needs to see me."

"Baby, I tried," he says, his voice pained. "The doctor says she's in shock and it will eventually pass. She doesn't say anything or react to much, except when I asked if she wanted to see you. She started to wail."

There is nothing that hurts as sharply as your child's pain. My hand comes up automatically, pushing hard between my breasts, as if to contain the building pressure on my heart.

"Bring her to me," I repeat. "Right now, Nick. I need to see her...No—she needs to see *me*."

Call it instinct, but I just know whatever is festering inside her will only become more damaging the longer we let it. The wound has to bleed clean before we can allow it to scab over.

"I'm not sure," Nick starts. "What if—"

"Please," I implore, cutting off his objections. "Trust me."

Nick pauses, staring at me intently before he finally gets up, and without a word, leaves the room.

It doesn't take long before I hear her coming down the hall. The low-pitched keening like an animal in pain. The sound cuts right through me and my breath stalls in my chest.

Nick marches in the door, carrying Mak in his arms, ignoring the nurse trying to stop him. He doesn't even pause, but comes straight to my bed, where he lays Makenna on top of me.

My arms immediately wrap tightly around her, and I bury my face in her hair, mumbling soothing nonsense.

Nick

It kills me, walking out of that room, hustling the nurse out in front of me. I trust Stacie, though. I trust she knows what she's doing, because I don't fucking have a clue.

"Sir, you can't just leave that child…calling security…" the nurse prattles on and I don't even hear half of what she says. I step back, so I'm blocking the door and turn to face her.

"That child has been through trauma most adults will never face in their lifetime," I bite off, getting into her space. "Twice in this year alone," I spit, holding two fingers up to her face. "She needs her mother. She needs to touch, hear, and smell her mother."

"But…"

"You'll have to go through me to get in."

I fold my arms over my chest in an attempt to show her how serious I am. It seems to work when she turns on her heels and stomps off down the hall. My legs feel suddenly weak and I slide my ass down the door until it hits the floor. I stare out the window that lines the hallway to see the day start to dawn.

Yet I worry. There's no way to know how much of what I said in that alley registered with Mak, but everyone else who was there sure as fuck got it. The idea of Mak having to go through life, carrying that as her burden, kills me. She's been through enough.

Fuck. I hate to think of my Anastasia having to deal with that, but I know it's only a matter of time before she finds out. I have no choice but to tell her. She'll likely hate me for it, but she would hate me more if she found out she was the only one out of the loop.

It takes a while for me to register that I no longer hear Makenna's crying, and I scramble to get up. Sitting down without the use of your hands is a fuckload easier than trying to get up again. I finally manage and gingerly push open the door to peek in.

The first thing I see is Stacie's beautiful blue eyes, staring at me over her daughter's dark hair. I can hear her continued soft whispers and Mak's occasional sniffles. Stacie nods her head almost imperceptibly and I inch my way forward.

"Mommy's right here, baby. Only a few bumps and bruises, but I'm fine. I promise. I'm not going anywhere. Mommy's going to be right here…"

The litany of assurances brings a lump to my throat, as I sit down beside the bed and rest my hand on Mak's back.

"Told you she was okay," I add my voice to the mix. Mak's head immediately turns to face me, and for the first time since Thursday night, when she kissed me goodnight, I see life in the little girl's eyes. "Hey, you," I coo, as Stacie falls silent, finally giving her ravaged voice a rest. "Is it okay if you sit on my lap for a bit? So Mommy can have a drink? I promise you can hold onto her hand the whole time."

I don't know what the right thing to do is here. All I know is that Stacie is hurting and Mak is scared, and I want to fix them both.

Initially it looks like Mak will balk, but then she surprises me with a little nod as she reaches out her hand.

-

"Are you ready to head home?"

We simultaneously turn to the door as the doctor walks in, a stack of papers in her hand.

"Well…" Stacie hesitates, as the woman's face falls.

"Yikes, dang, I'm sorry," she hurries to amend. "Do you have a place to go?"

"She has a home, yes," I insert, watching the two little girls, playing some game on the floor, paying way too much attention to the conversation to be healthy. Their nine-year-old worlds have seen as much devastation and uncertainty as I will allow.

I already tried to discuss it with my father, but I barely had a chance to get a word out, before Pops shut me up with a glare. "Boy, I may be old but I'm not too old to cuff your ears if you even think about asking stupid questions."

That had settled that. The girls were coming home.

It takes the woman fifteen minutes to go over the list of aftercare, prescriptions for pain medication and some supplements, and cautions on what to look out for.

"Are you sure?" Stacie asks once the doctor leaves. "I don't want to assummmm..." Her words are smothered when I cut her off with a kiss. "Okay then," she mutters when I lift away.

She brushes distractedly at the bandage around her head, looking cutely flustered. My hands may be out of commission for a bit, but my lips work fine.

I turn my head to the girls at the sound of soft giggles. Their heads are close together and both of them, like mirror images, have a hand covering their mouths. To my surprise I see, more so than hear, Mak talk to her little friend. I glance over at Stacie, who is watching them as well.

With both Stacie and I dressed in some borrowed scrubs, since our clothes were not worth salvaging, Neil walks in.

"Ready, folks?"

"Where's Pops?" I ask, looking around him down the hall.

"Gus is driving him home in your truck and he's letting me drive his badass Yukon." I have to chuckle at the big boyish grin on the younger man's face. "Took me forever, but when I suggested the girls would likely be more comfortable with me in the car, he had to concede."

Neil is pushing Stacie down the hall in a wheelchair, and I follow behind, each of the girls holding on to a wrist.

During the drive home, I half listen to the soft whispers of the two girls beside Stacie in the back seat. I wanted to insist she take the front, but she said she'd much prefer to be close to the girls. I gave in.

"I want to see the house," Stacie says when we drive into Dolores. I shift in my seat to look behind me.

"I'll take you," I promise. "But not today. Jen contacted me earlier; she is at the house, working with the fire department to try and salvage as much as they can. She'll be by later tonight."

I hope that would be enough to get that idea put on the back burner, because I don't want her to see what Jen warned me about earlier. Something Gus is on his way to deal with. Namely, Ben, who apparently has been camped out in his truck across from the wreckage of her house, passed out in a drunken stupor.

"Okay," she says quietly, looking back at me, a serious expression on her face. I'm willing to bet, if not for the girls sitting right beside her, she would have a few pointed questions for me. That'll have to wait till later.

"Stacie?" Becca suddenly pipes up. "Is it true that Nick is going to be Mak's daddy?"

Neil snorts loudly beside me, before reeling it in, and I twist even further in my seat so I can see Becca's little freckled-face. Mak, who is wedged between her friend and Stacie, has her head down and her eyes on her lap. Stacie looks a bit taken aback. As for me, I can't keep the grin off my face, because if I have anything to say on the matter, that's exactly what will happen.

"I don't know, sweetie," Stacie says, with an apologetic glance in my direction, before turning to the little girls. "I can't see into the future that far ahead, but for now, Nick and his pops are nice enough to let us live with them. That's kind of like a family, for now."

"Not kind of," I interject. "It *is* a family. We all belong."

Becca smiles broadly, Stacie's face softens at my words, but Mak—she looks up at me with that blank look back in her eyes.

CHAPTER 28

Stacie

"I can't get hold of Ben."

I stand up straight at the sound of Isla's concern over the phone.

We got home yesterday to find Henry on crutches in the kitchen, with a removable cast covering the bottom half of his leg. Apparently he got checked out sometime the night before, and although he didn't break anything, he's torn some ligaments in his ankle. The cast is supposed to give him some added support while he heals. Quite the motley crew we are.

We watched a bunch of lighthearted movies with the kids yesterday and ordered pizza for dinner. The girls went to bed early, exhausted from the lack of sleep since Saturday.

Everyone is still sleeping, even Henry, who often beats me to the Keurig in the mornings. Of course, I've had more sleep in the past couple of days than everyone else combined, which is probably why I'm up with the birds.

I lean on the counter while the Keurig sputters and hisses, signaling my second coffee is brewed, when my phone rings.

"Isla? He hasn't called you?" I know he's been avoiding me, since my calls all end up with voicemail, but

I thought for sure he'd have been in touch with his wife. "I mean, I thought it was odd he didn't show up in the hospital, but I was given the impression he was busy dealing with the authorities."

"Hospital? Authorities?" I wince at the shrill edge to her voice. "What the hell is going on? He never said anything! I haven't talked to him since Saturday morning. It's two days later without a word, and now you tell me there's a hospital involved? What the fuck?"

Before I have a chance to explain anything, I hear sounds of a shuffle and then Isla's Uncle Al is on the line.

"My niece is flipping the hell out, which in turn is upsetting the baby, so it'd be helpful if you talked to me, so I can calm this shit down."

Trying to be as concise as I can, I give him the Cliff Notes version of events. The thing about Uncle Al is that, being former law enforcement, he knows when to listen and when to ask on point questions. Therefore it doesn't take me long to get him sufficiently up-to-date, and Al asks me to hold so he can relay the information.

"Right," he says when he gets back on the line. "Glad to hear you're physically okay, and I promise I'll give you all the appropriate sympathies for what you've been through—again—but where the hell is your brother? You'll appreciate I'm not buying into him being busy and not calling his wife, when prior to this weekend he was calling her all hours of the goddamn day and night."

Suddenly I'm really concerned. It didn't occur to me to question the story he was busy. I may have even considered he might have been a bit peeved that Nick has taken over his role as my protector, but none of that would have kept my brother from calling his wife. Something else is going on.

"That's not like him," I agree.

"No, it's not. Now I recognize you may not be in any shape to go up the mountain and check on him, but is there anyone else?" he probes, and in the seconds following his question, I think, consider, and come to a conclusion that I'm not going to share.

"There is," I lie instead, which is met with a heavy silence that I quickly fill with a follow-up. "I'm staying with Nick and I'll ask him to go." My fingers are crossed behind my back, as if that would negate my deception.

"Tell him to call his wife—this morning," he grumbles before ending the call.

Protective as any of the men in my life, Al would not take kindly if he knew I am planning to head up that mountain by myself.

-

"*Jesus*. Close those damn blinds."

My brother is not okay.

This time of morning there were few people on the road on my way into town, and even fewer on the road up the mountain.

I'd thought to leave a note on the kitchen counter and managed to sneak out undetected. I was tempted to stop for a macchiato when I spotted the coffee shop in the distance, but figured I'd draw too much attention with my head bandaged and my face messed up. Not to mention my attire. Dolores is pretty casual, but I'm sure my *Hello Kitty* PJ pants would turn some heads. Tempting, but I resisted and turned right instead, up the mountain.

Ben's SUV was parked out front, so I knew he was home, but no one answered my knocks on the door. Luckily, Nick gave me back the spare I reattached to my car keys and I got in that way.

The place is dark and smells like a distillery. Even though it's getting light enough outside, little of it is filtering through the blinds that are closed everywhere. I didn't even notice my brother on the couch, leaning forward with his head in his hands, until now.

"What the hell is wrong with you?" I ask, clearly surprising him. His head snaps up, his eyes squinted to slits, as he takes me in top to bottom.

"The fuck are you doing here? You look like shit."

There are two empty scotch bottles on the table, and Ben is slurring his words, so I'm not taking what he says to heart. Instead, I place my hands on my hips and work up a good steam.

"Me? Let's talk about you! You're wife has been trying to get hold of you; she's frantic. I've been trying to get hold of you since I got out of the hospital where, for the fucking record, you were painfully absent." Ben's head sinks down again, his shoulders slumping and part of me feels bad. "What are you doing drinking? I've never known you to drink in excess. What is going on?"

"Isla called?"

"She's really worried, Ben. You're not answering your phone."

He reaches for his back pocket and tries to pull his phone free, and ends up toppling over, swearing up a storm.

"I'm hammered," he admits, running one hand through his silver hair, while fiddling with his phone in the other. "It's dead," he announces, tossing it at the table and missing by a mile. It ends up hitting the carpet underneath the table, luckily.

"Where is your charger?"

"Kitchen."

I bend over to pick it up when a wave of dizziness has me grab onto the edge of the coffee table.

"*Fuck,*" he bites off, leaning forward to grab me by the hips and pulling me down beside him on the couch. Then he drops his head back in his hands. I decide to let the silence speak and it doesn't take long before he breaks. "I'm a fucking mess."

I pull my own phone from my pocket and dial Isla's number back.

"Hey, honey," I tell her when she answers. "He's sitting beside me."

"Everything okay?" she wants to know immediately, and I decide not to pull any punches.

"I think he needs you here."

"Is that her?" Ben asks, turning to look at me, his eyes haunted. Instead of answering, I shove the phone at him.

I get up, giving him the illusion of privacy as I walk into the kitchen to find his charger, pretending not to listen to his side of the conversation. I don't care; I'm concerned about his wellbeing. He sounds defeated as he answers Isla with monosyllabic responses.

"Me too, baby. Me too." I hear him say and tears sting my eyes as I busy myself making a massive pot of coffee. He's gonna need it.

I hear his footsteps lumbering in my direction and resist turning around. He walks right up behind me and drops his forehead on my shoulder, and I wince at the wave of body odor and alcohol coming off him.

"I froze," he mumbles.

"What do you mean; you froze?" I don't move, bracing my hands on the counter, hoping he'll keep talking.

"You're lying there: soot, blood, debris covering you. I couldn't. I just couldn't. Not again."

Now I move. I turn around and with my eyes closed against the tears wanting to fall; I throw my arms around his neck and bury my face in his neck. Stench be damned.

"Still here," I whisper against his skin. "I'm fine. I'm still here."

"Yeah," he says, his arms tightening around my body painfully, but I ignore it.

We stand like that for what seems like a very long time, when he puts his hands on my shoulders and puts me back a step. His bleary eyes trace my face.

"Jesus, Sis. Jesus." He slightly shakes his head, before glancing over my shoulder at the coffee pot. "Good. Let me grab a quick shower."

"Excellent," I respond, pretending both our eyes aren't wet. "'Cause you reek." He starts walking out of the kitchen toward the back of the house, when I call after him, "We'll talk after?"

Instead of answering, he gives me a thumbs-up sign over his shoulder. I'll take it.

Nick

"I can't believe you knew."

This day started out with me angry at Stacie because she'd taken off without waking me. I won't easily forget the twenty minutes of sheer panic at finding her gone, before Pops came in from the kitchen, waving her note between his fingers.

I was going to get in my truck and follow her up the mountain, but Pops held me back. He didn't even have to say anything; all he did was point at the two girls on the couch, with eyes as big as saucers at my ranting. I shut my trap pretty fucking fast and dropped my keys on the kitchen counter.

Stacie showed up a few hours later, Ben's SUV following behind. The guy looked like he'd gone on a serious bender. When Gus and Neil dropped off my truck yesterday afternoon, Gus mentioned he'd been drunk when he dropped him home earlier. They planned to check in on him again when they dropped off his SUV. He'd left that parked across from Stacie's devastated house.

She was pissed, but when I tried to talk to her she'd cut me off, hissing, "*Later.*"

Well, it's later; Ben went home with promises he wouldn't drink again tonight. He'd wanted to clean a little, since Isla called this afternoon to say Uncle Al had packed up a U-Haul trailer, and they would be heading out first thing tomorrow morning.

The girls are in bed and so is Pops. He gave me a look before he made his excuses, knowing damn well I did something to end up in the doghouse.

"I thought it was under control," I tell her, guessing she's talking about the Ben issue, but with the way she's white-knuckling her hold on that picture I'd shoved back in the closet, I can't be one-hundred-percent sure.

It doesn't matter, it's clear from the way she rolls her eyes—or rather, her eye, since the other one is still pretty swollen—that I've clearly said the wrong thing.

"He's *my* brother, my responsibility. I had a right to know something was wrong."

"And you're *my* responsibility," I fire back. "When Neil gave me a heads-up, I made a judgment call, based on the fact that you were just released from the hospital." She opens her mouth to object but I raise my hand to stop her. "Let me finish; if anyone needed your attention and reassurance, it was those two, very scared and confused girls. So yes, I made that call and I'd make it again without hesitation."

Stubborn and independent woman she is, her struggle to accept what I'm saying is blatantly obvious, but she eventually nods. Her way of conceding to my point, and that's good enough for me. This isn't about *who's* right, it's about *what's* right.

I didn't expect her to be done, and she doesn't disappoint.

"Maybe you can explain then, why you had my picture in the closet in your bedroom. Paid a ridiculous amount of money for it, too. It's creepy."

I take the frame from her hands and hang it back on the wall, where I had it before. I lie down on my bed and fold my arms behind my head, my eyes on the gorgeous black and white print.

"Not creepy," I finally say, turning my eyes on her. "I won't lie, I'd have paid double that ridiculous amount to get my hands on that picture. Never thought I'd have a chance with you. I told you that. I still didn't at the time of the charity auction." She snorts derisively and I recognize this is something we'll likely always disagree on, but that's okay. As far as it comes to disagreements, I could think of much worse ones. "It seemed like the only way for me to have you close. I don't regret it for a minute."

"Then why did you hide it from me?" She wants to know and it's a fair question, but I don't know how she'll take my answer.

"You just had plastic surgery," I explain. "You were pleased with the results, I didn't think you'd appreciate being confronted with a *before* picture every night. That was the only reason. Nothing nefarious."

I watch closely for her reaction, but I can't see much as she takes a long look at the picture. Then she moves to the other side of the bed and lies down beside me, her hand finding mine on the mattress.

"That's a good explanation."

That's how we fall asleep, our fingers laced, lying side by side. A few things cleared up, but the big elephant in the room as yet untouched, and I don't know how she'll react when she finds out there is a far bigger, more damaging secret I've kept from her.

-

I have no clue what time it is when little hands shake my arm, waking me up, but it's still pitch dark.

"What's up, pumpkin?" I whisper when I recognize Becca's red hair. "You have a bad dream?" She shakes her head, her red curls bouncing around her face.

"Mak is crying."

I swing my legs over the side and am on my feet immediately. I lift Becca up on the bed, covering her with the sheets.

"You snuggle up with Stacie, okay? I'll go check on Mak."

The moment I walk out of our room, I can hear her whimpers. I walk in the girls' room and Mak is rolling from side to side, her face wet with tears, muttering unintelligibly. Rather than wake her, I crawl into the bed and gather her in my arms. The moment my arms close around her she starts to struggle.

"No, I don't want to go. No…"

"Wake up, Makenna," I encourage her, sitting her up with me. Trying to calm her down without waking her is obviously not working. "Come on, sweetheart. Wake up."

Her body still struggling, she slowly opens her eyes, looking at me with the ghosts of her dreams lingering in her gaze.

"Hey, you," I start, but I don't get any further.

"I don't want to go with him," she whispers; fear stark on her features.

"Go with who, Mak?"

"That man. He was mean."

"Yes, he was, which is why the sheriff put him in jail. And you're not going anywhere, sweetheart," I reassure her, curling her against my chest. "I'll make sure of it."

Some time passes and I wonder if she's drifted off again, when she suddenly speaks up.

"Will you stay?"

Somehow I get the feeling she's not only talking about just now.

"You bet."

"Why don't you bring her to our bed?" My head shoots up to find Stacie leaning against the doorway. "It's big enough for all of us. I think we could all use some comfort."

I get up and lift a very pliable and tired Mak in my arms. I lean in to press a kiss on Stacie's lips as I pass her. I put Mak in the center of the bed beside Becca, who is already fast asleep.

"Do you have a minute?" Stacie whispers behind me and I follow her back out into the hall. She reaches around me and pulls the door halfway shut before she turns to face me. "Does she know?"

"Sorry?"

"Ben told me what you did in that alley. What you said."

"Fucking hell," I hiss, tilting my head back and staring at the ceiling, trying to keep my cool. "I wanted to tell you myself."

"I knew," she says, putting a hand on my chest as she completely blows me away.

"How?"

"The tattoo on his back. It's the only thing I remember from that night."

I pull her into my arms and look down in her face.

"I'm sorry."

"Not your fault. None of it is your fault," she says, trying to smile but I can see it costs her. "But I need to know if Mak knows." I shake my head firmly before answering her.

"No. She has no idea. Trust me," I try to convince her. I'm not saying she won't clue in at some point, when she's older, but right now I really don't think she would've picked up on that.

"I trust you," she says, leaning her forehead against my chest.

After the roller coaster ride we've had—not to mention our earlier argument—those words anchor deep in my heart.

CHAPTER 29

Stacie

Settling into some kind of routine has been hard for all of us these past few days.

The only one who seems to take everything in his stride, is Henry.

Despite the cast on his leg, he's been out feeding the horses every morning; sometimes, taking one or both of the girls to help him out.

Since Monday night, Mak has had more nightmares, so the girls have ended up in our bed, just about every night. I don't mind. I feel better keeping them close anyway, and wouldn't even bother putting them to bed in their own room, but both Nick and his pops insist that might not be smart. The argument, which eventually convinced me to agree with them, was something Henry brought up. He suggested that being the independent woman I am, he figured I'd want the girls to grow up self-sufficient as well, clearly implying that coddling them too much might not be conducive to that.

Manipulative old coot. Too bad he's right.

Nick, very wisely, kept silent, although he had a hard time hiding the smug smile on his face. Needless to say, I was not in the best of moods after that discussion. Even the kids stayed out of my way.

Nick has been back at work since Wednesday, and I've picked up on schoolwork with the girls, so they won't be too far behind when they go back after the weekend. It was actually their teacher who suggested giving them some time to let life settle down around them, in a way they can trust, when I called to update her. It made sense.

Even Ben, since the return of his wife and child, seems to be finding his stride again.

The only person who still walks around, waiting for the next shoe to drop, is me.

That's why, when Drew called earlier this morning, asking if I could possibly come into Cortez to sign my statement, I jumped at the chance. Killing two birds with one stone, I checked with the hospital to see if I could possibly pop in today, instead of tomorrow, to get my stitches removed. Since Nick had to be in court this morning, Henry agreed to keep an eye on the girls.

I'm ridiculously excited to be doing something by myself. Don't get me wrong, I love having the kids, and Nick and Henry close, but I haven't been out of this house since Monday and I am getting a little cabin-fevered.

The best news I got though is that I was allowed to wash my hair. The prospect of heading into town with the dirty mop I've been sporting for almost a week now, wasn't exactly an appealing prospect, but the nurse I spoke to at the hospital gave me the green light.

Swelling on my face has gone down, and what is left of the bruising is easily covered with some concealer. Looking in the mirror, I'm shocked at how pleased I am with my appearance. The scarring, although better after the surgery, is nevertheless still present, but after the way I looked this past week, I'm struck at how welcome my reflection is this morning. A far cry from a few months ago; when I avoided the mirror or any other reflective surfaces.

The face in the mirror has become comfortably familiar. The face is me.

-

"You're alone?" Drew says, looking past me when I'm shown into his office. "Would've expected Nick, if not Ben, to tag along."

"Nick is in court and Ben doesn't know I'm here, which is fine by me," I snip, a little irritated he so easily deflates my balloon of independence. "Everyone seems to have forgotten that for many years I've worked on the legal side of law enforcement, and been a single mother to my daughter, without the *benefit* of a man to look out for me." I almost spit out the word benefit.

"Whoa," Drew responds, his hands up defensively. "I intended that to reflect on those two chest-pounding gorillas—not on you."

Embarrassed for overreacting, I still can't help chuckling at the comparison of Nick to a ape. The man has different sides to him, as I've come to discover. The Ferragamo and Bosch wearing side, and then the one wearing Wranglers and Henley. Add to that a sensitivity I can't quite place with either the confident corporate or the rugged rancher side of him, but it is as much a part of him.

"Who are you calling a primate?"

I swing around at the deep voice to find a smiling Nick walking in the room. Ignoring Drew, he closes the distance between us, wraps an arm around my waist, and pulls me close, before covering my slack mouth with his in a very thorough kiss. When he finally lifts his head, he immediately lifts his eyes to Drew, behind us, a big shit-eating grin on his face.

Ticked off, I shove both my hands hard in his chest, which sadly barely moves him.

"Did you just piss on me? Marking your claim? What are you even doing here?"

Drew's chuckle behind me, and Nick's fake look of innocence only incites me more. I growl my displeasure through clenched teeth, and plop down in one of the seats facing Drew's desk. From the corner of my eye, I watch Nick sit down in the chair beside me.

"Court recessed for lunch. Called home to check in and Pops mentioned you were coming here. It's around the corner, so I thought I'd drop in."

"Right," Drew says, amusement still clear on his face. "I need you to read through this and make sure it accurately reflects what you told me. If it does, I need you to sign it."

I take the papers he hands me and start reading. Scanning the written statement, I mark a few inconsistencies, while listening with half an ear to the guys making small talk. It isn't until I hear Nick mention Kevin Borland's name, that I start paying attention.

"He's just down the street in county jail," I hear Drew answer.

"Does he have representation?" I interject, drawing a growl from Nick's side.

"Please tell me you're not thinking of offering up as his defense lawyer," he grumbles.

"No." My answer is firm, but that doesn't mean the possibility didn't flash through my mind for a moment. "I want to put him away, not clear him, but given his connection to my daughter, you can't blame me for checking."

"He retained his own counsel, actually," Drew says, surprising me. "A Durango firm. Turns out Mr. Borland is not without means. Apparently money that he and his fiancée had saved up in a joint bank account for their wedding, and a down payment on a house for their expanding family."

A surge of guilt threatens to turn my stomach at the mention of his wife-to-be and their child, and I draw in deep air through my clenched teeth. Nick's large hand rubs up my spine and lands loosely around the back of my neck, calming me.

"He's talking some, though. Facing a combined sentence for his list of charges, including second-degree murder, first-degree kidnapping times two, and the probation violation, which would carry weight against him in court, can do that. Never seeing the light of day again is a distinct possibility, so perhaps he is trying to clear a path toward a possible settlement, should the DA be willing to consider." The former ADA in me immediately considers the benefits and pitfalls.

"I would offer to waive the probation violation and the smaller charges, drop the second-degree murder charge to manslaughter, in return for a guilty plea to all remaining charges, avoiding the need for a lengthy, painful trial," I muse, thinking over all the possible scenarios. "The girls would both be spared testifying, and he'd still get no less than thirty to thirty-five years in total."

"Want me to suggest that to the DA?" Drew jokes, a smile on his face.

"You could," I concede, shrugging. "He might even listen; I offer the added benefit of a victim's perspective on all of this. But be sure to mention the savings of a settlement versus trial as well. Money always talks."

"That it does."

Nick's been quiet throughout that exchange and during the time it takes me to initial my handwritten changes and sign my statement, but when I put my pen down, he finally says something.

"Can I take you out for lunch?"

"Excellent, I'm hungry," Drew quips, pretending to get up. "Mexican sounds good."

"Not you, you moron," Nick fires back; rolling his eyes. "Although I could go for some Mexican."

"Tequila's?" I suggest, that being the spot he took me to the first time he invited me.

"Where else?"

Nick

"I'm coming into the office on Monday."

We've just finished our tamales and are sitting back, letting the food settle. The waitress stops by to collect our plates and asks if we want to see the dessert menu. Both of us opt for a coffee instead.

"You sure you don't want more time?" I propose, but Stacie shakes her head.

"If this morning showed me anything, it's that I do much better on the move than when I'm sitting still, but that's not the only reason," she confesses, leaning over the table and taking my hand. "I want to find out exactly what is involved in adopting Becca. Pick Doug Grant's brain a little; I'm sure he knows more than I do."

I suppress a smile. Absolutely, Doug knows more, and what he didn't know before, he's fast finding out, since I already asked him to look into it. He also knows Rita Mayers, the social worker from the CPS, having dealt with her before, and offered to connect with her to find out how to proceed with a possible adoption.

"I'm sure he does," I agree, making a mental note to warn Doug not to let anything slip on the second part of my inquiries, since I want to find a good moment and the right time to bring that idea to Stacie's attention, but with only fifteen minutes to get back to the courthouse, now is not it. "I've already put a bug in his ear about the possibility, and he says he's happy to help."

The rewarding smile she gives me is open, happy, and untainted by shadows. I'm about to tell her how beautiful she is when my phone rings.

"Pops," I answer, after a quick glance at the screen. Across from me Stacie's attention is immediately piqued. "What's up?"

"Did you know that little girl's birthday is on Sunday?" Pops sounds gruff, almost accusatory.

"Becca?"

"Yup. I'd made them mac and cheese for lunch, and they both mentioned wanting it for their birthday dinners. She about blew me over when I asked when their birthdays were, and she said Sunday."

"Shit. Okay, I'm actually just finishing up lunch with Stacie. I'll fill her in. We'll handle it," I assure him, looking over at Stacie who is almost bouncing in her seat. "Thanks for the heads-up."

"Kid should have a birthday," he grumbles indignantly.

"We'll handle it, Pops," I repeat, before adding, "I've gotta go. See you later."

"What?"

Stacie almost launches out of her seat when I end the call, and I quickly fill her in.

"How did I not know that? Already I'm a horrible mother to that girl." I bust out laughing at the dramatic look on her face, which promptly changes to an angry scowl.

"Come on," I cajole. "We've had a thing or two on our minds, Anastasia. Surely that gives us a pass on perfect parenting." But my words fall on deaf ears, since Stacie already has her phone to her ear, tapping her nails impatiently on the table.

"I've got to go," I tell her, getting out of the booth and leaning over the table, but before I can kiss her goodbye, she presses the fingers of her left hand to my lips and turns her head slightly.

"Jen, it's Stacie," she says in the phone. "I have an emergency cake order for Sunday, I'll be there in about twenty minute to give you details. Be ready." Without waiting for a goodbye, she ends the call, gives me a peck on the lips and slides out of the booth. "I'm walking out with you."

I risk getting slapped with a contempt of court charge for being late, when I press Stacie against the side of her car and kiss her like I mean it. Call it payback for making me wait for it, although based on the little sounds she makes in the back of her throat this is not exactly punishment.

Her ass in my hands, her taste on my tongue; it's fucking worth every penny the judge will charge me.

-

A slap on the wrist, I got off easy.

It's four o'clock when I walk out of the building where Doug is waiting for me.

"Do you have it?"

He holds out a manila envelope to me and I take a quick peek at the papers inside.

"Did Stacie call you?"

"No? Was she supposed to?" He seems surprised and I mentally count my blessings at the distraction Becca's birthday apparently provides. It gives me time to do what I set in motion when I asked Doug to draft this document.

"She might. She wants to talk to you about the possible adoption of Becca, which is fine, but in case she calls you before the weekend, I'd appreciate it if you didn't mention this other matter."

"Gotcha. Hey, need me to come along?" he offers, even though I know he's eager to get home to his wife and kids. I clap him on the shoulder.

"No. I can take it from here. Appreciate the help with this."

"No problem. Good luck."

My next stop is the sheriff's office, for the second time today. In truth, I'd already been on my way to talk to Drew when I found out Stacie would be there. It was informative all the same, since I discovered the asswipe had retained a shark lawyer from Durango, and that drove urgency to the forefront.

Drew is just leaving the building when I pull in the parking lot. For all his posturing and teasing, Drew is a good man, who's instantly on board without needing much of an explanation. I end up following his cruiser just down the street, to the county jail.

"Why the fuck would I sign this?" Kevin Borland scowls as he shoves the papers I put in front of him off the table.

Keeping my cool, I calmly pick them up off the dirty floor and make a production of brushing them off.

"That's a good question," I tell him evenly, setting the papers back on the table but keeping my hand on them as I leaned in, invading his space. "One I'm happy to answer. It has come to my attention you are hoping to make a deal with the district attorney's office to avoid getting life."

"Yeah?" he scoffs. "What does that have to do with anything? With this?" He brushes at the papers again, but this time they're safely pinned under my hand.

"The DA and I go way back. I wouldn't say we're bosom buddies, but I'm comfortable declaring him a friend." I watch as anger drains from his face and is replaced by concern, with no small measure of satisfaction. "I see you are clueing in, but let me spell it out; I can put in a good word for you, and make that deal happen, or, I could put a bug in his ear about the danger you pose to the population at large. It's your choice in which direction you want to take this."

CHAPTER 30

Stacie

"Girl! I was getting worried you dropped me for Starbucks."

Jen is smiling broadly when I walk in.

"Blasphemy," I quip. "You know I worship at the altar of your espresso maker."

The sound of her chuckle warms me, as I consider how well I've settled in to this community. Not withstanding recent events, I feel like I'm making a good life here. I have friends, I have more family now than I ever had, and I have a man who only sees the beautiful in me. When you feel balance like that in your life, everything else becomes just a bump in the road.

"Who's the cake for?" Jen asks, as she creates magic with her shiny, hissing and sputtering, coffee machine.

"We just found out it's Becca's birthday Sunday."

"Poor little thing," Jen reacts immediately.

Dolores is a small community and everybody pretty much knows everything and everyone. The coffee shop and the pub would be the spots where most information is exchanged.

"You know what the kicker is? I'm not even sure what her favorite movie, or cartoon, or even color is. I know she's smart, she's sweet, and she doesn't complain about anything."

"Oh, honey. I suspect she may not have a clue yet what she likes, she's probably learned to be glad with what little she had. No one has taken the time to spoil that girl a little, or love her a lot." Jen hands me my macchiato and leans with her hands on the counter. "So…let's give her a cake that every little girl would love."

I smile at her enthusiasm. The cake, she insists, has to be multi-colored layers, to give that little surprise when you cut into it. Pinks, purples, and teals for the cake, covered with a thin layer of fondant, which she wants to top with cotton candy, like a cloud of confection. My teeth hurt, just listening to the description.

"I'll make some butterflies with sugar paste for decoration. I should be able to have that done for you late tomorrow afternoon, is that enough time?"

"Sure thing," I confirm. "I may drag the girls into town tomorrow. We haven't really been out much and we could all use a few more things before the real cold sets in. I'll try to get a drop on Becca's preferences, so I can try and get her something she likes. Maybe I can convince Nick to come," I suggest, chuckling at the thought of him shopping with three females.

"I'll pop out and grab her something too. Maybe a book?"

"That's a great idea. You know what? Do you have time to pop in on Sunday?" I ask her. I haven't really discussed anything with anyone, and am flying by the seat of my pants here, but surely Henry and Nick won't mind if we have a few people over for cake.

By the time I walk out of The Pony Express, I've made arrangements for Jen to bring the cake Sunday so we can keep it a surprise, and I've talked to Isla, who took less than a second to decide she, Noah, Ben, and Uncle Al would be there as well.

I feel pretty accomplished when I walk into the kitchen, where Henry is stirring a cast iron pot on the stove, creating smells that make my mouth water.

"What's for dinner?"

He looks at me, eyebrows raised.

"Stew. Nick talk to you?"

"Yum." I lean over his shoulder and take a deep whiff. With my mouth close to his ear, I whisper, "He did and operation birthday is underway." I quickly kiss his cheek and move around the counter, dropping my purse and keys on top. When I look up, Henry's eyes are on the pot, but he has a smile on his face.

"Where are the girls?" The TV is off and I can't see them in the living room.

"Exercising Maisy in the back paddock," the old coot says, giving me a heart attack.

"They're out there alone? With a big horse?"

"Like taking a dog for a walk with that horse. She's as docile as they come."

"But she's big. She could easily crush them," I persist.

"She's not gonna, and if these kids are expected to grow up on the farm, they'll have to learn how to take care of the animals," he says so matter-of-factly that it takes me a second to register what he's saying.

It brings back some of my current reality. I can't stop my mind from going where it wants to go; namely to an image of turning this temporary living situation into a permanent one. Would I want that? I love Nick, I love his pops, and God knows I've fallen head over heels for Becca. Is this what is best for Mak? For me? We slipped into life here on the farm with barely any ripple, and although I figure Mak might miss being close to the river, the horses and the rest of the animals would more than make up for it.

Jesus, listen to me, I don't even know Nick's feelings on this—although I have a strong suspicion—and I'm single-handedly dreaming up a future.

Henry is not the person I should be talking to about this, which is why I head down to the bedroom. I want to get out of these clothes, into something a bit more comfortable, and head out to check on the girls. One thing life has taught me is that you don't make every decision today. If your heart is in it, there is no reason to rush; another day or two will not change that. If your heart is not, it'll take that extra time to become clear.

In my more appropriate attire of jeans and one of Nick's flannel shirts, I head outside to look for the girls.

"Mom!" Mak's excited voice reaches me, just when I spot them on the far side of the fence. "Look! We've got Maisy."

I can see that. The girls look minute next to the big animal and I struggle to plaster a smile on my face.

"That's awesome, kiddo!" I yell back, stepping a little closer to the fence.

Becca is quiet, but looks quite content, walking beside Maisy's big head. I keep my distance, but watch as they bring the horse up to the fence.

"You should pet her, Mom," Mak invites when they get close enough that I can reach out and touch.

"She doesn't look like she likes me much, Makenna."

"Sure she does," Mak says, full of confidence.

"I think Maisy likes anyone who likes her," Becca suddenly pipes up.

"So you think I should try?"

"She wants you to." The look on her face is so serious, and expresses so much, that I get a lump in my throat.

I don't even attempt to answer and instead reach out my hand. The horse, perhaps sensing my trepidation, lowers her head and I gently rub the rough hairs on her large forehead.

"Look at you."

The sound of the deep voice startles me, which in turn startles Maisy, who suddenly jerks up her head and has me flying backward. Strong arms wrap around me from behind, holding me on my feet, and a soft familiar chuckle sounds in my ears.

"Sorry," Nick says, amusement in his voice.

Maisy's recovery time is better than mine, because even as I'm still catching my breath and waiting for my heart rate to return to normal, she is reaching her long nose over the fence and nuzzles at Nick's arm.

"Don't have treats on me, old girl," he apologizes to the horse, before turning me in his arms and kissing me hello. Quite thoroughly, I might add.

"Missed you," he mumbles against my lips.

"You just saw me a few hours ago."

"Time crawled." I snicker at his dramatic tone.

"Did you see us?" Mak, whose patience is being tested to the max, wants to know.

"I did see you," Nick answers, loosening his hold on me. "Was it fun? Maisy sure seemed to enjoy herself."

"She did."

"Good. Then let's get the old girl to her pen where she can have her dinner. Who wants to hop on her back?"

"Me!!" Of course, it's my spawn who has her arm stuck high in the air, jumping up and down, while Becca looks on from a distance.

Curious to see this play out, I step out of the way as Nick walks to the gate in the paddock and leads the horse through. Mak is right there; ready to climb on, when Nick leans down and whispers something in her ear. He straightens up and Mak's head turns to where Becca is still standing by the fence. She then looks up at Nick and nods, earning her his wide smile.

"You first, Becca," she says to her friend, and my heart melts a little, because I know it cost her.

My earlier thoughts come flooding back; this is what life could be like.

Nick

The moment Stacie walks out of the bathroom in her nightie, I toss the manila envelope on the bed.

It's been burning a hole in my pocket, but timing is everything. Now, with the girls in bed, and Pops watching the late news before he turns in, is the window I've been waiting for. I was informed earlier that shopping was on the schedule for tomorrow, and judging by the empathic communications Stacie's eyebrows signaled in my direction, participation was not optional. At least not for me. It meant though, that my original plan, to deal with this tomorrow morning, was no longer viable. Hence the sneak attack in the bedroom.

"What's that?" she asks suspiciously.

"Open it."

"Yeah, but what is it?"

"Only one way to find out," I tease.

Rolling her eyes dramatically for effect, Stacie snatches up the envelope and pulls out the stack of papers. The expression on her face as she scans the documents is difficult to gauge.

"I'll ask again," she says sharply this time. "What is this?"

"Hear me out," I start, noting there is call to tread carefully.

"I told you I'd spoken to Doug about adoption, but it wasn't just for Becca. I had hopes that sometime soon, when you and I can come to an agreement about our future, I'd be able to adopt Makenna. Those hopes were all but squashed when Borland turned out to be…"

"Don't even say it," she hisses. "I've decided he was no more than a vial from the sperm bank."

"Right. Be that as it may, when Drew mentioned he'd hired a hotshot lawyer and was looking to forge a deal, I decided to use that as leverage to keep my hopes alive."

"You arm wrestled him into signing away his parental rights before he had a chance to claim them."

"I did and I won't regret it, because even if you and me...*umpf*"

The force of her body, as she launches herself at me, causes me to stumble and hit the wall with my back. Not what I expected, but you're not going to hear a complaint from me, because I'm pinned against the wall by a soft, warm, and apparently very willing and able Stacie.

My arms come up, one rounding her waist and the other curling up along her spine. My hand burrows in her hair and holds her in place, with her mouth latched on my lips. Her tongue lashes an unadulterated assault on mine, and my body goes from zero to fully engaged, in a fraction of a second.

It's a frantic pace, with Stacie's hands clawing at my boxer briefs, trying to peel them off my ass, while I'm just trying to catch up. Kicking my underwear off, I manage to help her wrap her legs around my hips, and swing her around so her back is braced against the wall.

"Please," she mumbles against my lips. "Please, Nick."

"Condom." I surprise myself in the heat of the moment, but I'll have to move to get to the nightstand, and I'll need her cooperation for that.

"No," she says, tightening her arms around my neck.

"Anastasia," I plead, as much to her as to my own common sense to prevail.

"No condom. Whatever happens...happens," she whispers. "I love you, Nicholas Flynn, so very much."

And here I thought she'd been furious with me.

"All my heart, Beautiful," I give her back.

The thick head of my cock brushes through the slick wetness, searching for her opening before surging forward, burying myself to the root.

-

It's still dark out when something wakes me.

We ended up falling asleep sated, our bodies tangled underneath the bedsheets, still naked. It only illustrates how spent we were, because with the girls often coming in during the night, we make sure we're appropriately covered.

Not so now, which is perhaps why I hear Stacie rummaging in the bathroom.

I swing my legs over the side of the bed, grab a pair of PJ pants from the top dresser drawer, and slip into the bathroom, where I find Stacie sitting on the edge of the tub, her head in her hands.

"What's wrong?"

She lifts her head and I worry when I see she's been crying. With impatient swipes of her hands, she brushes at her cheeks.

"It's stupid."

"If it's stupid, you wouldn't be this upset," I suggest, sitting down beside her on the cold porcelain.

"It's not like I didn't know already," she says, speaking in riddles.

"Know what?" I try again.

"I know it was an accident and only that once. I thought I might be, when I was waiting for the house to explode around me. I'm ashamed to admit; I'd all but given up, when it occurred to me I could have a baby growing inside me." I wrap my arm around her and hold her close, because that thought may have flitted through my head once or twice as well. "The possibility is what gave me strength to move. That's what kept me alive, so when I found out in the hospital my blood work came back negative, I was only a little disappointed and put it out of my head." She chuckles a little, scoffing at herself. "Except it would appear I still carried a little bit of unreasonable hope."

"Is that why you said earlier, *whatever happens, happens*?" I pry, pressing my cheek to the top of her head. "You want to try and get pregnant?"

"Yes... Well, no," she corrects, confusing me even more. "I hoped maybe they'd made a mistake with the test since my period didn't show. I thought perhaps I already was."

She turns her head into my shoulder, and I take a moment to process and formulate before I speak.

"You got your period," I conclude. I'd like to claim it was because I have such excellent insight, but in truth, it's the box of tampons I just now notice on the vanity counter. "And you're disappointed." She doesn't answer, but nods her head under my chin.

"Come on, this tub is hard on my ass." I encourage her to get up with me. "You get back in bed, I'll be right there."

I quickly clean up and tug on my pants, before following her to bed. She curls up against my side and I cover her hand in the center of my chest with my own.

"I think the doctor prescribed supplements because she thought we were actually trying," she mumbles.

"So let's keep trying."

Her head shoots up at my words as she scrutinizes my face.

"Don't you think it's crazy soon?"

"Probably, but look at us; for all intents and purposes we're living together as a family, complete with two girls and one grumpy old man. It feels like the next logical step."

I roll to my side, touch my forehead to hers and look her in the eyes.

"Whatever happens…happens."

CHAPTER 31

Stacie

"Let's go, ladies!"

Of course, the girls first had to go say goodbye to Maisy, and I hope they won't stink the car up with *eau de horse*. Yesterday, when they'd come in from putting the horse in her pen, both ended up riding on her back. I died a thousand little deaths on the inside, while smiling back at the girls, who were clearly enjoying themselves, but they reeked to high heaven. Nick had laughed at me and swore that once Maisy was healed up, he'd take me out on a trail ride.

Right. Like that's going to happen.

We're taking my SUV, but of course, Nick is behind the wheel. I'm not sure what makes that a rule; that when men and women share transportation, the man automatically veers toward the driver's seat. Not only that, but women don't seem to mind giving them that control. Maybe it's a ploy.

I mean, I like to hold the reins of my own life, but handing over the wheel for a drive into town seems like a small symbolic sacrifice to give Nick the impression I'm letting him lead. Fat chance, since women in general, and myself in particular, are formidable backseat drivers.

"Don't forget the construction on the 145 south of town," I remind Nick, when we finally round up the kids and get on our way. "It's faster to take Lebanon Road into Cortez."

He doesn't answer, he just looks at me from the corner of his eye and smirks. That, of course, is like a red flag to a bull.

"If you don't agree, by all means take the 145. I'll be happy to prove you wrong," I challenge him.

"Who says I don't agree?"

I twist in my seat, but he's not looking at me, he's staring out on the road, his mouth still tilted up.

"The smirk on your face says."

"It's not a smirk," he disagrees, grinning even wider. "It's a smile."

"And what is there to smile about?" This time he turns to face me, his eyes lit up with humor.

"You. You're cute when you're bossy, but you're adorable when you get testy."

The gall.

"You know calling me cute and adorable does not win you any brownie points, right?" I glare at him, but he's clearly unaffected, putting his big paw on my thigh. I almost swipe it off, but it feels really good, so I just pretend to ignore it.

"What is *testy*?" Mak asks from the back seat.

"Is cute a bad thing?" Becca adds, and Nick bursts out laughing.

Rolling my eyes, I straighten in my seat and ignore Nick's explanation to the girls, holding onto my snit.

But my snit dissipates when I notice him skip the 145, and take the next turn off onto Lebanon Road. His hand gives my leg a squeeze and I sneak a sideways glance at him. He gives me a wink.

-

It's been a struggle keeping it a secret that we know about Becca's birthday. Especially since every time Mak declares liking something in the store, Becca immediately agrees. I still don't have a good grasp on what she likes.

We've just trudged through Walmart, and are about to head across the road to the Stage store, when I have an idea. With the kids walking in front of us, I pull on Nick's arm so he leans down.

"I need you to take Mak and find us some balloons."

"Balloons?"

"Yes. We're killing two birds with one stone. We'll need balloons and I'd rather keep it a surprise for Becca, but I also need to have Becca alone for a bit. Mak has a tendency to bulldoze right over her." Nick chuckles at that observation. I don't think anyone could miss the fact my daughter is a force to be reckoned with. As an afterthought, I add, "By the way, you need to threaten Mak within an inch of her life, if she spills the beans."

"Gotcha," he agrees easily. "So what's the plan?"

"You drop us off across the street and then I'm guessing The Dollar Tree for party supplies, or you could come back here to Walmart."

"Okay."

"There's a folded tarp with the spare wheel in the hatch. Toss that over the balloons in the back. Maybe give us half an hour?" He nods and leans down for a quick kiss, before we follow the girls into the parking lot.

As planned, Nick drops us off after he—quite creatively—tells Mak he needs her help with a present for me. The wistful look on Becca's face as they drive off kills me, but I remind myself it's for the greater good.

"You and me, kiddo. Let's go find something special for you."

It's tempting for me to buy anything and everything she touches or looks at. There's nothing I would like more than to spoil the kid, but I'd rather make her happy with a little thing every now and then, so she can hold onto the magic, than to give her everything at once, and leave her with nothing to look forward to.

It's funny how in the end, Becca's tastes are quite different from Mak's. Where Mak is more of a tomboy and loves jeans, logo shirts, Chucks, and *Doc Martens*. Becca's preference is more girlish, feminine, like the floral underwear she chose. She's into jeans too, but hers have little embroidered embellishments on the pockets, and her T-shirts have a touch of glitter or a little ruffle. She loves Chucks as well, but prefers them in purple or shiny, and apparently she adores jewelry.

I'm stacking the clothes on the checkout counter, when I notice her twirling the tabletop jewelry rack. One side of the rack in particular she keeps coming back to. It's a collection of silver charms, of all kinds, that are to be paired with a simple silver bracelet.

I hand the girl behind the counter my credit card, as I watch Becca closely as she slightly runs her fingers over a few of the charms. There are a few letter Bs, but one that is decorated with little pink stones she seems to like best.

It's an easy decision, and when the girl hands me my card back, I turn to Becca.

"Could you do me a favor? I forgot to grab one thing, but Nick and Mak could be here any second now. Would you mind waiting outside and keeping an eye out for them? I'll just be a minute."

"Sure," she says, smiling. "And thank you for my clothes."

On impulse I bend down and kiss her forehead. I've tried to be careful with too much physical affection, because she seems to shirk from it a little, but this time she doesn't flinch.

"Thank you, sweet girl, for being awesome." Hardly adequate words to describe how full my heart is right now, but I don't want to freak her out if I start gushing. Instead, I shove the bags in her hands, "Here, take these," and gently turn her in the direction of the door.

The girl behind the counter shares my enthusiasm, and soon we have a bracelet picked out, the B with the pink stones, and as she suggests a pretty butterfly, I find a horseshoe to add. Every so often, I check over my shoulder to make sure I can still see Becca.

It's tempting to buy every little charm, but the whole point of the exercise is to give her something that continues to hold promise. In the end, I buy one for Mak as well, with an M and another horseshoe, but I'll put that away for Christmas.

When I turn to the door, Becca's gone.

"Did you see where she went?" I ask the girl behind the counter, who just shrugs her shoulders.

I fly outside just as Nick pulls up in the Subaru.

"What's wrong?" he says immediately, rolling down the window.

"Becca...she's gone."

Nick

The balloons were easy enough; I just let Mak go to town, although I did put a halt on it when we reached ten. I had no idea balloons cost that much. They were all filled with helium and weighed down with the tarp in the back, as instructed. We'd have to work hard to keep Becca distracted, because it's not easy to hide balloons.

The Ute Gallery I took her to after, was a bit more challenging. I hadn't been lying when I told Mak I wanted to get something for Stacie, she just wasn't quite the help I'd anticipated.

The stuff she picked out was mostly colorful beadwork that was beautiful and intricate, but didn't exactly spell Stacie to me. For me, the classic combination of silver and turquoise was more appropriate, and we finally managed to agree on a beautiful rustic silver-molded wristband, with a floral medallion inlaid with different shades of the blue-green stone.

Mak almost jumped out of her skin with excitement, so when I told her we'd have to wait until tonight to give it to her, she was very disappointed. But with Mak that doesn't seem to last long, and on the way back she was prattling on about Becca's surprise party, Maisy, and her new *Doc Martens* boots. In that order.

The kid has the attention span of a gnat, but man, I fucking love listening to her.

I just pull up in front of Stage when Stacie comes running outside, looking around frantically. I roll down the window and barely have a chance to see what's up; when she says she can't find Becca.

"How long?" I ask, putting the SUV in park and getting out, because Stacie looks like she's about to lose it. "Look at me," I urge her, putting my hands on her shoulders to ground her. "How long since you saw her?"

A dark shadow steals over her face

"It's my fault. I asked her to wait out here. It was a ploy so I could quickly buy her present. I told her to be on the lookout for you. It's been maybe between five and ten minutes. Not long at all."

"Then she's close."

I scan the fronts of the stores and parking lot, but I don't see her. It's a Saturday, so the parking lot is full and I'm sure someone should've seen something. Although it doesn't seem like her, it's always possible she popped into another store.

"Okay, you go check the stores on either side, I'm going to drive around to the ones across the parking lot. Meet you back here. Don't panic. She's somewhere," I reassure Stacie, who nods sharply as she pulls herself together.

"What's going on?" Mak pipes up from the back seat.

"We have to look for Becca," I explain, pulling away from the curb.

"But I just saw her."

My eyes shoot up to look at her in the rearview mirror.

"Where?"

"She was just talking to her brother around the corner when we drove up."

I pull on the wheel and make a U-turn on the spot, ignoring the angry horn from the car behind me.

"Where around the corner?"

"By the dumpster in the alley."

I remember the narrow one-way alley at the end of this strip mall and turn in, effectively blocking it. My eyes land on Becca who stands in front of the dumpster, looking unharmed, but I can't see her brother.

"Stay in the car," I bark at Mak, as I get out. "Are you okay?" Becca nods her head, red curls bouncing.

"I'm fine," she says, before turning behind her. "It's okay, they won't hurt you."

I barely recognize the kid stepping out from behind the dumpster. Sure, he's still lanky, and his hair is even longer, but last time I saw him he was cocky and wearing a clear *fuck you* scowl on his face. Now his shoulders are slumped, his head is down, and the expression is one of fear.

Before I have a chance to say anything, I hear the crunch of running footsteps and turn around to see Stacie coming around the SUV. She doesn't stop for me, but goes right for Becca, folding her in a tight hug.

"Jesus, I was scared. What are you doing here? Why did you take off?" Then she spots the brother, who seems to be taking the spectacle in with some interest. "You!"

she spits at him and almost goes after him, but his little sister holds onto Stacie's arm.

"He was worried about me," she says in her little girl whiskey voice. "He's scared the sheriff will put him away."

"Why?" I ask. "I know he was looking to talk to you about what happened to your mom."

"I'll just get blamed for that. I know how it goes. I don't wanna go to jail." The poor kid is fighting tears.

"I told you they locked Kevin up," Becca tells her brother.

"It's true," I add, "They did. Last week, didn't you know that?" The instant relief on his face would be comical if it wasn't so tragic.

"Been hiding, living in the car. I haven't been back to Dolores. Saw Becca coming out of the store and wanted to make sure she's doing okay."

"She's staying with us," Stacie offers, looking down at the girl, who smiles back, her eyes happy behind her glasses.

"Listen, let me call the sheriff, he's a friend of ours," I suggest, thinking that Drew would likely know where a kid like this might get some help. At least he'd be a good place to start. "You probably don't believe me, but ask your sister; he's been good to her."

"I'll just go," the kid says, already looking for a way to get around us.

"Up to you," Stacie says, walking right up to him, unintimidated, even if the kid's about a head taller than she is. "But wouldn't you rather take this chance to do life the right way? Learn how to make a living you can be proud of, never having to worry where your next meal will come from, or where you'll sleep tonight? Not having to look over your shoulder all the time because you never know when it all catches up with you?" She puts a hand on his arm and I can almost see him stiffen. Christ, how long since someone touched him kindly? If ever? "I promise you, I'll look after your sister—*we'll* look after her," she corrects herself, looking at me over her shoulder. Next she digs through her purse, fishes out a piece of paper and a pen, and scribbles something down. "Tell you what; think about it. We're not going to hold you back. I've written down our phone numbers and also the sheriff's number. If you want to check how Becca is doing, call one of us. If you want to straighten yourself out and have a shot at building a good life for yourself, start by calling that number for the sheriff."

He looks up, from where he was staring at his worn sneakers, at the piece of paper Stacie is holding out to him. He turns to look at Becca, and then at me, before his gaze lands on Stacie.

"*Please. For Becca*," I see her mouth at him, and finally he takes the note from her hand and stuffs it in his pocket.

He walks up to his sister and pushes her chin gently with his fist.

"Be good."

"I will," she says, smiling sadly.

Without another word, he takes off on a run, disappearing around the SUV.

-

"What is this for?" Stacie looks at the pretty wrapped box I just put in her hand.

We're still at the table, having just finished dinner. Pops announced dessert, which the kids are pretty excited about. Especially since the apple crisp apparently comes with vanilla ice cream. So they are in the kitchen 'helping' Pops get it ready, and I thought I'd grab the moment.

"We've talked about a future, even making a family, but we haven't really discussed marriage." I smile at the way her blue eyes go wide. "Sooo..." I teasingly drag on. "If it were up to me, I'd have a ring in that box, but knowing how quirky you can be with surprises..." I get a thump on my shoulder for that. "I decided to get you this instead. Call it a promise."

"You gave it already?" Mak walks in, precariously balancing two bowls in her hands. "Did she like it?"

"I have to open it first," Stacie says, smiling.

Becca comes in with Pops following right behind, with the remainder of the desserts. She sidles up to Stacie on the other side of Makenna, and I smile at the picture the three of them make, with their heads bent together.

"It's beautiful!" Stacie exclaims when she opens the box and pulls the silver band out, fitting it immediately around her left wrist, the one with the scars.

"Looks so pretty on you," Becca says.

"I helped pick it," Mak announces.

"It's gorgeous. Thanks, honey." Stacie bends toward me and I meet her halfway, accepting her sweet kiss.

While she admires the bracelet with the girls, I look to the end of the table where Pops sits. He glances at me with the hint of a smile on his face, and winks before turning his attention to the bowl in front of him with gusto.

"Eat," he orders. "It's all gonna melt."

The girls scramble back to their seats and start eating. Beside me, Stacie is making the most distracting sounds as she digs in, moaning with every bite.

"This is so delicious," she mumbles with her mouth full. "Everything was delicious, thank you so much, Henry."

"Pops," my father grunts. "The name is Pops."

CHAPTER 32

Stacie

"Quick, bring it all into the kitchen." I wave Jen inside. "Nick took the kids up to Henry's fishing hole upriver. It about killed me this morning not to wish her a happy birthday, Jen—killed me."

"Jen," Henry greets my friend, as he relieves her of the boxes she's carrying and sets them on the counter. "What'd you all bring us? Looks enough food for an army."

"Three of those are the cake, which I still have to assemble, and I made sausage rolls. I thought it might go with the chili Stacie tells me you're making."

"Slow simmering in the Crock-Pot since last night," he says, proudly lifting the lid so Jen could take a whiff. "It was Stacie's idea," he adds, "although she'll soon discover why it was not necessarily a good one. Us Flynns have a very responsive digestive system."

Jen laughs while I roll my eyes. I've heard the jokes a few times already, and they can bring it on. They haven't met Mak on beans yet.

"Oh my God, it's beautiful!" I exclaim when Jen opens the biggest box and lifts out a large round cake, covered in what looks like a cloud of spun sugar.

"Wait until I'm done," Jen suggests, pulling a second, smaller cake out of the next box. And in the third box is a collection of intricately made butterflies. Their wings look like the edges of a doily, with beautiful perforated patterns.

I want to stay and watch, but there's another knock at the door, so I leave the cooks to their domain, and start playing hostess. Isla arrived early and helped put up the balloons and garland that Nick picked up yesterday, and already a few gifts have collected on the small table beside the couch. That is my sister-in-law; she does nothing in half measures. Evidence of which is standing outside on the porch when I open the door.

"Neil!"

"Are we too late for the surprise?" he asks, his arm around a pretty blonde woman I vaguely recall from Ben and Isla's wedding. "By the way, you remember my wife, Kendra, right?"

"Of course." I smile, relieved that he reminded me, and shake her proffered hand. "Nice to see you again, Kendra. And no, you're not too late, come in. Nick took the girls out but they should be back in the next ten or fifteen minutes."

I barely have their coats dumped in one of the bedrooms, when Drew shows up, a bouquet of pretty flowers in his hand.

"Girl's gotta have flowers on her birthday," he says almost sheepishly. I can't help but hope that one day, some woman is going to knock this charmer on his ass. Despite his teasing manner and player game, our sheriff hides a sensitive side a mile wide. It'll just take the right woman to tap into that.

"They're lovely. Let me put them in water." I lean in, kiss his cheek, and take the flowers into the kitchen. Drew follows me.

"Wow," I hear him say behind me. "That's some cake."

I notice, to my surprise, Jen blushing at his comment. I haven't known her that long, but I'm positive I've never seen her blush before.

The cake *is* stunning, the second tier is not centered, but offset to one side, so the edge aligns with the rim of the larger layer underneath. What looks like glass, or maybe clear plastic long dowels, are used to separate the layers. She draped more cotton candy over the little cake, with the odd tendril drooping off the sides to the base layer below. The entire design gives the cake a light and airy feel. To add whimsy, she is mounting the intricate butterflies with a dollop of gumpaste to long silver wires and sticks them randomly in the cake; the overall effect is a swarm of butterflies hovering over a cloud.

"Thanks," she mutters to Drew's words.

"It is stunning," I add, folding her in a big hug. "Becca is going to love it."

"I didn't see your car out there?" Drew pipes up. Jen steps out of my hold and turns to face him.

"I was dropped off," she says, turning back to the cake, but I notice her hand is a little unsteady.

"I'll drop you home later," Drew announces in a tone that does not invite objections, yet Jen does just that.

"No need," she says, her tone a little sharper. "I'm being picked up."

I look at Henry, who is looking back at me, one eyebrow raised. Okay, so I'm not crazy and something is up. Looks like it's time for me to stop by for a macchiato sometime this week.

The tension is broken when Ben barrels in the front door, baby Noah in a carrier in his hands and a diaper bag slung on his shoulder. It still makes me chuckle to see my badass, motorcycle riding, silver-haired, and tattooed brother, toting around that cute little critter.

Uncle Al walks in behind them and I walk straight into his arms, giving him a big hug.

"I'm so, so sorry about Ginnie."

"Better for her. Peaceful. Loved that woman something fierce, though," he says, and I have to swallow hard at the grief carving his face. "Having my girl around to help sort through things was good, although I don't think your brother was too happy. Helped me, though. That little boy of theirs sure brightens up the darkest of days." He smiles at a blinking Noah.

"Gimmie, gimmie." I already have my arms out and pluck my nephew right out of the carrier.

"You could at least grab the whole carrier," Ben grumbles and Uncle Al chuckles.

"Why would I do that, when all I'm interested in is the baby?" I fire back.

I barely have a chance to get my snuggles in when Henry's voice booms over the din in the room.

"They're coming down the driveway. Everyone in the living room and quiet!"

The next few minutes take forever; giving me way too much time to reconsider if this was such a good idea.

What if she freaks out? Maybe we shouldn't have done a surprise party, although most who are here are people she knows, so she's not walking into a room full of strangers. Besides, she'll be aware there are people here, from all the cars outside, she just won't know they're all here for her.

Pretty sure she'll be excited when she sees that cake, though.

Then the front door opens and I can hear Mak's voice chattering, but that's not what I'm focusing on. It's the small pale face of the birthday girl, peeking around the corner.

"Surprise!"

I almost slap my hands over my ears, it's so loud, and apparently it's too much for baby Noah as well, because he sets up a loud protest in my arms. I immediately hand him off to his mother.

When I turn back, I see uncertainty on Becca's face. It still hasn't registered, as Mak more or less shoves her further into the room. Nick follows slowly, a smile on his face until Becca turns and looks up at him in confusion. As if I needed more reason to love the man, he goes down on one knee, and pulls the little girl close, bending his head so he can whisper in her ear.

The next moment is one I don't think I'll likely forget; Becca's face lights up with the brightest smile I've ever seen on her, as she throws her arms around Nick's neck and laughs. A fat, juicy belly laugh, such a beautiful unrestricted sound, it brings tears to my eyes.

Nick

That was the longest morning ever.

Don't get me wrong, it was fun taking the girls fishing, but keeping Mak quiet was a job all its own.

I could handle the elbow jabs and dramatic winking. I could even manage the veiled, yet not so veiled references, which I hurried to deflect. What almost sent me over the edge though, was her incessant asking if it was time yet.

It reminded me of myself as a young kid, sitting in the back of my parents' car on some trip to visit a relative or, on one of the rare vacations, subjecting Pops and Mom to this nonstop litany of, "*Are we there yet?*" I'd ignore warnings to zip it until finally my dad's hand came swinging around from the front seat and cuffed my ear but good.

I don't believe in corporal punishment, and it was unusual a hand was raised when I was growing up, but I finally understood what could lead my father to lose his cool on those rare occasions. I just focused on breathing in through the nose and out through the mouth to settle the last nerve poor Mak was getting on.

Then when we just drove in and saw all the cars, I had to shake my head sharply at her, because I could see she was about to slip up. By the door, I pulled her back so Becca could enter first, or this whole production would fall in the water.

Mak is like a young pup: all adorable, happy, and excited, prancing through life, while knocking shit down with her wagging tail, and not even realizing it.

Luckily Becca remained clueless right up to the, "*Surprise!*" which is loud enough to wake the dead—and Noah. She realizes something is up now, but still seems unable to connect it to her own birthday, which about breaks my heart.

I grab her hand and pull her toward me, going down on a knee so I'm at eye level.

"Happy birthday, beautiful Becca."

I watch as her face morphs from tense confusion to the prettiest unfettered smile, making her eyes behind her glasses shine. She throws her skinny arms around me and laughs; a deep rolling, infectious sound that seems to come all the way from her toes. It doesn't take long for Mak to join her the moment I stand up, setting Becca on her feet. The next instant, the two girls, as different as they are from each other, are holding onto each other, jumping in circles, laughing, and giggling.

I walk over to Stacie, who looks like she could use a hug, and pull her to me. Over her head I lift my chin at Ben, who is closely observing us.

"Who wants cake?" Pops pipes up, looking like he's not unaffected by the scene.

"Me!" the girls yell, and for once I can't tell which one's which, they're both deafening. Poor Noah seems to think so too, as he adds to the chaos with his loud, indignant screams.

There are quite a few eyes that don't stay dry as Becca is suddenly overcome with emotion when we sing, "Happy Birthday," as Pops carries in the cake, dotted with ten little candles.

The cake is a piece of art and I give Jen a one-armed hug, kissing the side of her head.

"It's perfect. Thank you so much."

In response, she puts her head on my shoulder and wraps her arms around my waist, as we observe Stacie cut the cake. Mak is helping, handing out slices. When I watch her walk over to Drew with a plate, I notice his eyes are on me, and none too friendly. It's only a moment and then he looks down at Mak, smiling broadly as he takes the cake from her.

It's not until later, long after the cake is eaten and the gifts have been opened—which by the way, was another moment where Becca, and therefore Stacie, lost their composure—that I have a chance to ask him about it.

We're on the porch, the place where all the men apparently gather to drink beer and light a stogie. Well, at least Pops and Uncle Al are lighting up. Those two geezers seem to be hitting it off just fine. Knowing my dad struggled for a while after my mother died, he'd be closest to understanding what Al is going through.

Ben and Neil are discussing something to do with the dark web, with Drew offering an occasional opinion. The whole thing is something that is so alien to me; I tune it out. I lean against the railing and look out in the field, where Maisy is enjoying her first taste of freedom again, after being cooped up for weeks while recovering. She reminds me a little of Stacie in that sense, although for Anastasia it was the emotional injuries that kept her tied up, more so than the physical ones. Even Becca...who is only now starting to come out of hiding.

I'm lost in thought when Drew joins me at the railing.

"Kid called me this morning."

"Which kid—oh, you mean Becca's brother? Jason?" Color me surprised.

"One and the same. Good thing you gave me a heads-up, I was able to get him to come in on his own."

"That's faster than I expected. Figured he'd probably take a few days to mull it over, and that was best-case scenario. I didn't really know if he was gonna call at all."

"Guess the frost we had overnight helped," Drew explains, chuckling. "Must've been colder than a witch's tit, sleeping out in a car."

"So where is he now?"

"Catching up on some sleep in a warm holding cell. I've got some friends in Cedar Tree, not sure if you've met them, they run the diner there?"

"Arlene's?" The place was recommended to me once or twice, but I haven't made it out there yet. Something maybe I should rectify soon.

"That's the place. Arlene and Seb own it. Reason I thought of it, is because Seb is an ex-con. Good man who did a bad thing for a good reason. Anyway," he continues. "Neither of those two are exactly the warm and fuzzy kind. They don't take shit from anyone, but they both have hearts of gold and would be perfect to take on a hard-ass like Jason."

"Did you talk to them?" I ask, while he takes a drag from his beer.

"I did, briefly, but they were in the middle of Sunday rush. I'll call them back when I get to the office, but from the sound of Arlene's reaction, she's itching to straighten the kid out. If anyone can do it, it's that woman."

"Thanks, and once you know for sure, we should let Becca know, it'll likely be her best birthday present of all." I clink my bottle against his in a toast, before I ask, "Is that what that look you threw me inside was about?"

"Don't know what you're talking about," he denies turning his gaze in the distance, but I don't miss the little side-glance he throws me. Suddenly the fog clears and I clap a hand on his shoulder.

"Doesn't feel good when the shoe is on the other foot, right?" I tease him.

"Kiss my ass, Flynn," he grumbles, shoving his empty in my hand and stepping down the porch. "Give my thanks to the delicious, and always stunning, Stacie. I've got shit to do."

This time his provocative reference to Stacie doesn't invite even the slightest hint of jealousy. This time I know better.

-

The house is quiet.

What a great day. Busy, which is not something Pops or I are accustomed to, but man did it feel good to have the house full of people. Stacie beamed, Becca blossomed under the positive attention, and Mak, well, Mak was in her element. That kid kills me. If I didn't know for a fact she's Stacie's daughter, I'd bet my farm she belonged to Ben and Isla. She's cheeky, tough, and mischievous; the perfect blend of those two.

That became obvious after dinner, once everyone had left for home, and Pops and I retreated back out on the porch. Pops said it was to finish the stogie he'd left out there earlier, but I knew better, which is why I followed him.

I noticed Stacie peeking at us from the window at some point, a smirk on her face. Moments later, Makenna came outside and let one rip that about took the siding off the house, obliterating any attempts Pops and I made to kill the ozone layer. We could hear the laughter from inside, when Mak quickly slipped back into the house, leaving us with the collective fumes lingering under the overhang of the porch. Pops and I had a good chuckle when Stacie banged on the window and stuck out her tongue at us, two giggling girls beside her.

I look over at her now, her blonde hair spread out on the pillow, longer now than when I saw her at her brother's wedding. Light from the moon slipping between the curtains makes her hair look almost white, ethereal. She's never been anything but beautiful to me, but especially these past few weeks, I can see her start believing it. It's not just the healing skin that allows her to feel what I've always seen, it's the way she sees herself reflected in the eyes of all of us who love her.

Rebranding Beauty.

Glancing to the portrait on the wall, I see eyes that years ago captivated my heart and now guide me to my future—our future.

EPILOGUE

Stacie

"Can I top you up?"

I look over to the next table, where the woman who introduced herself as Arlene is pouring coffee for the elderly lady seated there.

Nick, who's sitting across from me, next to the girls, gives my foot a kick. When I glare at him, he slightly tilts his head at Henry, who is sitting beside me in the booth. I'm still trying to get used to *Pops*, he's been calling me on it almost daily for the past month. Pops is staring intently over the girls' heads, into the next booth. Apparently, he likes what he sees because even when Arlene stops at our table, offering to top up our cups with fresh coffee, his eyes are still fixed next door.

"Mrs. Henderson was just widowed a year and a half ago," Arlene whispers, leaning over the table to reach Pops's cup. "Too bad, because that new hip she just had replaced at the time, gave her a whole new lease on life. Sadly she's got no one to enjoy it with."

For a moment I'm worried Nick's father will blow a vessel, his face gets so red. Especially when he catches Nick and I struggling to keep our composure.

"She's cute," Nick stage whispers, adding fuel to the fire.

"Bathroom," Pops grumbles, tossing his napkin on his empty plate and sliding out of the booth.

"What's wrong with Pops?" Mak wants to know. The girls have picked up on the name much easier than I am. Even Becca easily calls him Pops.

"Too much coffee," Arlene says, smirking as she cleans away our plates. "Can I send Jay in here with some dessert? Girls?"

I was pleasantly surprised when Nick suggested we come here for breakfast. I've been back at work for four weeks now; the first week was part-time, but after that the cases kept coming and I've been pretty busy. We've all settled into a pretty easy routine since Becca's birthday, but haven't really done anything special since then.

It helps that it gives Becca a chance to see her brother, who's been in Seb and Arlene's care. Apparently they're making him finish high school, and have him working in the diner kitchen during the weekends. All in all, they're keeping a fairly tight leash on him, but as he told us earlier when we first came in, the carrot at the end of the string is the empty apartment upstairs, where he will be allowed to move into, once he's graduated. The agreement being that he continues to work weekends in the diner and keeps his nose clean.

"Apple pie for you too, or would you prefer peach?" Arlene asks me. Apparently everyone except Pops has placed their order already.

"Peach sounds good."

"Coming right up. I'll catch him when he finds his balls," she says, nudging her head in the direction of the bathrooms. I almost spew my coffee all over Nick, who throws his head back and barks out a laugh.

"What do you say?"

I'm sitting on the couch, the girls framing me on either side, as I look at Nick, who's sitting on his knees surrounded by shredded gift wrap.

It's Christmas morning and I'm on a high.

I was off the past week, stayed home with the girls who are off for the holidays, and for the first time I feel no guilt. That used to be different in my previous life. We shopped, baked, and decorated more than I ever have in my life. Last weekend we took the girls up the mountain to find the perfect tree, and last night we'd put on the final touches, the star on the top, and baby Jesus in the manger of the nativity set underneath. A tradition when Nick grew up, it's one I'd love to see continued in our family.

And now this.

I have butterflies in my stomach when Nick first pulls two envelopes from the gift bag he has wedged between his knees, and hands one each to the girls.

"Hold onto those," he instructs them, before diving back in the bag, and coming out with a small box.

"What do you say," he repeats, before adding, "to giving a man everything he's always wanted, but never thought he'd have? I fell probably the first time I saw you, but I had nothing to offer. I was flailing, I was shy, I was fat, and I—"

"You were fat?" Mak pipes up, but Becca immediately shushes her, which makes both Nick and I chuckle.

"Shhh, he's proposing so you have to be quiet."

Mak rolls her eyes, pretends to zip her lips, and with dramatic flair, then tosses the imaginary key over her shoulder.

"What I was trying to say," Nick continues, a glint of humor in his warm brown eyes. "Is that even when I didn't know it yet, you set a bar for me to measure up to. You challenged me to get my act together, barely having exchanged two words. And when I did, you showed up in my life again like the most amazing reward."

I can't help myself; I lean forward, cup his jaw in my hands and kiss him gently on the lips.

"Can you lot get on with it?" Pops gives his two cents, from the club chair beside the tree. "I've got a turkey in the oven that needs basting or else we'll have jerky for dinner."

Nick leans his forehead to mine, chuckling softly.

"I knew I should've done this alone with you," he mumbles under his breath.

"Your voice is all I hear," I assure him.

Nick

Every perfectly rehearsed word flies right out of my head when I look in her smiling eyes, her soft hands warm on my face.

"With all my heart; would you be my wife?"

I open the box that holds my mother's engagement ring, which Pops kept for me. It's much simpler than I would've picked for Stacie all those years ago, but today, sitting in flannel PJs with her hair in a messy bun, not a speck of makeup on her face, in the middle of a chaotic living room, it's the perfect ring for her.

"Finally," Pops grumbles behind me, and it's all I can do not to turn around and toss something at him. "That was Nick's mom's, just so you know."

"Hush from the peanut gallery," Stacie admonishes, before looking back at me and smiling. "It's beautiful and with all my heart; I would be honored."

I barely have a chance to slide the ring on her finger, and kiss her, before the girls start ripping open the envelopes I handed them.

"Easy, ladies," Pops cautions. "You don't wanna rip up what's inside.

A modicum calmer, they each pull out the sheath of papers and look at them, and each other, confused.

"What is this?" Mak pipes up first, while Becca is trying to decipher the words on the documents on her lap.

"It's a gift to all of us." I reach inside the bag and grab the last two boxes. Pops helped me pick these out, since I wanted to keep it all a surprise for Stacie, who is quickly clueing in. "Makenna, and Becca," I call their attention, before adding, "With all my heart; would you be my girls?"

"We're already your girls, silly," Mak says, giggling, but Becca looks at me, her eyes filling with tears.

"He means for real," she says solemnly as the first tear breaches her lashes and rolls quietly down her cheek.

"We're breaking ground next week," Al grouches, bumping his fist on the table. "But we can't do a damn thing if we don't have a permit in place."

"Calm your tits," Pops says, elbowing his friend as they pour over the blueprints for the addition these two plan on building onto the farmhouse. "Your son-in-law says he knows someone on the council who can speed it through."

I look at Stacie beside me on the porch swing Pops and Al installed last week. She's chuckling, one hand on her belly, as she listens to the two old coots go at it. It's nothing new.

Since Al moved back to town, those two have become the best of friends, even as they bicker every chance they get. Pops put the idea to buy Stacie's place by the river in Al's head. The selling point had been when he pointed out how much the girls enjoyed fishing there, and he'd probably never be rid of them. Al promptly put in an offer, just as Pops expected he would.

And when Al noticed one day, when they were grabbing a bite at the diner in Cedar Tree, that Pops seemed sweet on the widow Henderson, he went straight over to her table and put the charm on. It got Pops so mad, he forgot about staring at her from a distance every Sunday morning for months, walked up to Al, shoved him out of the way, and asked Mrs. Henderson out to Tuesday night Bingo in Cortez.

The two are a constant entertainment, the girls adore both of them, and other than their good-natured interfering; we love having them around.

This addition was their baby as well. Born just minutes after we announced our family would be expanding. For once the two agreed that we'd need more bedrooms, and they've been running with it ever since, only needing our input when it came to the actual design. All the practical stuff: the architect, the contractors, the permits, has been taken care of by them.

Good thing too, because since Stacie bought into the firm, adding her name to the awning, life has been pretty hectic. We've barely had time to ourselves, even since the wedding.

So tonight, since the girls are on the mountain, riding the ATVs with Ben and camping in his living room, I plan to take my girl out.

"Come on." I take her hand and pull her up from the swing.

"Where are we going?"

"Watch the sunset," is all I tell her.

"Truck's loaded, boy," Pops says with a wink as I guide Stacie to the pickup. He's responsible for the pile of blankets—it's still pretty damn cold when the sun goes down in April—and the picnic basket underneath the cover on the back.

Stacie sits quietly in the passenger seat as we head north on the highway, deeper into the mountains. Not far from Pops's fishing hole is a small dirt road that runs up to a small spring fed lake. Pops apparently discovered it a few weeks ago when he went exploring with Edith Henderson. I don't even want to know what the two of them were up to, parking on the side of a pristine lake watching the sunset, but I was grateful for the tip.

"It's gorgeous here," Stacie says, looking around her as I back the truck right up to the edge of the water.

"Stay here, I'll only be a minute." I slip out of the cab and quickly drop the tailgate, remove the cover, and smile when I see Pops even added a pile of pillows. A cooler with drinks, a basket with food, and he even thought of bug spray, even though we've hardly had any so far.

I help Stacie climb up in the back, and wait until she's comfortably installed herself before I get up too.

"Are you comfy?" I make sure, handing her a bottle of water while I grab myself a beer.

"It's perfect. Sit down." She tugs at my sleeve and I lift it over her head.

We sit like that—our backs against the cab, pillows behind us for comfort, blankets covering our legs against the cold—until the sun disappears behind the mountain peaks.

Then I slowly undress my wife, kiss our son in her belly, and in a nest of blankets and pillows, make love to her under the stars.

THE END

A WORD FROM KT

I am blessed with some of the most amazing friends in both the book world and real life. My circles are filled with incredible, strong women, much like Stacie. My book friends allow me to let my imagination fly and dream things I never thought possible, no matter what the obstacles. Everything in my book world traces back to being introduced to Tricia Daniels, who is one of the most resilient women it has been my honor to call friend. From that relationship all my bestie book friendships are forged: Trisha, Angie, Niki, and Patti. You have all faced adversity and have come through with your armor tarnished but your hearts intact. I love you all.

To Christine, Chris, and Diane, my real life cheerleaders. You have faced devastating life challenges and come out stronger than you ever thought possible. We've laughed, cried, and drank together to get through the good times and bad. You have supported me and been excited as this book journey unfolds, which is rare among real life friends. I love you with all my heart.

What is there to say to the world's most persistent mentor? Freya, you amaze me daily and if I ever grow up; I want to be you. I adore you, your words, your spirit, and mostly your incredible heart.

KT

A WORD FROM FREYA

When it comes to thanking folks, there is no other person for me to start with than KT, a woman who has become an essential component of my writing career in more ways than one. Not just a co-collaborator, but an engine, a motivator, a teacher, a sounding board and a friend. I love you to bits.

Joanne, who not only provides the necessary daily chuckles (the woman can be hilarious) and fabulous friendship, but she also very expertly does the final clean up of our stories. But more than anything else, Joanne keeps me humble, a task that can be challenging at times with one as strong willed as I am. Love your face.

My girls, I cannot ever forget my girls, most of who have been by my side for the past three years and then some. Catherine, Pam, Deb, Debbie, Lena, Sam, Nancy, Chris, all of you have given your time to help me put out book after book, and there simply aren't sufficient words to tell you how important you are. I adore each and every one of you.

A special thanks to Carey and Trish who jumped in and gave Ideal Image some fresh scrutiny before it was sent to final edit.

My Barks & Bites, a team of amazingly supportive and encouraging people I am grateful for every single day.

I have a posse, a group of book industry friends I can always rely on. We share books, smiles, laughs, tears, hugs and some of us even tattoos. I love all my peeps—so much.

My family and home away from home—Dana Hook—who freely gives her love, opens her house, donates her office and shares her family with me at the drop of a hat. I love you and yours so hard.

My family at home—always supportive, putting up with my ridiculous schedule and picking up the slack when I drop it.

You have my heart.

Freya

ABOUT THE AUTHORS

Freya Barker inspires with her stories about 'real' people, perhaps less than perfect, each struggling to find their own slice of happy. She is the author of the Cedar Tree Series and the Portland, ME, novels.

Freya is the recipient of the RomCon "Reader's Choice" Award for best first book, "Slim To None," and was a 2016 Kindle Book Awards finalist for "From Dust". She currently has two complete series and three anthologies published, and in addition to this Snapshot series, is working on a collection of Northern Lights novels. She continues to spin story after story with an endless supply of bruised and dented characters, vying for attention!

Stay in touch!

https://www.freyabarker.com
https://www.goodreads.com/FreyaBarker
https://www.facebook.com/FreyaBarkerWrites
https://twitter.com/freya_barker
or sign up for my newsletter:
http://bit.ly/1DmiBub

KT Dove grew up, and still lives, in the Midwest. At an early age she developed a love of reading, driving the local librarians crazy, and would plan plot lines and stories for her favorite characters. KT received degrees in English, Speech/Drama, and Education. And yet instead of becoming an English teacher as planned, she opted for an unexpected HEA.

Now married, a mother and still an avid reader, she stumbled upon the Indie author movement and became involved on several levels. Never in her wildest imagination would she have thought she would co-author a book. With the support of her family, she took the plunge, adding writing to an already busy literary existence.

She wouldn't have it any other way.

Stay in touch!

https://www.facebook.com/KTDove/
https://www.goodreads.com/author/show/16344207.K_T_Dove

ALSO AVAILABLE

SNAPSHOT Series

SHUTTER SPEED, #0.5
By Freya Barker

FREEZE FRAME, #1
By Freya Barker & KT Dove

Also by Freya Barker:

NORTHERN LIGHTS Collection

A CHANGE IN TIDE

A CHANGE OF VIEokayW

PORTLAND, ME, Novels

FROM DUST, #1

CRUEL WATER, #2

THROUGH FIRE, #3

STILL WATER, #4

CEDAR TREE Series

SLIM TO NONE, #1

HUNDRED TO ONE, #2

AGAINST ME, #3

CLEAN LINES, #4

UPPER HAND, #5

LIKE ARROWS, #6

HEAD START, #7

Printed in Great Britain
by Amazon